Lucky-Child
The Secret

Lucky-Child
The Secret

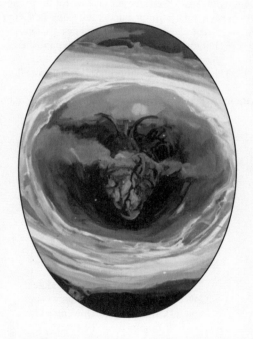

A Thrilling Indigenous Saga

Dr. Chelinay Gates
AKA
Malardy

Author and Illustrator

First pusblished in 2019
by
TellWell Publications

National Library of Australia Cataloguing-Publication entry

Dr. Chelinay Gates aka Malardy, author.
Lucky-Child: The Secret / Chelinay Gates

ISBN:
978-0-2288-2114-4 (Paperback)
978-0-2288-2115-1 (eBook)

Fiction/Fantasy.
Australian Fiction

Typeset by: Cadon Ayawentha Gates
Cover and Images: Dr. Chelinay Gates
Graphic Design: Cadon Ayawentha Gates
Printed by TellWell

Tellwell Talent
www.tellwell.ca

To all the *Julgia* Ones (Broken Ones) without whom,

this book would not exist.

To my father and his father.

This treasure-trove of memories is for my children,

Kiri, Cadon, Sharnee and Oni,

Forget Me Not.

In memory of my dear friends, Lee Millard and Drewfus Gates.

Their stories will live on.

Thank you

Many thanks to Ellen Zink who is my saviour; and to all those who offered financial, spiritual and physical assistance making it possible for me to write and mount the accompanying exhibition.

Bless you Laksar Burra for the long discussions on indigenous and spiritual issues and for understanding the journey to finding one's peace on country.

Sharnee, my daughter is always looking for opportunities for me and has never let me give up.

Oni, my youngest son, for the many insightful lectures.

Cadon my son, has been my gentle guide, mentor, life manager, typesetter, image editor and exhibition coordinator. He has been the strong shoulder I've rested my head on when I've cried, reliving these stories and facing rejection.

Tanya Finie, for being so touched by this story that she has partnered with the Lucky-Child to launch its message worldwide.

4 days before before going to print, Amanda Thackray was sucked into the Luck-Child vortex. She volunteered to proof and edit the entire book. She and Cadon working day and night to complete it.

The chance of meeting with Amanda has openned up a vision for a play and has offered inspiring imput for Lucky-Child: The Sacred.

Olivia Antonic, Lianna Fiocco and Winnie Hadad for thier enthusiastic support.

Special Thanks To

Paula Day

I set out on this journey, pencil in hand, in my tiny writing nook at the end of my bed. I could never have imagined the friendship I made with Paula Day who volunteered to type my book. Between the hours of 10pm and 1am, I'd ring her and read to her what I had written. Typing at great speed, she would laugh and cry, but more importantly, she would travel open heartedly with me into my past and there, meet my friends and family like no one else had ever done before. She is patient and kind, and I value her feedback and edits. Her paw print is on this book as much as mine.

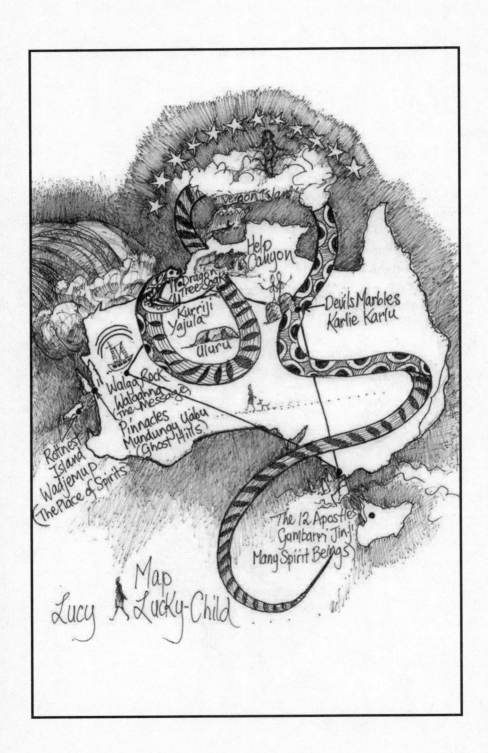

Acknowledgement to Ancestors and Country

Humbly, I offer my respect to Elders and the Traditional Custodians both past and present who have faithfully kept alive the Dreaming Stories and the Lore of this ancient land.

I wish to honour the first Language Speakers of each region for holding the primal sounds that form the words and sacred songs that uniquely describe the changing landscape in all her many hues. It is the mother tongue spoken and sung in Country that reconnects our human soul to this Sacred Land and the star-filled Heavens above.

I wish to acknowledge all the people who have touched my heart and whose stories now live on within the pages of this book. All names have been changed to protect the identities of those both living and passed. May you grow to love, laugh and cry with them as I have.

I ask for forgiveness for my child-like use of the great and noble languages of Mangala, a Pama–Nyangan Language of the Great Sandy Desert; Wajarri, from the Murchison Shire; Yawuru Ngan-ga, from the Broome region; and English, French and Vietnamese, from peoples far away.

Night after night with pencil in hand I have scrawled down the epic tales my family and friends have revealed to me in dreams. By recording their stories, I offer them the voice that others had denied them.

And to my dear twin sister, Helen, I've missed you since the day we were taken from our mother's breast and I wait until we meet again at home in the Milky Way.

Get Fear Off Your Back

Writing Lucky-Child has been a profoundly moving and cathartic experience for me. Veiled within the cloak of fiction and fantasy, I invite you to step onto my Life Board and meet those who have been precious to me.

I warn you, these lives have not been all sugar bags and honey ants. So, don't expect an easy ride. The journey from revelation to transformation is always painful.

Lucky-Child is all about the back story. Because it's the back story that furnishes context and meaning to life, and allows you to find love for those who wear deep scars. I trust that this book finds you at the perfect time in your life to be the catalyst for expansion.

Permissions have been collected for all but one story, for which I hold title. I share it with you, requesting your respect and love.

The extrapolation of Dreaming Stories reveals my Indigenous religious beliefs, and understanding of their meaning for the present age, and have been used as a personal devise for forgiveness and reconciliation.

Sensitive Material

This cautionary eye gives the reader the opportunity to avoid passages that me be confronting.

The image of the eye will appear at the bottom of the page and a single clapping stick will mark the beginning of the sensitive content, another will mark the end of the relevant passage.

Contents

1. The Call

It was a wicked day. The sun on the water shimmered like Mother of Pearl and the sky was the clearest blue I'd ever seen. We were fishing for breakfast, perched on a rock ledge high above the sea at Gantheaume Point in Broome—just Mum, my brothers Frankie and Jonnie, and me.

Mum felt a tug on the line, her strong arm flexed and suddenly she hoisted a writhing fish high into the air. The glare from its flashing silver body blinded me. Dropping my line, I closed my eyes and leant back against the hot, red rocks that towered behind me. The heat was pleasant against my back and I found myself drifting into an ocean of red behind my blood-filled eyelids.

'Lucky-Child.'

I recognised my *Jalbri's* (great-grandmother's) voice. I shut my eyes real tight so I could hear her better. The red intensified and I saw my *Jalbri* sitting under the Old Dragon Tree at the Soak.

1

Her long, bony fingers beckoned me. *'Come Lucky-Child, don't be messin',
get a move on! I'll be goin' soon.'*

With a jolt, I snapped back into my body! 'Mum! Muum!' My voice grew
louder and higher, 'MAAAM!' She was struggling to put another thrashing fish
into the bucket. She was stressed out cos Little Jonny was screaming his head
off at the big ugly fish Frankie was dangling in his face. Frankie was always
poking fun at everyone. But I was fed up. All I wanted was for Mum to listen
to me for once. 'MARMM!

'Wait, Lucy! Wait!' She said, not even lookin' at *me.*

'But Mum!'

'Lucy! Not now!' she barked, turning around to eyeball me with a clump of
Frankie's hair in her hand.

'Shit, that hurt!' he protested, rubbing his head.

Mum turned her back on me again to tell him off. *So typical. No one ever
listens to me. I may as well be dead.* As soon as I thought those words, my mind
flashed back to school the day after my Dad died …

Them rotten kids sang out, 'Lucy, Lucy, you're a Lucky-Child. Your Dad is
dead, and he'll be dead a while.'

That day I legged it and I was ready to run now. Yeah! Lucy Lucky-Child,
what sorta name is that?

My Aunty Rosie loves to tell everyone the story of my birth. She reckons I
was born in a shallow hole, dug into the creamy white sand at Reddell Beach.
Mum had laboured into the night beside Nyarluwarru; the Mother Sand Tower,
one of them huge seven red stone columns that rise up out of the sandy shore.
In our Dreaming stories, they are the Seven Sisters who fell to earth and were
set in stone forever cos they looked at that old Emu Man.

And as the sun rose behind them, I was born. Mum and Aunty washed me
in the shallows and a dugong swam up and snuggled into my foot. I giggled.
My aunty was shocked, she'd never ever seen a newborn baby giggle before
or since.

2

When they looked up, the water's edge was awash with bright-orange starfish. My Aunty Rosie believed that heaven was tellin' them to watch over this little bub, cos she's gonna be a real Lucky-Child.

'Lucy' was the name of my mother's youngest sister who died in childbirth. But 'Lucky-Child', well that's a whole other story.

In 1968, or near enough, my Dad was living on his mother's Country, a long way up north, past One Arm Point. They say his mother was a *Miwa*[1] woman and his father was a *Badi*[2] man, but Dad never found out for sure. We think Dad was only about seven years old when the German priests stole him from his parents.

When he drank, he'd tell us his story over and over again like a broken record. I knew he was afraid of losing those few painful memories, cos they were the only glue he had that connected him to his parents and his Country. I reckon if you don't know who you *really* are, you can never become who you're *really* meant to be. My Dad was meant to be much more than he became.

He said he knew for sure something bad was going to happen, cos for three nights before the Government truck drove into camp, he kept waking his parents telling them that a monster with bright-yellow eyes was coming to take him away. They believed he was seeing evil spirits, so they painted special makings on his body with white ochre[3] to protect him from the evil ones, and they kept him real close day and night.

Fast asleep, pressed between their warm bodies, he woke with a start to the strange noise of grinding gears as the Government truck made its approach. It drove over the sand dunes; its headlights bobbing up and down like the monster from his nightmare nodding its wicked head. He screamed, knowing that monster thingy had come to take him.

---

1   Miwa - Indigenous people from Ardyaloon or One Arm Point, Kimberley Region, Western Australia.
2   Badi - Indigenous people from Kalumburu, Kimberley Region, Western Australia.
3   Ochre - a natural clay earth pigment.

All the families that had settled around the campfires grabbed their sleepy children and looked for places to hide them. In hushed tones they pleaded with their kids to 'stay put' and 'be quiet'. A shushing sound rose high above the children's screams as all the adults tried to both comfort and silence their kids.

Dad reckoned the Lightning Brothers[4] were angry cos thunder boomed all around them and lightning lit up the night sky. Rain bucketed down like the Sky Gods were crying. Dazzled by the piercing headlights, wet, cold and frightened by the lightning and thunder, and choking on the thick blue smoke from the waterlogged fires, Dad stumbled out of his hiding place.

The first catch of the night, he was easy pickings.

He never forgot the sickly smell of the Government Man who snatched him up and held him real tight against his broad chest as he ran to the truck. Swinging open the huge metal doors, he dumped Dad inside. Lunging forward, Dad bit him like a rabid dog. I can imagine how the taste of cologne and cigarettes mixed with the rancid smell of beer breath would make a little kid sick to the stomach.

The Government Man forced Dad to stand up and then he punched him hard in the guts. Dad fell to the truck floor, winded and alone. But he wasn't alone for long. Each time the door opened, another kid was thrown inside.

When Dad told the story, he always added that the heavy clunk of that metal door closing sounded just like the door to cell #2 at our local lock-up. Poor Dad was taken prisoner at the tender age of seven—what chance did he have?

From inside that metal box, the kids could hear their mothers and fathers fighting the kidnappers.

Then Dad heard his mum scream, '*Alang! Alang*!' South! South!

They were taking the children south. He remembered hearing a thud as the truck moved forward. His mother's voice was suddenly silenced. The driver planted his foot and the truck lurched over a big bump. The kids heard the

4   Lightning Brothers - Legendary Indigenous Australian Dreamtime Story.

blood-curdling screams of their parents echoing in from all sides, as the truck sped off into the night.

The rains had come in early and the roads were difficult to cross. The Government truck seemed to drive forever. Then suddenly it stopped at a small landing and the children were transferred to a boat that set off into a raging sea. Terrified, the children knew they would never see their families again unless they jumped ship.

So, holding hands, all twelve kids jumped into the dark, choppy ocean. Petrified, the instinct to swim left them and they sank. Dad lost hold of the little girl's hand he was gripping, and as they sank into the angry sea, the boy's hand he was clutching in his right became cold like stone. He let it go.

Dad then heard the distant clap of thunder and thought he was going to die. Suddenly, a flash appeared in the water above him. Facing the light, he saw a *Jin.gi* (spirit being) reaching down towards him. The sea became electrified as if fire and water were battling for space.

In that dream-like state, he felt something soft snuggle up to him. In the inky blue water, he saw his mother's sweet face, and as he became lost in that sweet darkness, he felt himself rising quickly through the water into the light.

It was probably a dugong that took him to the surface, but to my Dad it was his mother's last embrace.

The next day he woke up in a bed at the Beagle Bay Mission Hospital, north of Broome, with a man from the Government standing over him asking him in English, over and over, 'What's your name? Blackie, what's your name?'

In shock, Dad kept repeating his mother's last words, '*Alang. Alang. Alang.*' He had been taken south, never to see his parents again.

'Okay. "Alan" it is,' said the Government Man in the suit. Writing my Dad's new name on the official paperwork, he turned to the priest and said, 'Poor bastard. Seeing as he was the only one to survive, let's call him "Lucky-Child". You reckon the lad would be about seven years old?'

The priest shrugged. 'Well, he's one of us now.'

With the stroke of an official's pen, Dad became 'Alan Lucky-Child', born at Beagle Bay Mission on 5 April 1961.

Poor Dad. Like most people in our community, he was given a name he hated. A name that reminded him of the night his mother was killed, and he was taken from the only home he ever knew.

Some say his father went mad with grief and took off into the bush.

You'd think that Dad would've got rid of that good for nothing name. But he kept it, just in case someone who heard it would remember his story and tell him how to find his family.

Now I keep that Lucky-Child name just to remember him, cos I miss him and love him and always will.

For us mob, when life throws all its shit at you and ya don't stop breathin' when ya shoulda, that's when people call you 'lucky'. But I've had enough of that sorta luck. I want that 'real good luck'. Not just for me but for that mob that went before me. I want to hear people say, 'Yeah, she's the 'real lucky one' from that "Lucky-Child" mob. One day I'm gonna be just like her.'

2. Fong's

Again, I heard my *Jalbri's* call. I jumped down off the rocks to the sand below. Glancing back up as I washed my face in the sparkling sea, I could see Mum and the boys still arguing.

Only *Jalbri* noticed me. To that mob on the rocks, I was invisible.

Setting off to find *Jalbri*, I made my way over the rocky outcrops and quickly up the red, sandy track picking minmin and crunching on their cool sweet-pea-like flowers, they're a cool treat in the heat of the day. Reaching the unsealed road to town, I passed Reddell Beach and waved as a sign of respect to the Seven Sisters on the shore. Running hard, it was hot, but I was free.

I'm a good runner, but Frankie's the best. He gets plenty of practice running away from trouble. He's always making fun of my skinny legs. 'Hey Lucy! You sure are Lucky! Lucky your matchsticks don't snap and go up your arse!' That's when I chase him. If my arms were longer, I'd catch him. No probs.

Lost deep in thought, I heard a car toot behind me. It was Steve Pigram, the footy coach from Anne Street. He'd just dropped some people off at the Point and was happy to give me a lift to Fong's store in town.

Yarning with him made time fly. Soon I was sitting on my lonesome out the front of Fong's. Last week, Frankie broke into the shop. He stole fags, soft drinks, chips, choccies, and a tonne of meat from the freezer. Then he trashed the place.

Suddenly I felt really hot and sweaty and realised I was hungry and thirsty as. I had no money to buy nothin' but it was too hot for sitting outside, so I mustered all my courage and went inside. Sprinting to the back of the shop, I pulled open the heavy glass doors to the drinks fridge, which let out a wall of cold air that made my hot body shiver with delight.

Unable to resist, I stuck my right foot in and then my left. Running barefoot had made my feet hot and sore. I leaned back, holding onto the long handles of the fridge doors and it felt like the most fun thing to do on such a stinking hot day.

Mae Fong screeched from behind the counter, 'Get out! You mob no good!'

Her husband ran in from the back room just as Jackie Burrup pushed open the front door.

'Hey sis, what's up?' Jackie asked.

Mae's sharp, high-pitched response cut the air, 'She no good! She bad girl! She open fridge to steal drink! Just like brother. Bad girl from bad family!'

'Chill out, little lady,' Jackie responded calmly.

I giggled nervously.

'I'm shoutin' this Lucky-Child and my money's good as the next man's.'

I put my hand on a large bottle of Coke and looked at him questioningly. He nodded. As I went to the counter where he was standing, he picked up a couple of packets of chips, some croc jerky, milk bottle lollies, and a pack of bacci for his roll-your-owns. He passed the money over to Mae, and I sheepishly stood behind him, under the watchful glare of Mr Fong.

'I don't steal, misses,' I said.

'You go!' she snapped, waving her hands at me like she was shooing flies.

Jackie Burrup was Frankie's best mate. He'd been working on a cattle station outside Derby. As we walked to his ute, he told me he was going home to see his mum and introduce his new girlfriend, Justine, from Alice Springs[5].

I surprised him by asking if I could catch a ride. I explained that I was going to see my *Jalbri*, who was dying at *Kurriji pa Yajula*.

'What? Dragon Tree Soak in the Great Sandy Desert?' he interrupted with a puzzled look on his face. 'Who are you going with?' Jackie looked at me as if he was checking the health of one of his horses.

'No one,' I said, welling up with tears. Suddenly, I felt all alone, like abandoned or somthin'.

'Bulldust! That's over 220 kilometres away. No shoes! No hat! No water! No food!' He shook his head.

'I'll hunt and eat bush tucker,' I bleated like an idiot.

'Get on! I'll go the long way around and drive you to the Gingerah turnoff. That'll leave you about fifty to sixty kilometres as the crow flies. We'll go onto Bidjy (Bidyadanga[6]) from there.'

I climbed onto the back of the ute and pushed his big smelly dog, Mutt, over to one side. I slumped down onto the swag that was all sticky with drool. Although still feeling wounded by the telling off, I was relieved he was driving me most of the way.

---

5   Alice Springs – A town in the Northern Territory, Australia, 2736kms from Broome, Western Australia.
6   Bidjy – Bidyadanga is a large Aboriginal Community, 190 kilometres south of Broome in the Kimberley Region, Western Australia.

As the car took off, my thoughts returned to *Jalbri*. White people call her Valeryi Dreamer. She's tall and elegant with dark, shiny skin. Her large, black eyes have an unnatural twinkle. She's got a mop of thick, wavy hair that she keeps off her face with a headband woven from reeds and decorated with small feathers.

When she comes to town, she wears a brightly coloured cotton skirt, with big pockets stuffed full of bush tucker for us kids. She never wears a top, instead she proudly paints her initiation scars with red and white ochre that highlights her small breasts.

My *Jalbri* commands respect. People always stop and stare at her. Not rude-like. Everyone knows they've never met someone like her before; she's a one off.

In her time, she's met lots of 'Big White People', even Prime Minister Hawk. He cried like a small baby when she looked into his eyes and told him all about his life and the things that were comin' his way.

Jalbri knows all about women's business and tribal magic. Animals *know who* she is, and they speak to her. She holds the tribal tongue Mangala, and when she speaks, even *kartijas* (*whitefellas*) understand what she's saying.

She's a real whisperer. Crying babies sleep in her arms. Aggressive men lose their fight near her. Animals follow her everywhere, and I love her.

She nags me, sometimes tellin' me not to think too much. Nothin' wrong with thinkin' I reckon. I like to listen to people's stories, and find out what's really troubling them. Everyone's got a story. The crazier ya look, the harder life's treated ya, and the sadder ya story. Them eyes tells ya everything. I told *Jalbri* how I see people, but she told me to be careful cos ya can be dragged into someone's life through their eyes.

I know it must be important for *Jalbri* to call me to Dragon Tree Soak. That's a real special place cos it holds the *living water* and is sacred to her desert mob. When *Jalbri* was born eighty-six years ago, the seed from a Dragon's Blood Tree was buried with her mother's placenta at just the right time, when them stars were lined up the proper way. That's our tradition.

Dragon's Blood Trees are amazing. Sister Clancy, our natural history teacher, was so excited when *Jalbri* visited our school to show us what she keeps in her *nguri* (drawstring bag made from kangaroo skin). She pulled out a big clump of red stuff that looked like a crystal made of blood. That's real important medicine for bushies.

'Eeww!' some of the girls shrieked, thinking my *Jalbri* was a head hunter.

Although Sister Mary Clancy was from Ireland, she knew exactly what that stuff was. Her chubby white face got redder and redder, like she was gonna explode. Suddenly, she grabbed her ruler, I flinched, thinking she was going to hit me. Instead, she brushed past me and raced to the world map on the classroom wall. With the end of the ruler, she made a long arc from a tiny little island in the Arabian Sea near Somalia and Yemen, past the tip of India, down past Sumatra, then Java, and all the way down to Broome.

She told us that she'd been to Dragon's Blood Island, and that Sinbad the sailor was born on there, and that maybe Sinbad himself sailed the high seas to our shores, mounted a camel, and planted the first dragon tree at *Jalbri's* soak in the Great Sandy Desert. How else did it get there? She gushed, lookin' *mamany* (crazy) as.

Sister Mary Clancy had to be from a different planet. Whatever disease she had, I'd caught it too and couldn't help thinking that Sinbad might be my great, great, great grandfather. How cool would that be?

Bored by Sister's fast talkin', *Jalbri* started to act out at the back of the class. She picked up a *malgara* (fighting stick) and pretended to hit Rachael on the head. Us kids cracked up laughing. *Jalbri* shouted out, 'This fella good for pain.' Then she squatted down, held her tummy and made farting noises. Poor Sister Mary Clancy had lost us to shrieks of laughter. *Jalbri* left our classroom and wandered off towards Town Beach.

That was the last time I'd seen her.

But with my mind, I could see her now, sitting at *Kurriji pa Yajula* (Dragon Tree Soak) waiting for me.

3. Town Beach

Mum married my Dad against her parents' wishes. She was from a different skin group to my Dad. According to our *manguny* (law), that's called a 'wrong way marriage'. Under this *Manguny*, *Jalbri* and Dad were not even meant to talk or look sideways at each other.

But *Jalbri* felt compassion for Dad because he was taken and raised by the church. So, in her mind, the *manguny* (law) shouldn't apply to him.

However, my mum should have known better. Her mum and Dad, my grandparents, have no contact with her or us because of this law, and have never even been to our house. Mum is dead to them, and she feels shame.

Mum doesn't talk much, except to scold us kids. She's often silent, even with her friends. Her eyes speak though. And my brothers and I speak for her. *Jalbri* talks with Mum in her mother tongue. They whisper to each other like softly struck tapping sticks. That's when I see Mum breathe and relax, and just for a moment the shame leaves her.

12

Gurndany is the word for shame, and our mob feels shame more than any other emotion.

Mum met my Dad at a cook up at Town Beach. Sheltered from strong winds and high seas, it used to be the safest stretch of water for us black kids. White people never went to Town Beach; they'd always go to Cable Beach at the rich end of town.

The vast Indian Ocean laps calmly on the surrounding reefs that leak into the mudflats and mangroves along Roebuck Bay at the bottom of the cliff, where the Mangrove Hotel perches. For us mob, it's a short walk from Anne Street, St Mary's, Fong's Store, the pub, and the lock-up.

Many years ago, things changed when the Farrells built the slaughterhouse on the jetty right on the point. Blood dripped day and night from the open floorboards, and all the offcuts from the meatworks were thrown straight into the once clear blue sea. From then on, Town Beach became thick with sharks looking for a free feed.

They put up a small enclosure made of steel netting that was fixed into the shoreline at the shop end of the bay. They called it 'Shark-Safe', but when high tide came in, the sharks swarmed over the top of the cage.

Aunty Rosie would laugh like a chook laying an egg when she told stories of them '*blackfellas* (Aboriginal people) leaping around trying to get out'. She's got the blackest sense of humour, but she's always got an add on story that brings you right back down to earth. Like when a young girl had her arm ripped off by a shark in a feeding frenzy when she was swimming in that cage. To make things worse, as compensation, that kid was given a job working for that same slaughterhouse, no joke.

That night at the cook up, Mum and Dad started chatting. He'd just done a long ride, herding cattle across the Top End. I saw a photo from that night, he and his mates looked 'real deadly[7]'. Dad said it was the happiest day of his life.

---

7   Deadly - Fantastic.

Mum went swimming in 'the cage' with her friends, expecting Dad to follow. But Dad never got over all them kids drowning when they jumped ship so instead, he just watched her swimming in the moonlight. His mates ragged him—what sort of coastal man couldn't swim? Mucking around, not knowing his past or why the water terrified him, they picked him up, ran down the old jetty and threw him in the drink[8].

Terrified, Dad panicked. Gulping water and waving frantically, he sank in the growing tide. His mates thought it was a big joke, but not Mum. She scrambled over the netting and dived into the dangerous water to save him, sharks and all. He grabbed hold of her so tight that she thought she was a goner too.

He was real *lucky* she was there.

He cried his heart out to her that night and told her his story. They held each other real tight and slept on the beach. That was the night her life changed forever cos Mum got pregnant. And she was only young like me, sixteen.

My Dad used to be the finest stockman anyone had ever seen. I saw him ride only once when a spinifex fire was threatening a cattle station just outside of Broome. In a whirl of dust, the stockmen rode fifty strong. Dad sat tall in the saddle leading his troop. He looked like someone out of the movies. As they thundered past, he turned to me and smiled. I'd never seen him smile like that before, and never would again.

I went with him to tend the horses that night. Dad blew out deep, airy sounds from his lips, like raspberries, and his horse Lightning, pricked his ears and came in close beside Dad's long, bony body. Then he tapped Lightning's flank and the horse raised his hoof for inspection and a clean.

As Dad brushed him down, they puffed and snorted at each other, and with each snort, they moved like a dance to 'a music of the wind'. I sat on a hay bale watching them, hypnotised by the rhythm. Finally, I fell asleep to the sweet, heady smell of molasses and chaff, and the airy sound of horse and man.

---

8 Drink- Aussie slang for 'water'.

Those were the times I liked to remember. When Dad was happy, we were all happy. He would light a camp fire in our yard and the billy[9] would be boiled for fresh tea. Dad made the deadliest damper ever—a tube of dough pressed around a stick, held over the fire until crispy. Piping hot, we'd pull it off the stick and fill it with a knob of butter and a blob of strawberry jam. Yum!

This was yarning time. He'd get his old bacci tin down from the kitchen shelf behind the flour bin and show us photos of himself with the lads, herding cattle from the old Country. He'd packed a million stories into his short life, and he'd ridden the miles to match.

There was no big, fat pension for him when he retired. His legacy from all those years in the saddle was bandy legs and rider's crotch and a fail-safe salve from an old tracker called Sniffer. 'It keeps the bones strong like steel, them muscles firm as. Stops the stiffness, pain and balding, and keeps a bloke's tackle working like a young buck's.'

You mix up:

2 cups of emu oil

1/2 cup of goanna oil

1 cup of camel testicle oil

1/4 cups of Dragon's Blood (the resin from the Dragon's Blood Tree)

Dad used this salve for everything—no kidding—skin rashes, sand-fly bites, and for keeping mozzies (mosquitoes) away. Dogs loved it. Even those savage police dogs would lick his hand and look at him lovingly.

Every Sunday was head massage day for the boys. The thick lard-like salve would melt with their body heat and trickle down their faces, making their skin shine like highly polished wood. He never did my hair cos he was worried that I would grow a beard and get a man's voice, 'like them Central Desert sheila's who eat camels' testicles'.

---

9   Billy - Tin can used to boil water.

Coming back from church, the neighbours always laughed at the boys dripping with oil, but Dad would point to his shock of thick, black hair and sing out, 'See everything's still strong', while grinning and gyrating his hips like Elvis.

Yeah, they were the happy times. I learnt to love that oil, and its gamy smell.

When the cattle stations fired the black stockmen, my Dad lost a part of his will to live. 'The deepest thoughts,' he'd say, 'come to a fella when he's on his own'.

I could imagine Dad riding the vast red land in tune to a different rhythm than us townies.

The rising sun would gently call him into the saddle and the heat of the day would make him rest up. Watching the colours of the setting sun always melted his heart and would bring a tear to his eye, and with a lump in his throat, he'd tell us, 'When the darkness comes in, all the little creatures find their voice. That's when ya know ya never alone.' Sitting round the fire, billy boiling, yarning with his mates about the old days took him back to his home out on the plains where the *bundarra* (stars) seemed so close, you could reach out and touch one.

It's a long way between drinks when you're herding cattle across the Top End, everyone ya meet's a real character, no one's normal. They've all run away from something or someone. Out there, in the land Beyond Beyond, our Country moulds ya, so ya become a part of the landscape. You become like the rock or the gnarled old tree. That's how ya find your totem.

Every stocky can sing and play the guitar. Even now the old fellas say that Dad had the mark of fame; a big gap between his front teeth and a beauty spot under his right eye. His voice had a special something. If he hummed in a certain way, thousands of bush cockroaches would line up side by side, head to tail, covering the ground. To them cockroaches and most animals, he was God.

But when you're *julgia* (broken) and lost, your luck sours and people know you for the wrong sort of acting out. When his mood was starting to head south, he'd get out his old mouth organ (harmonica). I'd feel my emotions rising up into my throat long before his big black lips touched its silver edge. When he'd gently breathe into that thing, a deadly sadness would flood into every corner of our house. Mum and us kids knew that the tin roof and four walls we called home, was just a prison to him that made his heart so sick. Living with us was killing him. Although he was free to go, he couldn't leave the only family he had.

So, to forget who he *really* was, he drank. But the drink never let him forget. Instead, it made him wild with rage and later, angry with shame. He was *julgia* and nothing could fix him.

Sometimes he'd get what he loved and what he hated mixed up. Although he hated the Church, because they killed his mother, broke his father, and abused all them kids, he couldn't help loving Baby Jesus and the Virgin Mary. When he was battling his demons and needed time out, everyone knew where to find him. If he wasn't in jail, he'd be kneeling in front of the statue of Mother Mary of Peace, holding Baby Jesus on the pearl shell altar at St Mary's.

Dad had friends, but only one father figure; his saving grace was Old Jimmy Howard. He lived in Broome with his thirteen kids, but after he buried his wife and five of his kids, he fell in love with a *kartija* (white woman), married her and went off to live in Noosa Queensland.

Old Jimmy played a mean guitar and all his songs were about herding cattle in Mt Isa. He was that real old-style cowboy with a big, white Akubra hat, long boots and a silver necktie ring. His manly hands were strong and gentle, just like him. He never said a bad word about anyone and was even grateful to the German priest for teaching him about horses, even though the Church stole him from his parents fifty years before they took Dad.

Taking kids from their parents started officially in 1910 and went on right up until 1970. And it's still going on today!

As Jimmy was being pulled from his father's grip by the German priest, his father's last words to him were, 'Son, don't look back, just keep looking forward.' That became the motto that Jimmy lived his life by.

When Dad was down, Jimmy would say to him, 'Son, don't look back, just keep looking forward.'

Those words made Dad clean himself up real good, wash and shave, and get Uncle Cedric to iron his pants. Dad would then go looking for work.

But nothing lasted long.

Even the rodeo gig ended in a fist fight, and he hitched a lift home, drunk as, looking like shit. Everything was a fight for him, he didn't know any other way.

4. Sorry Business

The thirteenth of October last year was a night we would never forget. Mum was frustrated because we'd all just come back from fishing, and Dad was already drunk. She threw her bucket of fish on the floor and yelled, 'Stop the fucking grog and get a job!'

'You don't know what it's like to be stolen,' he sobbed.

Fired up, Mum raised her voice like never before. 'Get over yourself! I don't know my father and my mother disowned me when I did *wrong way marriage* to you!'

'Fuck off!' he spat in her face. Looking real mean, he hissed at her through clenched teeth, 'I've had a gut full of people tellin' me what not to do...' He landed the first blow. Then beat her like never before. As always, she suffered in silence.

19

Frankie turned seventeen just two days before. He was six foot two and insane with rage. I saw him close his eyes and take an almighty swing at his father. Dad had taught him how to box. Frankie had learnt well and didn't hold back, he punched Dad with every bit of his strength. Crying and sobbing, blinded by tears he kept punching Dad again and again.

Frankie's survival instinct to fight his way out of every painful situation had kicked in mighty strong and he, like Dad, couldn't help himself.

'FUUUCKING STOP! STOP! YOU'RE KILLING HIM!' we screeched.

Crying and scared, we didn't know what to do. A neighbour called the cops and his sons, Big Ben and Fridge, grabbed Frankie and took him down with a strangle hold. Finally, Frankie gave up the fight. Breathing hard, he eyeballed Dad.

Dad's chest was heaving, crying softly he whispered, 'it's okay, son, it's okay.'

It felt like Dad was trying to tell Frankie that he forgave him. I reckon everyone knows that sort of forgiveness. It's like when your dog snaps cos you touch his bone. He can't help himself, even though he loves you.

The cops (police) stormed in all savage-like. No questions asked; they just put the boots into Dad over and over and over again. The thud of metal-toed boot against Dad's head and chest was sickening.

Frankie was shouting, 'STOP! FUCKING STOP! Dad, don't die! I'm sorry. Shit, please STOOOP!'

Wailing loudly, our grief made everything feel unreal. I felt like my soul had left the room and was listening from outside in the yard.

The coppers were in a frenzy. I even heard one fella shout out his wife's name as he sunk his boot into Dad's skull. Everyone seemed to be acting out a rage that had nothing to do with Dad. They couldn't stop themselves. With Dad's last bit of willpower, he looked at Frankie with love like I'd never seen before. He looked soft. Gentle-like. Compassionate like the Virgin Mary. Nah,

I think it was like how his mother's eyes must have looked at him under the water that night when he was stolen and almost drowned. The night he became a 'Lucky-Child'.

Dad tried to speak but he was choking on the blood pouring out of his mouth. He turned his head slightly, and his eyes rolled to the back of his head. He coughed a spurt of blood. His body suddenly looked heavy and strangely still. A blue mist rose out of his chest. It seemed to be attached to a gold thread that broke off and hovered in the air above him as if to say goodbye. I even think 'it' felt sorry for us. And then it was gone. Everyone stood for a minute in deadly silence, even the cops.

The spell was broken and the cops silently dragged Dad's sad, *unlucky* body into the paddy wagon.

All the while, Frankie was screaming, 'Oh God! No! No! I killed my Dad! I'm sorry, Oh God! No!'

It sounded like he was screaming into a brown paper bag, with the volume turned down by our grief. The misery of that moment shut out the noises of life. Poor Frankie felt so guilty. He loved Dad so much, maybe even too much. How could he, the favourite child, kill his own Dad? How could he live with himself now?

That night he punched his fist through every door and wall in our house. His hands were swollen and bloody and strangely, his gut instinct was to reach for Dad's healing salve. As he applied the salve it was as if he became Dad that night.

He still keeps up the oiling tradition and carries a photo of himself as a little kid riding bare back with Dad. That photo is like Frankie's relic. It's wrapped multiple times in GladWrap and he keeps it in his left shirt pocket close to his heart. He kisses it for good luck and rubs it gently over his lips when he is worried.

The coppers came back the next day to announce to everyone that, 'Mr Alan Lucky-Child from Beagle Bay died in his cell on the night of the thirteenth of October.'

However, we all knew differently.

But there was no point protesting about it. What could we say about that night that made us more innocent than them? Dad was *julgia* (broken), and if you're black and *julgia,* you're proper broken and your life ends up no good.

The Elders came to do 'Sorry Business'. Old Mr Rowe, the King of Anne Street, gently placed his hand on Mum's shoulder, he turned her around to look at him, and in a deep, soothing voice, he whispered, 'Hey *kurntal* (daughter), no more 'wrong ways' and *nyaan-nyaan* (secret whispers). It's okay, *buju* (finished), all that trouble.'

A long sound of grief escaped her body, like wind blowing through the gaps in the louvres above my bed. I knew they were talking about an *old secret,* but I didn't know what. I was lost in that dark space of not knowing when the King started speaking in a different language. I listened hard, but I couldn't understand what was being said.

Suddenly that moment was lost to the sound of men clapping sticks and singing, accompanied by the high pitch sound of women wailing. The singing made the grief more real, more physical. The air became thicker and we poured out of our little tin house. It felt too small, too rigid, too much like a prison to contain the expanding energy of grief.

Outside, the 'Sorry Business' song led us in a trance down to Town Beach and along past the old jetty to where the rocks left the mangroves. In the setting sun my heart melted into the piercing sound of the clapping sticks beating against each other. The harsh sounds of the men's *sorry* song wove itself into the women's shrill wailing. That vibration dragged out the pain and loss from every hidden crack in my body and spirit.

That monotonous, unrelenting sound undid all the threads that held me together. I couldn't think cos the clapping of the sticks was going against my heartbeat, setting me adrift like a small boat on a vast sea of sound.

Deep wounds healed and the emptiness made me feel free to *thubarnimanha* (straighten up) and start again.

Finally, I breathed in. It was as if the whole 'Sorry Business' was just a dream and it was hard to find where that unbearable pain used to live.

Suddenly, I saw him. 'Mum, there's Dad, no joken'. Look up! Mum…'

Dad walked across the water at Town Beach and stepped into that setting sun. Free of life's pain, he was reborn. For me, all the bad memories of my angry, misfit father slipped away and there, in the setting sun, him and me were washed in that same light. For the first time I understood that '*this blackfella belong me.*'

I slept. I woke and slept again. The 'Sorry Business' continued.

On the third day I saw Barbara, who was Dad's 'other woman'. I hated her. She lived off Gubinge Road at the far end of town. Her kid, Helen, was born on the same day as me. People even mistake us for each other, even though she has two freckles. *How dare Barbara come here with her bastard when we are doing 'Sorry Business'.*

Barbara walked up to Mum, hips swaying like some classy bitch. I ran up to see what was going down. 'He'd want you to have this, Mary,' she said, pressing two hundred dollars into Mum's hand.

Mum had given up her fight. Her face was still bruised and swollen, and she had dried blood through her hair and on the edge of her chin, but her tears had cleaned her face. Without a word, she just put the money into her apron pocket that she was still wearing, stiff with splattered blood from that night.

What was Mum thinking? Why did she stay with Dad? And how did she keep her pride with that bitch and her bastard living so close?

I glared at Helen, who was hanging back in the shadows.

'Now, piss off!' I yelled at Barbara, 'And take your bastard with you!'

They ignored me.

'He got you real bad this time Mary.'

'And what do you care?' I interrupted, 'You're the bitch he shoulda beaten!'

Barbara turned her evil eyes on me, 'He had no reason to beat me!'

'Shut up you whore!' My grief was replaced with rage.

'Let's go Mum,' Helen said softly, pulling her Mum by the elbow.

'Yeah, rack off, Dad loved us, not youse!'

I was so furious, I wanted to hit her. As they left, I turned to look at my poor mum.

I could see she felt shame, but the bruises around her eyes somehow made her look hauntingly beautiful. As I looked at her, my eyelids became heavy. I blinked slowly like a little kid fighting sleep. When my eyes finally opened, I was trapped in a strange *bukirri* (dream).

My mother stood opposite me, gazing into a deep rock pool. The dark still water reflected the full moon perfectly. Its eerie, greenish glow shone brightly against the purple night sky across which was strewn the Milky Way.

Strong and bewitchingly beautiful, like a black goddess from the Dreamtime, Mum stood tall and drew a single deep breath. Her full, black lips started to move, and to my disbelief I heard a song leave her lips. My ears struggled to separate this full, rounded high-pitched sound that soared above the men's 'Sorry Business' and the women's wailing. I'd never heard my mum sing before, but this song was so familiar. I'm sure I'd heard Sister Euphrates play it on her gramophone.

Mum's arms rose up as if embracing the moon. Her cheeks glistened with tears. As her piercing voice filled the air, I saw a girl on a white horse rise up behind her. Backlit by the huge full moon, I could see she looked a bit like me.

Distracted from the song, I ran forward, desperately wanting to get a better look at the reflection in the rock pool. Focusing my eyes, now filled with tears, I watched the girl on the horse turn away. The moonlight dimmed, lost in a thick smoke haze from a roaring bushfire.

Then, in the depth of the rock pool, something stirred. I thought I saw two glinting eyes. A cold shiver ran up my spine. I felt myself stiffen, as if I was

24

turning to stone. I gasped. From the rock pool's dark centre, an enormous ripple broke the water's mirror-like surface.

That girl, her horse, my mother, the moon, the Milky Way, and even my own image disappeared. My heart felt like it had been crushed like an empty Coke can. *Julgia*, *julgia*, broken, broken—all was broken. Confused and chilled to the bone, I returned to the 'Sorry Business' of my father's passing.

5. Sister, Saint and Lover

'Hey, Lucky-Child!' Jackie Burrup stuck his head out of the ute. 'Almost there. You okay?'

Jolted back into the present, I gave him the thumbs up. Going that little bit central and south-east, you realise how big this Country is and how few people live here.

Broome feels small because we were always looking out at the big sea in front of us and forgetting to look at the big Country stretched out behind us. The landscape had changed so dramatically from the Broome Township, with its avenues of frangipanis, boab trees, tourists and coffee shops.

The surrounding land is flat with ridges of rocky outcrops and little hills in the distance. Clumps of spinifex and other grasses are yellow against the bright-red sand. Spindly trees and scrubby bushes cling together in sandy ridges where the water collects.

I became aware of the ute slipping sideways and bumping over small ridges made by the recent rains. It's a slow drive avoiding large puddles on a cut-track road. The gentle rhythm and the warmth in the back of the ute seemed to make my life pass before me. The sound of Mutt's heavy breathing as he slept made me struggle to stay awake. Wiping his drool off my string bag, my thoughts went straight to Sister Euphrates.

Next to my *Jalbri*, Sister is the most inspiring person I've ever met. After school, three days a week, she teaches craft in St Mary's Hall at the back of the church. She's very old, tiny and French, and she wears her habit like a ballerina. She floats across the room with the lightness of a willie wagtail[10].

She draws the purple velvet stage curtains at the back of the hall to create a room for our class. On the drapes she pins photos from different parts of the world, as well as quotes from inspiring thinkers, and even her own sayings for the day.

We run noisily into her class. She's always standing near her wind-up gramophone, waiting for us. As soon as she says, 'Ladies', a hush comes over us and we leave Broome and travel with her, riding what she calls 'the magic carpet of our imagination'. That's how we share her amazing adventures through Egypt, France, The Congo. We've even had high tea with the Queen of England.

We all work on the floor surrounded by her treasures and lit by the warm glow of her favourite aunty's tall lamp. Its enormous red lamp shade has long, golden tassels that makes our room feel real posh. On the polished floorboards she places large handmade baskets filled with strings and cloths. And little baskets and bowls full of needles and beads. For each season, different cut grasses are brought in for us to work with. Dying and painting is always done outside.

Her little hands quickly twist and weave grasses and knot strings.

'What is this?' she'd ask.

---

10   Willie wagtail - A bird native to Australia.

'A bird', we might answer, and then she would launch into another story. Like our story-telling tradition, every lesson had a spiritual message. She recites quotes over and over in class both in English and Badi, and sometimes Islander. And as we stitch, we weave her messages into our hearts.

Last week, Sister gathered us kids in real close. 'Ladies,' she whispered, 'today is the fifth of January, my Remembrance Day.' We hung on every delicately accented note.

Sitting on the floor, every black eye followed her as she poured sweet black tea for us in her finest china cups. The hand-painted figures on the cups came to life, bathed in the warm lamp light that brightened the gloomy hall, darkened by the heavy monsoonal skies outside. Thunder, like a drum roll, set the stage.

'In 1968, when I was still a naive young girl from France, I went to Vietnam with thousands of other nuns and priests, both French and Vietnamese, to help those in the war.' She spread out black and white photos on the floor. Some were of children screaming and running in terror. Others were of bombs exploding, villages on fire, and bandaged children in the nun's arms. Her eyes filled to the brim with tears as the memories of these photos dragged her soul from Broome back to Vietnam.

'War is a terrible thing. There is no honour. There are no heroes. All good intentions sour on the battlefield.' She breathed deeply and tried to swallow. 'I was stationed in a tiny rice-growing village with four Vietnamese nuns. These women worked tirelessly and without complaint. They were Saints. Just innocent nuns caring for innocent children.

'We had such a sweet group of orphaned children. Binh, her name means Peace, was five years old, both her legs had been blown off by a landmine. Poor Cadeo and Yen were just eight and nine. They had been burnt horrifically by napalm. We cared for twenty-seven children, but these three were my special charge. Many had seen their parents shot dead, bombed, or burnt alive, and yet those little souls who had experienced such sadness brought us such joy.

'On the fifth of January 1975, the underground tunnel that was hiding every child in our village, was bombed by American Troops. None survived. The villagers believed that we nuns were informants who had betrayed them and revealed their safe place to the Americans. There was nothing we could do or say to convince them that this was not true. We had spent seven years caring for all the villagers regardless of political persuasion. Ah, but all our good deeds were forgotten. The locals had become *foux* (crazy) with grief. We understood that their rationale had left them. No more could they identify the true enemy—war itself.

'However, I was not expecting such cruelty. In the fields of rice near the tunnel they stripped my Sisters naked. Mother Angelica stood with dignity. The enraged men spat in her face, and without the slightest hesitation they raped her and slit her throat while she prayed aloud until death silenced her. Sister Mary Francis fell to her knees asking God to forgive them. In return they gouged out her eyes and cut off her tongue!

'Begging for mercy, I shouted in Vietnamese *"bân chúng tôi! bân chúng tôi* (Shoot us! Shoot us)!"* I wanted to offer myself up in their place. Suddenly they grabbed me. "This is it," I thought, but being white and a foreigner gave me special privileges. I was bundled into the back of the truck and taken to the notorious Ho Chi Min Prison.

'After being dragged out of the truck and through the courtyard, I was thrown into a tiny cell and forced to sit naked on a concrete block with my ankles chained to a metal bar at its base. I could not lay flat, and the cold, damp block was wet with urine and shit from the prisoner before. My bones ached and my stomach churned from the stench.

'The door banged closed. In darkness, I waited for the dawn. Hearing groaning from the other cells, I feared what dreadful things they would do to me. The feelings of suspense, overwhelmed me and shamelessly I sank into anxiety and self-pity.

'That night, in the darkness of that miserable cell, I lost my faith that God was good and that His Will was perfect. How could my Sisters' sufferings be a blessing? It was *nuit obscure d l'âme*—how do you say—Dark Night of the Soul. Then I heard the song of a single bird outside my cell announce the dawn. Oh, so normal. How did this little one not notice the war?

'But then, as if God would teach my desperate soul, a single ray of light illuminated the wall and made me cry with joy. *Non* (no), it was complete and utter bliss. The sweetest souls captured in this cell before me, had scratched into the concrete, perhaps with their fingernails, drawings, poems, songs, and bars of music. Someone even scrawled recipes that filled my stomach and my poor ribs that were so hollow with hunger. Such recipes reminded me of my mère (mother) and my hometown.

'It didn't matter anymore that I was sitting in—what you call—shit, for I was no longer a prisoner in a concrete cell. My mind and spirit soared with each newly discovered scratch. Then I understood that suffering reveals your true self. To find oneself is the true blessing and the sole purpose of why we suffer. Emerson [11]once said, "What lies behind us and what lies before us are small matters compared to what lies within us".'

Sister Euphrates' right hand laid flat against her chest as if to calm her heart. Looking towards Heaven, her eyes glowed brightly, and she looked beautiful. 'Your thoughts are your most precious possession; they help you manifest your Heaven on Earth.'

Then in true Euphrates style, she leapt out of that intense moment into the lesson for the day. 'Let's make a survival bag. A body and soul bag. It is useful to carry a small knife, matches, and some food and water. But the soul needs things to remind it of home and the people it loves. Put in the bag the things that will inspire you when you are truly lost.' She was radiant now. 'In this basket are some treasures of mine. Feel free to take the thing that touches your heart.'

Us kids sat for a while in stunned silence. No one touched our hearts like her.

11   Ralph Waldo Emerson - An American essayist, lecturer, philosopher and poet who led the transcendentalist movement of the 19th Century.

Suddenly, we were back in St Mary's Hall in Broome. Sylvee asked Sister if she could make a 'love bag'. Everyone screamed with laughter.

'Oooh, Sylvee and Skinny, kissing in the dark ...'

Sister clicked her tongue like gunfire, which she'd learnt to do in Africa. 'Ladies!' We quietened down, except for Rachael and Megan—the troublemakers. Turning to Sylvee, who was red with shame, Sister said, '*Non, mes chéries.*'

We knew that it meant 'my darlings'.

'Love is a beautiful thing, no need for shame. It is only right that love blesses the young. It takes you from being a child, and with its magic, transforms you into a grown woman.' Sister grabbed an armful of purple drape and held it close to her body. In that weird moment the drape looked like a tall man embracing her as she danced on those shining boards in the ballroom of her youth.

'Love *mes chéries* brings out the best in you. When he says '*je t'aime*,' I love you, your heart melts and every word he utters is then music to the ear, and to see him, it is like going from black and white TV to colour. His touch is electrifying, and his kiss is sweeter than the best chocolate in the whole of Paris. To be with him swells your heart and expands your mind because you know that with him, you are safe to reveal your true self.'

'What happened to him?' Sylvee interrupted, cutting through the moment, and bringing Sister crashing back to Earth again.

She dropped the drape, straightened her apron and picked up the war photos that were still strewn on the floor. 'Mother met with a car accident and the doctors said she wouldn't live,' Sister said in a matter-of-fact voice. 'I went to the Sainte Chappell Cathedral in Paris. On my knees I begged Jesus to save my precious mére's (mother's) life, and I vowed that if my mére survived, I would join a nunnery.

I uttered my pledge to blessed Jesus—may my life be a sacrifice unto him. At the very moment, a rainbow of coloured light poured down from the stained-glass window and illuminated my entire being. Instantly, my prayer

31

was confirmed and I was filled with the light and love of Jesus—the redeemer and forgiver of sins—and my mére made a full recovery.'

We all gasped.

'Well, well. That's that for now,' she said, slamming the door shut on her private life.

Everyone silently collected things for their 'body and soul' bags. We loved Sister's cool Mary Poppin's bag that was always either slung on her shoulder or sitting open at her feet, ready for amazing creations to materialise. It was her bag of bags. There was one for trinkets, one for scarves, another filled with threads and others for shells, stones and bones. Whenever we were mining for inspiration, our long, black fingers would reach down into the many bags of Sister Euphrates, searching for its treasures.

Sister had another intriguing bag, which hung on a crocheted choker that sat in the nape of her long, thin, white neck. It was a little black silk square bag with a tiny bone heart sewn onto a halo of brightly coloured thread. When asked if we could see inside that bag, she instinctively covered it with her hand, saying it held the relics of her heart. I wondered if it was home to a picture of her Sisters, her mére, her teenage lover, or some other dark secret.

Sitting on the cool, highly polished floorboards, I slid over to her basket of precious items. There, I noticed an old silver spoon with the words engraved on it: *Je t'aime*. I knew it meant 'I love you'. I picked it up and ran my thumb over the front and back of the spoon. I felt that whoever engraved 'I love you' had meant it, because the impression went through to the other side. Closing my eyes, I made a wish that I'd find that same sort of love—a precious, romantic love.

I opened my eyes to see Sister wiping hers. She'd noticed I had her spoon and smiled knowingly. Picking up a spool of unbleached cotton string, I went back to my spot on the floor to make my first 'body and soul' bag. Somehow, I felt a closeness to Sister now. The nun's habit had fallen away, and we were just two women understanding the stuff of the heart.

Sister came over and showed me how to crochet with the finest wooden hook. As she passed the thread over the hook, I noticed the scars on her wrists. Her little hands were so white against the string and my long dark fingers. Suddenly, I felt shocked by my own darkness, and I realised for the first time that Sister Euphrates never treated us like 'brown people'.

Our black families reminded us all the time that we were dark-skinned. 'Blacks don't do *this* or *that* because being black is the wrong colour.' They'd often say, 'You think you're so smart. You're just a *blackfella* like us. You're no different to us and never will be.'

No one expected us to want to know about faraway places and people and their thoughts. No one believed that we could understand how a teenage girl in Paris felt when in love. Somehow, our love was less lovely, less beautiful, and less romantic. Us *blackfellas* were prejudiced against ourselves. Sister Euphrates spoke to us like we were 'white'.

I crocheted my 'body and soul' bag with soft, fine unbleached cotton in the shape of a wind sock. It had a gentle point at the bottom and was as long as an A4 piece of paper. On the end of the drawstrings, there were two periwinkle shells that looked like a couple of moon craters that I reckon will always remind me of the sea and the reef at Gantheaume Point.

In the bottom I put Dad's white hanky that he used when he lived on the mission at Beagle Bay. I loved it because Dad had embroidered a big, poorly sewn 'A' on the corner when he was just a little kid. After he died, I nicked it, along with his old black, gold and red Luxor tobacco tin. Inside I put a small fishhook with a thin fishing line bound up with a lackey (elastic) band and a small folding pearl-handled pocket knife, which fit perfectly.

I found the knife a few years ago at the beach and imagined a Japanese pearler must have lost it when the luggers were still in use. Now I use that sweet little knife for everything, but most of all, I just love the feel of it in my hand. I also shoved a ring-pull cap from an old Coke can into my tin. I don't know why; I just gotta hunch that it will come in handy one day. And of course, I can't go anywhere without Dad's magic gloop which I plastered into an ancient Fullers Earth Cream tin that I found at the dump. It's perfect for the job.

Into a stumpy red metal cylinder, I put 3 pieces of rolled up brown paper and Dad's little TAB[12] pencil for drawing maps. I decided to take 2 tiny, white, naked porcelain dolls. I found a mob of them stuck in the reef at low tide.

Sister said the dolls are from from Germany and were probably lost at sea by the nuns who were shipwrecked fifty years ago. I imagine those nuns were real kind like Sister, cos they brought so many dolls for the mission kids to play with. It doesn't worry me that they're white, us kids are used to it.

My survival kit was looking pretty good, with the packet of Tiny Teddies that my best friend Louanna gave me, the jelly snakes that I nicked off Frankie, topped off with the little bag of black tea, tiny pot of cherry jam and small tin tea cup from Persia that Sister gave me. It's got no handle and is engraved with little flowers all the way round its rim, and it sits in ya hand just right. I love it.

As I put them in my 'body and soul' bag, I smiled to myself, then I folded up the plastic bag I'd used to carry all my stuff, and neatly slipped the plastic bag into the top.

'You're going bush in style. Nothing like drinking a fine tea and cherry jam under the Milky Way, ' she said, patting my shoulder. I felt real proud.

---

12   TAB - Totalisator Agency Board, a gambling organisation.

6. Bird Boy

Sister flitted around the room quietly, placing a special little gift in each girl's hand. Mine was a music box. I turned the handle, and it played a pretty tune. Sister sang a love song for me in English. It went something like this:

'Faraway over the sea

Somewhere, he's waits for Lucy

He stands on golden sands

Waiting to hold her in his strong hands.'

'Rark rark,' the girls sang out from the back of the room.

Sister smiled knowingly.

I felt shame cos everyone knew my candle was burning bright for Manu Tollie.

35

For many months I'd had a recurring dream about a handsome boy dancing like a bird. I told my family about this dream—big mistake cos now they won't stop ragging me. They jump out in front of me and do all sorts of crazy bird dances. I just have to pass Frankie and his friends, Megan and Rachael, and they squawk '*rark rark*' mocking me. It's all too much.

Last year, a boy called Manu Tollie came with his church group from the Tiwi Islands to dance at St Mary's for our Easter celebrations. When the purple drapes drew back, there on stage—with Bird of Paradise head-dress and full grass skirt —was the boy I'd seen so many times in my dreams. I recognised his eyes, the tilt of his head and his soft gentle nature in that strong, bronze body. As the boys danced in formation like the birds, I couldn't hold back my tears. He was literally the man of my dreams, my Bird Boy.

Since then, I've got to know a lot about Manu Tollie. He loves Mabo[13] and actively defends land and fishing titles for Tiwi Islanders. He wears his shark totem on a leather thong around his neck. The shark is finely carved from whalebone and seems to swim on the ocean of his bronze chest as it rises and falls with each breath.

That night we had a special community dinner at the hall and Mum did most of the cooking. Dad always said, 'Jesus caught them five fishes, but my Mary feeds the five thousand.'

Anyway, after dinner, we kids left the grown-ups and walked down to Town Beach. Along the way, some of the kids were throwing stones at houses and pushing over letterboxes. Louanna and I didn't want any kids bringing 'bad on us', so we turned around to head back home. When Manu noticed us leaving, he ran to join us and offered to walk us home.

The moon was full, and the tide was high, and I felt strangely comfortable with Manu by my side. I couldn't handle the thought of Manu meeting Dad and Frankie, who by now would have a skin full of grog. So playfully, I turned him

---

13   Eddie Mabo - An Indigenous Torres Strait Islander who overturned the legal doctrine of *Terra Nullis* (nobody's land) in his campaign for land rights in 1992.

away from Anne Street and pointed him towards the Mangrove Hotel. We went around the side, running under the twinkling fairy lights and past the tables dressed in white. The moon hung heavily, and its golden light made a path to where the sea kissed the sky.

Manu noticed a guitar resting against an empty chair. Picking it up and strumming it lightly, he sang softly, 'Listen to me sing, I want to change everything, and show you that you have my heart on a string.'

People started to gather around and some started dancing.

When he finished, everyone clapped. He suddenly got 'shame' cos he went bright red in the face, tripped up on a chair leg when he went to put the the guitar down and ran over to stand with us. He whispered in my ear, 'That was for you.' I felt my face go bright red too.

I'm actually scared of men, especially drunk ones. Ever since I was little I've had to fight my way out of many a man's grip. I've even had to bite a few drunken tongues that were trying to force their way into my mouth. I hate it. It makes me feel real dirty.

But Manu's not like them other guys. I awkwardly reached over and kissed his cheek. I'd never dared kiss a boy before. But he was different. There was kindness in his soft cheek. He was not a taker, or a forcer, or a demander, he was a thinker.

Kissing Manu made me think of all the bad things he wasn't, and I couldn't help feeling sorry for my friend Tina. She was so pretty and full of life, a huge flirt and 'deadly as' on the basketball court. That bastard Robbo, an ex footy player, thought he was hot shit, he beat her up and full on raped her. Tina was only fifteen. Robbo's lawyers went to court, moaning that he was depressed because now his big-time footy career was over. But it was her, Tina, who got the depression real bad.

She went properly off the rails, left school and started drinking heavily and sniffing petrol all the time. For a sniff of fuel, Tina would do anything those truckies wanted. She was my friend, but I didn't recognise her anymore. I couldn't bear to be near her or even look at her. She was drunk and high-as all the time, walkin' all crooked, drooling and talkin' rubbish like an idiot. She got so bad that even her mum couldn't stand it and went off to live with her Aunty.

One day when I was coming out of school, she came over and wanted to hang out with me. But she couldn't even focus her eyes on me. It was so embarrassing. I couldn't handle her talkin' to me and makin' a scene. Worst of all, I didn't want her fuckin' touchin' me. She smelt like shit.

'See you at six?' she mumbled, clutching onto me. I pushed her away. I was shaking and ran home furious. I'd had enough of her yapping on about Robbos' lawyers. I couldn't swallow her pity pie no more. I was gagging on it.

When I got to my house, no one was there. I was starving, but couldn't eat. I just sat at the kitchen table watching the clock and thinking about Tina. The little hand was passing six, I didn't budge. I was angry. I hated her for getting inside my head and trying to control me. I just kept watching the little hand as it reached seven and the big hand, as it made its way past twelve.

Suddenly, an icy chill ran down my spine. I'd messed up big time.

Breaking out in a cold sweat, my heart leapt up into my throat. I wasn't angry no more, I was scared shitless. Them skinny bloody legs of mine had a mind of their own and took off fast, real fast, faster than ever before, straight to her house at the far end of Anne Street.

The front door was opened wide. No music. No lights. I heard a strange spitting noise and something crashed to the bathroom floor. Struggling to open the door ... for a split second... time stood still... As I tried to open the bathroom door. My brain didn't want to believe what I was seeing or hearing.

Then it hit me. Shit!

Screaming, I kicked that door with every bit of strength my legs had in them. Tina's long, basketball playing legs jerked back and forth, kicking me as I pushed my way into the cramped bathroom. I was trying, but I couldn't get her down. The ceiling in their bathroom had fallen long before they'd started renting. The exposed beam was too high, I couldn't reach the knot she'd tied nestled stubbornly into the wooden join. Her purple, swollen tongue stuck out like she was mocking me for not coming sooner. I was too late.

Tina was fully dead. And with her blood shot eyes, she cursed me with night terrors that I know will stay with me forever. How can I ask her to forgive me when she couldn't trust me to be a *real* friend to her, let alone anyone else?

Robbo and those bastard lawyers had won. The case was closed. Tina had lost her claim for the emotional, physical and spiritual damage caused by the rape and beating.

Sure enough, he raped her, but me, Lucy, her only friend, murdered her and I want revenge for the murderer he'd made me become.

Truly, my rage at the injustice felt so real, so physical. I felt like I could hurl it at Robbo like a spear and kill him. I didn't want to see his fucking *walhi* (no good) face walking around town. I wanted him dead. Dead like Tina. A painful death. Not thinking, I told *Jalbri* what I was feeling.

Calmly, she said, 'Ya must be careful when ya take a life cos them fellas no good learnin' will come to ya.'

'Why don't we all get together and kill all the bad people in the world,' I asked, cheeks burning with excitement at the thought of using such power.

Eyeballing me, she firmly said, 'No. In your lifetime, ya can only "point the bone[14]" one time ....'

Shocked by her response, I remembered hearing about 'pointing the bone'. This was serious shit. I was just flapping my gums, but somehow, I knew now she'd done it.

---

14   Pointing the bone – A traditional curse performed by Australian Aborigines, the practice of condemning someone to death by pointing a sharpened bone at them.

7. Sacred Jilas

The ute pulled up sharply. I was slumped over with my head resting on Mutt's huge shoulder. As he leapt up and out of the ute, my head hit the back of the cab. Mutt quickly found a smoke bush to cock his leg on and let out a satisfying sigh as he pissed. To his surprise an enormous lizard ran over to have a drink from his steaming piss pond.

Jumping down off the ute onto the hot, crusty sand, I yelped and sprang sideways, landing in Mutt's piss. Unfazed, the lizard kept drinking.

'Prepared, are we?' said Jackie with a wicked grin on his face. 'Here, have these.' His girlfriend nodded as he gestured to the pair of thongs tied to the top of her bag.

With a tilt of his head and pointing his large lower lip blackfella style to the front of cab, Jackie ordered me to follow him.

'Got ya some goodies.'

'Wicked.' I smiled.

'Here, sis.' He grabbed the plastic bag from Fong's. In it were the things he'd bought. He gave me everything except for his 'roll your owns'.

I reached up to give him a big hug, but he was so long and bony, it felt real awkward. I wondered how his girlfriend managed cos she was a real short arse.

Reaching into his pocket, he pulled out two small cards of matches. Flicking them at me, he said, 'You might need these.'

'Deadly dude,' I said, bending down to pick up the Golden Fleece card. I noticed the big golden ram printed on the front of the purple sleeve. How ironic that Jackie should give me the sheep card. In 1907, the Canning Stock Route[15] cut through the sacred lands of The Great Sandy Desert and its neighbours, capping all the *Jilas* (soak, eternal water) en-route.

In the desert, there's surface water called *Jumu. Juljul* are freshwater soaks and *Pajalpi* are springs. These water sources are all seasonal. But then there's the *Jilas*, the most precious water source of them all. *Jilas* are not seasonal. They are *living water*—an eternal source from deep underground. They're real hard to find, cos they don't look like much, just a small patch of damp earth in a great big desert.

No one can live without water, but in the desert, water is more precious and sacred than city folk would believe. Dad spent many years driving cattle across Australia, so he knew all the different types of water sources. When Dad talked about water, he was never talking about the town water out of a tap, and not even the salt water our mob swim and fish in. He was only talking about pure drinking water, the precious stuff from underground.

15   The Canning Stock Route - A track that runs from Halls Creek, in the East Kimberley region, Western Australia, to Wiluna, which is in the mid-west region of Western Australia.

Last year I saw a black and white film at school about a *juja* (old man) teaching his grandsons how to find a *Jila*. The *juja* sang the directions to the *jila* from memory, as his grandson drove the truck through the desert. He told them to stop near a large sand dune. They got out of the truck and the old man burnt back the spinifex and called out to the spirit of the *Jila*, 'We are family. We have come to ask for permission to drink from the sacred *Jila*. See, we are here, we are your children.' Then, he turned to his grandsons and said, 'The smoke goes up to the sky and the Spirits know that the people with knowledge have come.'

Alone, the old man climbed up the sand dune and found a small, damp patch of sand about the size of his fist. He called out to the young ones to help him dig. They didn't believe there could be water up there.

The old man started to dig down. The more he dug, the muddier it became. Soon, water was gushing out of the hole and quickly formed an inland lake. The old man cried with joy as he jumped into the water with his grandsons, singing and dancing. It was awesome to see. That's our sacred water, our *living water*.

Anyway, them *kartijas* (*whitefellas*) who made the Canning Stock Route, wanted to tap our *living water* source with windmills to water their livestock as they drove them through the desert. To find the *Jilas*, they rounded up the *keepers of the soaks* and chained them together for hours in the deadly hot sun. Only when they were gasping for water and close to death, did the *kartija* let them go. Them poor *fellas* ran to drink one last time from their sacred *Jilas*.

In the end, fifty-one *Jilas* were stolen and capped. Heartbroken, the *Yiliwirri* (the old rainmakers) drowned themselves in the *Jilas* as they were being capped, preferring to die with the Water Spirits. The other *blackfellas* were taken far away from their traditional homeland to be slaves on the stations, and never returned home to their Country.

The Spirit of the Great Sandy Desert has become tired of man and his beasts. She has withheld her water and the desert has become hotter and dryer with each passing year. The Canning Stock Route is now useless and the livestock are few and feral. The stations are no longer profitable without our black labour. No one wants to live there anymore, except *Jalbri*, and four other keepers of the *Jilas*.

Jackie interrupted my thoughts, 'Are ya with us?'

I smiled, holding up the other card of matches, which read: 'Come again! You're always welcome.'

Jackie laughed. 'Nobody likes a *smart* black bitch.'

Looking at me again, he took off his hat and plonked it firmly on my head. He got his water bottle out of the cab and handed it to me. I was happy and felt ready for anything. Jackie then took off his t-shirt and put it around my neck. 'May come in handy to keep the mozzies off at night. From here, Dragon Tree Soak is about sixty kilometres as the crow flies. There will be small soaks along the way. You must keep correcting north/north-east. Do you get it? You know about *Jilas*?'

I nodded darkly.

'You may not be able to get it up on your phone here.'

I don't have a mobile, but I sorta knew what he was saying.

'When are Frankie and your mum picking you up?'

I didn't need to answer.

'Farrr Out!' he shouted, jumping on the spot and turning his head away from me enraged. 'You Lucky-Childs are always doing things arse about!' His words struck me like a spear through the chest. Turning sharply to eyeball me, he asked, 'Where's *Jalbri* meeting you?'

I couldn't look at him. I just wanted to cry and run into the bushes.

'Shit a brick! What's wrong with ya? So, nobody knows you're walking around the bush like a bloody lunatic?'

I couldn't control my tears. I thought my heart was going to jump out of my throat.

'Okay, sis. Get back in the ute, you can come with us. Everyone does bloody stupid things sometimes, and you, little sis, are no different to the rest of us.'

The words, 'I *am* different,' slipped out of my quivering lips. I desperately wanted to be different to everyone else, especially my family. I thought I was different, but Jackie made me see clearly that I was just a stupid Lucky-Child like the rest of them. I hated myself.

Letting out a loud groan and wailing like a dog on heat, I picked up the bags and ran into the bushes feeling like Lulu, the stupid, old bag lady.

Mutt was alarmed by the noise and chased me. I froze, frightened he was going to bite me. Jackie bellowed at him. Mutt cowered, and as Jackie put him on the lead and secured him to the ute, he yelled at me, 'You're about as bloody *different* as one of those black ants.' Then he must have felt real bad, cos he changed his tone and gently called out to me, 'Sorry girl, come on Lucy, it's okay. I know that sometimes us *blackfellas* need to do crazy stuff to work out our shit.'

I felt like he was trying to coax his dog out of the bushes, but I wasn't budging. 'Okay my girl, I'll get word to your mum when I get to Bidjy. Sorry girl, Frankie will come soon, he'll save you. Keep steady, don't go losing your mind in the bush.' Then his voice changed to teacher mode. 'If you feel like you don't know where you're going, *don't go anywhere*. Just stay put and camp. Frankie will come and save ya real soon. He's the man. It'll take ya four to five days walkin' full-on to get to *Jalbri*, righteo?'

'Thanks Jackie,' I said, half forgiving him.

He could see me turn around in the waist-high bushes, but he knew his words had trashed me.

He was right—us Lucky-Childs never did anything the 'right' way. That was why we were all failures. Why the hell would *Jalbri* call me to go to her when I didn't know anything about anything? Maybe she didn't call me. Maybe it was all in my head.

Dad used to get into all sorts of hair-brained schemes. He'd say, 'The Spirits told me I have to do it.' He'd go walk about and the only Spirits he'd meet would be pouring out of a bottle and down his throat before a fist fight.

Maybe I'm more Dad than I'd like to admit. Maybe I should've gone to Bidyadanga with Jackie. But, just like Dad, I'm too bloody proud for my own good. He'd never accept help from anyone either and ended up with his head kicked in.

I'm so stupid. I should be going to school tomorrow and here I am, out bush, on my own, proper Lucky-Child style.

A cloud of dust billowed into the humid air as Jackie drove off tooting goodbye and waving his long, black arm out of the cab. I knew he felt bad for what he'd said, and I felt bad that he was right.

Looking around me I felt overwhelmed. No tropical island paradise here. This was real dry country with low scrub and clumps of bushes along red silt ridges laced with poky spinifex. I walked a little way and then felt like I had to rest and sort out all the stuff I was carrying. Sitting down under a small minmin bush, I gulped down some warm Coke. *Errr, too sweet and gassy.* I laid back using Jackie's t-shirt as a pillow and covered my face with his hat and fell asleep.

Suddenly, I woke, frightened by the noise of branches snapping. My heart lost a beat and I lay real still, trying not to make a sound. I didn't even want to breathe under Jackie's sweat-stained Akubra. My heart was pounding and I could hear my blood rushing in my ears like breakers[16] in a storm. I couldn't hear nothing, except the pounding in my ears. I whispered to myself, 'Mother Mary, forgiver of sins, help me.'

And then something brushed up against my foot.

Oh! Sweet Baby Jesus, please! What the hell? Oh God, I'm Aboriginal, what's happening here? I'm on my own Country coming to find my Jalbri. What am I afraid of?

16   Breakers - Crashing ocean waves.

Shit!

I hadn't asked Country if I could be there. *Shame on me.*

I removed the Akubra hat from my face—there was no evil spirit standing at my feet, so I edged my way out from under the minmin bush.

It was black as black. Feeling my way between the spiky spinifex, I found a small clearing. Standing still and upright, I felt calm. Turning my face to the *bundarra* (stars), my eyes searched the sky for something familiar, and there he was, the Emu Man.

His form was a black shape surrounded by *bundarra*. We always look for him when we are at Reddell Beach. We stand near the stone pillars of *Nyarluwarru*[17], our *Muniwarri* (Seven Sisters in the Stars) who turned to stone after they looked at the Emu Man. Looking up, we call on them fellas from the 'cosmic drama' to guide us.

I was born right there, beside The Mother Pillar in Broome.

Now that I had found the Emu Man, I knew exactly where north-east was, and turning my face towards the distant Dragon Tree Soak, I picked up a handful of sand, stood up and called out, 'I am Lucy Lucky-Child. I offer my respect to Country and *Pulanyi Bulaing* (the Rainbow Serpent). I know it's wrong to be standing on Country without permission. Forgive me Ancestors, can you mob accept me and look after me and help me find my *Jalbri* (great grandmother). I am family, so please don't let any evil spirits get me. My Dad's dead, he was *Bardi-Garimba* skin group. You know, stolen generation, so he never knew his family, or who he really was. Mum is *Burungu* and I am *Barrjarri*.'

As I talked to the Ancestors, I threw sand into the air and found my hands moving in the ways I'd seen the Elders do when they did 'Greeting to Country'. A deep calm came into my heart and I was at peace within the darkness. Fear of being lost and alone left me. Now I was standing strong in Country and felt accepted by *Pulanyi Bulaing* and the Ancestors.

17   The Stone Pillars - Represent the Seven Sisters on Reddell Beach, Broome, Western Australia.

For the first time in my life, I felt like I belonged. I'd found my home.

I tell ya, it felt as if the Ancestors and Spirits were smiling at me. I stood in respect for a long time until the moment was over. Then, I sat on the cool sweet-smelling earth and sang all the old songs like 'Old Mission Road', that one always brought a tear to Dad's eye. And Islander songs like 'Pearly Shells', the one Mr Sammy Savage used to play on his uke with the Anne Street mob.

I was starting to get nervous cos I shoulda made a fire before nightfall. I felt sure them dingos were gonna attack me as soon as they smelt the jerky in my bag. Even camels and kangaroos are a problem to the stranger setting up camp, cos they're creatures of habit and always use the same tracks. Once, I fell asleep on a kangaroo track out bush when a *marloo* (big red kangaroo) in full flight was about to land on me. Dad screamed out just in time, and that big fella *marloo* did a backflip and just missed landing on me. I would've been squashed flat, like dead meat.

When my throat became so dry that I couldn't sing anymore, I took out Sister's little wind-up music box from my string bag. As I turned the handle, I could feel my face smiling broadly in the dark. 'Faraway over the sea, Manu was waiting for me, da da, da da da dah, one day we'll go sailing.'

That was the last thing I remember.

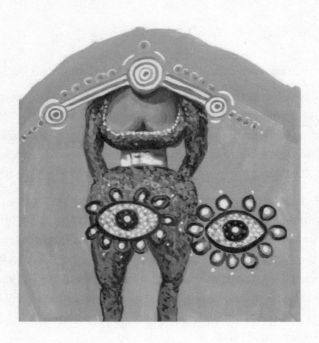

8. The Pearls

Woken too early by the screeching *biyarrgu* (galahs), my head was resting on my knees and my little music box had fallen to the ground. A *marloo* was helping himself to minmin flowers from the far side of the bush while keeping his eyes on me. The Coke bottle, still under the minmin bush, was swarming with big black ants. They loved that nectar in the centre of the flowers, but like us *blackfellas*, them ants think that Coke is best.

Trying to find a place to shit in the desert, away from ants and bugs, and the prying eyes of *marloos* and *bungarras* (goannas) was impossible. And I wasn't up for wrestling snakes first thing in the morning either. *Urgh!* Then I noticed mozzie bites all over my face, arms and feet. So, I got out Dad's salve. By the time I was done, I'd learnt that everything sticks to Dad's gloop.

Chewing on minmin flowers and a handful of *gubinge*, a small unexciting fruit, I realised why real bushies were so skinny. Already I was becoming a walking stick and I still had days ahead of me. I couldn't bear feeling hungry and gave in, finishing off the packet of chips and guzzling down the Coke after fighting the ants for it.

Keeping the chip packet and empty Coke bottle, I got my stuff together. Packed like a camel, I found where I'd stood last night during call to Country. Making sure I was facing in the right direction, I headed off towards Dragon Tree Soak. Trying to make up for lost time, I started running. Lugging my bags and stuff through the spinifex I got real hot and sweaty. Suddenly I heard *Juja* Jack's (Old Man Jack's) voice boom all around me, *'Lucy Lucky-Child! Thubarnimanha* (Straighten up)!'

Shit! I thought the Coke and chips were doing my head in. Or maybe I just needed a good sleep.

Juja Jack's voice boomed again, *'Hey daughter! Something bothering you? Thubarnimanha! You're already straying from the straight line. Thubarnimanha! Straighten up!'*

I swung around, expecting to see *Juja* Jack behind me, but instead I noticed that I had been following clumps of spinifex round in a circle instead of making a straight line. So, my hours of walking were wasted, I'd gone full circle.

Juja Jack would always tell us kids, 'You don't wanna be straying off that real straight line. The same thing you need to survive in Country, you need to survive in the big city. *Thubarnimanha*! Straighten up! Be on that real straight line.' Now I knew what he meant.

When that desert mob greets you, they'll ask in Language, 'Are you on the straight line?'

You should answer, 'I'm a bit off the straight line, but I'm trying to straighten up.'

Now I got it.

If you're not on the straight line between where you are and where you wanna be, you're lost. If you don't know it, you'll soon find out. The longer it takes for you to 'straighten up', the more lost ya gonna be.

'Far out, what am I doing?' I cried out to no one in particular. I was getting nowhere fast. Disappointed, I slumped down in the red dirt and and sobbed. A little *julirri* (blue-tongue lizard) ran up to check me out. In a flash, I had my pocketknife in my hand. *Quick lunch*, I thought, but looking at its sweet little face and eyes, I couldn't kill it. The *julirri* must have picked up my bad thoughts; he gave me a filthy look and raced off under a nearby bush.

'Shit, a vego Abo (vegetarian Aboriginal person)! I'm going to die for sure.' I really truly thought that cos I was Indigenous, it was in my blood to survive on Country and do tracking, and that all that shit shoulda come real easy, natural like. It wasn't like catching fish every day and heading off to Fong's for bread and milk. Nah, this was hard.

Fed up, I threw myself down on the ground, my bags flew in all directions. I was thirsty, hungry, tired, frustrated, and angry.

Feeling like a complete failure, I searched for my little tin cup, and poured myself a drink of water. It was warm and tasted like plastic. Then I chewed on a piece of hard, salty crocodile jerky. It was horrible.

From the angle of the sun, I could tell it was about midday. I started to doubt myself big-time, wondering if I should go back to Gingerah Road and wait for someone to save me. Then I had an idea.

I emptied everything out of my long silk bag onto the ground. Holding the raw silk in close against my chest, I felt it fall softly over my breasts and down past my knees, and I imagined it was my wedding dress. I closed my eyes and saw Manu Tollie standing in front of me. Breathing in deeply, I kissed the little soft turtle stitched into the top edge of the bag and said aloud, 'I do.'

Just at that very moment, a *biyarrgu* (galah) squawked mockingly.

'Get lost!' I squawked back. *Shame.*

The bag was crocheted from a twenty-thousand-yard spool of Persian carpet silk thread. My great idea was to unravel it as I walked. A bit like Hansel and Gretel, but instead of breadcrumbs, I would leave a fine silk trail

50

of thread, plotting a straight line from one small tree to the next. The thread would hang above the spinifex and low-lying scrub. That was how I would *thubarnimanha* (straighten up).

I ripped a long strip off the chip packet and attached it to the string on the first tree, so that if someone was looking for me, from a distance they'd see the silver and blue foil flashing in the breeze. I knew that any of the old trackers, like Arnie Bridge, would laugh at my tracks going nowhere—just round and round like a spinning coconut[18].

I was pleased with my handy work and sang out, 'Hey girl, you got kidneys and lungs.' That was what Mrs Mazie, our support teacher, always said when we did something smart. I was on a roll now. I was really doing it. The straight line made me feel smart and hopeful again. I set a good pace jogging along, watching my bag unravel.

By late afternoon my bag was half gone, *straight lining*. I felt so deadly, I shoulda been in the bush Olympics.

The shadows grew long, I knew I had to stop and make my first proper camp before nightfall. *Eat something, but what?* Clearing a spot, I collected dried twigs and spinifex, and using Jackie's matches, the fire took quickly. I was so happy to see a *gungkara* (conkerberry), as it was just what I needed.

Burning those branches keeps the mozzies away and chases off evil spirits, and to my good luck, the bush was loaded with berries. While gobbling down berries, I found a *kipara* (bustard bird) nest in the bushes with four eggs. I took two and left two for the mummy bird so she wouldn't fret.

I emptied the knickknacks from my Band-Aid tin, broke the eggs into it and put it carefully onto the fire to cook. Filling my billy with fresh water, I added a tea bag and waited for it to boil. Then I remembered the packet of Tiny Teddies that my best friend Louanna had given me. She lived with her parents, Aunty Toots and Uncle Cedric, three houses down to the right opposite us. They were not my real Aunty and Uncle, but I loved them just the same.

18   Coconut - Insulting term to an Aboriginal person—brown on the outside, white on the inside.

Aunty Toots is the strangest-looking woman you've ever seen. She has the biggest, widest, most humungous bum. Her bum hangs over a normal chair, but strangely, her waist is tiny. I saw old pictures of her when she was young, and boy, she was a stunner.

Even though her boobs are humongous and her bum's as wide as, she likes to show off her small waist by wearing tight-fitting lycra, buckled up and sucked in with a big, wide belt. It's usually so tight that if she breathed in too deep, you'd think she was gonna break in two. Aunty Toots is as mad as a meat axe and bossy to boot.

Poor Uncle Cedric is a giant with a face like a bulldog. But he is the kindest, sweetest, most patient man you'd ever meet, and he has to be. My Dad used to say, 'Another man would have killed her a hundred times over.' Every day Uncle Cedric wears large, creamy, baggy trousers, and a perfectly ironed white shirt, which is old stock from the mission days.

None of us mob have a washing machine, but Aunty Toots holds up the standard for us all. Early in the morning, I usually see Uncle Cedric carefully riding his bike around all the potholes on Anne Street on his way to the laundry, library, school and shops. He is the only man on the street with a full-time job as caretaker for our school. I watch him from my the classroom window, talking to the plants. The way he talks to them, I'm sure they're talkin' back.

A while back, their whole family joined some strange religion from Iran. The *kartija* (*whitefella*) say they're terrorists, but the people who came to their house were beautiful inside and out. The women looked stunning in their flashy dresses, bright-red lippy, jewellery, and strong makeup, and their eyebrows were plucked real sharp. They had tall noses, jet-black hair and eyes to match. They couldn't pass as *whitefellas*, and no way were they *blackfellas* like us.

They were real kind and always showed respect to Aunty Toots and Uncle Cedric. They were never ashamed to go into a *blackfella's* house and sit and eat *blackfella* food. Not like all the social workers and goodie-two-shoes who think they gotta dress down to come see us mob. Them social workers bring their own water bottles and snacks, and swear a lot, trying to get on side with us kids. It's so fake, nobody likes it and none of our mob trust them.

But the people from Iran were always polite. They called Aunty Toots and Uncle Cedric, Mr and Mrs Pearl, real respectful like.

Joining the *tall-nose* religion changed the Pearls forever. The day Uncle Cedric joined, he gave up the grog, went out bush and came back with a load of forty-four-gallon drums.

The passion vine went crazy and grew all over the front of his house and the little cyclone fence down the side. He even grew his own bacci for his own 'roll your owns'.

After some kids hacked at his passion vine, he called the whole Anne Street mob together. He told us that when he took up that religion, planting those drums was a symbol of him coming back to life again. He said, 'When I water them plants, I know that everything is going to be okay. No grog now, just a little bacci to calm me nerves.'

He was not a good talker, usually Aunty Toots did that for him. But that night, every one of us knew exactly what he meant.

Uncle Cedric got the lung sickness from working the mine at Wittenoom in the sixties when he was just a boy. The asbestos dust got him bad. I can hear him every morning from our place, coughing his lungs out at dawn when he's watering his tiny garden at his front door.

We are all trying to escape this wretched life on Anne Street.

In Aunty Toot's mind, the only way to escape is to act as if you already have. Hard job when you live on this Street. If ya stick ya head up higher than the rest, for sure someone's gonna chop it off. Aunty Toots isn't gonna let her only living flesh and blood, Louanna, turn out like us. She wants Louanna to be 'something special'. Like *whitefella* something special. Cos *blackfella* something special is the sorta special no one wants to be. Every morning, we can hear her yelling, 'Louanna, ready for school? Hurry up!'

I love Louanna. She's the sweetest, kindest girl I know. Although she doesn't talk much, you can't miss her. She is tall and chubby - wide like a boab tree - and she wears the thickest glasses ever that make her eyes look googly. She has honey-coloured skin, like an Islander, and long, straight jet-black hair that reaches down past her bum. She's always reading a book and is so smart. She knows everything about *whitefella* stuff, but nothin' about *blackfella* stuff.

She's the sorta person who always notices what people need. She knows that most mornings I don't have breakfast, cos we go fishing with Mum from dawn, and then I just go straight to school. She sits next to me in class for the first period, before going to the library to do advanced work by herself. I know she feels real lonely.

Every morning without fail, we play a game where she gives me a small packet of Tiny Teddies, and in exchange I tell her what it was like at the beach. I always bring back something special for her, like a bit of bright-blue nylon from the drag nets, some plastic, a shell, or a piece of coral to show her the exact colours of the sea and sky that change so wildly from the dry season to the wet.

More than any English teacher, Louanna has taught me how to describe things, like the sea, the land, people and their feelings. When she listens to my soul speak, she looks right through me. It's so spooky. Her face darkens and becomes as still as stone, like those giant black stone heads on *Rapa Nui*[19]. And for a moment I think she's blind and forget that she can actually see.

Louanna used to have an older sister who was only eight years old when she was kidnapped from Town Beach. The family never recovered. I don't know the details, but I do know it's bad for our mob to be silent on it. That's why Uncle Cedric turned to the drink and why they've had an 'exit plan' ever since. Aunty Toots watches over Louanna something chronic, like an emu guarding her eggs.

19   Rapa Nui - Easter Island, known for monolithic carved stone figures called mo'ai

Poor Louanna has become a lone captive in her home. Even at school she's imprisoned in an unreal world of letters and numbers that keeps her locked away from her Country, her Culture and her People. Our little game is her only escape.

When she goes to the library to work, she writes poems and stories based on what I bring her and what she sees through my eyes. If she ever gets out of Anne Street, she's going to be a famous author. She says I'm gonna be a psychologist, but I think I wanna be a *Mabarnyuwa* (Sorceress and Bush Medicine Healer).

9. Gulyi-Gulyi – Funny Looking

A spectacular sunset dissolved into darkness. Contented, I sat crossed-legged on the red earth, eating my eggs and drinking tea, sweetened with a jelly snake. Smiling to myself, I wondered what *Pulanyi Bulaing* (Rainbow Serpent) would think of me chewing on snakes. The firelight flickered dark purple on the orange sand. Bedding down for the night, I was warm and relaxed.

Turning my eyes to the night sky, I watched the *bundarra* (stars) shine so brightly that it made the Emu Man look as if he was dancing. Feeling sleepy, I became lost in the smoke from my fire as it hung thick and fragrant before my face. Then with the next smoke-filled breath, I could see nothing of the Great Sandy Desert. I was back in Broome.

I seemed to be standing outside and above our house in Anne Street, and I was shocked to see my mum crying hard with a mob gathering around her. Mum, hanky in hand, stopped sobbing, straightened up and said, 'The coppers have called off the search for Lucy.'

56

Aunty Toots let out a high-pitched wail. 'We're on our own again. We'll find her Mary. We can't lose another!'

Arnie Bridge, the old tracker, said, 'I told the coppers that her tracks stopped at Fong's. From there she's got in a car.'

Aunty Toots was inconsolable.

Mr Rowe, the King of Anne Street, clapped his hands and addressed the crowd, saying, 'You women do corroboree. If she's in town, we'll find her. Us men will drive around lookin'. We'll stop every car; search every man we see. If he's hurt her, we'll kill him.'

I felt real bad. I tried to attract Mum's attention, but no one could see me.

As I watched on from above, I saw my mum and the other women start to undress. I could clearly make out the deep scar on Mum's right shoulder from past beatings. She hated anyone seeing it.

In the streetlight, Mum looked beautiful and strong. Not a fisherwoman anymore—in my eyes, she was a warrior. Some young girls ran over to her with red, white and yellow ochre, and all the women, now bare breasted, started painting each other's faces, breasts and arms ready for ceremony. Even Aunty Toots' enormous boobs looked beautiful in that warm orange glow.

In the middle of Anne Street, a large fire had been lit and now the painted women danced in its flickering light. Looking to *bundarra* (stars), left and right, and then to *jama* (the ground) left and right, while doing *myambi* (knee-shaking dance), they called on the *songlines* to show them the way and asked the Ancestors to guide and protect me. The wind picked up and a huge *binu* (cloud of smoke) rose up from the fire. It looked like my Dad riding his horse, Lightning. Then it dawned on me that Dad was now one of my Ancestors, helping them find me.

The women danced for ages to the hypnotic rhythm of clapping sticks. I noticed a tall, graceful woman dancing timidly. It was Louanna. Aunty Toots was also watching her and smiled gently. Louanna nodded shyly to her mum.

57

Suddenly, a lone woman's voice sang out high above the clapping sticks, '*Alang*! (South) *Alang*! *Alang*!'

Their answer had come.

'She has gone south.'

Startled by those words, I fell back into my body. Jumping up quickly, I fed the dying camp fire, and that's when I realised that Jackie Burrup hadn't told them where I was.

The thought of being lost forever in the desert made my blood run cold and its chill made my bones ache. Squatting down close to the fire, I put Jackie's t-shirt on over my clothes and pulled it over my arms and legs, wrapping myself up like an Egyptian mummy. I tried to think of what to do next. I had gone south. When my Dad went south, he never saw his family again. No good comes to us mob when we go *south*. Frozen stiff, I fell asleep in that position.

The glancing dawn light made the spinifex turn gold against the sky like a swirling brush stroke of pink and lavender. In came the crazies of the desert, *biyarrgu* (galahs)—thousands upon thousands of them. Screeching as they landed clumsily on trees and bushes, and blaming the trees for their poor landing, they spitefully ripped off all the branches and nuts.

Marloos (big red kangaroos) bounded past in small groups, looking at me suspiciously, wondering who this stranger was in their path. Nearby, a *miginy* (kestrel), looking for a feed, circled a *mulgara* (bush rat) that was sunbaking outside his hole. A big fella *bungarra* (goanna) sidled up, but I kept real still because if they take fright, those buggers think you're a tree and run straight up ya. Last thing I needed was a face full of claws. Slowly the *bungarra* moved on.

In the distance I could see a family of wild camels; the baby was so cute. The *mirriyin* (crickets) chirped and I felt happy to be alive in Country. This is what my Dad had been talking about.

58

I had a bag of flour and a small jar of strawberry jam. So, in honour of my Dad, I decided to make damper. Fire lit, a beautiful dawn, some damper, strawberry jam and a cup of tea—perfect after last night's strange dream.

As I squatted down taking the first bite of my damper, I heard a strange yapping sound and felt something bump into my elbow. Swinging around I almost fell over. I laughed out loud to see a cute dingo pup nipping at me. He was camel coloured with white markings around his nose, chest and paws, and he looked like he was wearing long, white socks. His large pointy ears were white inside with black tips, but the tip of his left ear was bent over. Big black eyes looked intensely at me, waiting for my reaction.

I couldn't help laughing. His white-tipped tail wagged frantically, and he pounced on me, sticking his long nose into my damper. He bit off half and growled at me when I tried to push him off. He sure was hungry and cheeky. Strawberry jam was smeared all over his nose and chin. All he needed was a pink wide-brimmed hat to match and he'd look just like Dame Mary Durack[20].

'Okay, settle down. Sit!'

He licked my face instead.

I loved the smell of puppy breath. He was so happy to see me, and I was mighty happy to see him. His ears, nose and paws were far too big for his little body. He looked so funny, I decided to call him *Gulyi-Gulyi* (funny looking).

We shared the extra damper I'd made. I gave him some water from my cup. Happily, he started nipping my fingers and the quandong nuts woven into my bag. 'No *Gulyi-Gulyi*, cheeky boy!' He stopped and growled in protest. I realised how lonely I'd been, just me and my thoughts, even though it had only been two days. Now I had a friend.

'Well *Gulyi-Gulyi,* we're off to find my *Jalbri*. She'll love you. She probably knows your mum. Come to think of it, where is your mum?' Suddenly, I was really worried that an angry dingo bitch looking for her pup might show up and have a go at me.

20   Dame Mary Durack - An author, playwriter and pastoralist, an East Kimberley local identity from Broome, Western Australia.

I looked around nervously. '*Gulyi-Gulyi*, go home!' I ordered, standing over him pointing in the opposite direction.

He plopped his bottom on the ground. His legs folded under him, and then his head hit the sand and he started to *wayiliri* (cry).

'Poor baby. Come on *Gulyi-Gulyi*, we'll look for your mummy together.' I bent down and stroked him.

He recovered pretty quickly. Gee, he reminded me of my little brother Jonnie.

Trying to gather up all my stuff with *Gulyi-Gulyi* getting into everything was frustrating, but when we started walking, he was a natural bushman's dog. He ran off ahead, seeing off little creatures, and then he'd return and walk beside me, ears pricked and watchful.

I felt protected. For a puppy, he was surprisingly fast, and we made good pace. I gave up marking our trail. If us kids ever said we got lost, the Elders would say, 'How can two people get lost? You're only lost when you're alone.' I wasn't alone anymore. I was in Country with my new friend *Gulyi-Gulyi*.

All of a sudden, *Gulyi-Gulyi* took off barking madly and disappeared over a small ridge. I raced after him. He had found his mother. She had been bitten by a *milyura* (snake) that was also dead. She'd broken its back with her strong jaws.

Gulyi-Gulyi looked confused because his mum was not responding to him pawing at her breast and trying to suck milk.

I cried out, tears running down my cheeks, 'Come on, puppy. You're a good boy. Come on *Gulyi-Gulyi*, I'll look after you.'

Gulyi-Gulyi ignored me. He kept jumping onto her chest, stiff legged, trying to wake her.

Then, with his head close to the ground, tripping over his big feet, he turned around to face me. I ran over and swept him up into my arms. Kissing him, I sat down devastated. My heart went out to him and burst like a damn full of pent up tears for him, my Dad, Mum, me and the whole fucking planet. I felt like I hadn't cried properly before—not when Dad died, not at the 'Sorry Business', not anytime, not properly like this.

As if *Gulyi-Gulyi* knew I had cried enough, he started licking my tears. Looking at his mum and the *milyura*, he suddenly got mad with the *milyura*. He ran over, grabbed it by the tail and dragged it over to me. It was a big one, deadly as.

Gulyi-Gulyi's paw was on the *milyura's* body, and he was looking at me as if to say, '*You're the human, do something.*'

I decided to cook the snake for us to eat. We both needed some meat, and I literally couldn't kill anything to save my life.

I said a blessing for the mummy dingo:

Ngayalmanmanha jin-ga ngubanu Karajarri nyinyaan gu yagu.

I call on the Spirit Dingo of the Karajarri lands to look out for Mother.

Minjanmanha nyinyaan Gulyi-Gulyi.

I promise to look out for *Gulyi-Gulyi*.

Throwing sand into the air, the ceremony felt complete.

Gulyi-Gulyi sat respectfully as if he understood every word. Putting the *milyura* in a plastic bag, we set off over the ridge in silence.

After a long while, we stopped to set up camp. I was so proud of myself because for the first time I used *ngarnamin'gil* (the firestick tree). I rubbed the firesticks together to start the fire, instead of using Jackie's matches.

Gulyi-Gulyi and his mother must have had humans in their life before, because he showed no fear of the fire. In our Dreamtime story, the first fire was lit by a young sister, so fire belonged to women. Men have to ask for permission to light a fire. We ate the cooked *milyura*. I threw the bones and things far away

61

from our camp, but I kept the skull and skin to take back to Louanna. I'd love her to write this story.

Finally, the sun set and I made a rough bed out of *bilabirdi* (eucalyptus gum), *bardinyu* (pine), *barlura* (acacia) and *bilbiny* (grevillea) leaves and covered it with big sheets of *ngurlurrbi* (paperbark). It smelt delicious.

While I laid down gazing at the *bundarra* (stars), *Gulyi-Gulyi* tucked his nose deep into my armpit and I told him the story of the Seven Sisters, the *Muniwarri*. My *Jalbri* said that if a puppy smells your armpit, he's a 'one-person' dog for life. I lay talking to him and felt really comfortable being in Country. The more I spoke in Language, the more connected I felt.

Mum and Dad fought and talked in *Wajarri*[21]. Mum learnt to speak it when she was a little girl at the Dominican Convent School at Cue in the Murchison Shire. Dad learnt the Language many years later when he worked as a stockman and shearer at Wooleen Station near Mount Magnet.

At home, my brother and I speak *Yawuru ngan.ga*[22], and English, but at school and in the community, we speak English. But most of our mob speak many different languages because the Kimberley and Central Desert People still use their mother tongue over English.

Like *Jalbri*, her mother tongue is Mangala, but she also speaks some other regional languages like Juwaliny, Walmajarri, Karajarri[23], Wajarri, Broome Speak, and some others from up North and the Central Desert. English is her least spoken language. I reckon I could make *Gulyi-Gulyi* understand both Language and English.

Juja Jack was right. With pups by my side, I didn't feel alone or lost anymore. I decided to stop worrying about how long it was going to take me to get to *Jalbri*. I would get there at 'the right time'. Country time. Desert time. My time.

---

21   Wajarri - Indigenous Language from The Murchison, Western Australia.
22   Yawuru ngan.ga - Indigenous Language from Broome, Western Australia.
23   Karajarri - Indigenous Language from the Bidyadanga Region, Western Australia.

As I inhaled the sweet scent of burning *gumamu* (sandalwood) and *gungkara* (conkerberry), with my friend *Gulyi-Gulyi* beside me, I felt happy and protected and soon drifted into a deep sleep.

10. Battlement Rocks

The insane squawking of *biyarrgu* (galahs) seemed far too early as the sky refused to give up the night. I charged up the fire with some *nirliyangarr* (dune wattle) and then sat drinking tea while *Gulyi-Gulyi* ran off in different directions chasing little creatures.

Without thinking about it, I started to clap together two stones, and from a place deep in my throat that vibrated into my nose and forehead came that familiar nasal sound of women singing that I'd heard so many times before. For the first time I felt that I too was an Indigenous woman. I didn't know if I was singing the right words, but I knew the feeling was right. The sound belonged to this Country and to me.

Nearby I found some *lirringin* (soapy wattle) and I gathered the dried seeds that had fallen to the ground. Grinding them between my two stones, I made my first flour for *real* bush damper. It cooked so well and had a nice nutty flavour. *Gulyi-Gulyi* wanted to share my damper, so I thought I'd keep the jerky for harder times.

It was a new day and my urgency to get to *Jalbri* had been replaced with a contentment to be here in Country. I wanted to travel like a native of this land, instead of a lost Salt-Water girl. I noticed a small soak about 200 metres ahead and excitedly set off to get fresh water.

The soak looked deep but was only about the size of a double bed. It was fenced off with barbed wire to keep out livestock such as cattle, camels and brumbies. Propping open the barbed wire with a stick, I climbed through. The ground was thick with flowers, bush tucker and grasses, which felt like carpet under my feet. The little oasis made us travellers feel blessed. I had to hang on tight to the bull rushes, so I didn't fall in.

Reaching the soak, I filled my mouth with water and blew out a fine spray into the air. Then I sang out to *Pulanyi Bulaing* (Rainbow Serpent) to thank her for bringing the water to the surface from deep in the earth. This was the traditional way. *Gulyi-Gulyi* was busy chasing a variety of birds and goannas and other creatures who'd also come to the soak to drink, bathe and eat.

I snapped off some *lirringin*, our bush soap, foamed it up real good and just started to wash my private parts when *Gulyi-Gulyi* ran past me and jumped straight in. I don't think he'd ever seen a soak before, and this one was deep and freezing cold. He immediately sank. I saw his beady little eyes looking up at me and a couple of big bubbles came out of his nose. His ears were the last thing to go under.

Quick as anything, my hand shot in after him and grabbed his upraised paw. I yanked him out the way Mum pulled big fish from the sea. He landed heavily, staggered to his feet and shook and rolled in the red dirt. By the time he'd finished he looked like a red clay monster from a horror movie. The Return of the Spirit-eating Dingo. When he sucks your spirit out, you're a goner. Our mob would love a movie like that. I stood starkers, laughing my head off.

Drying off in the warm sun felt good. I wandered around collecting bush tucker and enjoyed being free from the prying eyes of humans. After a while I decided to get dressed. My favourite jeans were still a bit damp and looked a bit worse for wear, but my t-shirt smelt good now that it was washed.

I also washed Jackie's t-shirt, slung it around my neck to keep cool and set off again for a long days walk. *Gulyi-Gulyi* had a nice rhythm, running out in front, then circling back to walk beside me for a while, and then going out ahead again. Feeling safe and protected, we didn't talk, we just observed Country and walked through *her* and let *her* reveal *herself* to us.

I could hear the sound of bush bees and decided that we should stop to rest. We scaled the final ridge, and this time I had to sit down to catch my breath. Suddenly, I heard a rushing sound and the landscape around me became a blur. I felt like I was stepping through a fine spider web, and once again I was on the 'other side'.

My mother and the women, still bare breasted and heavily painted, were gathered around the St Mary's Shinju Matsuri festival truck. Sister Evangelist had driven off the side of the road, eighty kilometres short of where Jackie had dropped me at the Gingerah Road turnoff. She was a dreadful driver at the best of times. A deeply bogged truck spells big trouble in the bush. Wet silt is like quicksand. The mob of sheilas were talking about who was going to walk 120 kilometres to find me.

If you are talking about tracking, Old Patty Mae and her dog, Gofar, are legends. I was so happy to see her coming to find me, cos no one was lost for long with her on your trail. She could track your outward breath in a willy-willy (whirlwind). Her hair is wild and bleached desert yellow by too much sun, and half her face is covered by a full, thick, curly, orange beard and a mo[24] to match from eating too many kangaroo balls. All the desert sheilas eat balls.

---

24   Mo - Moustache.

Patty Mae isn't the marrying type, and you'll not see other women arm-wrestling big blokes at the local pub like she does. *Jalbri* gave her a little white clay pipe that looks cool against her honey-coloured skin. I love to sit and listen to her stories of bush life and watch her dark lips puff white clouds of smoke that circle up to her bright sky-blue eyes. She is a proper Broome 'mongrel'—A strong woman from a line of strong women.

The women must have been standing by the side of the road for a long-time cos Sister Evangelist had her rosary beads out and looked like she'd already done seven rounds. She was wearing a black armband, and then I noticed everyone was painted with the markings that we use when someone dies.

They think I'm dead. Poor Mum. Hang on! You bitch, I'm your only daughter! How come you're not crying? Cry you bitch! I knew you never loved me!

When the ute approached, I expected to see Jackie and Frankie, but it was that bitch Barbara and her little bastard, Helen. That made me so angry. The women were happy to catch a lift to the Gingerah turnoff with Barbara. I didn't want her and her manky daughter coming to find me. Why can't they stay out of my life?

Enraged, I jolted back into the present. I had to get a move on. I needed to be alone with my *Jalbri*, not have a bunch of women drag me back to Broome like a poor 'lost' girl. I was a *real* bush woman now. Jackie would be so proud of me. He'd obviously never walked to Dragon Tree Soak. I was sure I could teach him a thing or two.

In the distance, just to the right of the disappearing wheel tracks we'd been following, was an outcrop of massive boulders. Straight away I knew it was Battlement Rocks. *Jalbri* had talked on and on about this place one boiling hot day when we were fishing from the red rocks at Grantheaume Point. 'That big fella Battlement Rock. He's much higher than these rocks. Out there in the desert, he's our special Sacred Place.'

She didn't shut up for two hours, telling me how to *sing* out to the rock and what *signs* to look for before you climbed up. Then there was a big rant about when not to climb him. But I'd switched off by then. It was too hot for a lecture. But *Jalbri's* description of Battlement Rocks, 'Red with strong blue markings', was spot on. Proud of myself I yelled, 'Battlement Rocks, here we come.'

In spite of the water bottles being a hassle to carry, I decided that *Gulyi-Gulyi* and I would run as fast and as far as we could, making tracks to Battlement Rocks. *Gulyi-Gulyi* was a natural. He knew how to run without tripping me up, keeping watch out front and circling to my back.

I was overheating and had to stop our marathon run. Sweat poured off me and my heart and lungs were banging in my chest. Stopping to recover, I pressed my bum into the edge of an encrusted sand dune. Half sitting, half standing, I tried to catch an easy breath. I said to *Gulyi*, 'I've had it, I don't know about you?' I looked up at the sky for the first time in hours and was totally amazed to see how dramatically the weather had changed. But I pushed on regardless and soon we were standing at the base of Battlement Rocks.

In the far distance, the sky flashed pink and orange in a mesmerising light show. A massive, grey mushroom-like cloud erupted from a distant lightning strike, releasing a curtain of dazzling light that trailed to the earth like a neon grass skirt. High above us black clouds rolled in rapidly, as if being blown by some angry grumbling giant. The heat and humidity were unbearable, but I was on a mission and I was determined to climb to the top to see just how far away we were from Dragon Tree Soak.

'Come on *Gulyi-Gulyi*, up!' I ordered.

He wouldn't budge.

I tried to shift him, but he dug his paws in deep. 'Get lost then,' I shouted angrily at him and went up alone, leaving him whimpering on the red sand below.

I scaled to the peak of Battlement Rocks like a woman possessed. Standing tall, I felt like I'd won, and I'd done it all by myself. I took one long, deep breath, smugly raised my right arm and defiantly fist pumped the sky, shouting out loudly, 'Everyone, Lucy Lucky-Child has arrived!'

Black ants swarmed and birds darted off towards the patch of blue sky that we'd left far behind us. Then an all-consuming crack ripped the Heavens apart. Clouds of thick, grey vapour poured off the searing boulders. But strangely a cool current, like a snake's tongue, wrapped around me. Before I could snatch another breath, I was blinded by an intense blue-white flash.

Still standing, immobilised with my right arm locked stiff above me, an electrifying pain bolted down my right arm … across my chest … up my throat and smacked my right cheek. I fell hard, crashing like a tin soldier from one stack of smouldering boulders to the next until I landed stiffly on the muddy earth below.

Then there was another lightning strike.

Its terrifying forked tongue struck either side of my ridged body creating two chimneys of molten sand that spewed out plumes of blue smoke. I lay as still as death herself. My ribs jammed shut, unable to draw breath. My *rayi* (soul) decided to escape that pitiful, singed teenage *karrikin* (body). I felt the cord that connected us stretch thinner and thinner—so impossibly thin. I drifted further away from my Lucy, my Lucky-Child. As if to pay my last respects, I turned my eyes down to her, my once Earthly home.

Then, *Gulyi-Gulyi* ran at me, squealing as if to say, '*How dare you leave me.*' Desperately he pounced on my stiffened chest. His eyes flashed white, as if vividly remembering his dead mother. Over and over, in the pelting rain, he launched himself at my smouldering chest. He wasn't giving up on me, even if I was giving up on him.

Cold and aloof, I watched him. I was hovering even higher now in that dark cool space, just beneath the sombre heavily laden clouds where the Lightning Brothers were grumbling loudly, saying that I must leave that Lucky-Child behind and journey with them to the Milky Way.

Gulyi had heard them too, but he was not letting me go. Pricking up his ears, he became as still as stone. Then slowly he curled his spine forward, putting his forehead flat on the ground between his front legs so that his rear end was up higher than his head. A low, dark, painful rumble struggled out from somewhere deep in his being. Then in slow motion, he uncoiled until he was fully stretched backwards with his throat facing the electrified sky.

That dark, guttural rumble eerily turned into a shrill high-pitched wail. In one fluid movement he connected Earth and Heaven and was begging the Dreamtime Spirits to bring me back to him. The sadness in his high-pitched howl reached up that wispy cord that still connected my *karrikin* to my *rayi*. His love snatched me back into my smouldering body.

A breath came into my re-joined self and a cool trickling sensation filled my heart. I opened my eyes. I was back again with him. I *was* his Lucky-Child.

My funny-looking puppy became joy itself, whimpering and peeing uncontrollably. He created a fine shower of dingo pee by vigorously wagging his tail. Strangely the tickling sensation felt nice on my burning skin and it made me laugh. Then *Gulyi* lay on my chest, licking my face and eyes, and he put his head between my breasts and his nose against my chin. His left ear tickled my cheek as he breathed, so I tucked it underneath. Soon he fell asleep, his big paws pushed against my chin while his mouth made sucking noises.

I felt *warritharra* (sad) for my poor *Gulyi-Gulyi*. He was just a little puppy and should have been drinking from his *yagu* (mummy) and protected by her, not looking after me. I took his back paws in my right hand, and with my left arm resting on his back, I held his front paws with my left to stop them pawing my chin.

He was in a deep *nyubarr* (sleep). As I looked at the *bundarra* (stars), my heart swelled with love for *Gulyi-Gulyi*. *Nyubarrimanha* (falling asleep) I held my puppy in close to my heart and dreamt of swimming with him in clear-blue water at Gantheaume Point.

11. Sweet Warm Milk and Foaming Sea

I woke to the chilling sound of dingos howling. We believe that dingos are the keepers to the after-life. They are silent dogs, except when they howl to announce that death is near. *Gulyi-Gulyi* went ballistic. He'd fought hard to keep me alive and wasn't going to let his fellow dingos make me their latest kill. He was so deadly fierce, he frightened even me.

Unable to move and fearing death, suddenly I heard that familiar sound of pounding hooves—*nguurru* (brumbies) were on the move. The pack of dingos fled, and in the fading light I could see a brumby's eyes flicker against the dark outline of the gathering herd. The wild *nguurru* came in close, heads down snorting. Their sweet warm breath was a comfort to me.

In disbelief, as if he was standing next to me, I heard Dad's voice say, '*Hey daughter, you'll be okay. Get yourself outta that mud.*'

71

Dragging myself along by my arms, I didn't give a shit about the pain. I was just doing what my Daddy told me. It was dark now, and although I felt chilled to the bone, my skin was on fire. Exhausted, I rolled over and over, away from Battlement Rocks and the water that had pooled at its base.

Then I heard Dad's familiar tongue click, '*tnik, tnik'*, and to my surprise, a mare circled round the back of me and lay down. *Gulyi* pushed me towards her. I understood what they had in mind. Dragging myself in close to her to keep warm, I rested my head between the mare's rear legs. *Gulyi* and the mare's foal lay against my back to keep me warm. Fading in and out of consciousness, I heard my Dad saying, '*Drink daughta, drink.*' The mare's teat was leaking milk and I sucked long and deep.

I didn't know if it was drinking mouthfuls of sweet warm milk or the musty smell of the *nguurru's* loins that made my dream of Manu Tollie flood in sweet and strong. In that other world, I heard Manu singing, calling me across the sea, luring me like mermaids do. Then on that dark beach lit by a slither of a moon, he wrapped his gentle arms firmly around me.

Laying my head on his broad chest, I felt safe. Listening to his strong, steady heartbeat against the whooshing of his blood, the words, '*I love you, Lucy Lucky-Child,*' echoed in his barrelled chest. Reaching up on tippy toes, I turned my face towards his and planted a kiss upon his full, moist lips. His breath was sweet but I wanted more.

In one motion I flung my arms around his neck as he lifted me off the ground. I felt his erect *wirlu* (penis) brush against me. He looked embarrassed, but every part of me wanted him to enter me. I wanted us to be one body. Him in me and me in him.

'Lucy,' he started to say.

'Yes,' I responded, pushing my tongue past his full, soft lips into his cavernous mouth.

'Sure?' he struggled to say.

'Hmm,' I was too turned on to retreat.

Manu ran, carrying me to a sandy rise by the water's edge. I undid his *laplap* (sarong) and held his large, warm *wirrlu* tightly in my hand. Opening my legs, I pressed it against me, and pulling my undies to one side I sat the head of his *wirrlu* in the wet opening of my *mirni* (vagina).

'Are you sure ... We can stop?' he whispered.

'I want you. I'm almost seventeen.'

'What about *Jalbri* and the Pope?'

'Whaattt?' I said in disbelief.

We both cracked up.

'You've gotta be kidding me?' I asked, thinking there must be something wrong with me.

Manu climbed up the sandy rise and lay beside me. I snuggled into his armpit, just like *Gulyi*—I was now a one-man woman.

Snuggling in but a bit pissed off, I said, 'You're totally weird? Anyway, I reckon *Jalbri* and the Pope would be a perfect match.' Although I was ragging him, I felt like he was showing me respect in a strange way.

'Well, you know how we always have to ask permission for everything? Like, can we go onto Country or go up the rock? What about us? Do we have to ask for permission first?'

God, he was probably right. For tribal Catholics like me, sex was really complicated.

'Okay, let's ask the Spirits of the *Jirdilungu* (Milky Way),' I said, now aware that millions of Spirits were looking down at us about to make out on the beach.

Gazing at the *bundarra* (stars), Manu took my hand in his and raised it towards the sky. Then he spoke in a way that kept time with the sea lapping gently on the shore.

'I, Manu Tollie, Salt-Water man from Tiwi Islands, and Lucy Lucky-Child, Salt-Water girl from Broome, we call on the Spirits of the Milky Way to guide us. Sea Spirits unite us to be like the waves in of fine sand fell to earth. At first, I thought it was just red dirt from last night when I had to drag myself through the mud. But as the morning light increased, I saw a fine layer of white beach sand stuck all over me.

It was too scary to think that the dream of Manu Tollie was real. I became aware of feeling wet between my legs. Before I knew it, my right finger touched the edge of my undies. I was shocked when I looked at my moist finger to see a fine streak of blood. 'Oh God, what's happening? It has to be my period.' Reaching for my bag with women's stuff in it, I realised it must have been somewhere on Battlement Rocks. 'Shit, *Jalbri's* going to kill me.' Any moment I expected to hear her voice.

Turning to *Gulyi* and pointing at the rocks, I said, 'Bags! Bags!'

He pricked his ears and ran off as if he totally understood.

All I could think of were my precious bags stuck in the crevices, sopping wet. Looking to see where he was, I spotted his tail between one of the big boulders halfway up. Soon he bounced out of a crack and up and over the boulder like a mad thing dragging one of my string bags, the one with the jerky in it and all my special soul survival stuff.

By the time he dropped it at my feet, he'd dragged it through the dirt and it was filthy dirty. The cream cotton string knots were thick with red mud and bits of twigs and leaves. But I didn't care, this was my 'body and soul' bag and *Gulyi* was a legend.

12. Straighten up

'Lucky-Child, you'll be alright, thubarnimanha nganggu-nganggunmanhu (straighten up your thinking).' Jalbri's voice sounded like some old witch.

The last thing I needed was a lecture.

'What?' I hissed into the acrid air. My boiling hot body suddenly turned icy cold with rage. 'Shit! Here I am struck by lightning, dead, brought back to life by a dingo pup, can't move my legs, stuck in the bloody Great Sandy Desert looking for you, and you tell me to *straighten up my thinking*. Yeah, thanks for that!' My voice petered out cos my throat felt like I'd swallowed a hundred thousand razor blades.

Lying on the ground, trying not to swallow, cough or move, all I could think of was how much I hated the bloody bush, desert, or whatever you called this hell hole.

I wanted to go back home, swim, eat heaps of fish and hang out with my friend Louanna. I didn't wanna be a *blackfella* anymore. I hated Australia. I wanted to be a beautiful, rich, white French girl. I didn't wanna be Lucy Lucky-Child any more. I was totally pissed off.

Out of the corner of my eye, I saw something black scuttle across the red dirt. *Ganba* (giant scorpion)! Fearing that *Gulyi-Gulyi* would be stung, I flung him off my chest to my left-hand side. He squealed and ran under a nearby bush, thinking he had done something wrong.

I fixed my eyes on the *ganba* coming towards me. I felt trapped, lying on my back, unable to move my legs. I heard *Jalbri's* command: '*Balayi! Balayi! Watch out! Watch out! Ganganggamanha garndi* (take the stone knife), *mabarn* (have faith).'

As if by magic, an old piece of flint stone that had been carved into a knife, appeared beside my hand. I clutched it, and in a single sweep, I cut the body of the *ganba* in two. The front half of the *ganba* didn't know it was dead yet, and it scuttled towards me ready to fight, its big clippers still opening and closing forcefully. But its big curved tail, that was just about to strike, suddenly fell sideways to the ground, pulsating.

My body started to spasm. I'd lost control and I felt like I was going to pass out. It was like being struck by lightning all over again. Then I heard *Jalbri's* voice, '*Mabarn* (have faith), listen, pick up the tail and eat three parts. I am *Mabarnyuwa* (sorceress/healer) *Mabarn!* (Have faith!) *Mabarn!* (Believe!) You are a Lucky-Child.'

I grabbed the tail with my left hand and bit off three segments. Its black outer body stuck between my teeth and the white gooey stuff was sickening. The incredibly bitter, strong chemical taste was horrible. I started to heave my guts up.

Then, the strangest burning sensation spread from the tip of my tongue, down my throat and up to my brain. I felt my tongue and throat swell and go numb.

All at once, my eyes cleared and my body stopped shaking. A warm feeling travelled all the way down my spine, through my legs, and to my feet. Then, my feet twitched and my knees bent.

I couldn't resist the urge to stand, and *Gulyi-Gulyi* couldn't resist the urge to jump on me. He sent me flying. Yelping with delight, he tore around with his tail between his legs, running crazy like. He's not complicated. This little dingo was so happy, ya couldn't wipe the smile off his face.

I heard his tummy growl with hunger, so I grabbed my precious bag and gave him a big chunk of jerky. Feeling around inside for something else for me, I recognised the crinkling sound of the lolly packet. 'Oh sweet.' I stuffed six milk bottle lollies into my mouth all at once and then reached for Dad's Luxor bacci tin for my little pearl-handled knife. As I opened the tin, I caught sight of an image reflected on the inside of the shiny lid. At first, I thought the mirrored image was a trick by some evil sorcerer.

The she-devil that looked back at me had a mop of wildly matted hair, and strangely patterned skin, with the spookiest big, yellow eyes. Unable to break my stare, I suddenly realised that *she* was *me*. The *ganba* had given me my legs back, but it had also turned my brown eyes into a startling yellow. This was *mamany* (crazy).

At first, I wanted to cry, but instead I burst out laughing and yelled to my beloved, 'Manu Tollie how's this for a look? Our wedding will look like a proper horror movie.'

My scars were stinging like mad. Instinctively, I grabbed Dad's healing salve and smeared it all over them. *Gulyi* kept licking me. To distract him, I found the last packet of Tiny Teddies that Louanna had given me. I held up a single little teddy in front of his beady eyes. 'Sit,' I said, pushing his bum to the ground. 'I Knight you Sir *Gulyi-Gulyi*, The *Minhan* (The Brave).' Before I could finish knighting him, he swallowed the biscuit, snatched the whole pack from my other hand and bolted.

'Thief!' I yelled. '*Wheeuwrt*! *Wheeuwrt*!' I whistled for him to bring it back. I really wanted some. 'Not fair, *Gulyi, yanajimanha, yanajimanha* (come here, come here),' I called after him.

While I was shouting at *Gulyi*, a pretty chestnut mare trotted over and came in close. I thought the herd had left long ago. I stopped bellowing, slowly dropped my eyes to the ground, turned away from her, and made a soft clicking and shushing sound like Dad used to. She walked up behind me and nudged me in the back with her head. I stretched my left hand back towards her and she put her nose in my palm. She trusted me. I felt honoured.

I turned around to face her, keeping my eyes low. Dad told us kids that *nguurru's* (brumbies) were like *Wongi's* (Indigenous people from Kalgoorlie). 'Ya must never look a *Wongi* in the eye, it's rude 'til them fellas trust ya.

Nguurru's are same, same. You gotta be humble to get their trust. That's the proper way. Break 'em with a whip, and they'll never trust ya.'

When I finally looked up, her big brown eyes were looking at me like we'd known each other forever.

She didn't flinch when I stroked her strong, smooth neck. Holding onto a clump of her hair at her wither, I ran my other hand along her back and rump. She stood still but turned her head to keep her eyes on me.

'It's okay, girl, sshh, it's okay, *tnick, tnick*.' Smiling at her and blowing out long, lippy breaths like raspberries, I leant on her shoulder.

She didn't take fright; she just leaned back.

'Okay girl, let's go, *tnick tnick*.' I walked in front of her and she followed. Nearby I spotted a lolly bush. It was laden with shiny mauve berries that looked like waxy pink star-shaped flowers with lumps of bubble gum stuck to the centre. I imagined fairies eating them when no one was looking. I picked some and offered them to her.

Snorting softly into my outstretched hand, she ate them. Then *Gulyi-Gulyi* came running at her, nipping her back legs. Her ears went back and she kicked out at him. He ran off squealing with his tail between his legs. I tried to calm her even though I really wanted to scream at him.

She calmed down and started to eat straight from the lolly bush. I quickly went to see how *Gulyi* was. He was curled up in the hole he'd dug to bury my ripped-up packet of Tiny Teddies. He was trying to lick the lump on his shoulder.

'Bad *Gulyi-Gulyi*, you need to pick on someone your own size. *Carmon* (come on), let's see.'

He growled a bit when I tried to stop him licking his wound. It wasn't bad, just a bit swollen. '*Yanajimanha* (come on) Gul-Gul.' My great lump of a puppy was feeling sorry for himself, so I carried him back to where my bag was, even though he could have walked. I wrapped my 'sooky la la' in Jackie's t-shirt and pulled it up over his head to cover his eyes. He stayed still and was soon fast asleep.

I collected wood for a fire and made damper with the remaining flour in my bag. I filled the billy from a nearby soak and a simple meal was on its way. The mare approached me as I set up the fire. I wondered if she belonged to a stockman who had come to a grizzly end. Sitting near the fire, waiting for the billy to boil, I sang typical stockman songs, which she seemed to like. *Gulyi* stirred, wanting some damper. It looked like she'd put him in his place and a truce was drawn.

Sipping tea and eating damper, I watched the golden sun gently slide under the lavender sky. The earth was the deepest red and seemed to hold its breath as lavender turned into turquoise, and then into that familiar inky blue of a clear night sky.

Gan.gara (high above) hung a fine slither of *milara* (moon) and a thousand dazzling *bundarra* (stars). All the creatures, my deadly dog and an awesome *nguurru* (brumby) were silent as Mother Nature changed her gown for *nyubarr* (sleep). My last thoughts were of my mother. I missed her, and like a little girl struggling against sleep, my eyes finally closed.

Behind my closed eyelids I could see the mob of women following Patty Mae and Gofar. My mum and Barbara were talking to each other. Like an annoying fly, I hovered around them wanting desperately to hear what they had to say.

'Can you smell something burning?' said Barbara.

'Yes,' said Mum.

Both women looked around for signs of smoke. I had become like the *Jurdu* (spirit smoke). They stopped walking and let the others go ahead.

Barbara turned to mum and started having a go at her. 'You know the girls were meant to be mine! Alan was meant to bring both of them to me, that was the agreement!'

79

'You got Ellen didn't ya? Wasn't she enough?' Mum whined.

At this point, Helen piped up, 'Ellen, or me, Helen?'

Barbara ignored her, she was furious and started yelling at Mum, 'Don't try to play the victim with me! I took the ritual beating for you and your bloody wrong-way marriage!' She parted her hair showing Mum the massive scar. 'I was cast out of the family as punishment for you!'

'I'd just put them on the boob, they were having their first proper feed. He grabbed Ellen and pulled her off me. I fought him. I wanted to kill him,' she snarled, 'He stole Ellen, but he didn't get my Lucy!'

'Shit! What do you mean?' I pleaded, desperate for Mum to explain, Helen looked up, I'm sure she could hear me!

Helen, Ellen, whatever her name is, stepped away from mum and Barbara and just kept staring at me. The pain in my heart was overwhelming. Words had left me and all I could do was growl like a mad *duthu* (dog).

'I couldn't give my girls up, deal or no deal. Them babies were having their first feed,' Mum's voice trailed off, she looked pathetic.

'Are you deaf? I took all the punishment. The Elders said they would be mine and I was meant to teach them Language and Lore, and tell them all the secrets and give them their real names.'

Mum squared up to Barbara. Her face was hard as stone. Barbara was real uncomfortable. Mum's stare was deadly as.

Without blinking, or moving a muscle, she asked her straight out, 'Did he say he loved you?'

'Don't Mum,' I whispered from the other side, amazed at how just changing the topic could shift the balance of power.

Barbara smirked, 'Yes, of course, Alan really knew how to treat a woman.' Then with a stupid twinkle in her eye, she said, 'His shoes were always parked under my bed.'

'He never wore shoes, you moron!' I shouted from the other side. The galahs squawked back at me.

Mum was motionless, 'Did he ever beat you?'

'Of course not!' He had no reason to beat me.'

'Shut up you whore!' I screamed. Mum just stood there, her right hand closed into a fist. Her jaw tightened and she drew a deep breath through her teeth. I knew that look. She was ready to strike.

'Hit the bitch!' I yelled at the top of my lungs, excited at the thought of Mum giving that bitch a fat lip.

'Come away Mum, leave it alone,' Helen pleaded with the only mother she'd ever known.

'Yeah, rack off, both of you!' I yelled. Helen eye balled me. Shocked, I took a step back.

Then, Barbara noticed Mum's most recent cuts and bruises. Her face and tone softened, 'He got ya real bad this time Sis.'

'What do you care?' I whispered from the other side.

'*Gurndany* (Shame),' Mum whimpered, and then she collapsed. Barbara immediately knelt in the dirt beside her. Holding Mum's head on her lap she stroked her lovingly, just like a real good sister should.

I couldn't do anything but sit in the dirt and growl. *Gulyi-Gulyi* sat in front of me looking puzzled, wondering if maybe he'd done something wrong.

Some of the women spotted trouble and came to help.

I couldn't stop thinking about Helen… my sister.

Looking closely at her today, she really does look like me. I knew there was something fishy about us. I know the only reason I hated her, was because I thought she was Dad's other woman's child. We were always bumping into each other at school. I didn't understand the feelings I had when she was near me. I didn't even want to look at her, let alone speak to her.

We are both athletic and are always competing against each other for first place. At the last swim meet it was a dead heat. Helen and I even broke our left arms on the same day and ended up in hospital beds next to each other. Barbara couldn't visit her in hospital when my mum was there. I wanted to scratch Helen's eyes out when Dad came to see us, and she called him Dad. He gave Helen the biggest hug and kiss. I reckon they should have been mine, not hers.

That bitch Barbara is real wealthy compared to us. If ya ask me, she's probably a 'call girl' cos she's always 'dolled up' (overly dressed), like she is going somewhere posh to meet someone special.

Why didn't Mum fight for Helen after Dad took her? Maybe in the end she thought Helen woulda had a better life.

I couldn't get my head around how my Dad could take Helen from her mother when *he* was *taken* from his mother? Does history really repeat itself? If anyone knew the pain of separation, he did. Maybe that's why he took up with Barbara? To be close to both Helen and me?

Suddenly, the next thing I saw was Mum and Helen kneeling in the dirt, holding onto each other crying their hearts out. Barbara had turned her back on them and was in a heated discussion with Aunty Toots. Patty Mae was calling a truce to get everyone back on track. Overwhelmed, I lay on my side, rocking back and forth, growling softly to myself. *Gulyi-Gulyi* snuggled in close. His warm body and steady heartbeat were a comfort, and finally, I escaped into the land of sleep.

13. Blanket Stitch

Gulyi-Gulyi and I woke late by the desert clock. The *biyarrgu* (galahs) had come and gone and my *nguurru* (brumby) was grazing beside the nearby soak. I ran to that little soak feeling free as a bird and happy to have my body back. The spongy new *babarda* (grasses) felt so nice between my toes. My little chestnut mare was so pretty. She had a white blaze down the front of her face with a big white spot on her rump. I watched her lightly prancing on the spot, trying to shake off the long, wet, pieces of grass that were stuck to her hooves.

She looked just like a *Kaditja* Man—what we call *Birrinja*. They make feather slippers for their feet so they don't make tracks in the sand.

'*Yanajimanha* (come on) *Birrinja* (Feather Foot), I'll help you.'

Stepping out real light, she took herself onto the dry sand and I gently brushed the grass off her hooves for her. I remembered Dad saying, 'If you see

83

a *nguurru* with a light step, she'll give you a sweet ride'. I decided it would be much easier to get to Dragon Tree Soak if I rode her.

This was the moment. '*Tnick*.' I gave her the raised lip and head nod that us *blackfellas* do, and in a soft high-pitched voice, I said, '*Yanajimanha. Yanajimanha* (come on, come on).'

She came straight to me, side on as if she'd heard those words before.

Picking up a clump of hair on her whither, I raised my body weight onto the arch of her back. She didn't kick out so I knew she'd been ridden before. I threw my leg over and sat upright. '*Barndi barndi* (good, clever),' I said, patting her neck. 'Sweet.'

With a slight pressure to her flank, she was off and running. A real comfy ride. I called out to *Gulyi*, 'Catch up! Catch up!'

He could only just keep up with her a steady trot.

Then, with a '*tnick tnick*' and a firm heel, she broke into a gallop and left *Gulyi* for dust. 'Woah.' She pulled up snorting with her whither rippling, happy to be ridden again.

Trotting back to our camp, I had a real strong urge to get ready quickly and set off for *Jalbri*. It wasn't long before we were fed and exploring this *wandarri* (red sandy country) just like the old timers that used to call this place home. It was a laid-back, uneventful morning on Country.

We stopped regularly to check out bush tucker. *Birrinja* was such a great horse. I even had her jumping rocks and logs, but I was really surprised when she was willing to jump a fence for me. Barbed wire fences marked station boundaries and surrounding soaks to stop camels and other livestock destroying them.

Anyway, we covered good ground and were ready to stop and have a late lunch. Dismounting, I patted *Birrinja*, thanking her for a sweet ride. I heard a low growl. Thinking it was my tummy, I reached for another minmin flower. Then I heard blood curdling squealing … it was *Gulyi*.

I raced through the scrub using the narrow track made by the *nguurrus* (brumbys). There, standing tall on his hind legs was the biggest *marloo* (big red kangaroo) I'd ever seen. The front of his body was covered with blood. And laying on the ground with his stomach ripped wide open, was my precious *Gulyi-Gulyi*. Roos hold ya in real close to their bodies with their short arms, then they lean back on their tail and use the huge toe claws on their hind legs, like a butcher's meat axe, to slice you open from breakfast to arsehole.

Panicking, I screamed.

Luckily, the *marloo* didn't want to have a go at me too and took off. I raced over to *Gulyi,* shocked by how much blood was spurting out of him. I was dizzy as, and felt like throwing up.

'*Thubarnimanha tharlbarra (Straighten up, be strong),*' *Jalbri* whispered in my head.

'Shit! Shut up, he's my best friend!' I shouted at *Jalbri's* voice.

She shouted back ordering me, '*Thubarnimanha tharlbarra*!'

In a flash, I remembered that I'd packed a needle and thread in the band-aid tin in my bag. I don't know how I did it, but I got out the needle and threaded it, even though my hands were shaking like a leaf. I couldn't see for tears, and I had to swallow down a mouthful of vomit.

Gulyi was out cold, lying on his back like a dead dog, which was lucky cos it stopped the dirt getting into the gory rip.

I felt around inside *Gulyi* until I found the part that was pulsing out the blood. Using the thread, I made a loop, like ya do when ya start to weave a basket, looped it around the snake like thingy, and pulled it real tight to stop the blood spurting out. After that, I wound the thread around a few times, like when you close off a balloon to stop the air leaking out. Then I threaded it through the pull-ring from the Coke can, just to make sure it wouldn't come undone. It wasn't pretty, but it stopped him bleeding to death.

I remembered Sister telling us how useful blanket stitch was for joining ripped materials together. She'd even used it to sew up a soldier who had his stomach blown open. I'm not good at math, but I'm bloody good at blanket stitch. I reckoned I could save his life.

With a deadly confidence, I sewed up my puppy and remembered all the times I mended those horrible, old, grey woollen mission blankets that we were still using at home. Originally, they all had yellow stitching, but ours had a different colour for each new mend. Mum used to say it was like Jacob's coat of many colours.

But I hated those itchy, smelly rags, cos they reminded me of the American Indians and how they were given them same grey woollen blankets as a gift from the settlers who'd deliberately exposed the blankets to small pox. All the tribes that were given them poxy blankets were wiped out. Sister Euphrates told us that's what an 'Indian gift-giver' is. Big shame on them *whitefellas*.

I had straightened up alright, and now, like a master craftswoman, I applied Dad's salve to *Gulyi*'s long 'Z' shaped scar.

Birrinja was stressed to the max. Horses are very sensitive creatures, they feel another animal's pain. I called her in close to keep *Gulyi* warm, somehow, she knew what to do.

I noticed some good bush medicine in a nearby clearing. I picked *bilabirdi* (eucalyptus) leaves and *thumbuny* (sandalwood) branches, but I had no idea how I would be able to fit the large pieces of the *bilabirdi* leaves into my small billy.

As if by magic, I found a large old billy can with a water canteen hidden in the bushes. I'm sure it was left by someone who often visits this place cos there was a small camp site near the hidey hole. Indigenous I reckon cos there were heaps of roughly carved stone tools that were invisible at first.

Scraping together some leaves and twigs I started a fire the traditional way and used the billy to brew the herbs. Emptying my string bag, I found Dad's hanky at the bottom and dipping it into the brew of *binyj* (slippery jack mushroom) bark, I washed *Gulyi*'s belly and soaked the long line of blanket stitches, hoping it would kill the germs and stop infection.

Gulyi's jaw was shut tight with shock, so I used Sister's *je t'aime* spoon to prize his mouth open and feed him some boiled herbs. I'd watched the old people burn *thumbuny* (sandalwood) and use the ash on open wounds to stop a gash going bad and to bring down the pain.

So, I slathered a thick layer of Dad's salve on top of the ash to form a crust. Then I covered the crust with Dad's hanky and wrapped the plastic bag around *Gulyi's* tummy. Gently turning my whimpering puppy, I sewed it in place real tight. I prayed that it would hold his guts in place and keep the dirt out.

As I collected some *garnboorr* (paperbark) to make a stretcher for *Gulyi*, I realised we weren't far from Dragon Tree Soak, cos where there's *garnboorr*, there's ground water. Then I rubbed some tea-tree leaves together in my hands and held them over his nose to bring him round. Dogs hate that smell.

I picked him up, placed him on the stretcher and tied it onto *Birrinja's* back. Instinctively, she walked ever so lightly and quietly beside me.

From somewhere deep inside me, a song came to my lips. I was singing out to the spirits, asking them to protect us from an evil fate, and to open up the way for us.

We were like soldiers returning from battle, and after many hours, our sad procession drew to a halt. *Gulyi* let out a single howl. As I turned to face him, both my hands rose into the air and hovered over his body. An intense heat and energy flowed from me. My hands shook uncontrollably. The voice I recognised as *me,* was replaced by an older, darker voice. I understood the feeling of that sound, but no words could explain its meaning.

Suddenly, all the surface things I thought I knew, disappeared. It was *marbarn* (magic and faith). And there, in that spot, with my Ancestors as my witness, a deep rumble came up from the bowels of the earth, and a long, narrow crack appeared at the tip of my toes. The ground split open, and with my own eyes, I saw her, *Pulanyi Bulaing* (Rainbow Serpent), coiling herself back up to the surface of the earth's crust, just underneath my feet.

Then, a *willy-willy* (whirlwind) whipped around us and *Gulyi-Gulyi's* eyes opened wide as a *Jin.gi* (Spirit Being) materialised.

I trembled with both fear and delight, as she rose up and hovered above the ground. She looked at us with a deep compassion like I'd never seen or felt before. Her enormous eyes were intensified by the glow from her dazzling white face. She was trying to say something. Shocked, I realised she had no mouth.

A wispy cloudy-like haze enveloped *Gulyi-Gulyi* and rays of energy shone down from the *Jin.gi*. My hands had risen by a force not of my will and I felt the world turn one rotation. For a moment I felt dizzy and faint, and then a deep breath centred me and my raised hands lowered. Energy streamed from them into *Gulyi's* wound. The rest of the world had vanished. It was as if we were marooned in an island of isolation.

The atmosphere was electric. *Birrinja* was prancing on the spot and snorting. I started to chant words that were foreign to my ears and tongue. *Gulyi* howled. A *gurrgurgu* (mopoke owl) let out a loud hoot. The spell was broken.

The *Jin.gi* disappeared, leaving coolness in the air.

Everything looked normal again. The mist disappeared and the sun shone brightly. *Gulyi-Gulyi* was struggling to get out of the sling. *Birrinja* waited patiently for me to take the stretcher off her back. My naughty puppy had returned, full of energy. He'd ripped off the plastic waistband, and to my surprise, his scar looked sore but good. I left it uncovered, trusting that Dad's salve and the crust of ash would do the trick.

We started our journey again. We walked real slow so that *Gulyi* could keep up. I knew something special had happened and I felt like the *Jin.gi's* eyes were still watching over us. I would never forget how tall she was—more than twice as tall as me. But it was that familiar way she looked at me, like a close rellie (relative) who knew everything about me.

Maybe she was an angel, like the one that came to Dad when he was drowning. Just like Dad, I would never forget those compassionate eyes. It reminded me of old Sister Mary Teresa. Everyday she'd tell everyone she met that she'd seen angels—big ones that were over twelve feet tall. She was sure that *Jin.gi's* (Spirit Beings)—were angels.

'They don't have mouths,' she'd say, 'because a cruel unjust death had silenced them. These saintly women, the *Jin.gi's*, communicate their love and compassion more powerfully with their eyes than would be possible with spoken words.'

I must have heard her say it a hundred times, but now I believed old Sister with my whole heart.

Glancing down at my hand holding onto *Birrinja's* mane, I noticed how old it looked. Where was that girl I'd left on the beach?

14. Magician and Faith Healer

The thought of home reminded me that I was an identical twin. I wondered if my twin had felt all the *mamany* (crazy) stuff that I'd been through in the last few days. What if she was the evil twin like in the movies? Maybe she was the one who cursed me. *Nah, she'd have to be better than me.*

Thinking of her opened my mind's eye. I could see Helen standing alone on top of Battlement Rocks. A strange greenish-gold light surrounded her like an early morning mist. She was holding my other bags; she must have picked them up on the way to the top. Her face looked odd, like she was sniffing me out, sensing me, feeling my *songlines*.

The hairs stood up on the back of my neck. I coughed nervously.

'*Wanna talk?*' she said, facing me as if she were standing within arm's reach.

What the hell? There was no way her ears could have heard me. Battlement Rocks was far behind us. Feeling spooked, I squeezed *Birrinja's* girth and she picked up the pace.

The sound of Helen's high-pitched sing-song voice reached my ears. '*I know who you are. I've been watching you.*'

Shit! I dug my heels in. *Birrinja* broke into an all-out gallop. I didn't even think about *Gulyi* until I heard him protest. Pulling up sharply, I turned around and circled back to get him. I jumped off *Birrinja's* back before she drew to a halt, picked up *Gulyi*, remounted and took off again, heading for Dragon Tree Soak.

If she knows who I am, who is she?

A gentle breeze blew as *Birrinja* galloped, weaving between the spinifex. In spite of everything, I felt strangely powerful, like a female wizard with my wild hair blowing in the wind riding full pelt with my animal friends.

'*Mabarnyuwa* (magician),' my sister's voice surrounded me.

'*Jala-Jala Jura Mabarnyuwa*, Lucky-Child magician.*'

'*Jala-Jala Jura Mabarnyuwa*, Lucky-Child faith healer.*'

Birrinja pulled up sharp. The air turned cold. A *mara-irri* (animal with special powers) hooted. The *gurrgurgu* (mopoke owl) was sitting on a branch overhanging the tracks. *Gulyi* whimpered and *Birrinja* was restless.

'*We are yunba, yunba—identical, identical,*' my sister's voice boomed.

I dismounted as a sign of respect. I broke off a branch of wattle, placed it on the ground underneath the *gurrgurgu* and sat on the dirt, waiting for a message. *Birrinja* and *Gulyi* stood back in silence.

Helen's voice was now as clear as a bell. '*Lucy, I heard the women talking about you. When your mum didn't give you to my mum, one of the Elders cast the evil eye and cursed the whole Lucky-Child side of the family for disobeying the law.'*

'What law?' I cried, feeling overwhelmed.

'*I don't know, but don't worry, you're strong and you've got the power. You are mabarnyuwa (faith healer magician). Get to Jalbri as soon as you can. Love you, sis.'*

With those words she was gone and I felt the atmosphere change.

The *gurrgurgu* (mopoke owl) spread his wings and flew off. I sat weeping. *Gulyi* sweetly licked my face, and *Birrinja* stood behind me nudging me gently with her head.

Still sobbing, I got out Sister's little music box from my string bag that was now permanently slung across my shoulder. As it played, with a breaking voice I sang, 'Far away across the sea, Manu's waiting for me …' Feeling alone and too scared to go forward and too *malardi* (tired) to return, I had become a stranger to my own life.

A tiny little *willy-willy* (whirlwind) sprung to life a couple of metres away from my outstretched feet. I stopped crying, fascinated by the approaching red cone-shaped sand funnel. It fell apart in front of my folded legs, and there, in its centre, was a little white feather with a tiny spot of yellow paint on its tip. It was from Manu's headdress.

Excitedly I picked up my gift, kissed it, placed it in the waistband of my knickers, and called out, 'I love you, Manu Tollie.' I wasn't alone anymore.

Although I was feeling hungry and *malardymanha* (becoming tired of searching) for *Jalbri*, I decided I'd better *thubarnimanha* (straighten up) and head for Dragon Tree Soak. At a light trot I watched the landscape change from *wandarri* (the sandy red country) to a green oasis.

It was late in the afternoon and the sky above was the most beautiful blue. Light, wispy, purple clouds turned gold towards the horizon. My heart leapt for joy when I recognised the silhouette of my *Jalbri* sitting on a rock nestled between the old Twin Dragon Trees.

I sang out loud my greeting to her and Country, 'I am Lucy. I was a Lucky-Child. Now I am a Lucky-Woman. I am *Bardi*. Thank you *Pulanyi Bulaing* and the Ancestors for protecting me. I am here to see my *Jalbri*, Keeper of the Soak.'

'*Jalbri, Jalbri*, I made it!' I yelled, jumping off *Birrinja's* back and running to her. *Gulyi* almost tripped me up.

Jalbri stood to greet me, her thin, naked body looked beautiful lit by the setting sun. I threw my arms around her and hugged her tightly. The beautiful moment was shattered by the most disgusting wet fart sound I'd ever heard.

'Yuuck *Jalbri*!'

'It's not me,' she protested. 'It's *Winthuly-Winthuly* (Windy-Windy).'

'I know what it means,' I said, making fun of her.

'No, *Winthuly*, my camel.'

'Yeah, right,' I mocked.

As I turned in the direction of her pointed finger, sure enough there stood the strangest-looking ship of the desert I'd ever seen. Tall and bony, I couldn't tell if it was grey or black. Its coat changed tone seamlessly like a water-colour brush stroke, lighter grey in the bigger broader areas, bleeding into black on the ends of the limbs, nose and ears. Like *Jalbri*, it had a big set of chompers and a wicked gleam in its eye. *Jalbri* laughed. I didn't know if she was laughing at me thinking she had farted or at the way I looked.

'*Ngarnmanha*! (eat),' her old, bony hands took mine in hers and she led me to a clearing at the back of the soak where she had bush tucker cooking on her camp fire.

In an old, black, cast-iron pot, she was cooking her famous *marloo* (big red kangaroo) stew and on the open fire she was baking a *barnga* (small goanna). She'd also made a pile of wattle seed damper. I'd forgotten what real food tasted like.

I sat grinning as she served me tucker on a tin plate and handed me an old enamel cup filled to the brim with tea sweetened with condensed milk. *Gulyi* was a happy puppy too. He got the best part the *marloo* tail that us kids always fought over. *Jalbri* sat happily watching me scoff her food. This was living it up.

After I'd eaten my fill, *Jalbri* leant over and whispered, '*Thubarnimanha* (straighten up),' in my right ear.

Even though I was surprised to hear it said so softly, I still sprang to attention like a soldier. Hanging by a string around *Jalbri's* neck was a small, cylindrical carved wooden vessel that sat neatly between her breasts. Dipping her right thumb into the pot she wiped the fluid from the pot over my left eyelid and then my right. It made my eyes feel cool and took away the *malardi* (tiredness). She sang in soft tones as she applied the fluid and then ran her wet thumb over my lips. The juice was bitter as.

Then she told me to turn my hands over in front of her and she poured a little juice into each palm and the rest onto the crown of my head. 'You *mabarnyuwa* (female magician, faith healer, witch doctor).' Her words seeped into my soul.

She picked up one of her many tins, took the lid off and placed it near the fire to warm up. Running her hand over the back of my right arm and then onto my face, she told me to take off my t-shirt. Scooping out a handful of warm emu oil from the tin, she applied it to my neck, shoulders and back, and worked it right down to my fingertips. As she rubbed and pulled and twisted each finger, she asked me questions about my journey. She was keen to know if I'd kept the remains of the scorpion's body.

Jalbri then poured hot emu oil onto my scalp, which trickled down my face and neck, and as she massaged it in, she asked after Helen and my feelings about finding my twin sister. The rhythmic movement of her hands against my skin put me into a deep trance. I had no idea what I said and remembered nothing more of that night.

15. Walhi – No Good

It was great waking to the smell of hot breakfast, baked *wiri-wiri* (ta-ta lizard), flat damper made with grass seeds, and a big cup of condensed milk tea.

'*Kurntal barndi nyubarr* (Hey daughter, good sleep)?'

Mother, grandmother and great grandmother all call me 'daughter' in our culture.

'Like a rock, *Jalbri*, looks good,' I said as I took the damper that she gave me and waited for a bit of the *wiri-wiri*. The *wiri-wiri* is really fast, just look at it sideways and it's off and running, 'ta-ta'. You've gotta be mighty quick to catch a ta-ta first thing in the morning.

Jalbri can spring into action like a feral cat.

'We're gonna *yurla* (smoke) round camp today to protect from 'em evil spirits and make it real good, cos them womans are comin' in soon,' she said, pointing out past the soak.

'Yeah, ready when you are.'

Winthuly-Winthuly cracked another big fart as she slurped water from the soak.

'*Winthuly-Winthuly*,' *Jalbri* called, in a gentle high pitch.

The old camel lumbered up from her knees and trotted over to *Jalbri*. Wobbling her lower lip and puffing out, she rubbed her head against *Jalbri's*. Long, sticky lengths of spit flung out of her lower lip and copped me right in the face.

'Yuck!'

95

'Gotta respect your Elders,' *Jalbri* said, defending *Winthuly-Winthuly*. 'She's an old timer. Grew her up from a baby. She's been by my side b'fore ya mother's mother born you.'

I started filling her in on all the things that had happened on my journey. Every little detail—how I was fishing with Mum and the boys, and Mum wouldn't listen so I left without telling her. About how Mrs Fong screeched at me, and how Jackie saved my life by giving me heaps of food and water, some matches and a lift to the Gingerah turnoff. I'd been alone for so long I was just talking nonstop, on and on, I couldn't help myself.

The moment I mentioned Battlement Rocks, *Jalbri* started humming deeply, the sound rose up from her belly to her throat. Nervously, I kept talking about being struck by lightning. *Jalbri's* hum became like a swarm of mosquitoes— high pitched and intense. Still I couldn't stop talking.

When I mentioned the *ganba* (giant scorpion), she couldn't restrain her energy and started to dance, shuffling her feet in the sand. Picking up clapping sticks she beat them, dancing and singing like she was in a trance.

Then, I just blurted out the word, '*Jin.gi!*'

This was what she'd been waiting for.

Her dancing intensified as she called up the Spirits. I saw a man and a woman rise out of the dry, red earth. Struck dumb, I sat watching, not sure if I could believe what I was seeing. Clapping her sticks towards me, I got up to dance with her. Now *Jalbri* watched me closely. I tried to copy everything she did.

She held her feet tightly together, and as she dragged them rhythmically through the dirt, she disappeared for a moment in a cloud of red dust. She touched the skin on my bare tummy with her clapping stick and indicated that my breath and sound should come first from there. Then she tapped my knee, making me shuffle into dance. Then she tapped my tummy again and insisted that I breathe. She made me pay attention to the movement of her tummy with each inward breath.

Holding the sticks in her left hand, she slapped my chest firmly with her open right hand beating out the rhythm to our dance, demanding that I keep in time with her and fill my lungs so that I could imitate her sounds in song.

Slapping her hand lightly on my mouth, so I sang into her open palm, her hand moved up and covered my eyes from the light so that I would feel the sound of my voice vibrating in my face. Then she tapped her fingertips on the crown of my head. Every part of my body started to vibrate.

Suddenly I left my body and was travelling beside her. I felt the weight of my feet stomping on the ground but my head seemed to be high above the Dragon Tree Soak canopy and I was shooting off towards a lonely little cloud in the vast clear blue sky. The cloud cast a dark purple shadow on my face, and then, like a balloon with a leak, I contracted back to Earth.

Jalbri stood in front of me. Her eyes shone insanely. She looked younger, stronger and more alive because she knew I'd seen the Spirits and had learnt to dance their dance and sing their song.

'That was awesome,' I said, grinning. Thirsty, I looked for *Jalbri's minggarri*[25]. The long wooden bowl was wedged snugly into the red dirt so as not to spill a single drop of its precious fluid. The water reflected the bright-blue sky perfectly. Keen to see what I looked like, I knelt down and positioned myself above the *coolamon* (wood bowl for carrying water) so that I could see the scars on my face and my wildly matted hair. As I gazed into my intense, yellow eyes, my pupils dilated like dark whirlpools and sucked me into another world.

There I saw a lone figure, a woman walking with her left hand behind her back and a firestick in her right. The quandongs on her large string bag gently swayed and clicked against each other with each stride. The slow hypnotic rhythm of her stride made me lose myself in that simple act of watching this lonely woman wandering in a vast, empty, flat land. A subtle glint of light struck the edge of the medallion that hung on a plaited, leather thong, knotted onto the front edge of her bag.

---

25   Minggarri - Wood bowl for carrying water.

I knew that relic well. The little, silver medallion had Mother Mary Protector of Travellers on one side and a little aeroplane on the other. It was the only thing I possessed that belonged to my *Mimi* (grandmother). Confused, I opened my mouth to speak, but before a sound could leave my throat, the woman turned her head and looked at me.

She was *me*.

At that same moment, *Jalbri* splashed me, shattering the image of my reflection and severing that connection between me and that woman.

'Hey!' I said, reaching over and splashing her back.

'You kids talk, pac, pac, pac.' Her hands were held with palms together, opening and closing. '*Whitefellas* talk like small children playin' in water. Too much noise. Like you. I gotta take you by the hand, show you how to swim in the deep water. Deeper and deeper 'til you have no fear. Then you see spirit world and hear her messages.

'Ya see, when ya dance and sing, ya feel the energy of Earth come up into ya feet, legs, whole body, then ya can follow *songlines*. Each sound low and high calls up the energy. When I call *Winthuly–Winthuly*, the sound is high, cos she like the wind in the desert.'

Hearing *Jalbri's* call, *Winthuly* came over and put her great head on *Jalbri's* shoulder.

I laughed, childishly.

Jalbri and I chuckled as she planted a kiss on *Winthuly's* cheek. 'Ready, daughta?'

'*Tnick, tnick, Birrinja*,' I yelled.

'Don't you call me that,' *Jalbri* barked at me. 'How dare you? Respect!' she shouted, now standing over me.

'No,' I replied. 'It's the name of my *nguurru* (brumby).'

'Whaatt!' she spat at me.

I was in deep shit.

'You not call her that. *Walhi walhi* (no good, no good). *Maminy warlugura* (stupid teenager).' Taking a deep breath, she calmed down and said, 'You not use that word again. All the evil spirits, even the *mungawarri* will come out to get ya. *Mungawarri* 'em little people, live in hills and burial mounds, very dangerous. Give *nguurru* another name. You make too much trouble.'

It suddenly hit me that maybe all those bad things happened to me because I called my *nguurru, Birrinja* (*feather foot/the one that feathers stick to*).

'Sorry *Jalbri*, I called her that cos grass got stuck on her hooves and she looked like a ...'

'Aarh!' she snapped, cutting me off before that word slipped out.

I felt mighty big *gurndany* (shame).

'Sounds have power. You don't know nothin'. That *walhi* word has plenty big evil power. In them old days, them *whitefellas* had a man all covered up head to toe in black. He hanged all the bad *whitefellas* just near here. They called that fella *executioner*. That word you said means *executioner* in our language. Even though different, different communities use him to punish our peoples who break the lore. We know his heart is darker and much more evil than them fellas we make him punish.

'He walks this land a hidden man. With mask and shawl of feathers, and even his slippers are made of feathers all stuck together with blood and tied on with human hair string. Impossible to track. Too hard to see. If he stands beside you at night, ya can only smell him if ya down wind. But sometimes, when the moon is full, if ya lucky ya can catch the glint of his black, black eyes.

'He's one of us, like you and me from the Earth. But his magic is not from here. If he "points the bone" or "sings you", everythin' finished, you gone, bad way finish. No *marbarn* (witch doctor), no *kartija* (*whitefella*) doctor can save ya. If he spears ya from behind in the leg or somethin', the poison stays with ya, and ya whole life, you sick.'

I moved uncomfortably trying to lighten the weight of her words.

She continued, 'Four brothers used ta live near here. Just past our Burial Mound, other side of Help Canyon. Their *yagu* (mother) was a wicked woman. Married very young to an old, old man who already had three wives. The other wives say she put a spell on him to marry her. It was a "wrong way marriage", so he was kicked outta the tribe to go be with her. She had four children to four different men, all passers-by. Finally, she killed her husband so she could lay down with her eldest son. She taught him how to curse and do evil things. Soon the "feathers" came to him. He killed his mother and ate her flesh and kept her bones for "pointing". He's always plenty busy with black magic.

'Him and his brothers stole too many girls, specially 'em young ones going ta collect water and bush tucker. They take 'em and do bad things and when they finished with 'em, they kill 'em. I found one girl tied up naked on a *munggu* (anthill), left to die in the hot sun, a *minggarri* (wood bowl for carrying water) full of water beside her. Seeing water but can't drink made her *mamany* (crazy). Big *minga* (meat ants) found her, ate her alive. When I got there, she was dead. Alone, I did proper respect for her. Did singin' to the Ancestors ta take her away from here to her spirit home in the *Jirdilungu* (Milky Way).'

Shaking her head, she said, 'Not many people live out here no more, people passin' through or visitin' sacred sites have ta be real careful. Even 'em *whitefellas* with their Toyota Dreaming have ta be careful cos 'em *walhi* (bad) fellas have a taste for that soft white flesh.' She looked at me sadly. 'Ya understand how *walhi* a *Kukanyuyiti* (cannibal) is?' Her eyes darkened and swam in pools of tears.

I started to cry. I knew something bad had happened to her.

'When someone eats someone ya love, they steal a part of ya soul.' She drew a long breath and looked through me into the past.

100

16. One by One by One

Softly but clearly, she began, 'Long ago, when I was a little girl, me and my *yagu* (mother) left camp on her camel to find bush tucker and water for our desert mob. I hated doin' woman's work, hated sittin' in camp waitin' for someone to fix me up for marriage. I wanted to be *marbarn* (witch doctor). Ya know, *mabarnyuwa*, medicine woman and magic maker. My *yagu* knew me too well, she let me go walkabout[26] and did my work for me. It was gettin' late, I was following a track like I'd never seen before, real *wulkula* (soft), made with *jimpiri* (feathers). I was just a kid, pretendin' to be *mabarnyuwa*. I was thinking it was a Birdman I was trackin', but it was just a big trick to get me out of the way.

---

26   Walkabout - leaving the community to wander in the bush for short periods.

'*Winthuly-Winthuly* was with me. She was just a baby then and too young ta ride, and a pest to *Yagu*, always gettin' into the bush tucker we collected. So, I took her with me trackin'.

'*The one that feathers stick to* and them brothers caught my *yagu*. I could hear her screams from far away. My *yagu* screamed out, "*Wakuyanupirri! Wakuyanupirri*! (Hide! Hide!)." Her camel, *Munda* (Loner), was fightin' 'em hard. *Pulyarra* (Half blind) I ran and ran, but soon, I couldn't hear my *yagu's* voice no more. *Munda*, she went silent too.

'Them fellas killed my *yagu*, cut off her breasts and…,' *Jalbri* held up both her pointer fingers, 'Cut, one by one.'

She paused. 'They'd stuck a *jakiny* (barbed spear) up her *mirni* (vagina). *Munda's* neck and stomach, all cut right open.'

Jalbri's eyes closed and her jaw tightened, and *Winthuly-Winthuly* snorted and swayed from side to side, as if she remembered.

'Over and over I beat my head. Too much *yarlgu* (blood) but still, I couldn't die. Too much *gurndany gurndany* (shame shame). Ya know, my fault my *yagu* died. I lay holding onto my *yagu* and sang ta our Ancestors ta take her up ta her *Jindilungu* (Milky Way) home. That night my first *yarlgu* (blood) came. For three days I didn't move from there. No eatin', no drinkin'. I couldn't go back ta our mob. I *wakuyan* (hid) *miparr* (my face) from everyone. Must be *rantangka mangunkarraj*i (alone forever).

'The desert is not kind, I thought I would die soon. Every day, *Winthuly-Winthuly* cried and cried for her mother. Too much cryin' for too many days, she grew weak and sick. I thought she would die too. Baby *Winthuly-Winthuly* and me were *malardiyimanha* (exhausted). Lucky I found a small group of wild camels. The head female let *Winthuly* drink her milk. Slowly I learnt to talk to them camels and they became my new mob. They protected us and fed us for twelve seasons.

'Every day them animals learnt me how ta survive. *Mangunykarraji* (Always) movin' on ta new lands with the seasons.'

102

Jalbri had a far away look in her eyes.

'If I see people, I wakuyanupirri (hide) and watch 'em from far like that, not lettin' 'em see me. When darkness come, I studied the night sky and looked for my *yagu* in the *bundarra* (stars).

'One day, a *juja* (old man) came to the *Jila*. He wore a red *manngi* (headband worn by initiated men) and *naka* (loincloth) that had a *minyjil* (pubic tassel made of possum hair). Digging down deep with his *kana* (digging stick), I watched him call up the water. After some time, he sat himself down at the water's edge and started *kawanarri* (singing out). I hid myself in the spinifex, and watched 'im and listened up real good for a long, long time. He talked to the Earth and the Water in a way I'd never heard before. He was *mabarn* (witch doctor). Slowly I came out of hiding, but he didn't look my way, he just kept singin' and singin'. After long time, that fella got 'imself up and walked over to a high ridge. I followed 'im.

'He sang the Earth map as he walked, lettin' me learn where the *Jilas* were on our Country. Standin' on the highest point of the ridge, he clapped his hands and gave me a *jij* (plant) to eat. I looked out across our Country and everythin' became bright, like when ya lookin' at the sun. I seen my *yaga* and all my Ancestors flyin' above the ground. They say, "don't be afraid, be *kuliyiti* (brave) *kurntal* (daughter), you be *mabarnyuwa* (faith healer, witch doctor, magician). Kaj Kanarri (The Finishing), your *jarru* (womb) will give up a *kurntal* (daughter). She'll carry a *kurntal*, and that *kurntal* will carry twin *bundarra murungkurr* (star children)."

'Hang on, hang on, is that Helen and me? I interrupted.

'*Nganggurnmanha*, listen up.' *Jalbri* went on, 'Seein' far back ta past and long way ta future time, I knew I must take this *wulyu* (good) fella as my husband. He learnt me *wulyu* (good) ways of the Earth and Spirit world. And all them medicine things, and the magic things.

'It was *makurra* (cold weather) time and I was collectin' *lakarnti* (witchetty grubs) when husband gave me something wrapped in bark. I had a *walhi* (no good) feelin'. My full body turned cold. I opened the small packet. In there

103

was my *yagu's* fingers. Easy to tell cos a grindin' stone broke her *maaja* (right) finger when she was a little girl, so it pointed sideways. Just one word I said to husband, "*Jani* (Where)?"

'I followed 'im ta the camp site. Anger was eatin' me up inside.'

Jalbri grabbed at her chest.

'Husband whispered softly so the breeze couldn't hear him, "*Jinu* (be calm), we have her bones. Tonight, we will *point* and punish 'em for her. Be quiet and strong, together we finish 'em."

'We sat in the dark waitin' for 'em brothers to come. It was so cold, not normal cold... evil spirited cold. No *wilara* (moon) in the sky that night, and all the *bundarra* (stars) were dimmed by a *mandarrayimanha* (clouding over just before rain), and on the *kurr* (sound of the wind) we could hear the Sky Spirits *yayiliri* (wailing).

'An evil wind brought a sickly smell to our nose holes. Husband clapped his sticks and we called down the Heavens with our loud song. Our energy was strong and it trapped them brothers so they couldn't leave. Holdin' the feelin' of hatred and revenge, I pointed *Yagu's* bone.

'A hundred Spirit Men's voices sang with me
One by one by one.
I pointed my *yagu's* finger bone
One by one by one.
The bones broke through each chest and heart
One by one by one.
Frightened and cursed to death
One by one by one
Those men with their broken-hearts fell down
One by one by one.
And filled with grief was I to see
One by one by one
Is only three.
The *one that the feathers stick to*
Was still free.'

104

'A *gurrgurdu* (mopoke owl) hooted. Lookin' up, the sky had cleared and my *yagu's* star shot across the sky. We should've been happy but our hearts were heavy. Husband lit a fire and sang down our *mitily manga* (baby girl) from the night sky into my *yirarr* (womb). He took warm ash from the fire and covered my body to protect me from evil spirits. He whispered somethin' into my ear. The sound of his gentle voice made me sleep. When I woke, he had passed from this world to join my *yagu* in the *Jirdilungu* (Milky Way).'

'I want to kill that *walhi* (no good) man for you. Can I, *Jalbri*?' I asked, overwhelmed with emotion.

'No, it's better for you to be *mabarnyuwa* (faith healer, witch doctor, magician).'

She looked at me with great love, knowing that I'd meant what I'd said. 'This is my *yagu's minggarri* (wood bowl for carrying water),' she said, emptying the water. 'It is for you daughta.'

I took it in silence. Running my hand over the smooth wood, I nodded, accepting her special gift.

'Livin' alone with a small baby in the desert was mighty hard,' *Jalbri* continued. 'I used ta carry your *Mimi* in this *minggarri* (wood bowl for carrying water). But when the big dry came, livin' there was too hard. Just me, her, and *Winthuly-Winthuly* in the desert with no one to help us. Too hard, too hard. Too many *Jilas* capped and all the waterholes were dry. My baby got real sick, so I decided to go to Cue[27]. We arrived in real bad shape.

'As soon as we got to the town, the Government people took her from me and put her in the orphanage. I was her *yagu*! They took her from her *yagu* and told her she had no *yagu*! Her *yagu* was dead.

Upset, *Jalbri* continued, 'Took me six years to get her back. She's still angry with me. She thought I was some *mamany* (crazy) stealin' her from 'em. She forgot me. My only *kurntal* (daughter)! I was her *yagu*. Life was hard without food and water, but much harder without her beside me.'

---

27   Cue - A small town in the mid-west regions of Western Australia.

'How did you get her back?' I was dying to hear more about my mysterious *Mimi* who I'd never met and was never spoken of in our house or by anyone in our family.

'Me and *Winthuly-Winthuly* stole her from the school yard,' she said, with a wicked laugh. 'Your *Mimi* screamed her head off. Back in them days, *Winthuly-Winthuly* could run like the wind. She just kept runnin' until we were outta there. I did a big trick on the Government and hid at special *mabarn* (spiritual) place only for magic makers.'

'You mean sorcerers and witch doctors?' I asked, excited to hear more.

'I knew that no fellas white or black, not even them traitor trackers would go there. Thirty days and nights we stayed there hidden from everyone. In the daytime, I learned daughta everythin' about lookin' at the past and future from them stories painted on *Walgahna* (Walga Rock). In the night-time I learned her to read the *bundarra* (stars) and how to dream her stories.

'When all done, covered up by darkness, we travelled until the Government trucks couldn't reach us to snatch her away again. We didn't stop at Meekatharra, Mooloogool, not even Doolgunna. Instead we went the inland path all the way up to Bamboo Creek, up Pilbara way, two and a half days ride south-east of Warrmala.

'When we arrived at the tall gates at Bamboo Creek mine, the guard wouldn't let us in. I shouted out, "Mrs Lee! Mrs Lee!" She came runnin' and told him off good and proper. Straight away, Mrs Lee knew me. Long time ago their motor car broke down in my country. I gave 'em water, and Mr Ray, he went off to get his motor car fixed up. I stayed two days with Mrs Lee and her two boys, Scott and Myers. I was protect 'em cos man's *yuna* (circumcision corroboree) was happenin'. No womans, especially white womans, should hear the *mama* (sacred song) and them boys screaming, too loud for womans ears. She was so happy to see us after so many years.

'She gave us a little house just like the *kartija* (*whitefellas*). She was a good woman, gave us food and water, and me got job breakin' horses. It was good

106

for us. I knew your *Mimi* (grandmother) would be safe at the mine cos that Mrs Lee never let any children be taken from her place. Such a good woman, always thinkin' about the right way to do things. She even had her own school. *Miyarnu* (knowingly), your *mimi*, she learnt everything real fast, fast. Mrs Lee treated her like a proper *kurntal* (daughter), sew'n her beautiful dresses, takin' her to everywhere, even took her to the big city, way down south. Perth.

'Mrs Lee was like our people. Country got into her *rayi* (soul). She was always sittin' on a rock with her big sunnies on, fag in hand watchin' out for Country, seen how them rivers like to run, and where all them birds were goin'. She knew our *Jilas* made everythin' survive.

'Oh, but Mrs Lee, she could talk. Talk and talk, no stoppin' her. Never stopped to draw breath even. She reckoned she could pick the "bull-shit factor" a mile off. I'd seen her cut a man in two with her tongue if he lied to her. The Church, the Government, not even her husband Mr Ray could take that woman on. She was fierce. "It's all about the dark and the light," she'd tell 'em. "We are all angels with one black wing and one white wing. That's how we find balance. No one is pure. No one is perfect. There's a little bit of bad in every good and good in every bad." Mrs Lee's spirit totem was a black and white feather. She'd always have at least one sticken' up behind her left ear, held there by her big sunnies.

'Behind the other ear, she had a pencil for drawin' up all her plans and writin' her thinkin' down. She didn't sleep much cos her pencil 'n' paper and a black 'n' white feather was always beside her bed, watchin' her. I'd be always on the lookin' out for a black feather with white markings or a white feather with black markin' for her. She'd read 'em like a *mabarn* (witch doctor), each one had a whole 'nother story.

'She was a talker alright, but she was a hard worker too. She never got no one ta do stuff she wouldn't do herself. She was all eyes and heart for the land, and she learnt *Miyarnu* how to work hard with her hands and her head.

'One day, a herd of brumbies was rounded up. One wild, young stallion stood out, special like. Black like camp fire coals with a white face. That day 'em young fellas caned those *nguurru* (brumby) something wicked. They took the whip real cruel like to that wild one. Shiverin' with fear and drippin' with blood, he jumped outta the stall and took off. I've never used a whip to break *nguurru*. Me and Mrs Lee were angry as. She was givin' em what for when above the shoutin' we heard *Miyarnu's* voice: "Mrs Lee, can I ride him?" "No one can ride him, he's got the fear in him now," she said. "Mrs Lee, can I ride him?" "No, he's gone and he won't be coming back." "Mrs Lee, can I ride him?" *Miyarnu* asked again.

'This time, I answered, "If he'll let you feed him, you can ride him." Both Mrs Lee and *Miyarnu* looked at me. *Miyarnu* was happy. For two whole seasons I watched that girl go to the waterhole where he drank. She was in her final year of school and always took a book and some food for that big one she named *Ramu* (special patterns on a shield). By the end of the wet season he trusted her. *Ramu* ate from her hand and stood with his head close to hers as she read aloud to him. He walked beside her out in the bush, but when *Miyarnu* neared the big gate to the yards, he took fright and bolted. My *kurntal,* she'd watched me for years, whisperin' to *nguurru*, breathin' in and out like they do and showin' 'em soft hands. So, it didn't surprise me to see her talk to *Ramu* in my way. One day she mounted him. Strong young girl on a strong young stallion. They were one,' *Jalbri* said, locking her fingers together.

'*Miyarnu* became more and more beautiful. She was a wild one herself. Just like him, I had ta give 'err her head. I wasn't smart enough for her. She asked if she could live in the big house with Mrs Lee. She studied the white man's ways real hard and Mrs Lee and Mr Ray took her to Perth for proper *whitefella* schoolin'. *Ramu's* heart got broke when she left. For many days he hung around me and wouldn't eat. There was nothing for me neither at Bamboo Creek. *Warri-murdi* (homesick for my country), I left. *Ramu* followed, and when we came across his herd near the Gingerah Road turnoff, he joined them, leaving *Winthuly-Winthuly* with me.

'From time to time I'd hear about *Miyarnu* from passers-by who said she went ta Sydney University ta study the white man's law. They gave me a photo from a newspaper of her fightin' for our land rights and the right to vote. Front page, 1968. Made me real proud to see her photo there, smart girl that one. They said she changed her name to Lee when the old girl, Mrs Lee, died. No more *Miyarnu*. In our Language her name means *knowing*. Sad to fight for *rights* but give up your proper name. Real name lets people know *who you are*.

'Heavy with child, *Miyarnu* ... Lee, came ridin' home. She hitched a ride to Gingerah turnoff and there was Ramu, waiting for her. *Ramu* and I thought she'd come home to stay, but she'd only came to birth her daughta, Barbara. *Miyarnu* hadn't lost her strength and her labour was over quick smart. No sooner had she borned Barbara, my only daughta headed back to Sydney and left the bub with me. The papers say that Barbara Millard was born 5 April 1972. I asked who the father was, but she didn't give me no name, he was a one-night stand. She was so proud that he was an *ngarrungu* (Aboriginal activist). I don't understand this one-night business. Me and *Winthuly-Winthuly* raised that Barbara like she was our own.

'In 1975, my Lee Millard came back to Country ridin' *Ramu* again. She had another baby girl, Mary. This time, to her Uni professor. *Marlamarta* (mixed race) fella from that side.' She flapped her hand to the East. 'When she left, I was too busy with the girls. *Ramu* came often to visit, attracted to Mary.'

'Is that why Mum and Barbara look so different?' I dared to ask. Barbara has lighter skin and is heavy set with wavy hair. Mum is black with real straight hair. She's much taller and skinnier. It was all starting to make sense.

'Enough now. Time to go. Ta-ta,' she called, and *Winthuly-Winthuly*, who had wandered off to eat, came over and knelt down. *Jalbri* perched herself just behind the hump. It looked like a real strange ride.

'*Tnick tnick, Birri*,' I called, deciding that I would now call my horse 'Birri', and she trotted over for me to mount.

On cue, another fart and some stuff dropped from *Winthuly's* bum. I was glad *Birri* and I had moved forward. I'd forgotten all about *Gulyi-Gulyi*. 'Gulyiiiii!' I yelled. He raced in from the other side of *Jalbri*. He'd been off hunting. *Jalbri* smiled at my puppy. I'm sure he reminded her of when her camel was a baby.

We rode in silence until the sun was overhead. A lot had been said. Now I knew how my *Jalbri* became so strong. I felt honoured that she'd let me into her life. Mum never told me anything about herself. The sun was starting to get hot on my head and back. Old timers never carry water. I don't know how they do it. I was really really thirsty.

'Ta-ta,' *Jalbri* called again.

Winthuly–Winthuly went onto her knees. I dismounted and joined *Jalbri*, who was already rubbing firesticks together to start a fire. Breaking off a branch and lighting it, she walked around setting spinifex alight.

It looks pretty full on for *kartijas* (*whitefellas*). They think we're trying to fire up the whole place, but we're not. Watching the direction of the wind carefully, we burn down wind away from us, and then we go around the other side and burn back so the fire is contained. The smoke smelt good. Little creatures darted out from lumps of spinifex. *Gulyi* had a great time chasing them here and there. A few times he yelped cos he'd jumped on hot coals.

It didn't take long to burn back and smoke the boundary of our camp. We picked plenty of bush tucker while we were out. Everything was nice and easy. *Jalbri* waved, telling me it was time to go. We mounted and rode back, drenched in the changing colours of the setting sun. Arriving back at camp, I suddenly felt exhausted. Yawning and feeling dizzy, I lay down in *Jalbri's* bush bed and fell into the deepest sleep, unaware if she'd tried to wake me to eat.

17. The Tipples' Tale

The sun was up, but it was the sound of familiar voices that woke me the next morning. I opened my eyes to see my sister looking down at me. It was cool and misty and the fire was burning as if newly stoked. Surprised to hear other voices, I turned around to see that another fire had been built, and gathered around it was that big mob of women that'd been looking for me. Mum and Barbara were looking over real anxiously.

My sister and I acknowledged them, but it was clear that we were meant to do our thing, separate from the rest. It was really odd. I used to look identical to Helen, except for a freckle on her right cheek under her eye, and another on her chin, just down from the corner of her mouth, on the left-hand side. I didn't have any freckles on my face, but I had one on my right bum cheek, and another on the tip of my left big toe. But now of course, we didn't look alike because she was beautiful, and I looked like a freak show.

'Suppose you're the evil twin?' I asked, not knowing how to start the conversation.

She laughed, saying, 'Nah, if I'm not, you must be?'

'I can't be evil, I'm Lucky.'

We both giggled in the same way—so annoying.

'Actually, that scary look is cool, especially your yellow eyes. My freckles are boring.'

I would have said that too, if I was her, or she was me.

Somehow, that empty bit inside me that'd always made me feel alone, even when surrounded by mobs of people, had been filled. When I thought about it, we'd always been attracted to each other. I'd always spot her in a crowd and could single out her voice in the choir. But I repelled any feelings of wanting to be close to her with my rage over Barbara taking my Dad and hurting my mum. I thought Mum's shame and pain were just about Dad's affair and him having a child with Barbara. I had no idea that Helen was Mum's. We could have been the best friends ever.

Straight away I felt guilty for Louanna, my best and most faithful friend. I turned, glancing towards the women's group to catch Louanna's eye. She was looking at me and my sister, probably thinking that she'd already lost her best friend. I jutted out my lower lip and tilted my head back in typical *blackfella* style to ask her to come over.

With a wave of her hand, she declined. For a moment I imagined her finding her twin; they'd be like two boab trees gently waddling through the library together. I'm a proper bitch.

Looking back at my sister, I reached out and stroked her long plat. 'How do you do the whole bush thing and keep so neat?'

She ignored my question. Touching my right cheek, she said, 'Did it hurt?'

'Shit yeah, I thought I was a goner.' I burst into tears.

She flung her arms around me. *No shame*, I felt accepted in her arms like she'd known me forever. We didn't have to explain anything to each other. Mum always put me on the *outside*. It was almost as if to let me in was too painful for her. Even though she fought to keep me, it felt like she still didn't want me. She didn't let me *be* her daughter, so she lost both of us anyway.

We held each other and howled with grief for all those years of aloneness and for what could have been.

Before I could say what I was thinking, Helen said, 'We've got each other now and I'll never leave you again, Lucky.'

I was feeling anything but 'Lucky'. 'Don't call me that, I hate it'. I'm not lucky. I'm sick of it! 'Lucky' this and 'lucky' that. Lucky my legs don't snap and go up my arse.'

She cracked up laughing.

I took one look at her face and couldn't be mad with her.

'Nah, you're *lucky* your mum kept you and you got to live with Dad,' she said sincerely.

'You're kidding. Dad was the biggest booby prize on the planet.'

'Well, we're *lucky* we found each other,' she responded sheepishly. 'If you hadn't gone bush, we'd still be lookin' dark at each other.'

I was about to reply when *Jalbri* came over and said that tomorrow just Helen and me would go with her to Help Canyon to learn secret business. Just the name of that place made me nervous.

Us mob are weird—we call everything back to front. If you're the blackest, then you're 'whitey', the skinniest is 'fatty', and the fattest, we call 'bones'. So, I can imagine all too clearly what Help Canyon meant, you're on your own—scream, but no one's comin' to help ya.

Anyway, we had the rest of the day together to chill out. The women collected bush tucker and cooked lots of traditional food from different regions of the North West. When the cook-up started, all the old stories come outta hiding. Sad ones from the stolen generation, like Patty Mae when she ran away from the Missionaries and almost died alone in the bush at just six years old, or the horror story of Polly Tipple and her mum, Olive, living at East Arm Leprosarium.

Life was real cruel to the Tipples. Olive Tipple's mother, Maymuru was Mardu[28]. To this day, the old people still say that she was a real desert beauty— tall and slender with the biggest, brightest eyes and the widest smile. One day some *walhi kartijas* (no good *whitefellas*) kidnapped her from a waterhole in the desert. She was only a young girl, and her *yarlgu* (blood) hadn't come in yet. They had their way with Maymuru and threatened to kill her whole family if she made any trouble. They took her far away from her homeland and sold her to the dirty boss man at Bohemia Downs Station.

That man was a right bastard. He brought her up there and made her do everything for him. The cookin', cleanin', and she even had to sleep with him. Time passed and that boss got the TB[29] real bad and started spitting blood. But he didn't tell anyone that he'd got Leprosy too. The old girls say, that bastard passed all that deadly stuff onto Maymuru with his spit.

But that was not all he gave her. He put a bub in her too. *Maymuru* was pregnant with Olive and the leprosy took hold of them both real fast. Even though *Maymuru's* fingers and toes were numb and her eye got twisted inwards, and her lips looked ugly as, she still looked after him until his last bloody cough. The other people on the station got scared for themselves and sent her to the East Arm Leprosarium way up north.

There, *Maymuru* birthed Olive and the head nurse named them Tipple. It was a big joke cos everyone knew the boss man liked his drink. *Maymuru* died of the TB at the Leprosarium when Olive was just thirteen years old. That leprosarium mob kicked Olive out, telling her she was a free person now. For too many days she had no food, no money and no place to live. She didn't know

28   Mardu - Indigenous people from the Western Desert, Western Australia.
29   TB - Tuberculosis.

anything about nothin', how could she be free? A girl called Jesse Makewater got Olive a ride to Fitzroy Crossing to meet her Gooniyandi[30] mob. They became Olive's new family and looked after her real good.

Somehow, she found her way to Anne Street and used to live in a tiny closed-in carport in Tina's front yard. She was a collector of all things free and useless, and the men in her life fitted the bill perfectly. Olive was looking for love, but them *walhi* (no good) men helped her live up to her cursed name - Tipple. Although she got a taste for the drink, she was a kind, sweet-hearted, happy drunk. You'd always find her sitting in her old, wooden armchair that was plonked on the verge, just down the road.

I'd visit her most days after school. She'd always be waitin' for me. She was a real tall, slim good-looking woman with long, skinny legs like a seagull. She had high cheekbones, honey-coloured skin and strongly arched eyebrows that danced spiritedly as she changed expression. Her wide, purplish lips turned up gently, as if waiting, ready to smile. Her breath was sweet with the smell of red wine and her long, white hair was always clean and well brushed, in fact, a hundred strokes each. The leprosy had given her problems with her hands and feet, but I'd never heard her complain. Somehow, in the thick of it all, she had Polly about sixteen years ago and managed to look after her real well.

Polly's Dad, Paddy Malone, was as mad as a meat axe. A short, fiery redhead from Ireland with a sing-song voice that could make a crying baby sleep. In the dry season, he'd be on the luggers pearling, and in the wet he was a slaughterer for the meat works at Town Beach.

When Polly was ten, her Dad was sent to Fremantle prison for life for slitting Jonny Jack-Ass's throat. He'd called Polly a half-cast bastard. So poor Polly hasn't set eyes on her Dad since. She looks like him with her red hair and green eyes and all. She's a real short arse too. In spite of everything, she's as happy as, and devoted to the church like you wouldn't believe. If she wasn't *julgia* (broken), they'd have made her a nun by now. Believe me, when Polly sings hymns at church, even them statues of Baby Jesus and Mother Mary tear up.

---

30   Gooniyandi - Indigenous Australian people of Western Australia.

Paddy Malone was a hands on sorta Dad. Much better than mine. He loved cooking and was happiest telling tall tales, that is of course when he wasn't drunk and threatening to kill people. He had a thing about fairy tales. He believed they taught valuable life lessons. No one 'normal' lives on Anne Street—never have, never will.

When he was home from his pearling job, he'd get Polly ready for school. Knowing she was far too trusting, he tried to protect her the best he could. He made her believe she was Little Red Riding Hood. One day he threw a red tablecloth around her shoulders. He tied it in a bow at her throat and sent her off to school, yelling after her, 'Watch out for the Big Bad Wolf!' I thought my Dad was bad enough, gyrating his tackle on a Sunday morning, but Paddy took it to another level.

When Paddy was thrown in prison, Olive decided to show Polly off to the Warlpiri mob and introduce her to Gooniyandi Country. They went up in the dry, and when the wet season was finishing, a Broome fella called Darren offered them a ride home. That Warlpiri mob reckon it was mighty dark the night they left Fitzroy Crossing and a big fella *marloo* (big red kangaroo) jumped out onto the road in front of them. Darren swerved and drove head on into a freight train.

Darren and Olive were killed on the spot. But Polly was asleep on the back seat with no seatbelt on. She flew out the back window, cracked her head open real bad and smashed her right leg to pieces. No one thought she'd survive, not even the doctors. She was in a coma for ages. Finally, she came around but wouldn't believe anyone who said her mother was dead.

There was nowhere else Polly could go, except back home to Tina's mum's carport. The whole of Anne Street lined up to welcome her home. She looked a real sight when she got outta hospital. She hobbled home with a fair dinkum pirate's peg leg and a bandage on her head that looked like a turban. Her peg leg looks just like a thick wooden baseball bat covered in tan leather. It screws into a plate fixed to her stump. And as if she didn't look mad enough, to this day she still wears that wretched red tablecloth tied at her neck and draped down her back like a cape. Inside that head of hers, her mother is still alive and with her all the time, and they talk to each other nonstop.

I felt sorry for Polly, looking at her sitting by the fire talking to her invisible mum. I wondered what the mob back in Broome would say when they saw me. Remembering how crazy I looked made me feel uncomfortable to see Polly on her own. I called out for her and Louanna to come and join Helen and me, cos now I knew how important ture friends are.

18. Beyond Beyond

I turned to Helen random-like and said, 'I hate that name, "Helen".'

'Me too, it's never felt right,' she replied.

'Not right, not right, who's got a wrong name,' Polly interrupted, doing her looney thing.

'Why don't you both change your names?' suggested Louanna.

'Yeah right, Mum would be mad as!' we both blurted out at the same time.

'My mum's never mad,' Polly announced proudly.

We all cracked up.

We heard *Jalbri* call out in different languages, '*Jija nyumbarr, nyubarr*, sisters, sleep, sleep. Big day tomorrow.'

At first, I thought she was just talking to Helen and me, but all the women got up and made their beds from *kapok*[31] and *gungkara* (conkerberry) leaves. Some branches were also added to the fire to keep off the mozzies. Everyone 'smoked themselves', cos the bugs are fierce at the soak. We also rubbed ash on our skin to protect us against an attack from evil spirits.

It wasn't that late, but I was so tired after my walkabout the last few days, sleep came easy. This big mob of powerful women made me feel real safe.

I'm not sure how long we'd slept, but when *Jalbri* woke Helen and me, it was still real dark and quiet except for the sound of women snoring. Thank God Polly sleeps like a brick.

Jalbri led us away from the group and took us to a clearing. She was carrying a *mili* (firestick) to light the way. Standing the *mili* in the sand, *Jalbri* said, 'Lucy, you carry this *mili* cos you are the younger sister. You must lead the way and start the first campfire.'

A feeling of dread came over me, something was up.

Jalbri led us away from the firelight. She pulled off some small branches and swept the ground clear of bugs and other stuff. She asked us to lay on our backs facing the sky. It was odd being skin to skin with my sister. We giggled. *Jalbri* squeezed herself between us. '*Nganggurmanha widigunmanha* (Listen up and don't be forgetting).' Her long, bony arm pointed up to the Southern Cross. '*Dungdung* or some call *Djulpan* (Southern Cross).'

'We learnt about the Southern Cross at school,' Helen interrupted, trying to show off.

'I'm not learnin' you *whitefella* stuff. I'm learning you Dreaming Story.' *Jalbri* was not happy.

'*Nganggurnmanha*! *Nganggurnmanha* (Listen up Listen up)!' She was making sure she had our attention.

31   Kapok - Silky-cotton fibres from the kapok tree, used as filling in soft toys, mattress, pillows and warm clothes.

Then she began:

Wijiri banharnigardi, banharnigardi.
Once upon a time, beyond beyond.

Banharnigardi birla.
Even beyond the sky.

Banharnigardi wilu.
And beyond the sea.

The creation story began.

Jalbri continued to speak in Language, and this is roughly what she said, 'That unseen Creator, the Great Spirit of the Dreamtime, made a single sound, and as the sound spread out in the darkness, it changed to other sounds and those sounds turned into *mama*—the sacred songs. Then the *mama* created lines and shapes and after *yangarda, yangarda*—long, long time—the shapes gave birth to form. That was the time of the Great Peace when everythin' was calm and got formed up and became solid.'

She started to sing and draw shapes with her finger in the air. She nudged us and nodded that we should copy her. The sounds she made were deep and rich like a strong, sweet, black coffee, but there was an electric edge to the sound that made us feel like we were no longer lying on our backs on the dirt, but instead we were flying through the night sky with our *Jalbri*.

'The Creator saw everything before anything, and the Creator wanted all things to be good. He gathered up the Rain and poured it into a big *ngarn.ga* (cavern) in the centre of Australia. The Creator then plucked a *bundarra* (star) and gently breathed on it. The *bundarra* split in two and then, he blew life into both pieces. He put them *bundarra* gently in the water and he sealed the top, making a hard crust with his spit mixed with red dirt.

'In that deep, dark, watery place, two Great Serpent Spirits now grew. *Pulanyi Bulaing*, she took on the colours of the rainbow, soft and luminous, and she lit the darkness as she moved. Her twin, the Great Serpent, *Kulparn Karangu* was black like the dark waterhole, except for his red belly that flashed like fire when he moved. As time passed, the two Great Serpents grew and grew, fillin' the cavern until they could move no more. Archin' their backs under the Earth's surface, they broke through that hard crust.

'As *Pulanyi Bulaing* slithered out of there, she made the rivers and from her belly came out all the plants and animals. *Pulanyi Bulaing* brought all the daytime creatures to life and her light gave colour to all created things. *Pulanyi* was in charge of Water, Light and Life.

'Her twin brother *Kulparn Karangu,* he was in charge of Darkness, Death and Fire, and he was also the transformer of the land, pushing up the highest mountain, making rocky mounds and carvin' gorges. Darkness was a blessing for us mob, cos as the night fell it protected us from the hot sun and its coolness covered the Earth. In the darkness, all livin' things could rest, sleep and *Dream* their *Stories* and receive their *Lores*.

'In the darkness, nobody could see the different colour of another's skin. Nighttime blindness made them fellas trust that the Creator would protect all them fellas, even while they slept. *Kulparn Karangu* had the power over Fire that gave Light and warmth to comfort the peoples in the darkness of the night. But he was also in charge of Death.

'In this time of the beginnin' all things knew the Lore. The Great Twin Serpents moved between the different, different worlds, and Life and Death were friends. Under the cover of darkness, Death came gently to the people of the Earth because there was no fear, anger, hatred or want. They lived and died well. As they slept, their Dreaming returned them to their birthplace in *bundarra* (the stars) to journey on, in that big *Jirdilungu* (Milky Way).

'Time passed slowly for *Kulparn Karangu*. He became mighty jealous of *Pulanyi Bulaing's* rainbow-coloured arrival at dawn and vivid departure before his darkness crept in. Them days, this land was all green, and the leaves of the plants were real soft cos the sun was not harsh like now, and water was plentiful. Life was easy, and every heart was happy to be alive. People lived long, too long for *Kulparn Karangu,* he became bored and impatient. He wanted all the creatures to die. Joy left him and his hatred for the Earth, and all those who live on her back, grew and grew.

'*Kulparn Karangu* made his *yunganha* (gift) of Fire into a mighty weapon. As some women were returning from gatherin' food, their chatter and laughter made him angry. He roared and hissed, and his hot breath set the spinifex alight. Huge flames spread out across the lands bringing fear to everyone and everything. *Pulanyi Bulaing* heard the people calling out to her. She rose up high into the sky and saw too many once livin' things burn to death. Fear and chaos became *maaja* (boss) and our great Country turned red and black like *Kulparn Karangu. Pulanyi Bulaing* slithered back onto Earth to try to make more rivers, but the land was so hot that it burnt her belly and robbed her powers, and made her weak and *mardi* (sick).

'The great dryness came and the Earth was made *marurdu* (black), and her beloved Eromanga Sea[32] that once filled the red heart of this Country, was now bone dry, all gone. *Pulanyi Bulaing* once gave life to all the creatures on this earth. Them that survived the fires, now suffered the Great Thirst. Our once green lands turned into deserts, and the plants, like the people's hearts, became hardened.

'*Pulanyi Bulaing's* strength left her. No longer a magnificent rainbow-coloured serpent with power to create. All her livin' waters had dried up. Now she was just a small wispy form floatin' like *guba* (ash) from the camp-fire, higher and higher into the blackened sky, makin' her way to the other world up there.

---

32   The Eromanga Basin - A large Mesozoic sedimentary basin in central and northern Australia.

'On the fiery Earth below, seas of molten rock flowed and the Great Serpent *Kulparn Karangu* became *maaja* (boss). Every beating heart feared their fate. Terror had found a place on Earth, where it had never been before. Hatred, depression and despair filled each heart where love had been. Neither the good nor the bad could sleep and the spirit of the people, like the land, was all dried up, all *julgia* (broken).

'The Dreamtime Spirits felt the drought in our hearts, and told us to call out with one voice, *mabarn* (have faith).

'People from each and every skin group sang together. In song, they pleaded with the *Jirdilungu Jin.ga* (Milky Way Spirit Beings) to restore the balance and return *Pulanyi Bulaing* and her goodness to the world. Their song was so pure and sweet it made the 'songlines', which wrapped around the whole Earth and soared up and into the *Jirdilungu* (Milky Way), touching *Pulanyi Bulaing's* heart—this made her weep.

'One single teardrop, an ocean made, and in that one single drop, hope was restored. *Pulanyi Bulaing* stretched herself from the Heavens to the Earth. So glorious to see was her rainbow *manngi* (sacred headband) and its promise to those who live on the Earth. That goodness will never be *nyurlargunmanha* (extinguished) while there is life in her.

'*Kulparn Karangu* was insane with rage; he shot up into the sky after her. The battle continued for many Dreamtime days. Thunder rumbled and *Bindamanha* (lightning) flashed wildly. That night, *Pulanyi Bulaing* rolled over and over in pain and the *wilara* (moon) turned to blood, and all living things feared that our beloved *Pulanyi Bulaing*, the Life giver, had been killed by *Kulparn Karangu*. Then at the edge of the blackened clouds a silver light shone bright and a rainbow arched down to Earth from a crack at its edge. She gave our people her sign that she had not abandoned us. The skies opened and a *gathara* (torrent of water) fell to Earth and a golden light *ngalarn* (illuminated) the burnt places and made new life.

'*Pulanyi Bulaing* chased *Kulparn Karangu* across Australia. She had been *murlayimanha* (gravely) weakened and could not refill the inland sea. So, leaving the central lands as a desert, she protected her Waters by hiding them underground in caverns. Those caverns were just like the womb in which the two Great Serpents grew while the world was being formed up. *Pulanyi Bulaing* struck the hard ground and waterholes appeared, and the Great Spirits of the *Jirdilungu* marked each waterhole in the night sky with a *bundarra* (star), so that we need never *yurrun* (thirst) again.

'She drove *Kulparn Karangu* into Help Canyon and set him into the rock and turned his weapons to stone. Those weapons looked like the quills of a porcupine. So, we call this place *Kuji Warnku*—Porcupine Rock. Just as the central lands could not be restored, *Kulpan Karangu* had reached into every human heart and left dark scars of anger, hatred, lust and greed. When the night came in, only the pure could rest. Most humans had forgotten how to trust and because of this, they could not sleep nor dream their stories, nor receive their Lore. They were lost without love or laughter. Lawlessness consumed their hearts and they spread out across the Earth, infecting others with their disease. *Julgia, Julgia*, Broken, Broken, all was Broken.'

Jalbri shook her head and sighed deeply. 'Enough now, tomorrow we will learn more.'

We lay in silence for a while, and then, *Jalbri* got up to return to camp, and in silence, we followed her.

19. The Simple Truth

The sun was just starting to rise. Helen and I thought we were heading back to camp for a big feed, but *Jalbri* had other plans. She took us to the edge of the soak, stood in front of us, and called out loudly in Language:

'Ancestors, we are here to pay respect to the keepers of the soak.

'*Pulanyi Bulaing,* we bring our respect to you and your *living waters.*'

'*Pulanyi Bulaing*, your life flows through all living things.'

'*Pulanyi Bulaing,* as the sun rises and we wash in your waters.'

'We thank *Pulanyi Bulaing* and the Ancestors.'

Taking sand in her hand, she threw it into the waterhole.

We followed her actions.

'*Pulanyi Bulaing*, protect us from *Kulparn Karangu*. Stop him from chewing on our souls,' *Jalbri* said.

'What?' I blurted out.

Jalbri's eyes glinted like daggers at me. 'Undress!' she commanded.

'Whaatt?'

'*Kulparn Karangu* must have eaten ya ears and sucked out ya brain. Don't you know you stink? Ya gonna wash now, *jambarn* (quickly)!' *Jalbri* started to cackle at her own joke—it wasn't cool.

We stripped off. My clothes did stink, and that hole in my shirt where the lightning struck was pretty impressive. I had lost a tonne of weight. I was never fat, but now all my bones stood out. I glanced over at Helen; she looked gorgeous, slim but nicely toned. She undid her hair as she plunged into the water and she bobbed up looking like a proper mermaid goddess. I looked like some matchstick figure from a freak show. So not fair.

Jalbri looked worn but incredibly strong. Her dark skin glistened in the morning light. She waded over to a soap bush, picked some and gave it to us to lather up and wash. She let out a short sharp whistle for *Gulyi-Gulyi* to come. Obediently he bounded in, and she smiled approvingly.

My *Jalbri* could have been a sergeant major. She gave us a full demo of how to wash our private parts, how *gurndany* (shame). Then, like an annoying teenager, she started splashing us. Her arms were strong and her large, bony hands caught enormous amounts of water, which she flung at us. The war was on. We screeched with laughter when we weren't gasping for breath. *Gulyi* tried to eat the splashes; it was great fun. Mum never had time for fun. I really love this old stick.

'*Buju* (finished).'

It's always her way or the highway. Suddenly, it was clear to me that *Jalbri* lives in the moment, and really knows about the past, and looks out for the future. I reckon it has to be the best way.

'Come!'

We followed without question.

Jalbri stepped out of the water. *Gulyi* shook and sprayed her real good. She turned to check that we were following, as we both clambered out covering our breasts with our hands and bobbing down so our privates were under the water. She cackled. As she bent over to pick up her string bag, she gave no regard for what we saw. It was horrific. Anyway, as she turned towards us, she threw a fine string skirt at Helen, and another at me.

When it landed in my hands, my heart leapt for joy. It was made from the yellow *kapok* bush. I knew how long it would have taken her to beat the *kapok* and remove the fibre. Then she had to make the fibre into string and then knot it to make a skirt. I jumped out of the water to tie my new skirt around my waist, forgetting my shame at being naked.

I gave her a hand sign and shouted out, 'Cool! I love it.'

Jalbri gave me a wry smile and those old eyes twinkled with delight.

Sister Euphrates told me that I had a 'wry smile'—one side of the mouth turned up; one side turned down. It's like giving someone a look as if they're an idiot.

On the front of each skirt, *Jalbri* had made a pattern of different coloured seeds. Helen's was different to mine. Mine had lots of little red and brown seeds, but Helen's had a cascade of subtly changing brown nuts. In the centre of each waistband was a small empty pouch.

'Is this for our money?' I asked like an idiot, none of us mob ever have money.

Jalbri shook her head.

Jalbri, like Sister Euphrates, had a Mary Poppin's bag. I love that film, I've seen it thirteen times. From her bag she took out two very simple bras for Helen and me; they were just two triangles on a string, they were a real good fit. Helen started to shake her hips like an Islander and my thoughts flew straight to Manu Tollie. Suddenly, I felt shame to think of him in case *Jalbri* could read my mind.

127

Jalbri reached carefully into her old bag and brought out two discs of Mother of Pearl shell on a thick hair string. Holding one on top of the other, she stood in front of me and bent down low, holding out the top shell for me to see. Standing upright she took a step towards me and held the carved shell to my chest. I tied the string around my neck. My heart was beating hard and fast and tears welled up in my eyes. As she kissed my forehead and then my hands, I felt shame that such an amazing woman should honour me like this.

Stepping sideways, she held out the other shell to Helen. My fingers felt the engraving on the cool, shiny surface. The shells were like the *riji*[33] that my Dad got from an old timer. The men wore really big ones as pubic covers during magic and healing ceremonies.

Jalbri started to sing in Mangala, an almost extinct ancient language from the Great Sandy Desert region. She was trying to teach us as we travelled with her, fearing her precious mother tongue would be lost. There are only about twenty *First Language* speakers left in this whole world. The soak became silent except for her voice. The birds stopped their chatter, and even *Gulyi* bolted out of sight. Then as if responding to *Jalbri's mama* (sacred song), a loud hiss filled the air at the soak that shook the reads.

We turned to face the water and caught a glimpse of an enormous ripple coming out of the centre of the soak. It looked kinda like a rainbow oil spill as it darkened and sank down into the deep. We were not alone. A single whistle from the *mirrugurru* (a black-faced cuckoo-shrike) signalled that *Pulanyi Bulaing* was gone. From out of nowhere a fine mist of water sprayed onto our faces. We stood still in complete silence for a long time.

Then *Jalbri* grabbed her firestick. 'Time to go.'

It was dawn and we could smell the food cooking as we walked back to camp. I felt refreshed, even though we hadn't really slept all night. Something inside me had changed since *Jalbri* had been talking to me about her life and the

33   Riji - Body adornment traditionally worn in the Kimberley region of Western Australia.

Dreamtime. This knowledge was growing me up fast, but in a totally different way to my town life in Broome.

The women had prepared lots of food. As soon as they caught sight of us, Patty Mae, the tracker, put out a greeting call. The women formed a line and shuffled towards us, heads turning from side to side and arms swinging low, left and right, as they chanted in a language I didn't understand.

Jalbri gently pushed us forward from behind. 'Dance,' she said.

My feet felt stuck to the ground; we were not expecting this. The singing became louder and louder.

Stamping their feet, the women filled the air with red fine dust. Aunty Toots was a fantastic dancer, real light on her feet. Waving a stone with ground white ochre on it, she marked our foreheads, under our eyes, and painted a V in the crease of our breasts. Our mothers, Mary and Barbara, approached us from the side, each had a *grandi* (stone knife) in hand.

Mum grabbed hold of my hand and without saying a word cut two lines on my left arm up near my shoulder. Barbara did the same to Helen. Blood poured out onto the ground. It really hurt. I felt furious that no one asked our permission or even warned us. I wanted to punch Mum in the face for hurting me again.

As quickly as the ceremony started, it ended. Helen and I stood there dazed. Everyone went off to eat as if nothing had happened. Of course, nothing did happen to them, we were the ones left bleeding. The sound of yelping bought me back to reality. Someone had tied *Gulyi* up to a tree so that he wouldn't mess up.

I yelled, 'Let him go!' Feeling even more pissed off.

Freedom made him crazy. He ran around bumping into people and falling over. He ran at me, jumping up and nipping me with his sharp teeth. Finding the blood on my arm, he was happy licking it when he noticed my sister dressed just like me. He leapt back in fright, growling at her.

'It's okay, *Gulyi, mamany duthu* (crazy dog). *Mulgahu* (friend), *jija* (sister),' I said, while trying to get him to come to me.

Protesting with deep growls and small huffs. He must have thought that I'd gone off and cloned a new me from before the lightning strike. He thought hard before accepting her peace offering. Helen disappeared and came back with a *marloo* (big red kangaroo) bone. Cautiously he gently took it from her hand and then he ran between us as if he owned us both.

An enormous cook up followed by condensed milk tea was just what we needed. We hung out with Louanna and caught her up on why I had left Broome and all the things that had happened. I gave her the snake's head I'd kept for her. In true Louanna style she'd brought her pencil and notebook and was stoked to be writing down my stories.

Helen noticed our mothers walking towards us. 'I'm not talking to her,' she muttered.

I could see tears of rage welling up in her eyes. Barbara placed her hand on Helen's arm and a little blood seeped through her fingers.

'Don't touch me!' Helen yelled. 'I trusted you! You're not my mother, you stole me from your sister. You're my captor!' Her chest was heaving with the pain of this revelation.

'It was for the best,' Barbara replied.

'Fuck off!' I barked at Barbara.

Our mother Mary just stood there in silence. It was unreal. I wondered what else was going on? Why were they standing together on this?

Turning her back on Barbara, Helen stormed off shouting, 'I can't talk, or ever look at you! You make me sick!'

Barbara's eyes narrowed. I didn't know if she was speaking to me or Mum. 'It wasn't my fault Al died...' The whole camp had heard her speak Dad's name and were shushing her in shame. 'If he'd been with me, he'd be alive now.' Glancing at Mum, she said, 'Double broken Lore. Who brought the curse to the Lucky-Childs? Not me!'

'Enough!' Patty Mae bellowed.

My mum, Mary, started to cry. Barbara put her arms around her to comfort her. But it was all just a bit too lovey-dovey, and I didn't know what the hell was happening. 'You guys are sick in the head,' I hissed. I ran to the only person who really understood what I was feeling. My sister. *Gulyi* sprinted after me.

Jalbri had been watching the whole thing. 'Come girls, it's time to go.'

All the women were out of sight. *Jalbri* had two *malgar* (women's fighting sticks) at her feet. We naturally stood to attention in front of her. Picking up a stick and stepping towards me, she said, 'Lucy, you now *Bindamanha* (Lightning Strike),' as she handed me the stick.

I ran my hand over the smooth, hard wood while she picked up the other stick and gave it to my sister, saying, 'Helen, you now *Waranmanha* (Sacred Song).' Helen had a new name. *Waranmanha* was perfect for her. She had the best voice ever.

Clearing my throat, I asked *Jalbri* if I could be called Lucy *Bindamanha* .

'No, you are a Lucky-Child,' she replied.

My heart sank, thinking that I would never get rid of that hopeless surname. *Jalbri* stood to face me, eye to eye—she looked through me. '*Bindamanha* means Lightning Strike.'

I blinked. She knew that I was disappointed.

'This is your power. All the tribes of the Earth will know you. We have been waitin' for that Lightning Strike, our *Bindamanha* and the Sacred Song *Waranmanha* to come.'

I felt myself falling into the darkness of her eyes.

'Lucky-Child, you will keep. Be patient, children. Soon you will know who you are.' Breathing out deeply, she turned and walked off. '*Yanajimanha* (Coming)?' she muttered.

We followed her, and *Gulyi* quietly followed us.

Hundreds of different types of birds were darting around and *Gulyi-Gulyi* was very happy chasing them. I had left Jackie's thongs back at camp, so my feet were really feeling it. *Waranmanha* had nice runners; she always looked good. *Jalbri's* feet were a pale yellowish brown compared to her black-brown skin, and those old feet were hard, like worn leather. She walked barefoot everywhere. I don't know how she does it, cos every stone, stick, nut and seed, was seriously killing me.

Slowing the pace, *Jalbri* started telling us stories and singing simple songs. Going in and out of Language helped us learn. My concentration is poor at the best of times, and my head kept switching between *Jalbri's* chanting and my memories, both past at present.

Then suddenly the thought struck me, and before I could stop myself, my thoughts leaked out into words, 'Why didn't Jackie tell anyone where I'd gone?'

Both *Jalbri* and *Waranmanha* stopped in their tracks.

Before *Jalbri* had a chance to speak, my sister blurted out, 'He crashed head-on and died, just past the Gingerah turnoff on his way to Bidyadanga.'

I screeched like a speared feral cat. 'Oh no! Jackie, I'm so sorry …'

'No naming,' *Jalbri* interrupted, looking around nervously. 'No naming … shh shh,' she said, patting my back.

'It was my fault! He wouldn't have been on Gingerah Road. He went there to drop me. He was killed cos I'm *maminy* (stupid). What about his girlfriend?'

In tears, *Waranmanha* shook her head. 'Gone.'

'Why didn't anybody tell me?' I sobbed.

'We didn't know you knew him,' *Waranmanha* said softly.

'He asked me to go to Bidjy with him. He thought I'd die on my own in the desert. I'm a bloody jinx. Them Elders cursed me, didn't they?' I said, giving *Jalbri* a deadly glare. Rocking back and forth, all I could do was cry. Everything was my fault.

132

Jalbri suggested that we should head back.

'Nah, I don't wanna go back. Everyone will know Jackie ...'

'No name,' she interrupted.

'Even his girlfriend died cos of me. Anyway, I don't wanna see them bitches Mum and Barbara. What's up with them?' I had a head full of steam and *Jalbri* wasn't gonna fight me.

'*Gula warlugura* (Come nearby girls).'

We squished in close.

'For a long time now I've been holdin' the family story for you girls. Youse got big work comin', ya gotta clear ya minds. No more bad thoughts about your *yagus* (mothers). Lucy, your Aunty Barbara had a baby girl. Baby name Lucy, but she died at the birth time.'

'No, it was my Aunty Lucy who died in childbirth,' I insisted.

Jalbri glared at me. 'I was there. Where were you? Not born yet. Show respect. The trouble you young ones got is ya don't know how to *nganggurnmanha* (listen up).'

I shut up good and proper.

Waranmanha reached across *Jalbri* and grabbed my hand. This little talk didn't sound like it was going to be good for either of us.

'*Nganiggurnmanha*, hey listen up. Ya *Ija maraji* (true Aunty) is Barbara.'

'Why so many lies?' I whispered, looking at my sister.

'When her bub Lucy died, she went way down into big 'Sorry Business' and her husband couldn't stand no more. He left her and took up with another woman. Barbara was cryin' all the time cos her baby house got broke, so she couldn't hold a bub no more. She was called *Karrmina*, means "empty woman".'

Waranmanha corrected her, 'Barren woman.'

Jalbri was so bloody politically incorrect. 'The Elders knew that a great battle was comin'. They decided that Mary would carry the "Twin Spirit Children" and she had to give 'em to Barbara soon as they were born.'

I couldn't stop myself growling like a dog, cos every word that came out of her mouth made me more and more angry. So angry that my ears were aching at the sound of her voice.

'Both Mary and Barbara agreed and special *mama* (ceremonial song) called youse "Spirit Children" down from *bundarra* (the stars) in big *Jirdilungu* (Milky Way). The Elders wanted Barbara to raise youse kids together cos I taught her. She got real good knowledge of our Lore and speaks many languages. Away from the community, she was meant to learn youse all the special *secret* things.

'That's why Mary carried you girls, and Barbara took the punishment for Mary's "wrong way marriage". She agreed to the ritual beating, and even got cast out of the community so that she could have youse kids.'

This was hard for me to hear, but she went on anyway.

'Mary born you both at the feet of *Nyarluwarru*[34]. That Rosie, you call Aunty, the one that lives in the *ladies' house*. She's did proper good taken you babies out.'

Now I was super irritated with *Jalbri* and couldn't zip it up. 'Yeah, we know she's a lesbian. You can say everything else, why can't you say that word too.'

Jalbri continued as if she hadn't heard me, 'Your Dad went to get the babies for Barbara, but Mary fought him like a wild cat and only let go of Helen. That was how Mary broke our Lore again. Double broken Lore brought the curse of bad luck to the Lucky-Child family and you,' she said, looking straight at me.

A chill ran down my back. I jumped up screaming, 'Who are these Elders who *sang* us down from the stars? I want to know!'

My sister held me tightly.

---

34   Nyarluwarru - The Stone Towers representing the Seven Sisters at Reddell beach.

'*Walhi thabinmanha* (not good question),' *Jalbri* said firmly.

I knew there were family secrets, and I'd coped with not knowing all the details, thinking those secrets had nothing to do with me. But I really believed that the things I knew about 'me' were the truth. Who's the real me? I felt totally betrayed. No one told me the truth about anything, not even my birth. I felt sick knowing that everyone must have been looking at me and my sister with pity, when they made comments about me being a Lucky-Child. All along, them strangers knew more about my life than I did. What else did *Jalbri* know about us and our future?

Suddenly, I felt like throwing up. I loosened my grip on Helen and started running blindly into the night with *Gulyi* hot on my heels. 'Get lost! Go home! I don't want you anymore! Leave me alone!' I screamed at him as he nipped at my hand and skirt, trying to stop me running away. 'I hate you, go away!'

Gulyi-Gulyi froze. Looking at me he whimpered, turned around and took off through the bush.

Deafened by my own screams, I ran forward in the direction of Help Canyon. Out of the corner of my eye on my right, I noticed a misty form moving. But still I ran, desperate to be alone and get away from anyone who knew more about me than me. The bush was getting thicker and thicker, and I was getting more and more scratched. But still I pushed my way though. We were always told to tread gently on someone else's Country, but I wasn't listening to anyone anymore, I just kept thundering on.

I glanced upwards and was stunned to see a dazzling white light in the form of a stick figure hovering in front of me. It called to me. I froze on the spot. The hypnotic gesture of its hand summoning me to follow was hard to resist. My feet refused to move, but every part of my being wanted to obey. Confused and conflicted, I froze stiff with fear.

A single bloodcurdling shrill screech shot out above the bush line and seemed to drag the night sky down low. It was my sister, Helen. In a panic, I started turning around and around in circles, trying to tell which direction the sound was coming from. All I could hear was my pounding heart.

135

Deep inside me, from that space where my deepest fears live, rose a long-sustained wail. Just a single word, '*JalbriIII*!'

And then like an echo, I heard *Waranmanha* screech, '*JalbriIII*!'

Gulyi-Gulyi howled. It was an eerie moan, like a death spirit's, that rode upon our wails, and chilled me to the bone.

All of a sudden, *Jalbri* appeared in front of me. But she looked different somehow, not solid, airy like from a dream, except for her insanely bright eyes, that were way too bright to bring comfort to a frightened heart. Without a word, she beckoned me to follow her. The path I had chosen was so rough, like the landscape of my life.

After a while, we stepped into a small clearing. There in front of me was *Jalbri gardugardimanha* (sitting cross-legged) lit by the glow of a small fire with *Gulyi-Gulyi*, and our *malgar* (fighting sticks) beside her. I clearly saw *Waranmanha* coming through the bushes on the opposite side. Who had I been following?

'*Gula Warlugura* (Come nearby girls).'

We ran and sat on either side of her.

Her long arms reached around us and she held us in real close. The smell of goanna oil on her skin was comforting. 'You girls can't run away from who you are no more. Time for you to know everythin'. Special *mama* (ceremonial song) called you down from that old *Jirdilungu* (Milky Way) from our Dreaming place for a special job.

Who are you?

Who are *you*?

Who *are* you?

Soon you'll *know*.

Who you are.

136

'This one, that one, Mary, Barbara, your Dad, Rosie, and everyone else forgot *who youse are*, but not me.'

We were tired and almost asleep.

Jalbri nudged us. 'Wake up, we can't stay here.'

Getting up, we followed her into the night. Soon we heard women's voices calling us. They were carrying firesticks to light the way. It was good to reach camp and eat. *Waranmanha* and I crashed on our leafy beds, comforted by the earthy smell of crushed leaves and broken twigs and the heavy breathing of sleeping women. The ever-present smoke hung gently like an elfin blanket and hid us from wandering Spirits and kept off swarms of mozzies and midges.

The next morning the women let us kids sleep in. When we finally stirred, an enormous breakfast was waiting for us. Old *Jalbri* was on the prowl. She never rested. Before long she was organising another journey for us.

'We want to stay at camp and hang out with Louanna and Polly,' we protested.

'We are all going to *hang out* over there on that big fella canyon,' *Jalbri* insisted. No one could say no to *Jalbri*.

20. Rock Wall

It wasn't long before we came to an enormous rock that was higher than the craft room wall at the back of St Mary's Church.

'*Ju*! (Up) *Ju*!' she ordered, raising her right arm and flicking her wrist and hand.

'You gotta be kiddin' me,' I replied. After being struck by lightning on Battlement Rock, I wasn't real keen on being on top of any rock.

'Get the fear off ya your back!' she ordered, whacking my back with her strong, open hand.

'Ouch! Stop!' My shoulders sprang back in reaction to the hard slap. 'How do you expect us to get up there? *Ju Ju* yourself!' I barked back at her, overreacting because my back was still stinging.

'You respect *jarda* (old woman), watch!' *Jalbri* ran hard and fast straight at the rock. Her hands went up, and before we knew what was happening, she had run up the sheer cliff face like some great Daddy-long-legs.

'What the hell!' Not waiting for her to correct me, I yelled at the top of my voice, 'Yeah, I know, *nam jarri lirra* (shut up your face)!'

Waranmanha and I couldn't help laughing.

Jalbri's smiling face popped over the edge of the cliff. '*Thubarnimanha* (Straighten up)!'

I poked my tongue out at her, knowing that I would be safe with a whole rock face between us.

She shook her head. '*Waranmanha, ju* (up)!'

We were the best runners at our school. *Waranmanha* glanced at me and took off at full speed towards the rock face, but she stopped dead just before making contact.

'Again!' *Jalbri* squawked like some old crow.

Waranmanha ran again.

As she approached the rock face, *Jalbri* screeched from above, '*Wabarnanga* (Jump)!'

Waranmanha stopped sharply, banging her head hard against the rock.

Looking up I shouted out to *Jalbri*, 'It's too hard. Are you trying to kill us?'

We could hear *Jalbri* talking to herself. It sounded like she was swearing—oooh she was *mamany* (mad).

She disappeared from view, but we could still hear her 'going off her head'. Then there was silence. We were breaking our necks, trying to see what she was up to. Then we saw this *mamany jarda* (crazy old woman) lean forward over the edge.

'Oh God, OH NO!' we shouted. We thought she was going to commit suicide because I had disrespected her.

Ignoring our cries, she stretched out her long, black, bony arms, crossed them at the wrist, bent her legs and jumped forward, tucking her knees in tight against her thin, black body.

Waranmanha and I grabbed each other and screamed. *Gulyi* barked wildly.

She cleared the rock face and glided down freefalling in a standing position, arms gently curved behind her, hands pointing down and fingers open.

'WAHOO!' we screamed, in total awe of her.

She slid through the air, landed on her spread toes, powerfully rolled forward over her shoulder and amazingly rolled forward again back onto her feet.

'Ninja! Ninja!' we yelled, giving her high fives.

'Did you learn that from the Jackie Chan movies?' I asked.

'How do you think *blackfellas* get around out bush? City *blackfellas* fat, eating damper and jam, can't walk, bush kills them!'

Just the way she said it, she even sounded like a Ninja. *Awesome!*

'Shit. Yeah!' Of course, these bushies had to know the easy ways to get around and save their physical energy and time. This was wild. 'Respect to the *jarda thuthamarda Mimi* (old woman, little tits), she's the best! *Thubarnimanha* (Straighten up)!'

Waranmanha and I squealed. *Jalbri* was speechless.

'Okay, Okay,' she said, trying to regain some control. 'You *jaman* (run) at the *jabu* (rock wall). Not too slow, not too fast, or hit face, must do right way, then put foot up high.' She raised her foot above her waist to the rock wall. Her toes spread like fingers grabbing the wall. 'No this part touch,' she said, grabbing her heel with her hand. 'Kick into the *jabu*, you go *ju* (up). Otherwise you fall down. Kick *jabu*, you go up, next foot kick. Keep going *ju* and *ju*.'

She showed us a handful of times by taking a few steps. It looked easy when she did it. 'But you got hands. See, you place them right way, they help you. Move *ju ju*, at the top you pull *ju*.'

140

Waranmanha and I ran at the *jabu*. She did two steps up. I was impressed. I went down, not up.

'Kick wall, you go *ju*. Kick out, not down,' *Jalbri* ordered.

I tried a few times and failed.

Jalbri came to me and slapped me hard on the back. 'Get fear off your back! Look at me.'

I spun around; my back was still stinging like crazy.

She looked deep into my eyes, her nose almost touching mine. '*Bindamanha* (Lightning Strike), you can do it. You must do it.'

I felt undone. I wanted to cry, but then I felt a strange strength come into my limbs. I moved back from the *jabu*, took a deep breath and ran at it. Kicking out I went straight up and up, to the top and over, just as she had promised. I was elated. 'I did it!' I heard clapping from below, and when I looked down, I almost shat myself. That was a long way down.

I lay down with my head over the edge so that I could watch the action without killing myself. *Waranmanha* glided gracefully to the top and over with our master following behind her. That was wicked.

Giving us time to recover, *Jalbri* let us sit and chatter while she collected berries and other bush tucker for us to eat. As I watched her moving around, I became aware of how free she was. She was in charge of her life. Nobody told her what to do. She was herself - smart, strong and bold.

As we ate, we heard the sound of clapping sticks. Standing on the edge of the rock, we could see our mob of women gathering in groups at different points surrounding the rock. They were all painted up and their chanting went in waves, one group against another.

It was a strange and powerful feeling looking down on them. I felt like a pop star on stage.

141

Jalbri said, 'This is a *Bran Nue D*ae for our people.'

Waranmanha and I broke into song, singing out to the women below, 'There's something I just have to see, as an Aborigine, I wanna see ya hand my Country back to me.' We both made a mirror image with one-foot forward, one-foot back, one hand pointing at *Jalbri* and the other behind us.

'Ta-dah!'

The old chook couldn't help herself, she just cracked up laughing and laughing.

The women were giggling too.

Our voices boomed down to them and their voices echoed back up, bouncing off the rock face. 'There's something I just have to see, as an Aborigine…'

Dead set, I was feelin' at home on this great land. Town life seemed a million miles away.

'Okay, Okay,' *Jalbri* said, trying to shut us down.

But we were still in a cheeky mood and shouted out to the women below, '*Thubarnimanha* (Straighten up)! *Thubarnimanha*!'

'*Walhinanmanha* (Stop buggering up)!' *Jalbri* blurted.

We stood to attention, and so did the women below. Only a couple of young ones were brave enough to keep giggling.

'Are youse ready for me to learn you somethin'?'

'Yes,' we said confidently, thinking we were ready.

'Okay, look down. Imagine you are standing in the *Jirdilungu* (Milky Way) looking down to the Earth. You know how you look up and see the *bundarra* (stars) of the Southern Cross, there in the sky? Imagine you are on the other side of them *bundarra*, lookin' down. Got it?'

'Yeah,' we answered together.

Jalbri was excited. 'See that group top-end side, *Yaburu* (North people). They are *Kurriji pa Yajula*, our Dragon Tree Soak people. Don't be forgetting, okay? Now turn your back to the front.' She turned us around to face the opposite direction. 'See that girl, Louanna? Keep eyes on her group.' They seemed far away. 'Stay put,' she said, stopping us from taking a step forward to get a better look. 'You know the bottom of Australia?' she said, drawing us a picture in the air. 'Here at the bottom, *Gumbarri Jin.gi* (Many Spirit Beings Dreaming place).'

We were both confused.

'Get in,' she ordered, eyeballing us.

Waranmanha twigged, 'Oh, the Twelve Apostles?'

Jalbri nodded. 'Us fellas at *Kurriji pa Yajula* hold the North point of the Southern Cross. The *Girai Wurrung* people of *Gumbarri Jingi* place hold the most Southern point. Got it?' Her eyes shone bright with excitement. 'East that way, *Karlu Karlu*. Devils Marbles.' Her long right arm stretched out. 'The *Zalfinhi* (Twin Devils of Porcupine Rock) were born there from one of them fella's eggs.' Skipping to the opposite side, her voice got louder, '*Walgahna*, Walga Rock. Remember … Don't be forgettin'. Remember. That's why you know *Wajarri*.'

Before we could question her further, the clapping sticks got louder and faster and the *mama* (sacred song) coming in from all directions was making everything come to life. Insects, birds, all the little creatures stirred.

'See past that mob! See Barbara back there, she's the pointer star. They call it Pinnacles, but we know it is *Mundungu Yabu* (Ghost Hills).'

Now, old *Jalbri* looked like she was tripping on speed or something. 'See Mary down there, you know what she is?'

'No.' We shook our heads.

'*Wadjemup*. Ratsnest.'

'You mean Rottnest Island?' I corrected her.

'Yes, Noongar[35] land, them Noongars lived there before it broke off from the main land.'

Oops, I'd interrupted *Jalbri* in full flight. Pissed off with me, she rolled her eyes and continued, 'Place of *Jin.gi* (Spirit Being). Three thousand *jipi* (initiated men) were caught, chained one to another throat to throat, them *whitefellas* made them walk all the way down south to Fremantle from all the way up north in the Kimberleys. Then put in prison on Rats-nest, *kartijas* (*whitefellas*) killed 'em, every last one. Why? *Jipi* very important, you know why? Big learnin' for our people, that why.'

'Why?' I squarked.

'Because they had Secret Man's Business, have to save *Pulanyi Bulaing* and all the creatures and the land. If do nothin', no not be here right now. Everybody gone, even them *whitefella*, all gone.'

'Why are we here?' I blurted out, starting to feel scared.

The women had lit their *mili* (firesticks) and smoke filled the air. Soon all we could see over the edge of the rock was a blue haze, dotted with the dazzling red lights of the *milis*. I started to feel so sick.

'*Tharlbarra, tharlbarra* (Strong, strong),' *Jalbri* said kindly, realising she'd spooked the hell outa me. 'You draw picture.'

'My drawing gear is at the bottom of the cliff over there,' I said, pointing over the edge and realising just how high off the ground we were. *Gulyi* was curled up under a bush sleeping. He woke from his nap, took one look at me and started to whine.

'Okay, you jump.'

Shit, she wasn't kidding.

'Okay, *jarda* (old woman), show youse again.' She flew over the edge and rolled into an upright landing.

'You wanna go first?' I said to *Waranmanha*.

---

35   Noongar – Indigenous Australian from the South of Western Australia.

She hesitated as she went over the edge and hit the ground hard, landing flat on her back. *Jalbri* helped her catch her breath. She was winded but nothing was broken.

'*Bindamanha*, jump!' *Jalbri* ordered.

'Nah, I'll climb down.' I could hear *Jalbri* muttering to herself; I was the bad twin. The *julgia* (broken) one.

Climbing down was really hard. The rock wall was steep and I was partly skidding down trying to find footholds. When I got to the bottom, I was a total mess. My knees, toes, fingers and elbows were bloodied. I even bruised my chin, and my eyes were red raw from all the fine, red dust. I landed bum first right on a stone. It had taken me so long that *Jalbri* had given up waiting and had gone off to round up the other women.

Waranmanha stuck her head out of some bushes. '*Bindamanha*, this way. I've got your things. Come, there's a beautiful waterhole and everyone is swimming and preparing food.'

Feeling like a total failure, I limped into the clearing to see the sorta place *blackfella's* dream of. Deep within the cold, black waterhole, a dramatic stand of tall, red rocks reached for the clear blue sky. Shiny dark-brown bodies flashed white grinning teeth as they bobbed through the surface. I walked in very carefully, like some old war veteran. The icy water made my cuts and bruises sting.

Jalbri's head popped up like one of those scary deep-sea fish with the bulging eyes and big teeth. 'Ready? You draw!'

As if I could say no.

She swam in front of me doing *blackfella* crawl—arms moving like 'overarm', but head looking out everywhere for trouble. Nobody's dumb enough to put their face under the water and shut their eyes out here. If you did, you'd be asking for trouble.

We shook ourselves off like dogs and squeezed out our hair. I seemed dry enough to work on the drawings.

'You can see!' The sound of *Jalbri's* voice shocked me; for the first time she sounded like she had faith in me. '*Barndi, barndi* (good, good),' she whispered. '*Waranmanha*!' she screeched. *Waranmanha* was out of the water in a flash.

'*Guwa* (Yes), *Jalbri*'

Quietly we packed up.

'Have food first,' she insisted.

Aunty Toots and Marissa were dishing out tucker and they gave us heaps. While we sat and ate, *Jalbri* kept looking at me strangely. I had seen something she wasn't expecting me to. Louanna looked refreshed and was happy to eat with us. *Gulyi* had been for a swim earlier but was now covered in red mud. He was throwing stones and twigs in the air playing fetch with himself. Poor thing, nobody was paying him any attention. Polly was busy getting Sandy Gibb to help her screw her leg back on.

Jalbri hung around as we chatted. I knew she was checking that we didn't slip up and say the wrong thing. Aunty Toots started to dance, her big boobs bouncing in all directions. I had never seen her like this. She was so serious at Anne Street, always shouting at Louanna and poor Uncle Cedric, but here her spirit was free and she looked beautiful.

Jalbri tapped me on the shoulder. I grabbed *Waranmanha's* hand—it was time to go. We followed *Jalbri* to a clearing that looked as if she went there often. In the centre was a long, flat rock and besides it were some grinding stones smeared with red, white and yellow ochre. This must have been the place where people got ready for ceremony.

'Carmon.' I got out my old shaving cream tin. As I removed the lid, the sound of tin scraping against tin made me nervous. I feared that my drawings wouldn't be good enough for *Jalbri's* keen eye. I unrolled the long strip of brown paper and placed a red and white grinding rock at each end to keep it from curling up.

I put Dad's little TAB pencil in my mouth. My tongue explored his teeth marks. I could imagine Dad nervously biting down on the pencil, praying to Mother Mary that his nag would win. Him winning? Never happened.

Jalbri took a small firestick from her *nguri* (a drawstring bag made from kangaroo hide) and set light to a small branch. She circled around us until the air was heavy with the sweet-smelling smoke. *Gulyi* didn't like it and lay on the ground rubbing his eyes.

Even though I knew beyond a doubt that it was daytime, as the smoke began to clear, the sky seemed to open up and we were plunged into darkness. Veils of colour hung like heavy drapes in that vast cosmic theatre of the *Jirdilungu* (Milky Way). A cool purple mist moved around us, and as it cleared, we both saw her.

21. Mother Goddess Bulari and the Message Stick

A woman. A young, native woman. Her skin was as dark as camp fire coals, and her oiled naked body shone, clothed only by the sun. Standing upon a gloriously luminous blue moon, her dark feet and long toes glowed mysteriously, and spoke to me of other worlds, times and travels of which I could never know. Entangled in a mass of knotted curls, she wore a crown of twelve twinkling stars, and on both sides of her stood the ten faithful heroes and heroines of our Dreaming. She had to be the Mother Goddess of our Ancient Dreamtime Lore.

'Call me *Bulari* (Mother Goddess),' her voice was sweet and kind, and as she spoke, I could see her unborn baby moving in her belly. Seeing the child within her touched my heart and something tiny fluttered deep inside me.

'Where are we?' My thoughts materialised without leaving my lips.

'We are standing in that moment where today has finished, but tomorrow has not begun,' she said with a gentle smile upon her full black lips.

Our bodies felt strangely light as we effortlessly rose up. A cool breeze took *Waranmanha* and me higher and higher, until we stood hovering before her on a cloud of coloured vapour. Mesmerised by her beauty, my mind started to race, and I wondered how someone so young could be immortal. She only looked eighteen years old, just a year and a bit older than me.

My thoughts flashed to other iconic figures like Marilyn Monroe, Lady Di and James Dean, strangely they stay forever young in our minds. Even Mother Mary is always shown as a young woman, even though she had ta be fifty when Jesus died.

Like a thunderbolt it struck me. *Bulari* (Mother Goddess) was the mother of all Star -Children so she was our real Mother. We were her stolen children dragged to Earth by pleading Elders. I glanced at my sister and I could tell the same thing. The sweet sound of recognition vibrated through our beings and echoed within the vastness of space far beyond the *Jirdilungu* (Milky Way).

Adoringly we gazed at our dear Mother *Bulari* who had been waiting for us to come back home. Large tears pooled in the corners of her enormous black eyes. They hung on her lashes gathering volume and with a single blink, those droplets fell.

Instinctively *Waranmanha* and I cupped our raised hands to catch a single droplet of warm, clear, sparkling fluid. As if chemically reacting to my soul, the tear I caught instantly became black with fiery red and orange swirls that danced like firelight on a cave wall. As I watched in amazement the fluid became thicker until it solidified in my hand, turning into a smooth, shiny gemstone.

Waranmanha's stone was nothing like mine. It looked like a tiny *Pulanyi Bulaing*, coiled tightly, contemplating her next move. In the centre were two eye shapes that looked as if they were simply drawn using a fine stick dipped in dark purple paint. Those eyes seemed to swim beneath a translucent lilac surface marked like the scales of a snake. With each outward spiral, the colour changed ever so gently, so perfectly, from lilac, through light orange hue, to an intense bright crimson red. Its outer edge was spotted with iridescent lime green dots. Mesmerised, my jaw fell open in awe of *Waranmanha's* other worldly treasure.

Looking at our Mother, we asked, 'What are these stones?'

'My dears, they are *Milkanarri* (Seeing Stone). When you hold a *Milkanarri* against your heart, it will open your minds eye and show you the past, present and future.'

Bulari watched *Waranmanha's Milkanarri* touch the depression between her breasts. Within the *Milkanarri*, the lilac coloured snake-like head shape flashed yellow.

Waranmanha's eyes opened wide. She whispered, 'I can see it now. I know exactly what I must do.' She paused, and then as if she were talking to *Pulanyi Bulaing*, she said, 'I understand.'

My imagination was running riot. I'm not calm like my sister. I can't handle horror movies. *Blackfellas* are always talking about scary things. All I could think was that her rock was beautiful, but mine looked like an erupting volcano. Nothing sweet or enchanting about it. *Typical.*

I don't have anything beautiful and sparkling in my life. My clothes, and everything are hand me downs. Except for them things that *Jalbri* makes for me. I live in an old reserve house, real old and gloomy.

I was lost in thought, chewin' on my slice of pity pie, when suddenly, I felt a light thud on my chest. I hadn't noticed that I'd been unconsciously fiddling with my *Milkanarri* which I now firmly pressed between my breasts.

I blinked, and there before me, I could see my precious sister, sitting on the back of a massive white stallion, poised majestically on top of a large red Burial Mound. A greenish full moon hung low encircling them in an enormous halo against a lavender-coloured sky.

This vision felt so familiar to me. I was sure I knew exactly where that Burial Mound was. *Waranmanha* caught my eye and kept me fixed within her gaze. Suddenly, she released their hold on me as she turned away, the lavender sky blackened and the greenish full moon flashed red. Then I heard the crackle of fire and huge flames engulfed my vision of her and her stallion.

I knew what it meant. It meant death. I refused to accept this ending.

'NO! NO!' I screamed, 'Unfair! We've only just found each other.'

Bulari's voice was matter-of-fact, even remote, 'All things must return to the beginning. You too will return home to me one day,' she said.

In the darkness of my mind, I saw the red flash of *Kulpan Karrangu's* red belly, and for a heart stopping moment, I couldn't decide if it was real or just a dream, until I found myself once again, in the clearing with *Jalbri*. Then an urgency to draw took over me, I grabbed the charred *mili* (firestick) and began to score the brown paper with harsh straight lines. They were the roads that scarred the sacred places and let the mischief in. I felt unable to control the fury of my mark making.

With the blackened *mili*, I filled the area of Help Canyon and with rage I marked Battlement Rocks where I had been struck. A shiver went through my whole body and my fern-like scars tingled and began to itch. Their colour changed from purple to red, and the burning sensation became intense.

I couldn't stop drawing. I didn't even try.

Picking up a lump of red ochre, I smeared it wildly onto the paper. Fire, fire, fire, everywhere spreading across the land! Sobbing as I worked, my hand reached for a stick, and working it into the white ochre with some spit, I started to *pungarri* (paint in dots). As I painted, the heat left my body and my scars cooled and turned purple again. Then *pitimararri* (painting in lines), I calmly drew the *Zalfinhi* (Twin Devils of Porcupine Rock). Between the spaces I could feel *Pulanyi Bulaing,* hidden but not lost.

My hands started to shake. Overwhelmed and exhausted, I now knew what she and I had to do.

Jalbri came over with sweet bush tea, wild yam, and damper in hand. '*Bindamanha,* rest, must rest.'

Waranmanha squatted down beside me.

151

Wiping my hands on my legs, I welcomed the sweet tea and bush tucker. *Gulyi-Gulyi* wanted a feed too. He jumped onto my lap, knocked me down flat on my back, snatched my damper and high tailed it. I was too tired to chase him.

As *Jalbri* poured more tea from the billy, I asked, '*Jalbri*, what does all this stuff I've drawn mean?' As I spoke, my right hand seemed to have a mind of its own. Before I knew it, I had taken my *Milkanarri* (Seeing Stone) out of the little pouch on the waistband of my grass skirt and was holding the warm stone against my breast.

It was too late. I couldn't loosen my grip on the *Milkanarri*. I was searching for answers, trying to find myself in the future. *Jalbri's* eyes were awash with tears. She felt guilt and shame for the burden she had handed us.

Taking a long, deep breath, I felt the Earth turn a full rotation. It seemed to creak like an old ancient door not wanting to be opened by its key. From that secret place between the active world and the dream-filled one, I saw our history unfold from the beginning of time. Like watching a lava lamp, I saw the world ooze into being. The elements of Fire, Water, Earth and Air gave birth to Wood and Flesh, and so the drama of life began. I was standing before the great *Bamburdu* (Message Stick) of *Walgahna* (Walga Rock).

The messages inscribed by the *Bulya-man* (Sorcerer) so long ago on that mighty rock, were a timeline from past to the present and onward into our future. The battle between *Pulanyi Bulaing* and *Kulpan Karrangu* was clear to see—the two Great Serpent Spirits were drawn entwined around the Old Dragon Tree at the Soak. She in yellow ochre, and he in black and red. The *Bulya-man* showed *Kulpan Karrangu* leaving *Kuji Warnku* (Porcupine Rock) and entering the hearts of all the people near and far.

Etched into the next panel of the picture-gram at Walgahna Rock, was the great sailing ship that brought white people to our shores. Its sails were down and bulging, its nets were drawn, but there wasn't a single fish inside. Instinctively, I knew what this meant. This ship hadn't come from far away to fish, it had come to stay, and its huge nets would catch our souls.

152

As my eyes moved along the panel, I recognised *Kuji Warnku* (Porcupine Rock). Immediately, my heart felt engulfed by the picture of a man standing in a sea of flames, with his mouth open, screaming. His hands were raised up to the heavens, as if pleading for his suffering to end.

I closed my eyes tightly, and blindly shuffled away from that scene. When I stopped, I found myself in front of the enormous footprints of the Emu Man that traced the line of the river as it wound its way to old Dragon Tree Soak. Hidden behind the lines of the drawing, I could just see the image of a dark figure watching.

But the most unnerving drawing of all, was that of a lone figure heading East. Walking calmly through the chaos, that sad, lonely figure had two halos of light drawn in yellow ochre that encircled its whole body. And clearly painted in white ochre, a deadly lightning bolt striking the outer halo.

'*Bindamanha* (Lightning strike),' I muttered to myself.

As I stared at the *Bamburdu* (message stick), the lone figure turned to face me. The traveller trapped in that Dreamtime drama was *me*. Like a *junki*e, she was addicted to trauma, unable to break free. Cursed forever, she would wander through time, a voyeur to the struggles of humankind.

Saddened but resigned to my fate, I turned my attention to the final panel at the far end of the *Bamburdu* (message stick). In awe I stood before a simple drawing of my *Jalbri's* Old Dragon Tree, distinguished by its seven fronds. Around her tree, people gathered, encircled by a golden line of light that came from the East.

To the East, all looked well at *Karlu Karlu* (The Devils Marbles), and even further East in Koori Land[36]. But then I noticed that lone figure walk past our Promised Land, into the 'Beyond Beyond'.

36

Surfacing from my deep trance, I wasn't aware that *Gulyi* had wriggled himself between my arms. I must have squeezed him too hard cos he yelped and jumped up, licking a tear off my cheek as he went. I felt *Jalbri's* fingers run through my hair. I realised she had been sitting beside me the whole time.

'*Yanaji* (Come) *Bindamanha* .'

I elbowed myself along, dropping my head onto her lap.

She leaned over and kissed my cheek. 'I'm sorry I can't be with you. You are a strong woman. You will take my place.'

'I don't want to. I'm too young. It's not fair,' I protested, choking on the tears.

'I know, *jura* (child),' she spoke so softly, feeling my sadness.

'What about *Waranmanha*?' I cried, afraid of being alone.

'You are twin souls but your destinies are different. She will always be with you in spirit.'

I could tell she was choosing her words carefully.

'Not fair! Why am I always the one with nothing?'

Jalbri's silence was deafening.

Waranmanha threw herself on the ground beside me. Looking up past *Jalbri's* knee, she eyeballed me, saying, 'I will never leave you.'

We cried. But seeing *Jalbri* cry, made me really nervous. I needed her to tell me that everything was going to be okay. And that we'd be one big happy family. But there was nothing she could say to make me feel better. I had seen and read the story on the rock. I knew the ending.

'They're out,' I muttered, urgently.

Jalbri nodded. She knew I could see the *Zalfinhi* (Twin Devils of Porcupine Rock) emerge from *Kuji Warnku*. 'We go back to camp. You need rest.'

Waranmanha didn't question her either, she just quickly collected our gear and we set off.

154

The women had left the waterhole long ago. Silently, we walked. *Jalbri* took hold of my right arm, and *Waranmanha* took the other. Weak and unsteady on my feet, I felt like a soldier who had returned shell-shocked from an unrelenting war.

The *who* I thought I was had been shaken to the core.

Now I know *who* I am but not w*hat* I am or *why*.

In spite of everything, *Jalbri* set a fast pace through the bush, cos she knew the safest place for us was back at camp.

It suddenly struck me. 'Where are the men?' I blurted out, not expecting my thoughts to leave my lips.

'Woman's Business,' *Jalbri's* answer was matter-of-fact.

'Why no men?' I asked again.

I could hear her sigh. 'Woman's power different. Man's have too much fire. Only woman's can *barndijunmanha* (put things in right order).'

'What are you saying?' asked *Waranmanha*.

'You got it, sister. We are the sacrificial twin virgins.'

I thought it was funny, but no one laughed. In fact, no one said another word.

What if Manu...

Suddenly, I felt weaker, just seeing all the other women made me realise that they weren't here to find me or have a picnic or a black sheila camp. Nah, they were here for Big Women's Business. I knew the hard stuff was coming soon. Scared shitless, I got stuck to the spot and couldn't move.

Aunty Toots, Louanna and Polly carried me to a fresh leafy bed. The smell was delicious. It reminded me of Mum when we were out bush; she would always tell us to go to our *mangga* (nest), not bed. Lying in my nest I closed my eyes for a moment. The camp sounded like a *buiyi mangga* (hornets' nest). Something was up.

Mum and Barbara came over with sweet tea for *Waranmanha*, *Jalbri* and me. I felt real awkward. Sitting in my *mangga* with me, *Waranmanha* held my hand tight. *Jalbri* jutted her lip out towards Patty Mae and tilted her head back, telling her to bring whatever she was stirring in her cup over to us. I reckon *Jalbri* was drugging us. Lots of things were happening around us. Four women left the camp with Sandy Gibb, their *milis* burning bright. It looked like they were heading towards Help Canyon.

Only Sandy Gibb could lead those women. She is from the Gibb River near Derby. She's the greatest female stocky of her time, even rides in rodeos. She looks real mean. White people in town are frightened to look her in the eye. They even cross the street rather than walk near her. But what they didn't know is that she is the kindest person you could ever meet. She's not married but took on five kids outta the goodness of her heart. They were born with alcohol poisoning. Beth is eight years old, blind but super smart. James is deaf with a crook back and is in a wheel chair. Bella is four and so pretty, but her growth is stunted. Jimmy is two and doesn't speak but can scream the house down. Baby Emma is so sweet and happy, even though her eyes are really far apart and crossed, and her little feet are twisted in. Sandy Gibbs cares for them all on next to nothing. Mum sends fish to help 'em make ends meet.

Thinking about her took my attention away from the heavy shit that I thought was about to happen with Mum and Barbara. I had been looking right past Mum, now I turned my eyes on her. 'What do you want?' I was so annoyed that she was still in my face.

'We're sorry,' she said, speaking for the two of them.

'Sure! I said, glaring at her sarcastically.

'Respect!' *Jalbri* said, she couldn't help sticking her nose in.

'We were just kids Lucy. Your Dad and me did everything the wrong way. When the elders told me, I could carry "The Star Children", I didn't think of how hard it would be to give youse up. I fought like mad to keep youse. It wasn't Barbara's fault. I broke the Lore again and again. I went against the deal. All the "bad luck" is my fault. How could we tell you kids? So, we all ended up hating each other. We didn't talk to the Elders about fixing the problem because your Dad and me thought they'd take our Lucy away and give you to her.'

I now understood what Mum was feeling.

Barbara hung onto *Waranmanha*. 'We love you. I never wanted to hurt you kids. That day Mary and I agreed to let you kids be sung down from the stars was the happiest day of my life. I was going to be a mother. I wasn't thinking about the pain and suffering I was bringing to youse… Honest. Mary and me shouldn't have hidden your story from you. We're real '*pararrka talu.*' (sorry and ashamed).

Everyone was emotional, even *Jalbri*. Tears were flowing, and suddenly I felt exhausted. Mum and Sandy Gibb handed out more sweet tea. I sat in my *mangga* (nest) watching the relationships between this mob of women change.

This was heavy shit for *Waranmanha* and me. But I couldn't help noticing that something deep was happening for the others too. Some of these women had lived on Anne Street Reserve for over 30 years, but here on Country, the wind of change was blowing away them old troubles and lettin' their voices be heard.

I lay flat on my back and relaxed for the first time in a long while. As my eyes studied the heavens, my right hand raised all by itself, tracing the sky map I had drawn earlier. *Kurriji Pa Yajula, Karlu Karlu, Gumbarri Jinji, Walgahna, Mundungu Yabu, Wadjemup*. Again, and again I traced the Southern Cross onto the starry canvas of the night sky. And as I did, I recalled the images I saw on *Bamburdu* (the message stick) of *Walgahna*. I would never forget the messages from the *Bulya-man*. Into the night I drew and redrew until sleep took me.

22. Mimi Lee

Another day in paradise, I thought as I opened my eyes, dreading what plans *Jalbri* had for us. Sure enough, she was standing near my feet with her firestick in hand. I rolled my eyes.

'Okay, eat,' she said.

Waranmanha and I bolted over to Polly and Louanna, we needed a break from *Jalbri*. They were real happy to see us.

'Hey bushie, nice decorations,' Patty Mae teased, making fun of my string line and chip packet strips I'd tied to the trees. I knew she would.

I was trying to think of the perfect come back, when suddenly, Aunty Toots grabbed me and gave me the biggest hug.

'You're a smart cookie, don't listen to her,' she said, as I disappeared into her folds. Somehow my head worked its way down into her boobs. Seriously,

I couldn't breathe and thought I was a goner. She's a shocker, but I love her to bits.

I could hear what sounded like *nguurru* (brumbies). Sandy Gibb had rounded up the herd and was ordering them into the nearby clearing. My dear *Birri*, refusing to take instructions from Sandy Gibb, stormed through the bushes and pulled up in front of me, snorting. The whites of her eyes shone. She was not happy and probably thought I'd abandoned her. I threw myself at her, wrapping my arms around her smooth neck and planting my face into her cheek. I could feel her happiness ripple through her body. Nodding her head up and down, she whinnied to the others telling them she was happy to be reunited with her family. *Birri* thought of me as her daughter because she had looked after me in the darkest moment of my life. 'I missed you. Where have you been? I'd never forget you, *Birri*.'

Distracted by a deep snort, we looked up to see an enormous white stallion with a thick, white mane walk nervously past Louanna and me, and straight up to *Waranmanha*. They both instantly recognised each other like long-lost lovers. A chill trickled down my spine and a lump formed in my throat. I knew what song destiny was singing for them. His huge, gentle eyes were a transparent pale grey held in place by light-pink lids. He had an awesome stance and a rump like Beyoncé. An Arab for sure. He walked slowly around my sister, nodding and snorting, and then presented his side to her and lowered his head. *Waranmanha's* plait swung as she mounted her monumental horse. He pranced on the spot like a proper performance horse from some sort of circus. The *songlines* had been drawn and she could not resist its pull.

'*Bindamanha, Waranmanha*, your *Mimi* (grandmother) is here,' Sandy Gibb muttered as she hurriedly rushed to the back of the group.

A hush went through the mob.

Sitting tall and black on a wild-looking spirited stallion was a slim, wiry woman with short-cropped pure white hair and huge bulging black eyes. In her left hand she held a small, thin black cigar, which at first, I thought was a stick until she raised it to her painted red lips.

I felt like I'd stepped onto some *mamany* (crazy) film set. Her horse was unbelievable. Jet black except for its white mask like face. It reminded me of a photo Sister had shown us of Japanese kabuki[37] actors. To top it off, he had the scariest light blue eyes.

Drawing a deep chesty breath, she puffed out a large circle of smoke before saying 'So you're the twins?'

Crazy black bitch, I thought, looking up at her.

Then all snobby-like, she said, 'I'm your *mimi*. You may call me *Mimi* Lee and this is *Ramu*.' She patted his strong neck and added, 'Don't touch him. Where are your mothers?' She spoke like she fricken' owned the place.

Mary and Barbara were trying to be invisible, but she spotted them. Removing the cigar from her mouth, she blew smoke at our mothers and beckoned them to come over to her. Mum and Barbara shuffled over sideways, like crabs with their heads down, eyes looking at the ground. Then they both stood with their backs facing her, their mother. What the hell was happening?

'Long time no see *Bibi* (Mother),' said Barbara.

The atmosphere was so thick you could cut it with a knife. I understood that Mary and Barbara were forbidden to look at *Mimi* Lee, but I also thought they were forbidden to speak to her. Down-cast eyes, talking to someone's back—you'd think there'd have to be a better way. This was something else. I wouldn't have picked this bloody strong woman as their mother. Gee, I could imagine the fights Dad would've had with her. She would've won hands down. She acts like she's got bigger balls than her stallion, Ramu.

The moment she arrived everything changed, even the language. *Jalbri* had spoken to us mostly in Wajarri, because she wanted us to be able to speak to the *Bulya-man* (Sorcerer) from *Walgahna* (Walga Rock). She wanted us to understand his words and his drawings so that we could learn our true history, and know what was coming. Teaching us Mangala was how she could keep

---

37   Kabuki - classical Japanese dance drama.

her language alive. Although, we understood more of both languages than we could speak, and they were now firmly planted in our hearts and ears.

Now *Mimi* Lee was speaking to us in *Yawuru Ngan.ga*, Broome speak. *Bitch*. I knew she spoke Wajarri, Mangala, and the Queen's English.

'*Wang-gi li-yan mingan-ngany-janu* (Have you got bad feelings for me)?' she asked the back of Mum's head.

Mum *thubarnimanha* (straightened up) and said loudly, '*Marlu nirla nga-yu* (I don't know)!' She dared to answer back.

Good on her, I was so proud of Mum for standing up for herself.

Everyone else, except me, just stood with their heads down looking at the ground. I was the only one who dared to look the old *queen* in the eye. I needed another alpha woman in my life like I needed a hole in my head. She eyeballed me back, but I wasn't gonna to step down.

'*Marlu wayaluga* (Stop crying),' she ordered Mum and Barbara, breaking my stare.

I won that one, I thought to myself.

'It's time to put that *old trouble* behind us,' she said in perfect English. She must have had a convent education. 'It is finished!' The flick of her head was to add emphasis to her statement, but it was totally wasted on everyone but me, cos the rest of the mob still had their eyes on the ground.

I kept staring at her and then she smiled. It was a complete surprise. There was an unexpected kindness in those large, penetrating eyes. Just by looking at the curve of her forehead highlighted by her short, white hair, I could see that she was an intelligent, stylish woman unlike any other *blackfella* I knew.

She was wearing a red top with a sort of cut-away neckline and a black pair of fitted jeans with stars on the cuff. The earrings on her long earlobes flashed red and gold. As my eyes drifted up to her painted red lips, she smiled at me again. My instant reaction was to smile back. We'd somehow made a connection.

161

She was awesome in a way I couldn't explain. A real city woman. Fancy wearing red nail polish. The only other person I ever saw with red nail polish on in the bush was a crazy chick called Cecily who thought she was Marilyn Monroe in her last life and that Jesus was coming back to marry her. They say she got hit by a freight train at Halls Creek. She was totally out of her brain sniffing petrol. Poor Cecily. She was a white girl trapped in black skin. Beautiful as, no kidding, she could've been a movie star.

My thoughts were broken by *Gulyi-Gulyi*. He ran up to *Mimi* Lee's horse, and stood on his hind legs, singing to her in greeting. Just as he put his front paws on *Ramu's* side to reach up to *Mimi* Lee, *Ramu* kicked out and bared his teeth.

'Down!' she said. *Gulyi* hightailed it back to me squealing. He had a big lump on his hind leg.

'What's its name?' she asked.

'*Gulyi-Gulyi*,' I responded, stressed out to see my puppy in pain.

'It suits him,' she said with one of those wry smiles.

'He's not silly or stupid,' I protested.

'No, he's funny,' she replied.

Talkin' to this woman was like putting your hand into a bag of venomous snakes. *Kulpan Karrangu* was going to have a real battle on his hands, or belly, or whatever.

Sitting back elegantly, leaning on *Ramu's* huge rump, in a satisfied voice she asked, 'Where's my *yagu*?'

Jalbri stepped out. With a twinkle in her eyes she said, '*Miyarnu, wangnar* (happy) to see you got *waji jinjamarda* (no baby in arms) for me to raise.' *Jalbri* chuckled, but you could hear a gasp from the women.

Them were fighting words.

Mimi Lee's eyes narrowed.

162

'Bout time ya come to learn these kids somethin' about the Lore.'

Mimi Lee was too wise to answer her back.

Jalbri looked up past the enormous *Ramu*, who was obviously in love with *Jalbri,* cos he had taken a bunch of her hair in his mouth and was gently blowing raspberries. 'Come on *Maaja muni* (boss woman).'

A ripple of laughter went through the group.

'Let's go and learn them kids *Wakaj Kanarri* (The Finishing) story.'

Mimi Lee just nodded. No one took on *Jalbri* and won—she's a bitch and a half.

Jalbri signalled to the women to get some food and their stuff. *Winthuly-Winthuly* went down on his knees. We watched *Jalbri's* little bum find a comfy spot, and then *Winthuly-Winthuly* lurched into a standing position. Her camel stepped forward like only camels can, and the two giant stallions held back behind her. Poor *Birri* hung back even further. She was like a donkey compared to *Ramu* and *Waranmanha's* white stallion, who she'd name *Wilara* (Moon).

Going by what I'd learnt from Louanna, if anyone saw this mob going walkabout, they'd know for sure we were crazy. Louanna and I loved watching fantasy movies back at her house. Mum would give me a big fish to take for dinner, and Aunty Toots would make us the meanest scones. Louanna's got it into her head that I should be a psychologist. Annoyingly, she spends hours analysing the characters after we've watched a film. She's brilliant, and I love the way she shares the real deep, important stuff with me. She teaches me so much.

We had two black queens, one with a deadly sense of humour and the other one is just deadly. *Waranmanha* is our beautiful, innocent princess and the caregiver. Not fair, I'm the weirdo who learns lessons the hard way. I would like to have been the lover, but I think *Mimi* Lee is all over that with her red lippy and tight jeans. I'm sure men love her, even if they don't like her. I bet she bites their heads off like a praying mantis when she's finished with them. *Mimi* and *Jalbri* are both wizards, and I think I'm in training. Together we hold the wisdoms of the first people and the second people, of women and the universe. Adventurers we are and heroes we may become, but not by choice.

Up until now, the Country had been red and flat, dotted with clumps of spinifex. Lost in thought I didn't realise our motley group had already come to a halt.

'Okay, okay. Come,' *Jalbri* called out for me to dismount and follow her. '*Jambarn* (Quickly), *jambarn*.'

Gulyi was already with her. Lost in my thoughts, I didn't know how long I'd been sitting there like a stunned mullet. It was so hot; the sweat was pouring off me.

Behind a large band of trees and bushes, *Mimi* Lee and *Waranmanha* were digging out a *Jila*.

'You gotta learn stuff,' *Jalbri* said, pushing me forward.

I still wasn't moving fast enough for her. My Miss Goodie-Two-Shoes sister was there, head down, cute bum in the air, *junimanha* (laughing at something) with *Mimi* Lee—bet it was about me.

'*Nhangan, nhangan* (Go look, watch),' *Jalbri* said, poking my shoulder.

Suddenly the water rose, spurting up high above the hole they'd dug. *Gulyi, Birri, Winthuly-Winthuly, Ramu* and *The Great White Wonder—Wilara,* were there in a flash.

'Nah, nah!' *Jalbri* shouted, leading *Winthuly-Winthuly* out of the growing lake to stop her pooping in it. '*Bindamanha* !' she yelled.

'*Yanayimanha* (Coming),' I yelled back. I helped hold the animals back while she dug like a woman possessed. She was digging another hole to collect water for them so that our drinking water would stay pure. I felt shame that she was the one digging, but she was doing a better job than I could. *Waranmanha* raced over to help. *Sickening.*

164

'Okay, okay.' *Jalbri* indicated that I could let the animals go.

The hard work done, *Jalbri* and *Mimi* were now *kawanarri* (singing out) to the Spirits of the *Jila*. It was really moving to hear them. They drank first and then invited us to drink with them.

Stepping into 'the everlasting water', they danced, sang and played, splashing us and each other. They were mother and child again and we were their children's children. This was how the love of Country embraced the love of family—generations of strength and knowledge, and gratitude to the land, sky and its spirits.

Waranmanha and I were hanging out. The cold water was a relief from the harsh sun. Just being together having a swim was cool. We had competitions to dive down and feel the hole where the water was coming from. It was really cold and still had a slight upward pressure, which meant that the little lake was still expanding up past our waist.

I came up to the surface to see *Mimi* starkers, sitting on the edge smoking her little, black cigar. Although she was watching us, she was lost in thought. Her clothes were drying on a nearby bush. That old bird *Jalbri* was totally hyperactive. She was off doing something and soon returned with an arm full of stuff for a fire. *Blackfellas* love fires. They can't think straight without one.

'*Thubarnimanha* (Straighten up),' she screeched like some bloody *kuta barndagura* (naked bush bustard).

'In a minute,' I replied.

'*Guwardi* (Now)!' she squawked, stamping her feet in a little tantrum.

Mimi Lee looked over, smiled and blew out a big puff of smoke. She knew *Jalbri* like no one else.

We got out of the water, and by the time we had wrung out our string skirts and hair, *Jalbri* had the fire lit. She pointed to where we had to sit, even though it was still hot, we had to sit close to the fire. It's a *blackfella* thing. The *jurdu* (smoke) kept the millions of flies away.

23. The Twin Devils of Porcupine Rock

Jalbri stood on the other side of the small fire. She was trying to get our attention, but I'd already lost focus watching the little folds of old loose flesh hanging down between her legs either side of a scraggly patch of grey pubic hair.

'I've been watching you girls.'

That made me pay attention—I hated to think that she knew what I had been looking at.

'Youse young kids now days, don't know nothin' 'bout 'em *real things*, blackfella learnin'.'

I rolled my eyes.

She noticed, shook her head and kept going, 'I know youse girls got good hearts. Youse *barndi* (smart/clever). We can learn you up quick.'

166

Just at that moment the tip of my big toe started burning. I pulled it away from the heat of the fire. Holding my foot up near my mouth, I spat a big blob of gooz on it to cool it off. *Jalbri* shook her head. *Mimi* was trying to stifle a laugh.

'Are you okay? the smart twin asked.

'Yeah, I'll live.' I felt so dumb.

'Now *nganggurnmanha* (listen up), time for Dreaming story time. When you know your story, you know *who you are*.' The tone of her voice became smooth and dark, the squawking *barndagura* (bush bustard) took off.

Now we were hovering above the earth in a sound bubble made by her voice. Everything she said materialised before our eyes and our normal world slipped away. The flies, the heat, even the sunshine was switched off. All we could see were the flames of the fire flashing and flickering high in front of us. Its *jurdu* (smoke) filled the darkened sky, and *Jalbri's* white ochre-painted face talked to us through the *jurdu* like a vision from another world.

Watching her mouth move and her eyes gleam, we were enchanted by her ancient tale and moved by her haunting beauty. *Mimi's* strident voice drew the *songlines* that transported us to that other world. *Jalbri's* jet-black eyes glistened intensely, encircled by their rich dark-brown lids untouched by the dazzling white ochre smeared across her cheeks.

'In my *yagu's* (mother's) time, 'em *katijas* (white people) wore long dresses right down to their toes. Two girls came here, they had white, white skin and pale blue eyes, and down their backs, their yellow hair swung like a *milyura* (big snake), way down past their *bumma* (bum).'

As she spoke, the girls appeared in the firelight before her.

'Just lookin' at their eyes you could see that their hearts were *walhi* (no good). Sweet smilin' faces to the front, big trouble to the back. Old people from them days said that *Kulpan Karrangu* made their mother bring 'em *walhi* girls here specially for makin' "big trouble" for us mob. That evil Fire Spirit went deep into their hearts, 'em girls were perfect for his *walhi* work.'

167

As she continued, we could see everything she said in the flames of the fire, just like a movie. 'That time too many people were passing through our Country doing mining, makin' camp and takin' kiddies. All that *walhi* energy destroying Country and families. Them girls and their mother came with 'em *punku* (immoral) people.

'But one of them *barndi wayilpila* (good white man) came. His name Derwen, mean big tree (oak tree). He had long hair and a big, curly beard and green, green eyes just like *Pulanyi Bulaing*. He was *jalajala* (really good) to the old people and always protected our children from all the *walhi* people comin' with their two faces on.

'All us desert people, we loved him. Them central desert mans called him *gagi mupinjarri*, meaning bird medicine man. *Gagi* (birds) loved him *wayilpila* (good white man), even tiny, tiny *gagi* would fly right down and sit on his big gentle hands. He'd talk and talk to *gagi*, and he learned them kiddies ta be kind and not hurt 'em little *gagi*. All them old desert womans watched him real close and named him *Karparli* (Grandmother). 'Cos we say, "a kind grandmother always raises up good children", so everyone called him *Karparli*.

'Our *Karparli*, that Derwen, went out early every mornin' to draw in his big, black book. That *walhi* (no good) mornin' he went walkabout to Help Canyon, right to the faraway end, to him *Kuji Warnku* (Porcupine Rock). It was *Wilburu* (September) and the spinifex was tall against *Kuji Warnku*. All the flowers opened up for that there fella. He sat on that *barlu* (rock ledge) high up lookin' out over Country, watchin' the sun comin' up. He got all his stuff out to do paintin'.

'But *Karparli* did not feel good in his heart, somethin' wrong. He didn't ask no one for permission to go up *Kuji Warnku*. Not ask *Pulanyi Bulaing*, not ask Nature Spirits, not ask no body nothin'. He passed by the yellow flowers growin' on the bush at the base of *Kuji Warnku*. He was meant to break a branch and strike the rock with 'em and ask for permission to climb up. That would have kept him safe and kept the *Kulpan Karrangu* trapped in that rock. See, *blackfella* knowledge means somethin',' she said, looking right at me.

168

'That evil *Kulpan Karrangu* was so happy. He'd been waitin' long time for some fella ta free him. He called that *walhi* woman, the *Zalfinhi's* (Twin Devils of Porcupine Rock) mother, to feed our *Karparli* to her *kurntals* (daughters). "Derwen! Derwen!" she cried out. "Please help me, I've lost my girls. Could you please see if you can see them from up there?" He'd heard many *walhi* things about her, but he was a kind man and did not want to think *walhi* of her.

'So *Karparli* stood tall, not knowing that the *Zalfinhi* were hiding under the *barlu* (rock ledge). Looking out across the plains, *Karparli's* heart was filled with joy.'

As *Jalbri* spoke, in the *jurdu* (smoke) I could see the red earth of the desert awash with the colour of a billion flowers in bloom. Must have been so different from his homeland.

We watched him looking for the girls to the East, West and then to the North. But then from the South, we heard the howl of a *kuli kunyarr* (wild dog). As he turned to face the sound, a chill went through him and all of us too. For an instant the desert became silent and a strange darkness crept up from the Canyon below.

The *Zalfinhi* lit their *mili* (firesticks). A loud crackling sound split the dry desert air. Huge flames fuelled by spinifex leapt out of Help Canyon. He was trapped. Facing the fire front on, a single cry came out from his heart and passed his burning lips. 'Lucy!' It was his wife's name from his homeland, Wales.

While I was watching Derwen, somehow, I became hooked into his drama. When he screamed Lucy's name, it was my soul, not hers, that was wrenched out of its dark hiding place beneath my ribs. I entered the scene as a small, blue ball of energy hovering in front on his moist lips.

We, he and me… our souls melted into an amorphous blob that was both a comfort and a curse.

I was invisible yet exposed. In this smoky Dreamtime world, I was more real than the fleshy form I'd left sitting on the sand watching from the future. In an instant I knew that I, this teenage Lucy, would never be the same.

169

As the fire towered over us, the searing heat devoured the air. We dared not breathe. He swept me up with his right hand still covered with paint. With a stroke of genius, he grabbed his trusty wide-brimmed hat with his left hand and covered his painting hand and face. In one swift movement, he captured me there.

His greying moustache cushioned my fall in that dark hot space just above his top lip. I quivered, trapped in the depression underneath his nostrils, dreading that his next inward breath would suck me into a world from which I could never escape.

The flames burnt down from *Kuji Warnku* (Porcupine Rock) and spread out along the spinifex planes. Still hovering in front of his lips, I whispered from that place where pleasure never goes, 'I am sorry.' And in the next breath, I added, 'I wish it happened to me.'

From his rosebud lips, a faint, breathy reply shook my soul, 'It has happened to you.'

Desperately, I looked from the past to my body sitting in the present. I could see *Mimi* Lee and *Waranmanha* holding onto a hysterical Lucy, but I couldn't hear their words or feel their touch. I had become his Lucy, and his soul was clinging onto me like grim death.

Flames lashed over, past and through us. His burnt left hand dropped his smouldering hat. *Watali* (Poor fellow), my Derwen sat on the *barlu* (rock ledge). His hands and fingers were blackened and stiff. His clothes had evaporated and his skin had melted. His beard had burnt down and his nose hung off its bridge red raw.

Suddenly, his blackened eyelids opened and his green, green eyes looked compassionately at me. Those eyes were too green, too bright. He had been to the other side, *Banharnigardi, Banharnigardi*, Beyond, Beyond. He had been where no man should go and seen what no mortal eye should see.

Still hovering before him, knowing that somehow, I had to stay, I started to sing in the old traditional way. The harsh nasal sound seemed to calm his physical pain. I sang the same chant over and over. I called on *Bulgardu* (God of the Universe), on Jesus and the *Muniwarri* (Seven Sisters) the *Jin.gi's* (Spirits) of the *Mangarikarra* (Dreamtime), the *Jila* and all the Ancestors to help us. I didn't ask for much, but like the relentless wind, I chanted over and over and over again:

Bulagardu	God of the Universe
Panu rankunarri	Enough is to take a breath
Panu waninyarri	Enough is to live
Galinjumanha	Look after (save) him
Bulagardu	God of the Universe
Panu rankunarri	Enough is to take a breath
Panu waninyarri	Enough is to live
Galinjumanha	Look after (save) him

From beyond the smoke of that camp fire, 120 years in the future, I heard my *Mimi* join me in my chant. Her voice was surprisingly sweet, its tenderness melted my heart. *Waranmanha* joined in, and each tone of this strange and ancient harmony seemed to carry the grief of the ages past and present.

Then *Jalbri's* voice quivered like a bow, heavy with tears, 'Long, long ago the Lore told us, *Balayi*! (Watchout), *Thuribirla* (The daytime sky) will turn *mamukati* (dark) and *Ngardubirla* (The night-time sky) will shine *pily* (red). *Nila* (You will know) *marduwayimanha balbaru* (growing madness time) is here.'

A lone *kuli kunyarr* (wild dog) howled from the highest point of the now blackened *Kuji Warnku* (Porcupine Rock). Through the *jurdu* (smoke) from the fire three men appeared. They had strikingly beautiful faces and thick, long beards, and their strongly sculptured bodies were smeared with blood-red ochre.

171

Each man wore a *manngi* (headband worn by initiated men) dressed with long, straight black and white feathers. Below their *manngi* just above their eyebrows was a single white line that lay thickly on their *yuna pulkun* (initiation scar). Dressed in *jani* (pubic tassels), each carried a long *mangul* (hunting spear) with a *mirru* (spear thrower), as well as a *karrpina* (combat shield) strung to their backs.

I knew who these giants were. I was sure I'd seen them before in a dream. These were the Spirit Men and they had come with their Spirit Dingos who in a flash gave chase to the *kuli kunyarr* (wild dog). The Spirit Men moved like dancers as they rounded up the *Zalfinhi* and their mother.

The whiz of a single spear was barely audible above the yelping of the *kuli kungarr*, the hissing serpents, the crackling fire, the laughter of *Zalfinhi*, the wailing of women, and the gentle moaning of my three women from the future sitting around their camp fire.

But those hovering between the worlds like Derwen and me, we heard that *mangul* (hunting spear) cut the air like thunder on a summer's day. The *mangu* showed no mercy. I heard its sickening thud as it cracked open their mother's ribs, penetrating her heart, and wriggled its way through her back half escaping into the acrid air.

Alive and aware, she saw her *walhi* (no good) life pass before her as the last bit of air shot out of her lungs. A horrific scream was a vain warning to her twin devils. She reeled backwards. Her dead weight fell onto them, and that one *mangul* (hunting spear) pierced those twin devils, pinning them onto the great *Kuji Warnku* (Porcupine Rock).

The Spirit Men sang out a single sacred sound. The surface of the rock became fluid and the *Zalfinhi* were sucked into the rock. *Kuji Warnku* (Porcupine Rock) became solid again, but I could still see those devilish girls' ghostly shapes moving just under the surface of the rock. Before I could loosen my tongue to speak or close my eyes to blink, the Spirit Men and their dingos had disappeared.

172

Shit! I felt like I'd been holding my breath. Taking a deep breath, I was relieved to see the women and men from Derwen's time carry Derwen down from the rock and fix him onto a bush stretcher that they'd attached to their *nguurru* (brumby). The fire still raged, driven on by the easterly winds. *Alang* (South). They were heading south to the nearest station and then onto Perth Hospital.

The sky was electric and thunder rolled out, but no rain fell upon the scorching earth. *Pulanyi Bulaing* fought the dreaded *Kulpan Karrangu*. All day and all night, and then another day and night that fire burnt across our land onto other people's land and on and on, and still we continued south looking for hope.

Time passed slowly. The Mangala people of the Great Sandy Desert moved Derwen carefully, feeding him and dousing him with herbal concoctions to heal his burns. As they headed south, they crossed the tribal boundaries of the Juwaliny and Yulparija, and still they continued. Each tribal group added their 'Sorry Business' song to ours.

I was still a tiny blue orb hovering above Derwen, connected to his heart by a thin, golden thread. His pain was my pain, and through his eyes I learnt to fear life and loss. I was lost in his sea of sorrow. So deep I was sure I would drown. So vast I wished I would. I was drifting attached to this man's life and I didn't know why.

My connection with *Jalbri*, *Mimi*, *Waranmanha*, Manu Tollie, Mum, *Gulyi* and *Birri* had been cut off. Our procession was in search of *kartijas* (*whitefellas*) to mend Derwen's body and send him back to his homeland.

The travellers muttered among themselves, debating where they should take him. Then a familiar name, Dr Pilawal (Bloodwood) was mentioned. They decided that because Dr Pilawal was white and a medical doctor, and Derwen was white, she should look after him real good.

All us *blackfellas* knew about Dr Pilawal. In the north-west, *her* name has been woven into camp fire horror stories. Dr Pilawal was no saint. She ran away from Poland after being caught doing human experiments on orphans. Dr Pilawal continued her 'work' in the Lock Hospitals on Bernier and Dorri Islands off the coast of Carnarvon.

Most of her patients were grieving parents who had just had their children stolen from them. Metal dog collars were fixed around their throats and attached to heavy chains that weighed down their long limbs. Large groups were chained together and then transported to the segregated islands. Few survived the horrific medical experiments. Us *blackfellas* became living lab rats. Daisy Bates[38] described the Lock Hospital as 'tombs of the living dead'. The Locks were finally closed in 1919, but the terrifying memories of that place still live on.

It was in the land of the Mardu people where the travellers found Dr Pilawal's cave. They knew they were coming close because of the weird-looking dead animals hanging in trees nearby. Legs, heads and other body parts had been swapped over to make ugly new creatures.

Juja (old man) called out, 'Dr Pilawal, a *whitefella* needs your help.'

There was much mumbling and carrying on, but finally Dr Pilawal came scuttling out to see. 'What's up?' she asked. Old, hunched and hideously ugly, but her eyes gleamed with delight. Just like a cockroach she scurried over to the stretcher. Her breath stank of rotten flesh. 'Bring the patient this way,' she ordered.

The path was cleared for the horses.

Suddenly, she lunged forward and bit off one of Derwen's fingers. He screeched. Blood dripped from the finger dangling from her mouth. As she scurried back to her cave, all but two of the old *blackfellas* ran off screaming, believing that Derwen was 'cursed'.

Terrified, I shot up into the air, snapping the golden thread that connected me to Derwen's heart and fused my soul to his and to this weird dreaming place

---

38   Daisy Bates - Irish journalist, welfare worker and lifelong student of Australian Aboriginal Culture and Society.

from so long ago. 'AHRRR!' I screamed, as I was propelled like a comet into a black hole. I was in a dark, dark space but it wasn't empty.

The darkness had texture so fine and beautiful to the touch like a Somali's skin. It wasn't empty out there. I was surrounded.

The darkness was alive. My unravelling began. Light seemed to be trailing off me, weakening me, disorienting me. The energy source that was propelling me began to stutter, and in slow motion I ground to a halt.

I was falling apart.

In a sharp, breath-taking moment, I was snatched at nauseating speed out of that textured darkness and crashed heavily back into my body on the red dirt beside the flickering camp fire in front of *Jalbri*, *Mimi* Lee and *Waranmanha*. A high-pitched sound rang in my ears, and I was sure I could hear voices whispering, but for the life of me I couldn't make out what they were saying.

Waranmanha hugged me tightly, but I was still stuck deep within my body and couldn't feel my skin because my *rayi* (soul) hadn't leaked out that far yet. I saw the fire flicker and was petrified that I would be dragged back to be a part of Derwen's drama.

Jalbri said something to *Mimi,* who got up, lit her cigar from the flames and poured water on the fire, snuffing it out.

A surge of panic ran though me. I grabbed hold of *Waranmanha* and clutched *Jalbri's* hand so tight I could hear her bones creak. This surge of adrenaline drove me to the surface of my skin, making me feel hypersensitive and alert.

Mimi squatted in front of me. 'Focus on the light of the cigar tip. Breathe in and out slowly. Don't lose focus.' Her tone was calm and strong like nothing was a big deal. '*Barndi* (Good),' she said, looking straight into my eyes.

Instantly I felt my mouth soften and turn into a smile, and I started to feel more normal again.

Mimi started to sway her cigar from side to side. Occasionally she'd stop it in front of her face and take a deep drag. The fag lit up the tip of her strong nose as a cascade of tiny sparks fell from its tip like falling stars.

175

'Do you think he died?' I asked, my mind racing back to Derwen.

"'For mortals vanished from the day's sweet light. I shed no tear; rather I mourn for those who, day and night, live in death's fear.'"

'What?' I responded to *Mimi's* deep voice.

'It's a Greek Proverb,' she replied. I could almost feel her shake her head.

'How can I stop being afraid?' Shocked by my own question, I waited for her reply.

'*Mabarn* (Have faith) and your fears will slide off your back. You're being prepared, made ready for greatness; you must gather your powers and believe that the ultimate course of universal destiny is good. There is no choice, you must be obeyed.' Her words cut through to the truth like a hunting spear.

Jalbri started talking to *Mimi* Lee in a language we didn't understand. There was a warmth and agreement in their tone.

Waranmanha patted me on the back and whispered into my right ear, 'She's right.'

We sat quietly, trying to catch a word here and there. I heard *Jalbri* call *Mimi* Lee, '*Miyarnu*.' *Mimi* didn't correct her. To her *yagu* (mother) she would always be *Miyarnu*. The slow, long arc of light the cigar made on its way up to *Mimi's* pursed lips and then down again helped me drift off into a deep sleep.

24. Diamonds in the Dust

I was aware of *Jalbri* and *Mimi* talking as I slept, and it made me feel safe. I wandered back to that other world to see if Derwen was okay. The *kartijas* (*whitefellas*) had arrived and taken him to hospital.

'Ya don't wanna be strayin' off the straight line.'

Startled by *Jalbri's* voice, I fell from that dream state and sprang to my feet wide-awake. I went to speak but she stopped me.

'*Muta wanti* (Just sit down)! *Nganggurmanha* (Listen up).' *Jalbri* signalled to her *kurntal* (daughter) to light that fire again.

The sky was just starting to get lighter.

Jalbri started to draw in the dry sand. '*Thubarnimanha* (Straighten up),' she squawked like a *gagi* (bird).

177

I rolled my eyes so hard I thought my left eye was going to get stuck.

'Somethin' the matter with you or you just got a big mental problem?'

'No, I'm okay. My eye just got stuck.' I didn't mean to say that.

Everyone burst out laughing. *Mimi* laughed so hard; it triggered her smoker's cough.

'You're like a bloody *wintiki* (curlew).'

I tried to salvage some dignity by saying to *Jalbri*, 'Something got stuck in my eye.'

'Shuuush,' she hissed, placing her fingers to her lips. She stood up and stepped out lightly.

I grabbed *Waranmanha's* hand tightly, fearing that something was about to grab us. My heart was pounding. *Gulyi-Gulyi*, who I'd completely forgotten about, raced off like he knew what he was doing. I wanted to be invisible, cos my imagination was taking hold and the warning system inside my head was out of control.

Warning! Warning! Dangerous universe ahead! *Balayi* (Watchout)! *Balayi!* I couldn't hold it in anymore and started screaming, 'Shit! Shit! Shit!' I'd become a *shit* machine.

'*Nam jarrilirra* (Shut up your mouth),' *Jalbri* whispered with as much force as she could muster while whispering. She swung around and eyeballed me. '*Walhi* (No good) you speak on Country like that. You know respect?'

I felt big-time *garndi* (shame).

Suddenly, *Jalbri* started running towards Help Canyon. *Shame or no shame.*

'Shiiiit!' I screeched, running with my sister in the opposite direction.

Gulyi saw us running and took chase. He tripped me up. I fell onto a *gubinge* bush taking *Waranmanha* down with me. We crawled underneath—spiders, scorpions, ants, centipedes, mozzies, snakes and *doublegees*, we didn't give a shit. Talk about panic, I grabbed *Gulyi*, shutting his mouth tight. He was whimpering, but that was just too bad for him. Us girls were lying under the bush, eyes closed, holding our breath.

Then we heard the strangest sound. It was definitely *Jalbri*. It sounded like someone was strangling her.

My blood was rushing so loudly in my ears I thought my head was going to burst and my brains would fly out. *Waranmanha* started tapping my head with her fingers. It sounded so loud, it made me angry. 'Stop! What's wrong with you?'

'Look,' she said.

Frightened of what could be standing in front of us, I took a big breath and got ready for the worst. Terrified, I opened my eyes, half expecting to see Dr Pilawal standing there with half a dozen of *Jalbri's* fingers hanging out of her mouth like fags.

There stood *Jalbri*, large as life, with a huge *bungarra* (goanna) draped over her shoulder like a fur coat. She cracked up laughing and sounded just like one of Uncle Cedric's chooks trying to push out an egg.

'Not funny!' *Waranmanha* proclaimed, all high and mighty like some bloody upper-class princess.

I tried to roll out from under the bush elegantly, but one of my dreadlocks got stuck on a twig. I had to yank out a huge clump of my hair just to get free.

Jalbri lost it, killing herself laughing, she said, 'You kids made me piss water.'

'What did ya take off for?' I asked.

'Tucker!' she exclaimed, proud of herself.

'*Mamany* (Crazy) bitch!' I snapped.

'Thought you knew that already,' *Mimi* piped up

'No eat, no think, no live.' *Jalbri* acted out her words like a Kindergarten teacher.

I scowled at her, feeling like a dumb bum.

We heard someone call out in greeting. The rising sun backlit three troublesome women: my lanky mother, the curvaceous Aunty Barbara and the hourglass Aunty Toots.

'We're coming!' *Jalbri* squawked excitedly, handing me her bloody *bungarra* to carry.

Gulyi was already running circles around them yelping with joy. *What a traitor, he'd do anything for a good feed.*

We must've looked like a real deadly mob. *Mimi* and *Jalbri* walked in front with the traitor, *Gulyi-Gulyi*, between them. *Ramu* strode on the left-hand side of *Mimi*. He was looking out in all directions and snorting, just to make sure everyone knew he was the one protecting us. I reckon he thought he was a pit-bull, not a *nguurru* (brumby).

Behind them, Toots was leading *Winthuly-Winthuly* with Mum, Aunty Barbara and *Waranmanha*. Her white stallion, *Wilara* (Moon), pranced perfectly beside his princess *Waranmanha*, who walked the desert like a dancing diva from one of those black and white movies.

I couldn't take my eyes off her; she was fascinating to watch. As I trudged behind everyone carrying the bloodied *bungarra* and trying to avoid the endless poop coming out of *Winthuly-Winthuly's* rear end, *Birri* walked behind me with her head down. I reckon she was depressed, looking at the 'show ponies' in front.

I couldn't hear any of the conversation going on until *Jalbri* stopped to address the mob, '*Kantiyala* (Ride him)! *Kantiyala*!'

In a flash, *Mimi* Lee was sitting tall on *Ramu*. '*Yagu*,' she said, offering *Jalbri* her hand so she could sit behind her.

I felt like crying at the thought of *Mimi* and *Jalbri* sitting skin to skin, just like they would've in the old days when *Mimi* was a little girl. But *Winthuly-Winthuly* wasn't having her *Jalbri* ride *Ramu*. She broke free from Aunty Toots and started spitting and showing her teeth.

Ramu was tensing his rump, ready to kick the teeth right out of that drooling mouth of hers, when *Jalbri* made soothing camel sounds. *Winthuly-Winthuly* then calmed down. 'Ta ta,' *Jalbri* commanded. *Winthuly-Winthuly* dropped her rear end, and to our surprise, *Jalbri* swung her leg over her neck.

She then turned to Aunty Toots, asking her to get on. *Winthuly-Winthuly's* eyes almost popped out. Talk about breaking the camel's back. Groaning, she struggled to stand with the weight of Aunty Toots. Then, as she straightened her long legs, the most enormous fart escaped and I copped a mouthful.

Mimi Lee faced Mum and said, '*Bidi-Bidi* (Butterfly), ride with me?'

Mum mounted with little protest from *Ramu*. I was shocked to see her place her arms around *Mimi's* waist. It didn't add up. What is 'Butterfly?'. And what about all the 'wrong way marriage' business? They were not meant to be talking or looking or being next to each other.

What the hell? I must have missed something.

Waranmanha and Barbara looked gorgeous together on *Wilara*. I chucked the *bungarra* onto *Birri's* rump and jumped on feeling pathetic. *Gulyi* had made a powerful friend in *Ramu* and chose to stick to him like a blowfly.

'Ride on!' *Jalbri* commanded.

Birri took off; she wasn't going to be shamed. Wow, it was great, we galloped full pelt leaving a red dust storm behind us.

I remembered Dad and Frankie's favourite film. I started singing at the top of my voice, '777 The Magnificent Seven[39]'. Mum, *Waranmanha*, Barbara, Toots and even *Mimi* Lee joined in. '777 The Magnificent Seven,' they sang. 'We are only seven but we're fighting to bring justice to our world.'

That was us alright. 'We are fighting to make a safe future and wipe away our past.' We all laughed. Suddenly I felt proud to be with this mob. We stormed into our new camp. A feast of bush tucker had been prepared for breakfast.

---

39   *777 The Magnificent Seven* – A 1960 American Western film.

Tea sweetened with condensed milk, wattle seed damper and bush fruits with baked *bungarra* were a delicious start to the day. Everyone was happy to be together again, except for Loke. You could never tell what was up with her. I don't even know why she came. She's a real user. I don't like her or trust her. She's not coping out here cos she's a druggie, and we have no grog, no pills and no petrol for her. And what's worse, she's been cutting herself again.

Jalbri called to the mob, 'Come in close and listen up.'

Everyone did except for Loke, who was sitting under a bush with her head down and back to us.

'This is a special time; you mob have to work together to save the future for our children.'

The theme song from 'The Magnificent Seven' kept running through my head. 'Yeah, and we're gonna wipe away the past.'

'*Bindamanha*,' *Jalbri* called out, trying to keep me in the present.

'You all know about the battle of the Great Serpents?'

'What happened to Derwen after he got burnt? Did they fix him in the city? Where are *Kulpan Karrangu* and the *Zalfinhi*?' My questions shot out of my mouth like bullets.

'*Barndi, barndi* (Good, good). Wait up. Just you listen. Then you hear right thing, proper time.' As *Jalbri* took a long deep breath, her scrawny tummy bulged, filling with air, and her eyes were no longer looking at us. Instead they were gazing into the distant past.

'*Kulpan Karrangu* had been waiting since that big trouble in the *Mangarikarra* (Dreamtime) for someone to come who didn't know nothing about our Lores and traditions to climb up that *Kuji Warnku*, cos that would set him free. Us fellas know the proper way to go up. Ya gotta break some branches off that special yellow bush. That one, he only grows there at the base of *Kuji Warnku*. Ya gotta shout out greetings to the Spirits and the Ancestors, same time beatin' the branches on the rock. No stoppin', keep going'. When all 'em little flowers fly high up into the sky, then ya know ya got permission to climb up. Not do proper job, then that *walhi* (no good) *Kulpan Karrangu*, he be set free. That Derwen fella, he just did that simple climb up there, didn't know nothin' about nothin', and he undid a hundred generations of asking for permission, all gone to dust and *Kulpan Karrangu* free.' As she spoke, her head shook.

And all I'd seen came back real vivid-like.

Her voice became deep and gravelly, I couldn't recognise it as hers anymore. All of us women huddled in closer. I started to panic cos some spooky kinda shit was going down.

'*Gurland* (don't be forgetting) that big fella *Kulpan Karrangu* was in charge of darkness, sleep and fire. Too many days that fire burnt right across the land. Too many animals and plants died, gone forever, finished. The sky was red, all day and night for a long time until darkness came and fear filled up everybody's heart. After big fear, then came big anger. Darkness covered up the whole earth, but still no one could sleep. No sleep, no dreaming their stories. Us *blackfellas* couldn't receive our Lore. Even them *whitefellas'* law lost all its power. All the peoples near and far got mad and sick with the sadness and fear. Anger and hatred filled up the human soul... still too many people, can't sleep.

'*Pulanyi Bulaing,* she made the rivers curve through our Country. But *Kulpan Karrangu* scarred the country with straight lines that cut through our sacred places. Those long, straight roads brought different, different troubles. They took our land and destroyed the Spirit of our people.'

In the sand in front of her, she drew the winding rivers making their way to the sea, and then she drew straight lines from the cities that criss crossed the whole country. Her lines even went beyond the land into the sea, straight lines, everywhere straight lines; the gentle curves of nature seemed lost. I knew what she meant. *Kulpan Karrangu* had reached out far beyond Australia. By boat and plane, he had infected the whole planet. Our planet was drying and dying. And humans everywhere on the planet found it hard to Dream and receive their Lores.

'Our Country's not the only one crying; the whole world's screaming and crying out. Sacred waters are poisoned, making everyone sick. And still, nobody's children can sleep. All the peoples have lost the way, or lost themselves, all *julgia* (broken). You kids doin' nothin', like the *marloo* (big red kangaroo) sitting under the tree in the hot midday sun, scratching themselves. Just sittin' there, ya heads noddin', listening to that *walhi* (no good) music thing stuck in ya ears like chewin' gum. Can't hear ya Country cry. Don't hear "Sacred *Jila*" cry. No one even hear their *yagu's* (mother's) cry. All deaf, blind, lost and *julgia* (broken). All *julgia*.

'*Wakaj Kanarri* (The Finishing) is here. You womans gotta end all this trouble. Turn ya eyes to "What's Up". The *Jirdilungu* (Milky Way) to the *Muniwarri* (Seven Sisters) and the *Djulpan* (Southern Cross). Youse don't need to be afraid, cos we got the *Bundara Murungkurr* (Star Spirit Children).' She pointed at *Waranmanha* and me.

Shit, I thought.

'Them girls got them *Milkanarri* (Seeing Stone), they gonna guide youse mob. Bring all them *bundarra* (stars) back to the Dreamtime. You girls must be big like a big *yagu* (mother) for all the different, different peoples. For the whole world. Get me?

'The *mitimiti* (full moon) is coming. Youse know what ya have ta do and youse *Murungkurr* (Spirit Children),' she said, looking at *Waranmanha* and me. 'We got to learn you too many things before *Wakaj Kanarri* (The Finishing).'

Suddenly I had *kalakala* (diarrhoea). I leant over and told my sister. My guts were rumbling. Jumping up I ran. *Waranmanha* followed with *Gulyi* hot on my heels.

I was dumping a truckload of poop behind a small bush while trying to keep *Gulyi's* nose out of it.

'Are you okay?' *Waranmanha* asked.

'Are you kidding?' I snapped back.

'Did you look?' she asked.

I knew she had seen me hold the *Milkanarri* against my chest.

'Of course I did. You can't leave me!' Now I was on my knees praying for the *Milkanarri* to be wrong.

'Whatever happens, I'll never leave you.'

'Bullshit! You are so full of it. I've seen everything. You think I'm an idiot?'

'I'm not scared,' she said, trying to reassure me.

Suddenly, a *Jin.gi* (Spirit Being) appeared in front of us. Instantly my tears of anguish melted into awe.

'Who are you?' *Waranmanha* asked.

The *Jin.gi* blinked her soulful eyes. Her translucence fluttered on the wind and she disappeared.

Passing me some leaves to clean myself, *Waranmanha* looked straight at me and said, 'See, that's a sign. What more do you want? Let's get out of here, we need to be alone.'

I nodded.

'I'll get some tucker. Be back in a sec.' She ran off and *Gulyi* chased after her.

I stood there alone, in silence.

25. Junki and Nypni

Waranmanha ran back with my 'body and soul' bag slung over her shoulder and *Jalbri's minggarri* (wood bowl for carrying water) in her arms full of yummy bush tucker, and she had the biggest smile on her face. At that moment, I realised how much I loved her.

'Let's go?' she asked. The billy hanging from her little finger fell to the ground.

'Ya think of everything.'

'Yeah, pretty much.'

I picked up the billy and offered to carry the *minggarri* for her. She held it tight and started to jog. I ran beside her.

'Ya know if I'd been the one with the fancy shoes, you would have eaten my dust in the 400 metres last year.'

'C'mon then, show me what you've got.' She sped off.

'Not fair, I'm not ready,' I shouted, running after her. I didn't really want to win.

Just being together felt so good. Our new camp was a bit too close to Help Canyon for my liking, even though we were on the opposite end of *Kuji Warnku* (Porcupine Rock) on the easterly side.

'What about there?' *Waranmanha* asked.

'Looks good.'

A small waterhole hugged the bottom of the enormous rock face. The reflections made the rock look like it was floating on water like some ancient stone ship.

Waranmanha got to the water's edge first. She'd filled the billy and washed her hands and face. Scraping up some dried twigs, she set up the fire. I stood watching her, amazed at how good she was at this sort of thing. It took me ages to work out how to start a fire without matches.

'Are you still crook?' she asked, looking concerned.

'I just feel a bit sick.'

'This will make you feel better,' she said, handing me some damper.

'Oh, guess what I've got,' I said reaching down into my bag that was on the ground between us. 'Sister Euphrates' tea and a tiny bit of cherry jam.' I was excited to show her my stuff. I sprinkled the tea into the billy.

'It smells beautiful,' she said, sniffing in deeply over the boiling billy.

Handing her Sister's little tin cup, I bowed my head in respect and said, 'Princess *Waranmanha*.'

'No, that's fine, you have it,' she protested, trying to grab the enamel mug that I was going to use.

'Stop it! Look at this.' I passed her my *je t'aime* spoon.

Straight away she ran her thumbs over the indentation. 'It's beautiful,' she said with a faraway look in her eyes. 'Oh no!' she interrupted. Then I saw her wince. 'I think I've got my period.'

'Got stuff?' I asked her.

'Noo!' she rolled her eyes, annoyed.

'I do.' Reaching again into my string bag, I pulled out a little packet of tampons. Mum hated me using them, but too bad.

'Thanks Bindi.'

'Don't call me Bindi.' I laughed.

'Should I use paperbark to line my knickers?'

'Yeah, do that if you don't mind a bug in ya bum. Hang on a minute.' I found Dad's cotton hanky. Even though I'd washed it after using it on *Gulyi*, it was badly stained by the herbs, mud and ash. I felt shame handing it to her.

She tenderly raised it to her full lips and kissed the 'A' Dad had sewn on when he was little.

'You sure?'

'Of course, it's yours.' What else could I say; she obviously loved him, maybe more than I did.

'When's yours due?' Her question immediately made me throw up.

She walked me back to the fire and poured me a mug of tea sweetened with cherry jam. I felt better straight away.

'I think I'm pregnant,' I blurted.

'What?' she responded. 'Who to?'

'Manu Tollie.'

She smiled, and then I told her the whole story with her 'oo-ing' and 'ahh-ing' all the way.

'The *Milkanarri* (Seeing Stone) showed me you were pregnant, but I didn't understand what it meant.'

188

'Really!' I was shocked. 'Do you think *Jalbri* knows?'

'Yeah, of course she does. But don't worry, she'll help you.'

'Oh God, she already thinks I'm stupid.'

'Stop it,' *Waranmanha* insisted. 'She knows exactly *who you are*.'

'Yeah, thanks,' I said sarcastically. 'Maybe Manu won't want me. I might be a lousy mother and wife.'

'*Bindamanha*,' she said firmly, looking straight into my eyes, 'he knows *who you are* and is rowing across the sea to be with you.'

I was sad, excited, happy and sick all at the same time.

I was getting hot and my energy started to soar. 'Wanna go swimming?'

'You check it out first,' *Waranmanha* said, smiling at me.

'Are you admitting that I'm the best diver?' Before she could answer, I started to scale the rock, heading for the highest ledge.

'Show off!' she shouted from the bottom.

Standing with my tippy toes on the edge of the rock ledge, I breathed in, bringing my hands into position, when suddenly I caught sight of movement in the water below. Whatever it was, it quickly sunk down into the deep and left a large ripple that lapped out to the edge of the water.

Instantly, all thoughts of diving in vanished. Instead I sat on the ledge and dangled my feet over the edge, peering into the deep pool below, trying to spot that thing again.

'You okay?' *Waranmanha* yelled.

'Did you see it?'

'No,' she yelled.

'There's somethin' big in the water and it looked right at me!'

'We didn't ask for permission!'

We both started to panic.

'You do it!' I begged, feeling the panic settling in. *I dare not move.*

'I am *Waranmanha*. I'm standing on Country with my twin sister *Bindamanha*. We are sorry we forgot to ask for permission to be here on your Country. We are *Bardi* people and humbly ask for permission to be on Mangala Lands. Would all you Spirits and Ancestors protect us? Please?'

Just then a palm-sized rock on the ledge beside me fell into the water. As I moved, trying to block its fall, another fell. The loud plop sounded like gunfire. I managed to grab the next one before it fell and noticed that someone had painted a *Jin.gi* (Spirit Being) on one side.

'*Waranmanha*!'

'What's up?' she yelled, looking distressed.

'Someone's painted *Jin.gi's* on all these rocks,' I yelled as I turned over the rocks lying beside me.

'You're kidding me,' she yelled, scaling the rock to join me. '*Bindamanha*, look here, I reckon there's something behind this?'

There was a large rock about waist height that seemed to be blocking an entrance to a small cave.

'Give us a hand,' she said, trying to push it aside by herself. Together we pivoted the rock onto its edge and opened it like a door.

On the inner face of the rock there was a beautiful painting of a *Jin.gi*.

'Wow, look at that!'

'It's beautiful,' *Waranmanha* replied, running her long finger over the area where the *Jin.gi's* mouth would be.

'Shit, look in there!'

'No swearing!' she snapped. 'You'll bring trouble on us.'

As our eyes adjusted, we could see two skeletons lying on bush beds. Both skulls were surrounded by long, white, wavy hair. Studying their dress and tools, we could tell that they were women. But the weird thing was, they had hundreds of small rocks piled next to them and each had a *Jin.gi* painted on one side. These women must have been alive in Derwen's time.

'What are you thinking?' *Waranmanha's* voice had a ring of excitement to it.

Tired of standing, I moved one bony foot over and cleared a little space to sit.

'You can't do that!' she protested.

'By the look of these old girls, they seem pretty happy to have me sit with them.'

'Don't be stupid, skulls always look happy, you need skin to look miserable.'

We burst out laughing.

The cave was dark and musty. Little creatures had been feasting on the old girls and pooping everywhere!

'*Waranmanha*?' I asked. 'Could you get my bag and some twigs? I wanna get the fire going so we can have a real good look around.'

She was back quick smart. We started our fire in their old fireplace on the pile of old ashes. There was even an old billy can.

With the fire lit, the cave became real homely. The smoke was drawn outside by a large crack near the entrance. The fire's light danced on the walls and made the painted stories flicker like an old movie.

'I'm going to try talking to them,' she said.

'How?' I asked.

'With the *Milkanarri* (Seeing Stone).'

'I didn't know you could do that. I thought it just showed you stuff. Who else have ya spoken to?' I asked.

Ignoring me, she got out her *Milkanarri*, and I followed her example. She asked a question and before we knew it, we were there, talking to the old girls.

Junki and *Nypni* were beautiful. Their long, wavy, white hair was stunning against their dark-brown skin. Their eyes shone with excitement as they told us they were keepers of Help Canyon. Their long fingers moved gracefully, pointing this way and that as they recounted amazing tales.

Watching them, I was flooded with a great sadness that *Waranmanha* and I would be separated again. The *Jin.gi* had been painted to protect themselves and any strangers who came to Help Canyon because *Kulpan Karrangu* and the *Zalfinhi* were not the only evil forces here.

We knew that the *one that feathers stick to* still lived at the next rocky outcrop, and Dr Pilawal used to live south-east of here. But now, *gulyba* (sick) ones had come to this sacred land to make trouble.

While we sat with them, *Junki* and *Nypni* sang us past the boundaries of day and night, Heaven and Earth, past the billion stars of the Milky Way and into the Silence, thick with possibilities. I couldn't tell if I was awake, asleep, entranced or in fact dead. All timeliness ended and *I was*.

Like the striking of an ancient gong, I heard my name 'Lucy Lucky-Child' repeat its never-ending chime through all the worlds of time. Falling like a shard from a stone spearhead, I sliced through the past and future and landed clumsily back in the present.

Suddenly, we could hear *Jalbri* bleating from the canyon floor. Quickly thanking *Junki* and *Nypni*, we cast our eyes down, showing our respect. Then *Waranmanha* and I ran out of the cave.

'We're up here!' we yelled in unison.

'I know where youse are. Come down,' *Jalbri* ordered.

We thought we were in deep shit. As we clambered down, all the women stood watching us.

'Have we missed something?' I said under my breath to my sister.

'Beats me,' she answered nervously.

As soon as our feet hit the sand, we 'straightened up'.

'You met *Junki* and *Nypni*?' *Jalbri* asked, looking unnaturally happy.

'Yes, they said we should take the *Jin.gi* stones for protection,' *Waranmanha* hastily added.

'That's what we came for. All campin' here now. Come, I learn you stuff, show you special place. Eat, drink first.'

Waranmanha ran on ahead with *Jalbri* to get food.

I followed slowly, weighed down by all the painted stones I'd stuffed into my string bag. I thought the heat of the day was playing tricks with my mind cos I felt like I was being watched. Glancing back up to the opening of the cave, I saw our two friendly *pulyarr* (ghosts) *Nypni* and *Junki* waving at me. Smiling, I waved back at them. From the highest ledge, a large rock plopped into the water below. I heard sniffing and caught sight of a flicker. I thought I saw something break through the surface and taste the air.

Scared, I ran.

26. The Keeper's Tears

We set, off leaving the women at the waterhole. As usual, *Jalbri* started to sing. In spite of trying to pick up some words by imitating the sounds, it was way too hard. Besides, we just sounded like a swarm of mozzies.

Mabandaya hardnay wangla yabadda.

Haitrai yabadda haya nagnada.

Mabandaya hardnaya wangla yabadda.

Haitrai yabadda haya nagnada ...

It sorta got into our bones and we started a hip-hop battle behind *Jalbri's* back as we followed her to somewhere around the back of Help Canyon.

194

Breaking first was *Waranmanha*. She pulled off her lackey (elastic) band and her long, wavy hair looked super cool and sexy as she swayed her tight butt in a crisp moonwalk. Her long arms emphasised the gestures she made with her elegant hands. She was *mamany jambarn* (crazy fast).

Compared to her, my moves were more Indi. My bum and boobs seemed to have gotten bigger already. I was right in the middle of a horror move with my legs spread in a deep knee squat, my left hand doing a heart pump and my right doing a strangle hold around my neck when *Jalbri* turned around.

I fell backwards landing on my bum. *Jalbri* looked straight at me and started to dance. Foot stomping, hand and head waving *blackfella* style, all the while chanting:

Mabandaya handnaya wangla yabadda.

Haitrai yabadda haya nagnada ...

She didn't miss a beat; she was awesome. That foot stomping looked almost like a moonwalk as she shuffled right up to my toes. Stopping, she gave us a wicked smile. We clapped, wishing we had filmed it. *Jalbri* had won that round. We showed her how to do a high five and the Yankee fist knock.

'*Yanajimanha* (Coming)!'

Happy now, we followed her.

'Just over there,' she said, pointing to the back face of Help Canyon.

We had walked real far. This side of the Canyon had a different energy to the other side. It seemed brighter and freer, as it lay open to the vast plains that led north to the Top End.

Without warning, *Jalbri* started running—something was up. We followed close behind, our imaginations running ahead of us. At a deafening pitch, she yelled out the call to Country, the Spirits and the Ancestors. The sound of her voice was amplified as it echoed off Help Canyon's sheer iron rock wall. We were freaking out.

Enraged, she broke off some branches from a *bilabirdi* (eucalypt) and started to sweep a path up to the rock, wailing nonstop.

We thought someone had died.

'*Jalbri*! How can we help?'

Our question seemed to make things worse. She started running, screaming and crying. We'd never seen our *Jalbri* like this.

She threw herself onto the ground at the base of the Canyon and curled herself into a little ball like a baby in the womb and sobbed uncontrollably.

'Get help!' I ordered *Waranmanha*.

She took off like the ground was on fire.

Mimi had already heard her *yagu's* screams. She'd mustered the women and rode full pelt. *Ramu* was snorting hard as she dismounted. *Mimi* immediately broke into an eerie wail.

Shit, we didn't know what was happening or what to do.

Waranmanha and the other women poured into the clearing. Everyone was wailing and beating their chests except my sister and me. Wailing wasn't giving us anything to go on.

My anxiety was too much to handle.

'What the fuck is happening?' I yelled at the top of my lungs in a desperate measure to get some control.

Everyone gave me the 'evil eye', except *Jalbri* who was still lost in her own stuff.

Mimi spoke clearly as a torrent of tears tickled down her well-defined black cheeks like a spring rising out of the deep. Pointing to the rock wall, she said, 'See that dark-blue stain on the rock?'

I nodded.

'This place is the source of our sacred water. Never before has there been a story of this Living Spring drying up. It marks the beginning of a new time in history for our planet. It will take the tears of this tribe for generations to come to replenish its source. If we do not weep and do *mama* (sacred song) then the Spirit of the Living Spring will leave our planet forever and all the peoples of the earth will perish.'

I stood in stunned silence. I wanted to ask why *Jalbri* was so upset. But *Mimi* must have read my mind. '*Jalbri* is the keeper, so she feels responsible. If the Living Spring dies, none of *Jalbri's* descendants will live to see *Wakaj Kanarri* (The Finishing). Her lineage will come to an end and the gates of the *Jirdilungu* (Milky Way) will be closed to them forever more.'

My mind screamed *what the fuck*! But I dared not give voice to my outrage.

The thought of *Jalbri* leaving us like this was unbearable. Choking on my tears, I calmed my mind and asked, 'Can I die instead of her?'

'No baby, this is not your job.' If *Mimi* had called me 'baby' before, I would have been angry with her, but now it made me feel loved. I threw my arms around her and wept like her little grandchild would.

Jalbri's frail voice grabbed our attention. She had propped herself up as best as she could. *Ngurliyimanha* (Crying together), we gathered around.

'*Nganggurnmanha malardiyimanha* (Listen up, I am becoming tired of searching).'

She looked really tired, not like the woman who'd just been dancing with us.

Looking at *Mimi*, *Jalbri* said, in Mangala, '*Mamikatija wajarrirna nyawayi mulnyi* (I can't see the Country in the dark).'

The sun was up real bright. *Mimi* left me and ran to her *yagu*, yelling in Mangala and English, '*Marraja ngapa kurntal*, get me water, daughter!'

Mum, Barbara, *Waranmanha* and I were meant to respond to her call, but Mum didn't go for the water, instead she went and sat beside *Jalbri*, letting her rest her now old, heavy-looking head on Mum's shoulder. Barbara wasn't leaving either; she sat down and started rubbing her grandmother's feet. *Waranmanha* and I stood frozen to the spot.

Water appeared, from where I didn't know, and Patty Mae carried it reverently in a small, wooden bowl. *Mimi* carefully took the vessel. The red nail polish on her fingers looked like a cluster of gems around its tiny base, and then our *Mimi* placed the wooden lip against *Jalbri's* and fed her gently, sweetly, like you would a tiny bird you feared might take flight.

With each sip, she sang softly, '*Yagu kunanyarri. Yagu kunanyarri* (My mummy is drinking. My mummy is drinking).'

Every time *Jalbri* took a sip, she said under her breath, '*Miyarnu.*'

The next thing I knew, the old girl came to life. I don't think Patty Mae had special 'life-giving' water in that tiny bowl. I think it was *Mimi's* words and love that brought her *yagu* back.

The light had come back into *Jalbri's* eyes. Her long, bony finger beckoned my sister and me to come in close. Mum's hand reached out from behind *Jalbri* and squeezed my shoulder. Somehow it softened my heart towards her.

Waranmanha sat next to her mum who kissed her lovingly on the cheek. We'd both grown up over the last few days, and the family boundaries had grown too. Now I understood in our Language that *yagu* could mean your biological mother, your Aunty, your grandmother, your great grandmother, or even a friend or respected Elder. The feeling of 'mother' transcends just pushin' a baby out ya bum.

Sitting beside *Jalbri*, I looked at the mob gathered in front of her and it felt like she was getting me ready to take her place. She spoke in Mangala and English. Even though you could see she was weak, her power was still there rumbling like a volcano about to erupt.

198

'*Minili wantula*. We will always stay together.'

'*Mingala ngana wutan*. Our tears are running.'

'*Minili turlpu kunpulu*. We are together in heart and blood. We are family.'

'Who's ready to battle with *Kulpan Karrangu* to get back our *living water*?'

Waranmanha and I shouted the loudest, 'We are!' Our hands shot into the air like revolutionaries.

Louanna and Polly Tipple echoed our cry. Aunty Toots was fired up too. Waving her hands in support, she called out something in the Language from the tall-nosed religion, '*Ya Baha* ...'

I noticed that *Mimi*, our mums and the older women all sat real quiet.

'This battle is not with *Kulpan Karrangu*.'

'Typical,' I whispered to *Waranmanha*.

Mimi leant over and tapped me on the shoulder. Gee, this was like being with the nuns in church.

Jalbri continued, 'The battle between *Pulanyi Bulaing* and *Kulpan Karrangu* is inside us. The sacred *kartiny* (sandalwood tree) is dead. Our people's dreams have died with it. We have become the people of *ngapa yakurr juljul* (the dirty water soak).'

Silent tears rolled down the faces of *Mimi* and her *kurntals* (daughters), Aunty Toots and hers, even Patty Mae's and Sandy Gibb's. But not Polly Tipple's, she was too busy trying to screw her leg back on straight.

'You womans must become the new keepers of our *living waters* here in your hearts, and here where your *yagu* carried you inside her.' Her large, thin, black hand reached out and placed itself firmly on my tummy. I could feel myself turning red with shame and the little one inside my womb moved towards her great, great grandmother's cool hand.

I couldn't appreciate the moment; all I felt was shame.

'When youse all living inside your *yagu's* tummy, youse were swimmin' in the *Mangarikarra* (Dreamtime) safe and peaceful like.'

Mimi, Mum, Aunty Barbara and the other women sang the *mama*—that ancient sacred creation song spoke to my baby. My eyes connected with my sister's and instantly I knew that I should name my baby *Waranmanha*.

'Youse womans come back home cos youse *are* the new *Jilas*. My work is finished. You be the *living waters* for that big world mob.' Her eyes were sparkling. 'Lucky-Child,' she said, pointing her lower lip at me.

'What?' I had almost forgotten that name. In reaction, I blurted out, 'You know us Lucky-Childs are *julgia* (broken)! Why were our kids stolen if we're so great?' Talk about going into fight with a knife in both hands.

The women gasped.

Again, I felt so much shame. I never thought that question would just pop out, especially right now.

Trying to avoid my question, *Mimi* asked us girls to get some food.

Jalbri stopped us leaving. 'No more food. Me finished with eating.'

'Come on, *Jalbri*,' I pleaded.

Mimi stopped me too, explaining that this was the 'traditional way'. *Jalbri* was preparing herself to leave.

'But that's suicide!' I glanced at *Waranmanha*, but she was sitting on the ground folded up, sobbing into her knees. Her arms were wrapped tightly around her long shinbones; she'd seriously shut down and it didn't look as if she was coming out any time soon.

I felt *mamany* (crazy) that everyone was accepting *Jalbri's* decision. I couldn't hack it. I ran up and grabbed her hand. '*Jalbri*, I don't want to live without you!'

With a simple motion of her bottom lip, she indicated that everyone should leave us.

As *Mimi* was turning to leave, *Jalbri* beckoned her to come close. She asked her to get some sap from the Twin Dragon Trees at the soak.

200

'What's that for?'

Mimi answered me, 'She will drink it instead of water until the end.'

'You're not fucking poisoning her!'

'No, I'm not fucking poisoning her. This is her Mother Tree and will give her energy and clarity until she passes.'

Her posh voice and calm manner put me right in my place. 'Sorry, *Mimi*.'

Before I could say more, she added, 'I know you are. Don't waste time. *Jalbri* wants to talk to you. *Ramuuu*!' Her voice echoed against the canyon wall. *Ramu* could be heard arriving and then heading for the soak at great speed.

'Daughta, come close.'

'I love you, *Jalbri*. I don't want you to go.' Trying to look at her and not cry was super hard. I kept blinking to clear my tears so I could focus, and when I did, her bright eyes were looking straight into my *rayi* (soul).

'I'm going back home to my *Jirdilungu* (Milky Way). My work here is all finished up.'

'What about me?' I pleaded.

'You see that star up there, *kara* (west) side of *Kurriji pa Yajula* (Dragon Tree Soak)? That's *my* home. You know where my home is now, you can come visit me anytime.'

I smiled at her words, even though my heart was breaking.

'How do I get up there?' I asked, feeling a great loneliness creep into my heart. I felt like a tiny wooden boat without a rudder, lost in an endless sea of grief that was slowly seeping through the crack in my broken soul. *Jalbri* took my hand, saying, 'Look up, if you hook your *rayi* (soul) onto my *bundarra*. You will never drown.'

I woke from my daydream with my hands raised and my head facing the sky. Dropping my arms and feeling dejected, I looked into *Jalbri's* eyes again.

'*Bindamanha,* look for my star in the night sky. When the big rain comes, ya drink that one and you'll taste my words. It be like medicine for ya. In the *jurdu* (smoke) from your camp fire, you'll see this old face in there. When you hear *kurr* (the sound of the wind), listen for me. I'll be singin' the *mama* (sacred song). Talk to me, I'll be listening for ya.'

'What do I do when you and *Waranmanha* have gone?'

Although *Waranmanha* looked shut down, her ears were still working. 'I'll always be with you, *Bindamanha,*' her muffled voice slipped out from between her knees.

'She and me are going Home. Not easy to go up. Lot of pain in here,' *Jalbri* added, beating her chest. 'Hardest thing, to leave you.'

My ears ached hearing her words and my tongue was tied real tight.

'You got big journey in front of ya with that little *Waranmanha* inside ya.' Her smile looked strangely bittersweet. 'In this world, many things *julgia* (broken) for long time now. Even long before the *kartija* (*whitefellas*) came. Every time ya do somethin', always be thinkin' *thubarnimanha*, straighten up. If ya lookin' for a *Jila*, ya can't be strayin' off the straightway. Goin' this way and that, ya not find *Jila*, ya get proper lost. You not find the straightway, ya die, all finished up. That's life.

'Everyone want ta go home, but the closer ya get, there's no more this way or that, only one way to ya front door. The trouble between the Great Serpents made the mans and womans make their own laws, but *walhi* (no good) for people anymore. From that time 'til now, children been taken in different, different ways. The straightway gone, lost long ago.

'You, Lucy Lucky-Child, will change up these things forever.'

Interrupting, I yelled, 'I hate that name!'

'Yes, I know,' she said softly. 'That is your name in the *kartija* world. Here and at Home, on Country, and upstairs,' she said pointing to the Heavens, 'you always *Bindamanha.*'

202

I was breathing heavily and my ears were on fire, but I had to keep listening.

'*Bindamanha,* that wrong-way pattern has happened and is happenin' to our children. You will know it too. Too much hard lessons.'

My hands gently rubbed my tummy, and silently I sent a message of love to my baby *Waranmanha.*

'First ya gotta make up ya mind to LIVE or DIE. If DIE, then finish, but still not go straight Home. If LIVE, then be alive, not half alive, half dead. I go Home soon. You must LIVE, no choice.'

Rolling my eyes, I felt tricked again. *No choice.* There was never any choice for me.

Jalbri continued, 'Thoughts must be straight, not crooked. Have ta be knowin' who ya really are. No doubt. No hidin'. No lyin'. No cheatin'. Must be pure like the *living water* from the *Jilas.* You will wait here in nowhere land until your proper time. No choice. Ya bring back the right-way, the *straight-path.* Your *Mimi* will help you.

'Time here feels too slow, but in *Jirdilungu* (Milky Way), your life and all the peoples before you, one blink, all finished. Soon I will blink and you'll be Home with us.'

My sister and I sat tongue-tied in stunned silence.

Jalbri dismissed us, asking us to bring our *yagu's.*

Like robots we got up, and without speaking a word we motioned to them to go be with her.

'*Bidi-Bidi.*'

That must've been Mum's traditional name, although I'd never heard anyone use it before.

Mum knelt closely to *Jalbri,* took both her hands in hers and leant over so that her *yagu* could kiss the crown of her head while she kissed her mother's hands. My senses were in overdrive as I strained to hear what was being said.

Finally, when Mum sat upright, she looked tall, graceful and more radiant than I'd ever seen before.

Barbara moved in close. *Jalbri* said something to her that made her turn around and look at *Waranmanha* with tears in her eyes. She turned back to *Jalbri* and nodded her head repeatedly.

I was starting to feel annoyed that we were not included in the discussion. I didn't notice *Jalbri* throw one of *Nypni's* painted stones at me until it hit my cheek. 'What's that for?' I asked as I picked up the thumbnail sized painting of the *Jin.gi*, and without thinking, I held it against my lips and kissed it like a relic.

'If you want a good life,' she said in a loud voice so that everyone could hear, 'you gotta learn how to say *sorry*. You have ta forgive, even if they don't deserve it. You gotta love without wantin' nothin' back and you gotta be thankful for everythin' cos everythin' happens to learn ya somethin'. It's easy to be thankful for good things. Many good learnin's from *bad* things.'

Jalbri's words hit me like *malgar* (women's fighting stick).

'What about payback?' Oh God. I couldn't believe I'd said that. What was wrong with me? How dare I ask that when she's done revenge against *the one that feathers stick to*.

Before I could draw breath to apologise, *Jalbri* said, 'When you do revenge, killing and payback, you've gone off the straightway, doesn't matter who you are. Ya trade ya good heart to win, always big with punishment in the end. Someone or somethin' will be taken from you. Then ya have ta stay down on Earth until you find *the way* again, otherwise can't go up.'

'What punishment did you get?' As soon as the question left my mouth I couldn't believe what I'd said!

The sound of shocked women tutting was light on the air. In an attempt to distract myself, I put the little *Jin.gi* stone I'd been clutching back into my pouch and shifted around nervously. That's when I felt something stiff underneath my knee. Sitting back slightly, I reached down and pulled out two small playing cards. A black five of Spades and a red nine of Hearts. Before anyone saw them, I quickly shoved them into my pouch.

The first thing that leapt into my head when I saw the five of Spades was Dad's grave-digging job. It paid well but he threw it in after two weeks cos he couldn't handle thinking that maybe he was burying his family. He'd come home, stand his spade inside the front door and start effing and blinding, saying 'Nobody's gonna shove me underground in a dirty great hole.'

Finding two playing cards in the middle of the Great Sandy Desert had to be some kind of omen. As I gathered my thoughts, I noticed Polly Tipple standing in front of *Jalbri* all lopsided, her wooden stump sinking into the soft sand.

'Mummy says hello Mrs *Jalbri*.' That's Polly, she's a real funny bird. Back in Broome, she chatters nonstop to her mum. If she's not brushing her hair, she'd be polishing the trinkets she'd found to sell at the markets. That's how she makes a crust. Not bad, considering. My mum tried to get her Government help, but with no family and no birth papers, she couldn't prove that she existed. So, we all look out for her. Crazy thing is, there's lots of people living out bush who can't prove they were ever born.

Jalbri smiled at her real gentle-like. 'Hello Olive,' she said, looking to Polly's right-hand side as if Olive was standing there. 'Your mummy's real proud of ya Polly, and she wants me ta find ya an earth mummy ta help look after ya.'

'I want my mummy,' she said, holding on real tight to her tragic-looking cloth teddy. It's made out of old bandages from the Leprosarium. Its head and legs hang limply either side of her closed fist cos most of the stuffing has fallen out. Its eyes are now two grubby marks where the buttons had been, and its left ear is gross cos she sucks on it to get to sleep. I felt sorry for Polly. Her undies always smelt of urine or worse, but she's got a smile that hardship can't wipe away; the smallest things thrill her.

205

Barbara's hips swayed confidently as she walked up and stood on Polly's left. Everyone knew Polly's right side was permanently occupied by her mummy, Olive. Barbara looked like a two-bob watch with a Rolex complex. That was how Dad described her when she waltzed into the hospital in front of Mum that time *Waranmanha* and I both broke our arm.

'Polly darling, Olive wants me to be your earth mummy, do you?' Before Polly could answer, like a typical sales woman, Barbara made a devastating pitch. 'I have a sewing machine at home and I'll make you the prettiest dresses. You can have *Waranmanha's* room.'

Polly accepted the offer with a *maminy* (stupid) grin.

Waranmanha let out a screech of sheer pain. Confused, her eyes followed her new sister and her fake mum. I knew she felt like that bitch Barbara was replacing her before she'd even died. 'That's not fa ...' My sister stopped herself, choking on the word 'fair'.

Our mum, Mary, grabbed my sister by the arm, and smiling like the Virgin Mary, she said, 'You know I'm your mother and always will be.'

What about me? This was proper *mamany gurna* (crazy shit). *Oh My God!* I started to spew.

Those words were like raindrops in a drought for *Waranmanha*. She smiled *divinely* at her Mum. But for me, they were like molten lava that seared my soul. An overwhelming sense of aloneness flooded in until my skin felt tight with sadness. I could see myself destined to walk this earth alone and unloved, just like that sad figure etched into the rock by the *Bulyaman* (Sorcerer) at *Walgahna* (Walga Rock).

27. What's Up?

Mimi returned hurriedly with the Dragon Tree nectar. She smiled as she passed Barbara fussing over Polly Tipple. Watching her approach, I was itching to know what would become of Polly and Barbara. My fingers reached into my pouch for my *Milkanarri* (Seeing Stone).

Just at that moment, *Mimi* strode past. 'Don't do it!' Her sergeant major voice bounced off my eardrum.

The *Milkanarri* slipped out of my fingers, but I quickly swooped it up and popped it back into its pouch.

'Has she been troublesome?' *Mimi* asked *Jalbri*, who just smiled as she sipped the sap from her Mother Tree. Straight away the 'life' came back into her. It was magic.

'Can I have a sip?' I wanted to try it.

'No fucking poison for you!' *Mimi* snapped back. She was in a bad mood about something. In her left hand she was holding two mining lease stakes. The short four-centimetre square pegs had a metal band over the top imprinted with site numbers '56' and '49', and there was Chinese writing across the top.

'*Yagu*, I found this one,' she said, holding up number fifty-six, 'sticking out of our Burial Mound and forty-nine at the back of our sacred *Kurriji pa Yajula* (Dragon Tree Soak). *Yagu*, did you see the Chinese?'

'Yes, four Chinamans came with two *walhi kartija* (no good *whitefellas*). They told me I finish here. Already land sold to Chinamans.' *Jalbri's* eyes were flashing like daggers. 'I told them fellas, this Our Land, Our Ancestral Land. Told him about the Twin Dragon Trees, Chinamans look real interested, but them *kartija* rude to me. He push me, say, "All you *blackfellas* want somethin' for nothin'". I tell 'em no, I'm Keeper of the Soak. I look after.' They said, "You boongs don't look after nothing". Then he said, "See these fellas," pointin' at the Chinamans, "they will look after real good. Next year there'll be a whole city here, what've boongs done in 40,000 years?"'

'Shit, how dare he! Who were they?' *Mimi* was furious. 'What did they buy?'

Sadly, *Jalbri* said, 'Our Sacred *Jila*.'

'WHAAT!' *Mimi* interrupted. 'Our Burial Mound?'

An ever-increasing chorus of rebellion rose up from our gathered mob.

'Them fellas really know what they want. *Kartija* (*whitefella*) says they pay plenty big money for good sweet water. Them Chinamans want all the good stuff, copper, iron, and I told 'em we got no gold but they want gas. I told 'em *Winthuly* got plenty.'

'Fracking! You're kidding me!' *Mimi* erupted.

'That's what the Bossman said, deal with Prime Minister, all done.'

Mimi was as cranky as a cut snake. 'We've been fighting for over a hundred bloody years for the right to look after this land. What fucking difference has it made?' She hissed as if possessed by *Kulpan Karrangu* himself. 'I want to curse them.' *Mimi's* tight butt fell on the red earth. The little stars on the cuff of her black jeans created their own landscape on the desert floor.

It was distressing to see her like this—our iron maiden was melting like butter.

'What's up?' *Jalbri* said, from out of nowhere.

'Not now, *Yagu.*' *Mimi* sighed.

'What's up?' *Jalbri* insisted.

'Big things,' *Mimi* said in a childish voice, eyes looking up and her arms spread out wide hugging the sky.

'What's down?' *Jalbri* continued.

'Small things.' *Mimi* relaxed, grinning as she bent over to touch the red earth with the palms of her hands.

'What's in the middle, *Miyarnu*?'

'Nothing,' *Mimi* said with her strength and vigour returned.

'Hey *kurntal* (daughter), you know all about the *kartija* (*whitefella*) law from Uni. You must look at 'what's up', to the heavens, to our *Jirdilungu* (Milky Way), our *Djulpan* (Southern Cross). Look to the 'big things', our Dreaming and our Lore. That'll guide you proper way.

'Them mans lookin' at 'what's down'. They are after the 'small things'— money, dirt, air and water. All these things are easily lost without the Spirit, the Dreaming and the Lore! Those fellas lookin' at what's 'in the middle' make nothin' of their life and are led by others to nowhere. They live this day to that day. They never look up and know nothin' bout nothin'.

'*Miyarnu*, my *kurntal*, now you are the traditional custodian of *Kurriji pa Yajula* (Dragon Tree Soak). Patty Mae will live here and protect our Sacred

209

Soak.' *Jalbri* then called *Mimi* by all her traditional name and titles, as recorded in the *Jirdilungu* (Milky Way). *Mimi* sang *mama* (sacred song) in words for our ears only. And then, as if responding to an ancient tone, the high-pitched angelic voice of Polly Tipple soared to 'What's Up' like Yunupingu[40].

'The South Wind has come into my life once before

It brought pain and sorrow

It took my mother from this shore.

'Sing out my sisters to your loved ones gone before

Cos I've seen the dark clouds rising

Like never before.

'Sing out them Spirits like never before

Sing for our Country and our Culture

Our Dreaming and our Lore.

'Sweet North Wind' take our *Jalbri* and sisters high above

Bless us with your gifts of Forgiveness and Love

We sing out for your help to make the world a better place

For Country and our people and the whole human race.

Struck dumb, our mob just stood gawking at her. She looked like an idiot, but she's deep as. For the first time I realised how she'd suffered. Because us mob didn't take her seriously, we thought she didn't feel pain as deeply as us.

Shame on me. Shame on all of us.

---

40   Dr Geoffrey Yunupingu - Indigenous Australian singer and musician.

Her voice was incredible. It made me feel like a bullfrog. Watching her standing there with her old rag doll, simple and pure, I knew she'd seen the other side. Maybe even been there.

From the bushes we heard a loud rustling sound. Aunty Toots squealed and ran behind Sandy Gibb who had her spear ready for action. I almost pissed myself when this dark thing came out of the bush and headed straight for me.

It was *Gulyi-Gulyi*. I was stuck in my own stuff and had totally forgotten about him. He dropped something at my feet and jumped up onto my lap. Phew, he stunk. As I pushed him off, I noticed a frayed rope tied around his neck. He must have chewed through it and then taken off with that huge rotting pig's trotter. Gofar was there in a flash wanting a piece of the action. *Gulyi* growled—he wasn't sharing.

'Bloody Chinks, they're at the soak,' said *Mimi*. Spinning around like some she-devil, she eyed us mob and asked, 'Who's coming?'

Snorting loudly and raising his magnificent head, *Ramu* was the first to answer. His massive neck and shoulders rippled as he nodded his readiness for action. *Mimi* clicked her fingers and *Ramu* trotted up looking mighty and strong.

I was exhausted just watching their display of grunt. I wanted to stay with *Jalbri*.

Waranmanha echoed my thoughts. 'I'm staying here.'

'Okay, you two stay,' *Mimi* ordered, needing to show there were no rebels in the camp.

In a flash, Mum ran to her mother and was sitting behind her on *Ramu's* broad back. Her arms hugged *Mimi's* waist firmly. I felt odd seeing them together; maybe I was a bit jealous.

Polly was ready to follow the mob, but Barbara wasn't risking anything for anyone. She grabbed Polly's arm, saying, 'Sweetie, your mummy wants you to stay with Barbie. Come Lovie.' All that old rage I had for that woman was coming back real strong. She needed a good slap.

'Ta ta,' *Jalbri* called *Winthuly-Winthuly*, who lumbered over and put her great hoof right on my foot.

Maminy (Stupid) camel. 'Get off! Fuck ya!' I yelled, punching her shoulder, trying to make her lift her foot.

Instead she leaned in deliberately, putting all her weight on her one hoof, crushing my left foot. Then she turned her great head, laid her ears back, bared her teeth and spat in my face.

'*Winthuly-Winthuly*,' *Jalbri* called sweetly.

Winthuly turned her massive head and then lifted her great hoof off my foot. Then, swaying her great hips, she let rip a disgusting, sloppy, green fart on me as she waddled off to be with her *Jalbri*.

I reckon that bitch of a camel was grinning. Honest to God, I was as mad as a cut snake.

Mimi looked back at me. 'Are we done?'

'Sorry for living,' I snapped, trying to walk—my foot was killing me. Pretty sure it was broken. *Jalbri* was stroking *Winthuly*, telling her what a 'good girl' she was and asking her to let Sandy Gibb and Patty Mae ride her to the soak.

That bitch of a camel looked at me real smug-like as she gently knelt down to let them get on.

'Can I come?' Louanna piped up from out of nowhere.

Waranmanha called *Wilara*. 'Take him.'

'Really?' Louanna looked scared but excited. As she pulled herself up onto *Wilara's* back, I didn't recognise her anymore. Like an Islander Princess she was tall, elegant and wise.

I felt pretty shabby in comparison.

They were just about to head off when a *jindi-jindi* (willie wagtail) flew into the clearing. Our mob believes that if a *jindi-jindi* lands on you, you'll die soon. It fluttered over *Mimi* and landed on Mum.

I was shocked.

Then it flitted off, passed over Patty Mae and Louanna, circled around and landed on *Ramu*. Off it went again, briefly landing on *Wilara* and then Sandy Gibbs.

Aunty Toots shooed it off, saying, 'I'm not going.'

We all laughed nervously. It went past Barbara and Polly and touched down on Marissa, who pushed it off quietly. It flitted over to *Waranmanha* and landed firmly on her shoulder and nestled into her hair. Gently she parted her hair and it hopped onto her finger. *Waranmanha* handed the little *jindi-jindi* to *Jalbri*. *Gulyi* wanted to eat it.

'*Kantiyala* (Ride him)!' *Mimi* ordered, as they set off, leaving us behind with our tiny messenger of death.

I noticed Marissa sneak off. 'Where's Loke?' I yelled.

Mimi turned and yelled, 'We'll deal with her later!' Pausing for a moment, she sucked deeply on her thin cigar. 'Ready *Bidi-Bidi* (Butterfly)?'

Bidi-Bidi nodded and tightened her grip around her mother's waist, nestling her cheek into *Mimi's* back. Hooves clopped and thundered, and soon that mob was out of sight.

I sat thinking about how the *jindi-jindi* had landed on Mum and not Barbara or *Mimi*. I wondered if it would have landed on Loke, had she been here. She's a tripper that one. She's not one of our Anne Street mob. Her mum used to camp out at the slaughterhouse at the end of Town Beach, but she died when Loke was only seven. Loke was taken into 'care', if you could call it that. When she turned thirteen, she got knocked up by her 'carers'. As soon as she was showing, they dumped her at the park in town with no money, no food, nothing, and told her to get lost. Not the first time that's happened to one of us mob.

She got proper lost. That *walhi* (no good) mob she fell in with took heroin. They had her sniffing glue and doing drugs, and she paid with sex. She birthed a baby girl, but the word on Anne Street was that it was a monster and died after

213

nine days. Loke tried to be a good mother. She nursed her baby but it made her crazy.

And then some Christian mob from down south brainwashed her and made her even crazier. Told her that Jesus said, 'If your hand causes you to sin, cut it off', or 'If your eye makes you sin, pluck it out.'[41] Even worse, they said, 'It's better to go to Heaven without an eye than be cast into hell.'[42]

One day my Dad found her on the street. She'd tried to pluck her eye out and was a bloody mess. He carried her home to look after her. She was a wreck. I remember Dad gently washing the blood off her hair and face. I can still see Loke's head lying on Dad's lap, tears running down his face as he told her about his Mother Mary of Peace at St Mary's Church and how Mother Mary was so kind, she would never punish anyone, no matter what they did.

That night she slept in Mum's bed and Dad slept on the couch. I had forgotten how kind Dad could be and how much I loved him and missed him.

He was always bringing home stray dogs and waifs. Mum never complained; they stood on common ground when it came to lost souls. Loke really improved. When they were going to church every day, just the two of them, I'd stop off there after Sister's craft classes and hear Dad talking about Jesus.

Dad should have been a priest. Our parish priest, Father O'Shanesy, was a shameless drunk. Even at the altar, he'd be knocking 'em back. Sister Ignatius would say with red-faced Irish fury that, 'He was a heathen with ungodly ways'. He wouldn't even come to Anne Street if you were dying. But you'd always find my Dad sitting at the bedside of the sick and dying, listening to their every word. Thinking back, people used to call my Dad a 'mongrel bastard'. Although his pockets were always empty, his heart was full of gold.

'*Bindamanha,* come here' *Jalbri* insisted.

'Yeah, coming,' I said, as I limped over and plonked myself on the ground.

41   The Holy Bible, King James Version, Mathew 18:8
42   The Holy Bible, King James Version, Mathew 5:29

Then *Jalbri* sang out, 'Toots!'

She came running, kicking up small tufts of grass with her chubby little feet, flushing red and real sweaty. She stood before *Jalbri*, rearranging her breasts.

'Toots, you're a good woman. I've got something to tell ya from the other side'

Aunty Toots' face became even redder and she started sobbing.

'Don't cry, my girl, *thubarnimanha* (straighten up). You done real good job with Louanna. Jessie's in the *Muniwarri* (Seven Sisters), but she *nguwinatu* (a person who comes back all the time). She's comin' back soon cos she's gotta message for our mob. After *mitimiti* (full moon) your Jessie is comin' home.'

Aunty Toots fell onto her chubby knees and put her head on *Jalbri's* feet.

'C'mon, c'mon, she'll be here soon. Enough.'

Aunty Toots sat up with the biggest smile on her face, comforted by *Jalbri's* words. 'Thank you, thank you,' she said, looking straight into *Jalbri's* eyes. 'Will she recognise me?'

Jalbri nodded with a smile. That was all Aunty Toots needed. Hoisting herself off the ground, she trotted off excitedly telling everyone, 'I'm going to do a big cook up for when that mob get back.'

Barbara and Polly Tipple followed Aunty Toots while *Waranmanha* and I stayed with our *Jalbri*. *Gulyi-Gulyi* lay at *Waranmanha's* feet chewing on his bone. *Waranmanha* and I softly sang our favourite songs from school. It was easy to harmonise with her; our voices were a natural fit.

Before, when I would sing songs in my head, I'd always hear another girl's voice singing in harmony with me. I often wondered if it was just my imagination. It was sweet to know that she was real.

It was a perfectly delicious moment, being on Country together, singing and looking out across the vast plains. A mirage of gold and purple danced on the horizon, luring the dazzling crimson-red sun into its darkening abode.

215

Suddenly, gunfire echoed against the canyon wall.

Jalbri sprang to attention. 'Where's *Birri*?' she demanded.

'I don't know, *tnick, tnick, Birri*,' I started to shout, but *Jalbri* stopped me.

'Use your mind,' she ordered.

Straightening up, I closed my eyes and I could see *Birri*, but she was far away … my concentration was broken by the sound of galloping hooves.

Ramu entered the clearing at great speed. Pulling up sharply, *Mimi* shouted, 'The lost girl has been shot by the *kartija*. She's dead. Mary and the others are back there preparing her body.'

We all knew it was Loke.

Yanking on *Ramu's* halter, turning him on the spot, *Mimi* dug in her heels and was off, heading back towards the soak.

Moments later Louanna appeared on *Wilara*. '*Waranmanha*!'

With that single word, *Waranmanha* swung herself up behind Louanna and they left.

'What about me?' I yelled after them. Looking at *Jalbri*, I asked if we were going too.

'No, not your business.'

This made me real mad.

'My girl, you still got things to learn. Where's *Birri*?'

'Forget *Birri*, what about this baby I'm having?' I felt scared and frustrated.

'That one in there.' *Jalbri* placed her hand on my belly. 'She's a special one.'

All the fight left me and my heart felt soft like clay. 'Yeah, I know. I reckon I can feel her listening to us right now, and sometimes I swear she's talking to me.' It felt good to open up; I needed to talk.

'Little *Waranmanha*.' As *Jalbri* spoke, she bent down putting her lips close to the skin of my little bulge. 'I'm your *Jalbri*, I'll be lookin' out for you. Look to the stars little'un. Your mummy, she's a good girl, she will never lose you.'

I could see the skin on my belly move as my tiny baby pushed herself right up under *Jalbri's* lips. But her words were no comfort to me.

'You,' she said with her hand on my tummy with Bub nestled under it, 'must rest, soon too much work for you. The others will deal with the lost girl.'

Suddenly I felt very tired, like I was in a trance. Rolling over to face the fire, I fell asleep instantly.

My dreams took me far away from Loke's death. I saw my beloved Prince Manu Tollie standing on the shore. He was looking out to sea calling my name. 'Lucy Lucky-Child, I am coming for you and our baby.'

Even though I was asleep, I felt myself smiling. I watched him respectfully kiss his mother and father, the King and Queen of Tiwi Island. Saying goodbye to his sisters and brothers, he then pushed his canoe into the sea at Van Diemen Gulf. His family sang the *mama* (sacred song), and every eye held back a tear as they watched him row over the break and out of sight.

Although still fast asleep, *Jalbri's* words echoed in my mind: *'Where's Birri? Where's Birri?'* Then, I saw her galloping full pelt towards Dragon Tree Soak. To my delight, riding her like a jockey was Sister Euphrates. Her veil had blown off and her locks of white hair were sticking out of her coif (cap worn under a nun's veil). Her rosary beads were wrapped tightly around her neck and the crucifix flew high on the wind behind her. Slung over her shoulder was her 'body and soul' bag.

I woke with a start. 'Manu and Sister Euphrates are coming,' I blurted out. Hearing the news, Aunty Toots made me a mug of hot sweet tea. Sipping it slowly, I watched *yalibii* (emus) in big family groups heading west, and I half expected Manu's head to pop up over the horizon. Then my senses switched from seeing the mesmerising sunset to hearing the thundering of hooves and the voices of the women returning.

Cocooned in sheets of paperbark, Loke's swaddle was tied onto two large branches that trailed behind *Winthuly-Winthuly* like a stretcher. As soon as *Jalbri* saw the procession, she started singing the *mama* (sacred song).

Apparently what had happened was, Loke was hiding in the bushes near the soak. *Mimi* and the other women were arguing with the miners when Loke screamed like a stuck pig. The *kartija* (*whitefellas*) shot into the bushes, thinking they were gonna get a free feed of wild boar, but shot her dead instead. *Mimi* reckons they were showing how tough they were and warning the women not to mess with them, cos they had guns and weren't shy to use them.

The men stepped into the clearing to claim their trophy. There, slumped over dead in the centre of a spiral made of hundreds of crucifixes, crudely fashioned from twigs, was Loke. The Chinese landowners and their mates bolted. This was a bad omen for their new empire.

The scream they'd heard before was poor Loke trying to hack off her left hand. Just like the bible said, 'If your hand causes you to sin, cut it off and throw it away.' Some might say the devil had got hold of her and was making her kill herself. But nah, she just wanted to go to heaven, and I reckon Baby Jesus would've let her in just for trying to be good. I can imagine her up there right now, yarning with my Dad.

More fires were lit, and our hearts were heavy like the air around us. Marissa was shattered. The only one she was close to was Loke. She'd been pacing up and down when suddenly she stopped and said she wanted to take the 'punishment' for Loke. That was really heavy shit. You never want to be facing *blackfella* Lore.

After lots of muttering and head nodding, the clapping sticks beat out a hard, sharp rhythm. Patty Mae positioned herself about twenty paces in front of Marissa. She raised her *jakiny* (barbed spear) onto her shoulder and started to run. Marissa stood real still, and her eyes were turned up to *Muniwarri* (the Seven Sisters). I gasped, feeling sick. I could hear *Waranmanha* trying to stifle her cries, but the older women kept singing louder with more and more determination.

As Patty Mae did a run up, each foot fall was heavy on the earth and made me feel more anxious. But Marissa was completely calm and resigned to her fate. With a soft whirr the *jakiny* hurtled through the air. The sound of it penetrating her was like ripping GLAD Wrap [43]as it cracked through her thigh bone and awkwardly wriggled its way out the other side.

The clapping sticks stopped, and in total silence Marissa fell back, the *jakiny* impaling her leg to the ground but her eyes were fixed on the *bundarra* (stars) above.

At that very moment, Sister Euphrates and *Birri* entered the clearing. She dismounted and ran to Marissa, calling me to follow. No explanation was required. I felt shame that she'd think we were uncivilised doing tribal 'punishment', but Sister had seen this kind of thing before.

In spite of everything, it was good to be near Sister again. I had missed the sweet smell of her lavender soap.

As Sister stemmed the bleeding with her fingers, she looked up at me. Her eyes darted around my face and down my arm to my hand. 'You've changed', she said knowingly.

My eyes got sorta watery and I just wanted to tell her everything, but now was not the time.

'Come beside me, *môn chérie* (my dear).'

I knelt down beside her and my black skin rubbed against her white arm.

'You remember blanket stitch?'

'Yep', I replied. 'I've already saved a life with my blanket stitch.'

Marissa was groaning loudly. Strangely, I seemed so far away from her groans with Sister by my side.

Sister got *Waranmanha* and Louanna to get all sorts of stuff out of her bag. Sandy Gibb brewed up a strong painkiller from plants, and in another tin she had a disinfectant boiling like the one I'd used for *Gulyi*.

Marissa is a real negative, aggressive woman who hates the world and everyone in it. She hates to miss out on anything and always wants something

---

43   GLAD Wrap - Cling film, thin plastic film typically used for sealing food items.

for nothing. And being a total gossip, she always has her nose stuck in other people's business. I couldn't believe it when she came to the desert to help look for me. Loke and her were definitely the odd ones out.

When that *jakiny* (barbed spear) left Patty Mae's hand, Marissa's face changed. That bitterness that dragged down the corners of her mouth and made her dark eyes mean, vanished. It was as if sacrificing herself for Loke gave her a new joy, maybe you could call it 'grace'. A new 'amazing grace' like Old Jimmy Howard used to sing about.

I tugged hard on the last stitch to the front of Marissa's thigh, forgetting for a moment that there was a human on the other end of the thread. She winced. That would have killed. I glanced up expecting to see her looking daggers at me, but instead, she had a softness and kindness I'd never seen before. Somehow, something deep down inside her had changed. She looked real holy-like 'cos she'd taken on the pain for Loke.

Leaving Sister to finish off, I went to feed and water *Birri* who'd been standing near us waiting patiently. I hugged her and kissed the blaze on her forehead. She snorted back contentedly as I hummed into her ear. *Gulyi* came over and licked my bloodied hand. I'm sure he was thanking me for sewing him up when that roo cut him open.

Even the night air felt strangely holy, and for a moment I looked around and realised that every one of us mob had changed. I too had found my family and my home in Country. But I couldn't help but wonder *who* these animals were and how they managed to find me at a time in my life when I needed them most.

Aunty Toots and Sandy Gibb are great cooks and had laid out a magnificent feast. I went over to listen to Louanna and *Waranmanha* yarning. *Waranmanha* was telling Louanna about all the extra juicy bits of our adventures so far. I thought I'd be jealous, but I was happy to see Louanna scribbling like mad filling up her notebook.

I sat stuffing my face wondering if this would be our last meal together. Marissa was still being fussed over by Sister. Polly Tipple and Barbara were hanging out with Patty Mae. Sandy Gibb and Aunty Toots were cooking even more stuff. *Mimi* sat alone on a rock puffin' her cigar, looking like her thoughts were a million miles away.

Sandy Gibb bought over two enamel cups full of some kinda murky fluid *Jalbri* had told her to brew for us.

'Drink!' *Jalbri* ordered.

Sandy Gibb laughed as she watched us trying to down the bitter brew. Instantly I wanted to throw up.

'Drink, Drink!' *Jalbri* insisted. She looked a bit annoyed that I was wasting it.

We gulped down the last of the foul-tasting stuff.

Then *Jalbri* asked me to make a nest away from the firelight so we could get a good look at the *Jirdilungu* (Milky Way). She suddenly looked real tired and fragile. We eased her up and slowly walked with her into the darkness and helped her lay down on her back.

When she was all settled and comfy, she got us to lay down either side of her. We were mucking around and giggling when in desperation the words, '*Thubarnimanha* (Straighten up)!' left her dry, old lips.

The tone of her voice changed our mood completely.

'Remember, listen up, *nganggurnmanha*! *Tantalpal* (Clap your hands)!'

We clapped as she sang a familiar song.

28. The Dark Night

Mamikat (The dark night) came in close. Lost in *Jalbri's* rich, sharp voice, the *bundarra* (stars) came down to Earth, and *Jalbri's* outstretched arm touched each constellation—*Muniwarri* (the Seven Sisters) and the marker *bundarra*, *Karlu Karlu* (The Devils Marbles), *Wadjimup* (Rottnest), *Walghana* (Walga Rock) and even Help Canyon.

Soon we were flying between the *bundarra*. Beyond our sun and planets, we passed through other orbits, just the three of us: *Jalbri*, *Waranmanha* and me. At the edge of the *Jirdilungu* (Milky Way) was a lone star dazzling in the night sky.

'Is that your home?' I asked *Jalbri*.

She looked elated. 'That fella my birthplace.' She sounded young again and like a teenager going off on a date. 'I'll keep going. You girls know your way home. Yes?'

Just like Superman she shot off at the speed of light, leaving us tumbling back to Earth through a thick, black mist. We'd slipped between realities, between worlds. Between the Dreamtime and the Dreamless place. We tumbled and tumbled as if our tumbling would never end.

Then with a heavy jolt we landed back into our bodies.

Suddenly the night had grown colder. *Ngubanu* (Dingos) howled, a *gurrundu* (mopoke owl) hooted, and *kurr* (on the sound of the wind) *Winthuly-Winthuly* moaned. My great grandmother's hand felt icy in mine.

'*Jalbri*,' I whispered nervously.

'*JalbriII*!' *Waranmanha* echoed.

The chill of death startled us.

I rolled onto my elbow to get a proper look at her. There, reflected perfectly in *Jalbri's* open, lifeless eyes was the *Djulpan* (Southern Cross) and beside it, her home star.

'CPR!' *Waranmanha* yelled. We'd both learnt it at swimming lessons. She started pushing on *Jalbri's* chest. I took the biggest, deepest breath and put my lips to hers.

'Now!' *Waranmanha* shouted.

For a second, I was stuck. I couldn't breathe out.

'NOW! NOW!' she urged, whacking me hard on the back.

That slap released my breath into *Jalbri's* mouth. The strangest thing was that my breath had become like a tiny bat, flying into the dark depths of an enormous cavern. My breath and I felt so small, so insignificant. I tried to take another breath but couldn't. *Jalbri's* energy had caught me like a fish on the end of her line.

'What are you doing?' *Waranmanha* screamed.

All of a sudden, I drew a deep breath out of *Jalbri's* lungs. Somehow, her soul entered me. My lungs, throat, tongue and nostrils were filled with an old musty taste like an old nun in a rest home. I'd sucked up a hundred years of *Jalbri's* pain. My head became heavy and flopped down onto her chest. I coughed uncontrollably.

'Get off her! Get off!' *Waranmanha* shouted, sobbing her heart out. She pushed me to the ground, and I lay there choking.

Our *Jalbri* had left us.

I was trying to make a sound, but nothing would come out. Not even tears. My chest was aching and felt like it was going to explode. My mouth kept opening and closing in slow motion like some bloody weird talking goldfish in a silent movie.

Then the sound came in and the volume was turned up high. '*Jalbri*!' erupted from the depths of my soul. Its force hurtled me like a great comet through the *Jirdilungu* (Milky Way) searching for our *Jalbri*. I wanted to fly anti-clockwise around the universe with my dead *Jalbri* in my arms and rewind time back to the fun times long before her death. I wanted to go back to those times when she would visit us in Broome with pockets full of bush tucker. If we could just go back to then, I'd tell her I loved her and would never let her die again without me.

Speeding into the 'Beyond Beyond' where the creation story began, in the darkness I heard the first sound, the *mama* (sacred sounds) that gave birth to all shapes and a hundred thousand things and their offspring.

Past 'Beyond Beyond' was the Most Great Peace and in that soft, fuzzy dispersing darkness I saw only the back of my *Jalbri* racing away from me. 'Come back ... *Jalbri*!' The void stifled the sound of my words so that even my own ears couldn't hear my screams. They disappeared like *Jalbri*, consumed by the ever-expanding cosmos.

For an instant I hesitated, confused and lost. Glancing down I saw the elements of Fire, Wind and Water entangled in a cosmic embrace, and beyond that I saw our bright little planet Earth.

Suddenly, the *mamas* (sacred sounds) of that faraway place were shattered by a great hiss. *Kaplan Karrangu's* serpentine form shot up from the Earth through all the layers of the other worlds. He barred his fangs and twitched his hideous tongue at me. Startled, I plummeted to Earth, screeching as I fell, landing heavily into my body. I sprang bolt upright.

To die now and travel with *Jalbri* was not to be my destiny.

A *walypa* (bitter wind) blew in from the east, and fine, red sand pelted us and reddened the sky. We women huddled together, and although we were *ngula jimaha* (crying together), we felt so alone. A *miginy* (kestrel) screeched above us, hovering like the Afghan death kites that cameleers fly when they send the departed souls of their loved ones to their heavenly home upon the wind.

Gently kneeling beside *Jalbri, Winthuly-Winthuly* rocked herself back and forth. Her big head swung like a pendulum across *Jalbri's* body.

Waranmanha was grief stricken. I sat as still as one of the stones from Battlement Rocks, but a mighty fire was smouldering inside me. Without warning, I erupted. Grabbing a *gurndi* (fighting stick), I began smashing my own face over and over as punishment for still being alive. Blood poured from my open mouth, and as I spat, a tooth rolled out onto the dirt. I just sat there, bludgeoning myself and feeling numb.   *Waranmanha* jumped over *Jalbri* and sat on my right side trying to comfort me. I was lashing out in a frenzy, and I landed a sickening blow to the back of *Waranmanha's* skull. She fell heavily against my shoulder.

I raised my stick about to land another blow when *Mimi* shouted, 'Stop!' and punched me in the face.

Stunned, I returned to my senses.

Looking at us girls, she sweetly placed her open right hand ever so gently on my left cheek. The weight of my head fell trustingly into her hand. '*Kurntal* (daughter),' she whispered. Her sweetness undid me.

'My *Jalbri's* gone,' I howled loudly.

'No name, baby, no name,' she responded gently. *Mimi* placed her other hand on *Waranmanha's* neck.

Out of the corner of my eye, I saw her look adoringly at our *Mimi*, who was kneeling in front of us so we could rest our heads on her chest. She craned her head around to talk to the stunned women gathered behind her. 'Okay, we will start "Sorry Business",' her voice echoed in her chest.

Patty Mae and Sandy Gibb came over to look after us.

Mimi got up. She was an impressive figure with her straight back and white cropped hair that seemed to give the impression she was moving forward, leading the mob from wherever she stood. She's real classy and sorta better and smarter than any of us mob.

Jalbri was still lying on the ground with her mouth and eyes wide open. She didn't look like my *Jalbri* anymore; something was missing. Above the strident sounds of women singing and wailing, I could hear *Mimi's* loud, commanding voice ordering different women to collect various things for the ceremony.

'*Jalbri* looks so different,' I said to *Waranmanha*.

Mimi stopped suddenly, leant over and whispered, '*Gurndany* (Shame), no name,'

Waranmanha and I wanted to help. *She* was still stiff, as if *she'd* been made from bush bee's wax, and had a strange dark-brown yellowish colour. *Her* face seemed longer, and *her* jaw looked so hard and pointed, and *her* eyes were real sunken, not like before. Everyone cried loudly when they neared *her* body.

Our mums came over rolling an enormous ball of human hair string. It stands waist height and carries the history of *her* mob for hundreds of years. It's kept hidden in a secret cave and only brought out for ceremony. Men can't touch it. It's a real honour for us to even see this sacred hair.

The persistent wind made it difficult for Polly Tipple, who was attempting to carry several enormous pieces of paperbark for wrapping around *her* body. The paperbark was laid flat, and *Mimi* and our mothers reverently picked *her* up off the ground.

226

'We want to …' I started to say, but then *Mimi* glared and shook her head. I didn't feel shutdown like I would have before. Now I understood what respect for tradition meant.

They laid her on the creamy pink paperbark. *She* now looked strangely beautiful. The *walypa* (bitter wind) dropped and a fine, red dust fell softly as if the great giant Sky Spirits were dusting the flour off their hands after kneading the dough for damper.

Leaning over her, I blew the fine dust off *her* wax-like face, half expecting *her* to blink or say '*Thubarnimanha* (Straighten up)'.

Our mothers drew the paperbark cloth around *her* firmly leaving *her* head sticking out of the swaddle. *Mimi* closed *her* eyes and tried to close *her* mouth, but it stayed open just a little showing the top edge of *her* bottom teeth. *She* was resting peacefully now. We took it in turn to kiss *her*. I kissed *her* cheek; it was surprisingly cold and felt like plasticine. The realisation that *she* was gone forever struck me.

Sobbing I watched *Waranmanha* kiss *her* forehead. *Mimi* spent some time whispering something in her *yagu's* (mum's) ear. Then she took a single white-tipped black feather from behind her ear and placed it on her *yagu's* chest. It was the perfect touch. Her *yagu*, our *Jalbri*, looked like a proper queen.

Suddenly, *Winthuly-Winthuly* moaned and *Gulyi-Gulyi* howled. Through the paperbark wrapping in the centre of *her* chest, a warm golden ball-shaped light began to form. It rose up from her chest, hovering briefly above *her* dead body, and then it flew higher and higher over our heads. As our eyes followed the mesmerising golden ball of light, a comet came into view.

As the comet flew past, its long tail trailing through the star-filled sky, *Jalbri's* spirit, in the form of that beautiful golden ball of light, joined with the comet's fiery tail and flew out of sight.

Aunty Toots let out a joyful high-pitched wail and beat her clapping sticks. That sharp and hollow sound made each inward breath cut deep into my heart. Louanna started chanting. Her deep, rich voice grounded the high-pitched nasal sound of the other woman as they joined in one by one.

Sandy Gibb and Patty Mae stood with their *mili* (firesticks) burning bright. Polly Tipple ploughed into the clearing carrying an enormous pile of mixed plants: *bilabirdi* (eucalyptus), *bardinyu* (pine), *gungkara* (conkerberry) and *gumanu* (sandalwood). She had a big smile on her face, and she looked so proud of herself. In the middle of our sadness she was grinning and chattering to herself. I wanted to slap her. But then I remembered Sister Euphrates' lesson from her time in the prison cell: 'The gift from the spirit world is joy.' Maybe that's why Polly always looks so happy.

I was deep in thought when Polly's stupid wooden leg gave way and she fell flat onto the pile of stuff she was carrying, landing at *her* feet. The chanting fizzled out into laughter, and us mob started to talk about our *Jalbri*. The funniest stories came out and that laughter dissolved into sad tales, and again we were 'Sorry'. Truly 'Sorry' that *her* life had to end now.

The strongest women in our group attached more hair string to her swaddle and made handles to carry it. The *minggarri* (wood bowl for carrying water) *she* had given me was full of water, and *Mimi* cradled her *yagu's minggarri* as if it were her newborn. Standing over *her*, she poured some water between *her* breasts. Over and over in hushed tones, the words *pararrka, pararrka, pararrka* (sorry, sorry, sorry) were spoken, and rivers of tears flowed down *Mimi's* cheeks, wetting *her* dry, cracked lips.

Catching my mother's eye, I whispered, '*Pararrka.*'

Sandy Gibbs' eyes glistened with respect for *Mimi's* grief. She handed her *mili* (firestick) to Barbara and walked over to pick up the string handle of the swaddle near *her* head. Patty Mae passed her *mili* to Louanna and took hold of the handle at the foot end. These two strong women carried the swaddle all the way back to Dragon Tree Soak. Everyone followed singing 'Sorry Business'.

Arriving at the soak, Patty Mae and Sandy Gibb placed the swaddle on the soft, green grasses growing at its edge. In Mangala, the chant went out again and again, a thousand times over, until suddenly, I understood.

228

Pina-manarri nganga kankarni warlu.	Thinking is lost on top of fire.
Marrayin rayi ngapatu.	Round up this soul with water.
Yalawarra,	Upward Facing,
Yalawarra.	Upward Facing.
Nganyjurrula kawanarri.	To the stars we are singing.
Nyuntu Wirinykarli, warinykarli.	You're Coming Home, Coming Home.

Our Elders were always telling us that we couldn't forget our two great twin powers: Fire and Water. For us mob, they are the life force of *Pulanyi Bulaing* and *Kulpan Karrangu.*

When we want rain, we burn the land and the *jurdu* (smoke) takes the heat high up into the Heavens and makes the clouds. Then, in comes the rain.

When we find a *Jila*, a fire is lit. The *jurdu* (smoke) goes up to ask the Spirits if we can dig for their precious underground water. So, 'Thinking is lost on top of fire,' means that if your thoughts are fiery, the 'straightway' is lost, so you gotta cool off and be still like water.

Fire is action. Water is calm.

When we are 'Upward Facing', looking to Heaven for guidance, that's when we can use Fire and Water the right way. For them, that's looking Upwards for the Knowledge. Fire and Water become friends and everywhere is home. Them fellas who forget to look Upwards, both Fire and Water become their enemies and nowhere is home.

Sweet-smelling thick plumes of smoke coiled their way into the sky. We call this smoke, *putijputy*. It announces someone's arrival upstairs in the *Jirdilungu* (Milky Way). A large fire was started right on the edge of the soak to burn some of *her* precious things. The fire crackled, spitting out the water, and its embers became softly airborne.

229

One by one the women added wood and twigs and fuelled the fire with kangaroo oil. Lost in trance, we watched the flames lick high into the star-laden sky. The clapping sticks and 'Sorry Business' song continued throughout the night. That sharp relentless sound blended easily with squawking *biyarrgu* (galahs) that announced the rising sun. Then that same sound became heavy at noon, and although every eyelid drooped, it went on for three more days and four whole nights.

Her body was treated in the traditional way, the 'secret' way. At some predestined moment, *Mimi* went forward. Looking more 'bushy' than 'city slicker', she sorted through the embers picking out *her* bones and placing them on a clean piece of *ngurlurrbi* (paperbark). The women carrying the *mili* (firesticks) stood them in the ground beside *her*. They lit up the water's edge and the reflection of the Twin Dragon Trees danced across the soak.

Piece by piece *Mimi* placed each bone into the water to wash them. She was speaking in words I didn't understand to someone invisible. Turtles with webbed feet pawed through the water to nibble away small bits of remaining flesh from *her* bones. As they moved through the water, the green moss growing on their flattish oval shells swayed as if blown by a gentle breeze. It looked strangely beautiful.

When *Mimi* put *her* skull into the water, *her* jaw was wide open, and it looked like the old girl was having a lend of us. *Her* old chompers seemed to have more character now that they had been stripped of lips, fleshy cheeks and chin. When the turtles with their long, fine serpentine necks explored the inside of *her* head and started nibbling bits of leftover brain, I started to heave.

When all was done, *Mimi* dried the bones, carefully painted each one with red ochre, wrapped them in paperbark and tied the parcel with reeds. She called *Ramu*, who'd been hanging at the back of the clearing, listening and waiting. *Mimi* and *Ramu* set off at a very slow walk. *Winthuly-Winthuly* followed, moaning loudly.

230

Wailing and clapping sticks, our mob followed *her* remains until we were at the rock that marked the way to our burial grounds. *Mimi*, *Ramu* and *Winthuly-Winthuly* continued on, until *Winthuly's* moans blended with *kurr* (the sound of the wind).

The soft hues of dawn and the waxing moon reflected perfectly in the water at the soak. As I gazed at the moon's reflection, I could hear the Twin Dragon Trees murmur softly as if noting the end of another era. Just at that moment, a large turtle poked its head out of the water, right in the middle of the almost full moon's reflection. It looked like a flying snake. I knew it was a message from *her*, telling us not to forget why we were here.

Louanna called me, and as we walked to camp, we could see *Mimi* riding like fury into the distance past Help Canyon. *Winthuly-Winthuly* kept pace, her long neck jutted forward running like the camel of her youth. A long, red dust cloud made by the thunderous hooves hung heavily on the landscape.

29. Don't Look Back

Back at camp, food and sweet tea was quietly handed around. We sat in small groups talking but soon everyone slept, everyone except *Waranmanha*. When I woke in the late afternoon, *Mimi* had not returned. *Waranmanha* was standing near the soak. *Gulyi* was lying on top of me. Pushing him off, I went over and asked, 'What's up?'

'Something's up. Things are on the move. *She's* left a rip in the fabric!' *Waranmanha* seemed far away.

'Think about it. Obviously *Mimi* has taken *her* place.'

She shook her head.

'You've looked,' I said, angry that she'd used the *Mikanarri* (Seeing Stone) without asking me. 'I thought we were in this together.'

232

'It's not long now, *Bindamanha*,' she said, squeezing my hand. '*Mitimiti*, the full moon is coming. Sweet destiny is calling me. I know what I have to do.'

'I know what's going to happen. All that sacrifice stuff is shit! Don't believe them. It doesn't have to happen,' I yelled. '*Jalbri's* gone, fat lot of good that's done any of us!'

'Shame, no name!' *Waranmanha* snapped at me.

'It'll only happen if *we* let it. It's all in our heads, that's why they call it Dreaming. We're gettin' outta here now!' I grabbed my sister by the arm, but she wouldn't budge. I grabbed her plait and pulled her away from the soak. Mary, Barbara, Toots and Patty Mae heard her squeal and came running.

'*Tnick tnick*.' In a flash, *Birri* was beside me. 'Get up!' Don't be pathetic! You're mental!' *Waranmanha* wouldn't move. 'You wanna die? There's a million other ways! Nah, not for a princess! You wanna bloody mythical snake to burn you to death. I used to think I was mad. But I'm the sane one. You're a bloody lunatic. Ooh, Saint *Waranmanha*!'

Mum ran over to comfort her. Obviously, she didn't give a damn about me.

'Okay, stay! See if I care! Loser! You're all losers!' I yelled as I pulled on *Birri's* mane to mount her. I dug my heels in deep and we were out of there with *Gulyi-Gulyi* racing flat out behind us.

I was *kali* (furious). I just wanted those stupid women to fuck off and go back to where they came from. 'Bloody Abo's, you're so full of crap, your brains are all fucked up!'

As I hurled the abuse, I felt my posture change. I sat real straight; my knees spread a little further apart like a proper bloke. My mouth was turned down hard at the edges. And then, when my bottom jaw jutted out, I felt like I'd finally become 'Steve', the bloody red-necked pommy chippy.

His job was to fix any problems we had with our council houses. Everyone hated calling him out cos he'd clock-up a three-hour call out, just to fix a blocked drain but would spend two and a half hours shitting on us. I was getting a real taste for what it felt like to be Steve.

Feeling deadly as, I rode for hours, trying to work out how to put an end to this *mamany* (crazy) stuff. I pulled up sharp in a little clearing between the low-lying spinifex and dismounted.

Still *kali*, I used the last of Jackie's matches from the Golden Fleece sleeve to set the spinifex alight. As the plain lit up, an amazing feeling of exhilaration ran through me. My soul ignited. I was on fire.

'I am powerful! Fuck you, Country! Fuck all of you. Fuck off!' I punched the air feeling like a deadly Empress watching her city burn.

Great plumes of *jurdu* (smoke) rose up from the burning clusters of spinifex. 'RARHH!' I roared, *wirinykarli* (upward facing). My body started to move as if possessed. The slow, jerky movements brought out a different sound from my throat. It moved into my face and ran down my spine and into my feet. I was lost in a trance, shuffling forward with my hands moving this way and that.

Kurr (The sound of the wind) seemed to carry the ancient sound of song on its breath. The *winthu* (wind) changed direction and my nose caught scent of a sickly evil smell.

Bajayimanha (Becoming wild with anger), I opened my eyes and there he was, *Birrinja* (the *one that feathers stick to*).

The *jurdu* (smoke) in the changing *winthu* (wind) took on the forms of those I loved. My Dad moved in and out of focus like a mirage on a hot road. 'Dad,' I called, confused.

The crackling voice of *the one that feathers stick to* responded.

Then I saw Tina, with the noose around her neck, smiling at me. 'Go away!' I shouted, in fear's tight grip.

I stood lost, alone and scared in this *jurdu* (smoke)-filled place, no longer the deadly Empress feeding off her rage. On the verge of panic, my voice barely audible, I began, 'Ancestors …' but I was interrupted by an evil vision

234

of *Jalbri's* mother being killed. I didn't want to look but I couldn't turn away. The sound of his awful crackling, mocking laugh left me stunned. *Gulyi* was biting me, trying to get me to react to him. *Birri* bolted.

The pain in my heart was too much. My right fingers felt inside the little pouch for *Jalbri's Yagu's* (mother's) finger bone. Just as I gripped it between my trembling fingers and raised it into the air, my Dad showed me another vision of our kitchen back home in Broome. My heart leapt for joy to see my brother Frankie. But something didn't feel right.

Frankie was standing as stiff as a board, his head raised slightly, like he was staring at something. Without Mum and me there to look after him, the place was a mess, dirty dishes and crap everywhere. I suddenly realised what Frankie was staring at. It was the flour bin on top of the kitchen cupboard. That's where Dad used to hide his old bacci tin that had his special photos inside.

I hadn't forgotten about that tin and was wondering if Frankie was going to get it down and reminisce about Dad. But instead, he reached behind the flour bin, pushed aside Dad's tin and pulled out something wrapped in an old, red and white striped tea towel. He plonked himself down in his chair at the kitchen table; his face was wet with tears. He wasn't crying over dishes, he just sat staring at the thing in the tea towel on the table in front of him.

Right on cue, I heard Old Jimmy Howard's voice, 'Frankie, me lad, are ya home?' Old Jimmy bent down and peered through one of the holes in our front door made by Frankie's fist that night Dad … Dad left us.

Frankie turned to look at Jimmy, eyeballed him for a moment and grabbed the object off the table. As the tea towel fell away, there in his trembling hand was Dad's gun. He opened his mouth real wide and shoved the barrel in deep. I heard him gag when it pressed against the back of his throat. Then, he pulled the trigger and blew his brains out.

'NO!' Jimmy's scream echoed mine.

Gurndany (Shame) on me, *gurndany* on me. It's all my fault, Frankie was alone because of me.

Old Jimmy kept talking to Frankie through the hole in the front door. 'Son, I told you not to look back. Keep looking forward... that's all ya had to do. Just keep lookin' forward.' His mournful wail amplified his grief. 'Ahhh, no son no ... Not You ... I've buried everyone ... All my thirteen kids are gone now, my first wife and my second ... Your Dad and now you, my boy. Oh Frankie, why did you look back? No good comes from lookin' back.' He slumped forward sobbing, his head resting against the door.

Straightening up, still talking to himself, he said, 'Ain't no reason for this old man Jimmy Howard to live no more ... Nuthin' to *look forward* to. Nuthin!' Sticking his long arm through the hole, he turned the key from the inside and unlocked the door to our miserable life. He looked around at the state of the room. Calmed himself down. Straightened his white Akubra. Removed his necktie and wiped his eyes and face with it. Then he bent down and placed his necktie over Frankie's open eyes. He undid the top three buttons of his shirt. He picked the gun up off the floor, and as he stood up, tall and proud, he started singing with that familiar country and western twang:

Amazing Grace, how sweet the sound, that saved a wretch like me.

I was, once lost, but now am found.

Was blind, but now, I see.

Thru many danger, toils and snares.

Twas Grace that brought us safe thus far.

And Grace that'll lead us home.

And then he continued, 'Mummy and Daddy, your boy Jimmy's comin' home. Daddy, I did what ya told me. I promise I didn't look back. Now I'm really lookin' forward to comin' home ta youse mob. Long-time no see.'

Old Jimmy was smiling like he could see his folks standing right there in front of him. He carefully placed the barrel of the gun on the mass of thick, white chest hair over his heart. Ever so slowly he pulled the trigger. I think he died before the bullet left the cocked barrel. Falling backwards with a heavenly expression on his face, his hat flew off and landed gracefully on the floor covering a large lump of Frankie's brains.

I dropped *Yagu's* finger bone.

Shrieking laughter pierced the smoke-filled air. Panic stricken and unable to breathe, I fell to my knees, searching for the finger bone. The sound of women's high-pitched voices floated high above the *jurdu* (smoke) plumes. I couldn't tell if they were friend or foe.

That sickening stench intensified until it became overwhelming. *The one that feathers stick to* was standing beside me. I was petrified, frozen stiff, waiting for his filthy hands to touch me. His hot, foul breath made the skin on my neck crawl but still, I couldn't move away from his approaching lips.

Suddenly, I felt pressure from the tip of a cold knife at the base of my throat. Instantly, vomit came up into my mouth. I moved my head back against him, trying to release the pressure on my throat. A clump of bloodied feathers stuck to my cheek. Repulsed, I swallowed. Acidic bile burnt my throat on its way back down. I wanted so badly to move my body, but I was paralysed with fear. I had lost all hope.

I felt something light skim over my eye, graze my cheek, glide past the corner of my lip and fall to the ground.

'*THUBARNIMANHA*!' my *Jalbri's* voice shouted loudly.

'AHHH!' I roared, unable to form any words.

'*SHARGARR*!' he shrieked from behind me.

There, hovering in the *jurdu* (smoke) was my *Jalbri*.

I lunged forward to pick up *her Yagu's* bone, and as my trembling fingers clutched it in the dark, I noticed a small white feather with a yellow dot drift right down in front of me. 'Manu Tollie,' I whimpered, snatching it up from the ash-covered ground.

I sprang to my feet, ready to face *the one that feathers stick to*. Realising his spell was broken, he backed up ready to flee. I looked up, and to my surprise, I saw *Waranmanha* on the other side of him. Our eyes locked as she slowly raised her arm. She had *Jalbri's Yagu's* other finger bone in her hand. He had nowhere to go.

My hands were steady now. With Manu's feather pressed hard against my chest, I *pointed the bone*.

Watching him take punishment for *all* his horrific deeds was an ugly sight. Squealing like a rat caught in a trap, he scuttled off into the darkness, his wretched life leaking out of him with each step.

As his putrid energy dissolved before me, the night sky bent down to kiss the warm, blackened earth. My sister and I clung to each other, sobbing out the word 'Sorry'. We cried ourselves out.

It struck me how often us mob are *sorry*. *Jalbri* had told us about revenge killing, and now *Waranmanha* and I had *pointed the bone*, I was scared shitless. What would our punishment be? How could we stop this revenge bullshit?

Bulari (Mother Goddess) answered my thoughts in tones thick like honey that trickled slowly into my heart and gave me understanding. 'Revenge is only finished when you forgive. Long before your life began, way back in the Dreamtime, the seed of forgiveness was planted so the troubled ones could *JutinKarra Kawanarri* (sing out for forgiveness to undo the past).' I got it. That's how some people could forgive really, really bad things.

Mimi suddenly appeared; she must have heard *Bulari* too. She came over and wrapped her strong, sinewy arms around both of us. '*Barndi barndi kurntal* (Good clever daughters),' she whispered.

I caught sight of Mum and Barbara approaching. *Mimi* released her grip on us and we ran to our mothers.

'Mum!' I shouted. 'Frankie's shot himself and Old Jimmy's dead too.'

'WHAAT!' she screamed, slapping my face and grabbing my arms really tight. Looking directly at me, she screamed, 'What about Jonnie? Where's poor Jonnie? Look for him!' she ordered, poking me as if that was gonna help.

With my heart thumping in my chest, I stilled myself and looked into my mind's eye. I told her everything I saw. 'Jonnie's in the kitchen, in the corner near the stove rocking backwards and forwards, not saying nothin'.'

Mum's sobbing was painful, and I felt gutted.

'Uncle Cedric has just come. He's talkin' to Jonnie. He's offering him his hand. But Jonnie won't look up. Uncle Cedric has just picked him up and is getting him outta there. All the Anne Street mob are sobbing and wailing. Aunty Rosie and her partner Sally have just come. Jonnie's gone mental, he's flapping like crazy. Uncle Cedric's handing him over. Rosie's got him. Mum, he's safe. Aunty Rosie's takin' him back to the Lady House. They'll look after him real good.'

Mum was rocking from side to side, just like Jonnie.

'Mum … Frankie had to go to Dad. You know he couldn't live without him. It's better this way.' As soon as those words came out of my mouth, I knew I couldn't take them back. All I could say was, 'Sorry Mum. Soorreee!'

Her strong hand swung out and slapped my face again. 'He was my son. I loved him. Who the fuck do you think you are?'

Barbara held onto her, probably thinking she was going to beat me black and blue.

My mind rewound to memories of her and Frankie. It was true. She did love him more than me. He'd poke her ribs or pull her apron tie while she was cooking dinner. I'd forgotten how she'd smiled at him, but never at me. She'd let him do whatever he wanted. But I had to do his jobs and mine. If I'd stolen stuff from Fong's, she woulda come down on me like a tonne of bricks. But even when Frankie killed Dad, she forgave him straight away. She really loved him.

239

'Lucy ...'

'Don't call me that!' I snapped.

'Okay, I'm sorry,' she said, looking over at *Waranmanha*.

'Oh yeah? You should've kept her instead of me!'

'No, that's not fair.' Her words had a hollow ring. 'You're just like my *Yagu* (mother), she never wanted to be close to me.'

'What? *Mimi* Lee? You've got to be kidding!' I was shocked. How could we both be feeling the same thing?

'Yes, you're *Mimi*,' she said, looking down with *gurndany* (shame).

Then *Mimi* uttered just one word, '*Bidi-Bidi* (Butterfly),' and Mum flew into her arms.

They wept; I wept; we all wept. All was forgiven between them. *Bidi-Bidi* was *JutinKarra Kawanarri* —she was ready to sing out for forgiveness to undo the past—all was forgiven.

Mimi's long arm reached out and grabbed my arm, pulling me into their love fest. She turned to look at Mum. 'She loves you, and I love you. I won't leave my *kurntal* (daughters) ever again,' she said, gently stroking Barbara's arm.

Mum was just looking at me with her eyes wide open. After all we'd been through, there was nothing to hide. '*Kurntal* (Daughter), I'm *pararrka talu* (sorry and ashamed), forgive me.'

Off to one side, Barbara and *Waranmanha* watched us in silence. They looked so awkward, like tits on a bull. I was expecting Mum to include *Waranmanha*, but she didn't, she just kept looking right at me until she got into my *rayi* (soul).

A long time passed until the hard bit in my heart cracked open. Then I felt the trust flow in. Forgiveness washed the past away; we were starting fresh.

Mimi sensed it was time to move. She bellowed out to the mob, 'C'mon, can't stay here forever, we need to set up a new camp. I'll ride back to

Kurriji pa Yajula (Dragon Tree Soak) to collect the lost girl's bones when the fire has burnt down.'

The moment *Mimi* said she was going back to fetch Loke, the lost girl, instantly I was there, watching from above. The many layers of *ngurlurrbi* (paperbark) snugly wound around her, forming a giant heart shape that was burning brightly. The reeds that so carefully held the bark together were now black and twisted like the crown of thorns that Jesus wore. The circle of simple crosses she'd made out of broken twigs and vines was on fire. And those little flames spread out their light, engulfing the Twin Dragon Trees and the vast, dark plains heading south.

The Twin Dragon Trees were ablaze, their fronds twisting and crackling in the raging inferno. Small explosions erupted in the crackling fire as seedpods released their loads. For a moment the ash-filled air cleared enough so that I could see down into the crown of the Dragon's Blood Trees. There they were, reaching towards me, gigantic spears of waxy, creamy white flowers. In the innermost heart of the flower-laden spears, fruit was forming. Once in every hundred years, we are blessed to see fruit form on our beloved Twin Dragon's Blood Trees[44].

I offered up prayers for Loke. No more *pararrka talu* (sorrow and shame). She was forgiven. Returning to the mob, I sang out, 'The Twin Dragon Trees are in flower and have fruit!'

Aunty Toots let out a catcall and started dancing. She took Mum by the hand, forcing her to dance, saying, 'It's gonna be alright, Mary. That's the sign. Don't look back.'

In the middle of our happy moment, *Mimi* shouted, 'Okay, everyone, time to move on!' Looking at me, she said, '*Bindamanha,* can you count?'

---

44   The Dragon's Blood Tree - *Dracaena Cinnabari*, is native to Socotra Island in the Arabian Sea, and it came to Australia with the cameleers. According to legend, the first Dragon's Blood Tree was created from the blood of a dragon when it fought an elephant. Its red sap is used for medicinal purposes to treat pain. It's also used in treatment of the AIDS virus.

'Of course I can count,' I said like a *maminy* (stupid idiot).

She raised her eyebrow waiting for me to start.

'*Waranmanha*, Mary—sorry, Mum—Barbara, Louanna, Aunty Toots, Sandy Gibb, Patty Mae, Sister Euphrates, Marissa and Polly Tipple. That's ten.'

'Did you count me?'

'Oh yeah, *Mimi*, that's eleven.' I could feel myself turning red with *gurndany* (shame).

'Did you count yourself?' *Mimi* asked shaking her head.

'Yeah. Nup. Me, Lucy, that's twelve.' *So dumb.* I was shocked that I'd used 'Lucy'. My face was burning up. I was so *gurndany*. I could have slapped my own face.

'Patty Mae, find a safe place with water. We've got to wash and rest this mob before …' She stopped herself short. We all knew the *wilara* (full moon) was near.

'Yeah, there's a place, just that side,' Patty Mae said, jutting her bottom lip out in the direction. 'Not too bad a walk. Good *Jila*, plenty tucker and no *Mungawarri* (very dangerous little spirit men that live in the hills).'

'*Barndi*! *Barndi*! (Good! Good!)' *Mimi* agreed.

Patty Mae set off quickly, making fast tracks with Sandy Gibb and Gofar as company.

'*Kurntal* (Daughters),' *Mimi* said, 'you ride *Winthuly-Winthuly*.'

Waranmanha and I looked up.

'Not you two,' she said dismissively. '*Bidi-Bidi* and *Pulpurra*, they rode on *Winthuly* when they were littlies.' *Mimi* was looking at them, but Mum was looking down and half turned away. She wouldn't look up or say anything. She'd shut down after Frankie. I felt real bad to see her going back to her old ways.

242

Mimi strode up to her and took her by the shoulders. Straight to her face, she said, 'I'm your *Yagu* (mother), always have been, always will be. We don't need fighters anymore, we need healers. I'm asking you to forgive me. Then in Mangala she continued:

My girls, my daughters, *Bidi-Bidi* (Mary) and *Pulpura* (Barbara)

Pararrka talu I'm sorry & ashamed I left you.
Pararrka talu I'm sorry & ashamed I didn't protect you.
Pararrka talu I'm sorry & ashamed I let the Lore divide us.
Pararrka talu I'm sorry & ashamed I made you afraid of me.
Pararrka talu I'm sorry & ashamed I never showed my love for you.
Pararrka talu I'm sorry & ashamed I am your Yagu.

There was deadly silence on all sides. It felt like she was speaking for every mother who'd felt *pararrka talu*. Mum and Barbara fell into *Mimi's* arms like small children. Mum raised her head from their embrace to look at *Waranmanha*, and then me. I nodded my forgiveness and I felt a weight lift off my chest and a darkness leave my eyes.

Waranmanha was acknowledging Mum when Barbara looked up and caught her eye. Barbara mouthed, 'I love you'.

I glanced over at Louanna; she was lost in a big hug with her mum. I felt a gentle lick on the back of my hand. Looking down I saw two large, dark-brown eyes looking longingly up at me. 'Forgive me *Gulyi*, I'm *pararrka talu*.'

This time those words were light on the air like a cool, early morning breeze in *parranga* (hot weather time). He opened his mouth wide and tried to tell me all was forgiven. *Birri* snorted loudly, and then she came over and stood in real close. I hugged them both. Healing for us mob was happening out here on Country.

Even Patty Mae, Sandy Gibb and Marissa, the toughest women on the planet, were hugging each other. Patty Mae's great desert-yellow mop of hair and her orange beard flowed over Sandy Gibb's thin, black shoulder.

'Time to go. *Thubarnimanha* (Straighten up).'

Waranmanha and I glanced at each other; *Mimi* was the new *Jalbri*. '*Kurntal, Winthuly-Winthuly*, ta ta,' she said, just like *Jalbri*.

Winthuly-Winthuly immediately fell to her knees and her big head rose expectantly. Barbara got on first. Mum wrapped her arms around Barbara's waist and held on tight as the old camel lumbered off her knees into a standing position.

Little Sister Euphrates sat with me on *Birri*, with *Gulyi* tailing us. *Waranmanha* took Louanna and Polly Tipple. *Mimi* took Aunty Toots. Poor Aunty Toots felt shy to hang onto *Mimi* because of her massive boobs. Her arms were flapping all over the place. *Mimi* wasn't impressed, so Toots put both her arms back behind her, resting on *Ramu's* broad rump for balance, but still her boobs bounced up and down against *Mimi's* back. I couldn't help laughing. Although Marissa had a bit of a limp, she was one tough bitch and recovered well enough to walk it with her new mates, Patty Mae, Sandy Gibb and Gofar.

30. The Slipper

It was lovely to have Sister here with me. I had missed her sweet French accent.

'*Ma chère*, I am very proud of you.'

'Really, Sister?'

'*Oui,* my dear. I can see that you have been through a lot and that you have grown into a beautiful, wise young lady.'

'Nah! Sure you're talkin' about me?'

'Tell me *ma chérie*, what things have been lessons for you?'

People didn't usually talk to me like that. I felt shy, but I started telling her the whole story from the beginning.

Sister's little white hands clutched my waist tightly. Time passed quickly with her at my back. I felt so loved and respected by her. I even had the guts to tell her, a nun, about Manu. She laughed, asking me if we got permission from the Pope. She was a real friend, none of that 'shoulda, woulda, coulda' stuff. She gets me and I love her for that.

We arrived at the most beautiful waterhole you could imagine. It was hot and humid, and all us mob were filthy dirty. We shouted out the call to Country and jumped into the icy-cold water. The older women got their energy back and started splashing us young ones.

Aunty Toots made us laugh when she tried to bob down under the water and her boobs popped up around her ears like a pair of floaties. She laughed so much she almost choked to death. I listened to the laughter bouncing off the rock walls and saw 'happiness' like I'd never seen it before. It had to be that forgiveness stuff—it must have pushed the sadness out and let the joy come right in.

Even the animals were swimming in the soak. *Winthuly-Winthuly* was on a mission to drink the waterhole dry. She had to keep shaking her head cos her eyelids were heavy with water. Polly was splashing *Ramu* who was stuck to *Winthuly-Winthuly* like glue. They sure had a stack of history together; nothing would separate them now. *Ramu's* scary pale-blue eyes had softened, and he was shaking and rocking his head, like he was beating out the time. His strong jet-black bottom lip pressed against his snow-white upper lip as he playfully sprayed water at Polly. He was a good shot too.

Gulyi and Gofar were busy trying to catch the spray in their mouths. *Wilara* and *Birri* were staying right out of trouble. They had waddled in shoulder-deep and were happy to cool off, hanging out together. I watched *Mimi* playing in the water like a little girl, happy and free. She'd found her real home with family on Country.

Sister Euphrates was really short. Her baggy long johns and bonnet were so waterlogged and heavy, they were holding her down. We took it in turns to swim over and hold her up while she cupped her hands and took aim at her next target. She's a gutsy one and gave as good as she got. I reckon that's how we all should be in life.

There we were, out in Country, eating well, talking about real stuff and doing important things. Learning how to *forgive* and how to accept being *forgiven*—it's so important for our mob. Life in town is always too serious, and it's too hard for us mob to fit in. School teachers tell me I'm *maminy* (stupid), and the Townies let me know I don't belong. Out here, all us mob belong. Out here we can Dream and receive our Lore.

The water made me think of my Bird Boy, and before I knew what I was doing, I could hear the eerie moan of conch shells and the sound of his people singing on the shore at Rebi Island—his clan's traditional home land. Manu had shown me Rebi on a map, so I knew exactly where it was—a tiny island in the Tiwi group about eighty kilometres off the coast of Darwin. Manu is the eldest son and his parents are the Chieftains of Tiwi Island.

On the beach, conch blowers announced Manu's departure with puffing cheeks and rising chests. The King and Queen were standing like stone statues drenched in the golden rays of the afternoon sun. A group of women in long, brightly coloured floral dresses swayed and sang, surrounded by other members of their tribe. There were pots of food still boiling on open fires, and flowers were strewn along the shore. Twenty to thirty dugouts were out on the beach.

Just as I turned my eyes to the sea to search for him, I copped a mouth full of water from *Mimi*. Gasping for breath, I decided it was payback time. But, she was too quick for me. Before I knew it, she was standing at the edge of the water, stark naked, announcing it was time to get out and set up camp before dark. When she shouted, nobody dared hang back. Everyone got out, even the animals. Playtime was over.

It didn't take long to get several fires burning and collect a heap of bush tucker. Patty Mae was an awesome hunter, so us mob were set up for a real good feed. After collecting a bunch of stuff and making our beds, we settled down to sing, waiting for the meal to cook. The mozzies were out in droves. *Jurdu* (smoke) from the fires hung heavily in the air, keeping them at bay. The bugs were insane. It was noisier near a waterhole at night than it was in the open desert plains.

Those *mamany* (crazy) birds were back, but as the darkness rolled in, they fought for the best perch. Closing their silly eyelids, they peeped themselves to sleep. The chirping of cicadas, croaking frogs and the howling of dingos, seeing off wild dogs and feral cats, set the scene for the bats.

Screeching and twittering as they launched themselves out of deep crevasses in the rock face, their rubbery wings flapped loudly as they swooped down taking a sip of water before swinging around and flying off above us—their wing tips almost touched our heads. Louanna and I were freaking out. We shook our heads madly and waved our arms, afraid that these winged vampires might bite us with their horrible little teeth.

Once the bats had cleared off, we ate and drank bush honey tea under the almost full moon. Sister Euphrates started to sing. Her sweet French accent made me feel relaxed and I fell asleep.

It was still dark when I woke with a start. My neck was really stiff. Patty Mae and Sandy Gibb were having a snore off, and Polly Tipple was fast asleep still chattering to her mummy. My eyes slowly adjusted to the dark. *Gulyi* was laying on his back, legs apart, balls on show. No *gurndany* (shame).

'Something bothering you?' All those years in Vietnam during the war made Sister a light sleeper.

'Yeah, I had a bad dream.'

'Tell me, sweetheart.' She got up, stoked the fire and put the billy on.

The once huge, bright full moon that had hung low in front of the waterhole and called the bats out to play, had now left the waterhole. Along with all the night creatures, it had followed the *tingari* (migratory song cycle), heading *kara* (west) towards the sea. The moon was now just a tiny thing hanging silently just above the horizon. I reckon it must have been about 3am. Proper Salt-Water men would have been out in their boats pulling in their nets right now. It was a perfect morning for a big catch.

The firelight comforted me as I told Sister everything. 'I dreamt I was asleep in my bed back home on Anne Street. *Gulyi* was there too, curled up on the end of my bed.' Sister nodded. 'I woke to go to the dunny (toilet) and noticed the moon shining through my long, narrow sash window. Sitting on the edge of the bed, I went to put my feet into a pair of embroidered turquoise-blue velvet slippers. You know the type?' I asked, using my finger to draw the curved top and the flat bottom.

'*Oui, oui* (yes, yes), Turkish slipper.' Just mentioning fabric made Sister's eyes twinkle.

'Sister, I don't even have slippers, especially not those sorts of slippers. They were made for a princess, not me, they were real posh scuffs.'

'Oh, *c'est magnifique* (that's wonderful), go on.' Sister was really getting into it.

'A deadly black snake was coiled inside one of the slippers; its mouth sprang open to attack me. The weird thing is, I knew it wasn't my foot. It was a little girl's foot. Honey-coloured like Manu's, not dark like mine.' I took a deep breath, realising what I'd just said.

'*D'accord*! *Bien sûr!* (Okay! Of course)!' Sister was always saying that.

'Just as the snake was about to stick its fangs into my foot, *Gulyi-Gulyi* sprang into action and grabbed the snake sorta sideways behind its open jaws. I screamed; I thought the snake was gonna kill him. *Gulyi* wouldn't let it go. He shook his head so violently that he broke the snake's jaw. The snake wiggled off real fast and disappeared. Then I noticed a large, dead, black rat beside the other slipper. I hadn't noticed it before.'

Sister cringed. '*C'est horrible!*' (That's horrible!)

'All of sudden, I don't know how, I was in a car, driving to pick up my friend Paula. Even though I don't drive, I was taking her to my book launch. Don't ask me what my book was about. I was driving real slow, super careful-like. Paula was super annoyed and kept poking me real hard over and over. She was in a big hurry to get home, cos she'd left her son Braden all alone. He's autistic like Jonnie. So, I understood why she was real worried about him.

'Eventually we arrived at this big posh meeting to launch my book, but there wasn't just one book, there were three. I was meant to sign them but I couldn't remember my name. Paula kept saying, "We gotta go, Braden's on his own." She wouldn't stop nagging me, so we had to go. On the drive back to her place, I had to keep stopping cos every time I looked out the window, we were in a different country and I kept getting lost. It was so frustrating. Then I thought, *What's up?* I looked up and drove my little car into the *bundarra* (stars). *Miniwarri* (The Seven Sisters) gave us directions to get back to Earth. Finally, we arrived at Paula's house, and she just ran inside, she didn't say goodbye or nothing.

'I reached over to get something off the back seat and my hand grabbed the blue velvet slipper. The snake stuck its fangs into my hand and I let the slipper fall. Then I noticed that the whole car was filled with dead rats—black ones, brown ones, white ones, and many without fur. The last thing I remember is being hypnotised by the black serpent's gentle swaying. His longing eyes pleaded with me to follow him. Seduced by his call, I was drawn into the slit of its pupil like a bat returning home to its cave before dawn. As I glided into the abyss, I wondered who had killed those rats, him or me. What do you reckon, Sister?'

As she poured our tea, her hand shook slightly. Sister looked up at me— something had changed in her. All French pleasantries were gone; she was real serious and straight to the point. '*Bindamanha,* there are three major chapters to your life. This one is about to close. The little girl who was putting her foot into the slipper is your daughter, *Waranmanha*.'

I felt like throwing up cos I knew she was right.

'You will protect her, but in the end you too will pass.'

'What about Paula and Braden, is something going to happen to them?' I was super stressed now.

'Your life will be a very long one. So many will hurry into and out of your life. When we are given a person's name in a dream, it means they are of great significance. Watch out for each other. Paula will always be there for you in spite of her responsibilities.'

'Really?' I interrupted. 'What's with the full moon?'

Her eyes were moist with tears now. 'Those you love will come and leave, illuminated by its light. When the sky is dark, your heart will close and you will be alone.' She reached over and squeezed my hand. She offered me a piece of *bilabirdi* (eucalyptus leaf) to chew on to stop me feeling nauseous.

As my stomach started to settle, I asked, 'When did you learn to read dreams?'

With a sweet turned-up smile, she said, 'I never told you that my parents were Romani Gypsies. We ran what you call a "sideshow". Ah, my mother was the best fortune teller and dream seer in the whole of France.'

Forgetting the horrific fortune she saw for me, I asked excitedly, 'Did you have a caravan?'

'*Oui, oui, bien sûr!* (Yes, yes of course). We all had horse drawn caravans. That is our Romani way. My horse was Christos. Ah, he was so beautiful and strong. But that was so long ago, my dear. Too much water has passed under my bridge.'

'I knew you could ride. I could really feel it when you were sitting behind me on *Birri*,' I said, smiling broadly.

Mimi must have been listening cos she turned over and said, 'Today we rest. Sleep, you'll need it. We're gonna set off after dinner.' There was softness but nervousness in her tone.

'Yes, *Mimi*.' I got up and headed to the bed I'd made earlier. Passing Sister, I bent over and kissed the top of her coif (head cover), it was still slightly damp. 'What do the dead rats mean?' I whispered so that *Mimi* couldn't hear me.

'The rats are all the difficultés (difficulties) you will face—some from your mob and other *Aborigène* (Aboriginal) people, too much problémes from white people, even others from faraway lands looking for profit and to take advantage.' She took my hand in hers and kissed it like a subject would her queen. 'You come from a noble line, don't ever forget all your people who have and will go *up*, they will guide you.'

I could still feel the impression of her lips on the back of my hand.

Manu was from a noble line; I'd never thought of myself like that until now. Our unborn daughter is a true princess. I lay in my nest looking for my *Jalbri's* home star and fell asleep with her words ringing softly in my ears:

'What's up?'

'What's down?'

'What's in the middle?'

31. Breathe

When I woke it was late, almost midday. The sun was high in the sky and all the fires had burnt out. I must have slept like the dead. Everyone was lying around like they'd only just woken too. The air felt still and sorta empty like the oxygen had been sucked out of it. I found it hard to breathe.

Looking around I noticed Sister Euphrates struggling to get up. She was sunburnt real bad, even though she was wearing more clothes than the rest of us. I could hear Patty Mae and Sandy Gibb talking behind me.

'Everything's just got up and gone,' Patty Mae said.

'What do you mean?' I asked, with my back to her. My energy was totally zapped; I couldn't even turn around; it was just too hard.

'All the animals have left, even the insects.'

'You're kidding? Yeah right, pull the other one,' I said mockingly.

'Look! Out there, in front of you.'

Patty Mae was right. In the distance I could see flocks of birds and huge grey swarm of insects off to the north. *Yalibii* (emus) and *marloos* (big red kangaroos) fled in droves, and even *malji* (tomcats) and *kuli kunyarr* (wild dogs) ran side by side. On the ground there were usually thousands of *milyura* (snakes) and *bungarra* (lizard), but there was no evidence of a single slithering or scurrying creature in sight.

It was as if we were sitting at ground zero. 'Any *jindirala* (dragonflies)?' I asked. The soaks in the Kimberly's are thick with *jindirala* this time of year.

Polly Tipple started chattering, 'No fly-flies, all gone. No pretty fly-flies, all gone.'

We took the hovering flashes of iridescent reds and blues for granted. Now I missed them like family.

My arms and legs were so heavy, I couldn't lift them. I felt totally spaced out and my speech was slurred, I sounded like a druggie.

'No fly–flies, all gone. No fly-flies—'

'Shut up!' I hissed, trying to bark at Polly. Turning my eyes, I could just see *Mimi* lying flat on her back.

From that position, she commanded us, 'Patty Mae, Sandy Gibb, Louanna, Barbara, Toots, Marissa, get out of here. Head towards Help Canyon, light your *milis* (firesticks).'

Sandy and Patty slowly dragged themselves to the nearest snuffed out fire and tried to relight it.

'It's no use, it won't take.' Patty Mae was worried.

I remembered the Golden Fleece matches in my bag near the fire. 'Use the matches in my bag,' I said.

Insulted by my suggestion, with a grimace she struck one, then another and another. It was no use; the matches wouldn't light either. Where had all the oxygen gone?

Struggling to her feet, in a raspy voice, *Mimi* ordered, 'You mob get your horses out of here now!' She stood hunched over, gasping for breath in front of *Ramu*. 'Come *Ramu*.' With each order she shuffled back a step and *Ramu* dragged his enormous body along by his front legs. He whinnied softly, pleading with her to forgive him for losing his strength. It was painful to watch. They did about a hundred paces before they were out and managed to catch their breath again. Aunty Toots had an interesting technique. She kept rolling over and over until she reached *Mimi*. Then she stood up looking all proud of herself.

Gulyi-Gulyi was barking wildly, running from left to right as if blocked by this *mamany* (crazy) sorta force field airlock thingy. He must have gone off on his early morning hunt before the air got sucked out. 'Stop! Sit!' *Mimi* barked, trying to focus on us. Surprisingly he sat down and shut up.

Waranmanha was slowly pulling herself along the ground using her arms. *Mimi* was pleading with her to get up and lead *Wilara* out. I could hear *Birri* stomping and snorting on the opposite side of the airlock. Suddenly, she thundered in, went straight over to *Wilara*, took his mane in her teeth and pulled him to safety.

'*Barndi*! *Barndi* (Good, clever) girl.' *Mimi* patted and kissed her.

Snorting in deeply, she trotted back in. She must have been holding her breath or something. She lined herself up behind me and started pushing and nipping me lightly, forcing me to move forward. It wasn't long before I was out too.

Now only Mum, Sister Euphrates and *Winthuly-Winthuly* remained. *Mimi* wasn't having a bar of it. She drew a breath and ran in grabbing her daughter by her arms and dragging her out of there. Puffing up her lungs again, she took *Birri* in with her and lifted Sister onto *Birri's* back and let her trot out. *Mimi* followed exhausted.

All eyes were on *Winthuly-Winthuly*. She'd shat herself. Her tongue was lolling out of the side of her mouth and her eyes were starting to roll to the back of her head.

'I think she's finished,' I said.

'Rubbish!' *Mimi* was furious. 'What's up?' I heard her say under her breath. Suddenly she cried out, '*Yagu pararrka talu* (Mother, I'm sorry and ashamed),' like she felt guilty for not looking after *Winthuly*. And then, honest to God, like gunfire from Heaven, we heard, 'TA TA!'

Winthuly-Winthuly groaned and raised her massive head. Like magic, she stood up and stumbled out of there and back to life. We erupted in celebration, jumping around, hugging *Birri* and *Winthuly-Winthuly*. Sister fell to her knees in prayer.

Waranmanha and I shouted, '*Thubarnimanha* (Straighten up)! *Thubarnimanha*! *Thubarnimanha*!' We broke into some pretty cool break-dance moves. Everyone was shouting '*thubarnimanha*' and cutting loose with some moves of their own. *Mimi* was real Woodstock and Mum was bopping. Who'd believe that?

'Eyes to the right!' *Mimi* yelled.

Something was racing towards us, shifting the atmosphere. An enormous serpentine form hurtled through the sky. It was so big it looked like a massive storm cloud. It cast a long, purple shadow on the ground that slithered towards us at great speed.

'It's *Pulanyi Bulaing* and *Kulpan Karrangu* racing to the battle ground,' *Mimi* yelled, waving her arm madly to urge us on. *Mimi* raised her voice, '*Kantiyala*! (Ride him). *Kantiyala*! *Kantiyala*!'

My blood ran cold. '*Tnick tnick*.' *Birri* was beside me in a second. Grabbing her mane, I hoisted myself up. 'Sister!' I called, extending my hand to her. We were galloping flat out but we couldn't keep up with the others. *Gulyi* ran behind us yelping.

'Ease up, *Bindamanha*, I'll pick him up,' Sister said.

I slowed a little.

With real circus style, Sister loosened her grip on me, swung her lean body over to my left, hooked her right foot into my waist and let herself flop backwards off to the left side. By the time *Birri* had taken another pace, *Gulyi* was snugly sandwiched between my back and her chest.

'YA-WHOO!' I exclaimed.

Big trouble was coming. We seemed to have lost the whole day. The sun was already setting as we galloped towards Help Canyon. We were not alone. In the elongated shadows of spindly trees and spinifex, we could see an array of our tribal warriors keeping eyes on us and watching our backs. *Waranmanha* was up the front with *Mimi* and Mum. *Winthuly-Winthuly* was hot on *Ramu's* tail. I couldn't help thinking how beautiful my sister looked. I wondered if this was it. Soon she would be gone. Soon I would lose her to be forever alone. She felt me looking at her and turned for an instant to acknowledge me.

Stepping into the darkness through serpentine shadows, it was really hard to see while cutting through the bushes. I imagined anything that moved was an evil spirit. Fear blinded me. We'd fallen behind the others and my anxiety was growing with each step. I heard voices calling out. Terrified, I dug my heels in and pulled *Birri's* mane to turn her around. She ignored me and lightly stepped through the bush, sure-footed and courageous.

Sister must have felt me. 'Think of Manu,' she said, and then she started to sing, 'Manu's over the sea. Somewhere he's waiting for Lucy …'

I suddenly felt light and airy. Taking any excuse to escape my body, I found myself floating above Manu rowing out onto the high sea.

'Lucky-Child, is it you?' his voice carried across the swell.

'I love you, Manu Tollie.'

Illuminated by the full moon, the carved shark pendant almost looked alive as it swayed from side to side on his rippling chest muscles glistening wet with salt water. A hundred waves broke in endless lines, their crests like white lace on a dark-green velvet tapestry.

'I'll go sailing,' Sister's singing eased me back into my body.

'Where are we?' I asked. *Milis* (Firesticks) were burning brightly; their flickering light caught the ridges on the Canyon's rock wall making them look like scary faces. We'd come to a halt and were standing with the others, ready to take instruction from *Mimi*.

'You all know Help Canyon one way or another.' A shudder went through me. 'The *Zalfinhi* are out, but they are not why we are here. This is the time of *Wakaj Kanarri* (The Finishing) and you are the chosen ones.'

I let out an anxious squeal.

'*Bindamanha* ! Stop it!' *Mimi* barked, instantly shutting me up.

Everyone had dismounted except for Sister and me. I knew she was staying to comfort me. I'm never good with scary shit.

'Get down,' *Mimi* insisted.

Sister dismounted, but I dug my heels in again and flapped my hands, wanting my wretched horse to turn around and head off. To where, I didn't care. *Gulyi-Gulyi* stood on his hind legs with his front paws on *Birri*, whining softly and licking my toes.

'Patty Mae, get her down!' *Mimi* ordered.

Patty Mae strode over, grabbed my left arm and leg and yanked hard.

I flew off *Birri* and landed heavily on the ground.

Mimi composed herself and said calmly, 'Everyone stay and hold the sacred space. Be together and expand your energy out until I get back. I'm going to get *Yagu's* (Mother's) remains.'

I jumped to my feet covered in creepy crawlies and started to cry hysterically.

'Don't leave me! I want to come with you.'

'*Bindamanha* stay! Stay!' she said firmly, as if I was her bloody *duthu* (dog).

258

The Secret

An assortment of flying insects were swarming around the *milis* and our ears were humming cos the air was thick with mozzies. Flapping my arms, I ran straight through them to my *mimi*.

She'd already mounted *Ramu*. I held onto her foot 'Pleeease ... I want to go with you. Don't leave me here!' I was leaning on *Ramu*, and *Gulyi* was licking and mouthing my hand, trying to get me to come away. I felt *Ramu's* rump tense as he turned his head towards me.

'*RAMUU*!' *Mimi* said firmly, knowing he was getting ready to kick my teeth out. I saw her squeeze her knees into *Ramu's* broad girth. He moved forward, but I refused to let go of her foot.

First I staggered, and then I just let *Ramu* drag me along. I had a real strong grip on *Mimi's* big red-painted toe and I wasn't letting go.

'SHIT! Let go!' she yelled, completely forgetting about the *Zalfinhi*.

Ramu pulled up abruptly, thinking she was yelling at him. The force of his halt loosened my grip and I fell face first into the dirt. *Gulyi* jumped on my back and started licking my ear. 'STOP!' I yelled, flicking him off with a deadly roll. He went flying through the air and hit Polly, knocking her off her stump. Everyone cracked up laughing.

A long sigh escaped from *Mimi's* lips. 'Okay, get on.'

I think I totally rattled her.

She got out her lippy and applied it like a pro. Then, with an impatient, fed up look on her face, she pulled out a cigar, lit it and inhaled deeply. 'I'll be back soon. Hold the space,' she told the women.

Ramu was so big that I needed Sandy Gibb to help me get up. I hung on tight behind her, too tight for her liking but that was too bad, I wasn't letting go for nothing. I was still bawling[45] my head off when we left.

'Could you not snot on me?' she said through clenched teeth.

45   Bawling - Crying

259

'I know you think I'm stupid,' I said, feeling sorry for myself.

'Yes, and?' she said sarcastically.

'I've got the anxiety real bad, and you make it worse.'

'Get over it,' was her response.

'You don't know what it's like to be struck by lightning and die.'

'That's your lesson, not mine, I got other fish to fry,' she said coolly.

'Oh yeah? *Ja ... she* said you're meant to teach me and look after me!' I was sparking up now.

'Grow up. Learn this… look after yourself!'

'What does that mean?' I snapped at her, snot still pouring out of my nose onto her special red top that hung off her skinny, rigid back like elephant skin. She'd lost a lot of weight too.

'Grow up! How can you be ready if you don't grow up? No one can hold your hand all the time.'

'I am grown up!'

'Yeah, sure. Are we talking bra size 12 or shoe size 7?' she said sarcastically. 'Stop with the snot, I can't bear it!' *Mimi* pulled *Ramu* up sharp and jumped off him.

Suddenly, panic hit me again, fearing she was going to leave me sitting there with *Ramu*.

'Move forward!' She sprang up behind me and reached forward for the reigns.

Her long arms were now on either side of me. Immediately I felt different, less like an outcast desperately clinging on to the stiff bitch.

Quietly, she whispered into my right ear. 'You only have to remember two things. Who you are and what you are here for.'

'Why don't you respect what I've been through?' I questioned.

'I do. You're more than that.'

'What do you mean? Don't preach to me when you went off, got knocked up twice, dropped the babies on your *yagu* and then rejected your own daughters. And my mum, you punished her for doing what you did, except she stuck by her man and would have raised both of us kids if she was allowed to. Yeah, ya even rejected us kids. What did we do to you? You were meant to be our *Mimi* (grandmother)!

I was fuming, but she cut me off. 'Get off!'

'Nah! You're not leaving me here, like you did your kids.'

'Get off!' She jumped off. *Ramu* reared up and I fell off. She patted his strong neck, rewarding him.

I sat on the ground crying. '*Parraka talu* (I'm sorry and ashamed).'

Mimi stretched out her open hand to me in silence. Helping me to my feet in one action, she wrapped her arms around me and held me tight. I wanted her to say that she forgave me. But she was still trying to recover from the shit I'd just dumped on her.

Finally, she took a step back, held me firmly by the shoulders, took a deep breath and said, 'Stay here. I'm going to get *her* remains.' She turned and walked off briskly.

I ran after her screaming, 'You're not leaving me here!' I grabbed the waistband at the back of her jeans.

She turned to face me. I thought she was going to take a swing at me, but instead she grabbed my hand and almost yanked it off. 'Come on then! If that's what you want, come!'

She was furious, walking at a running pace. I was finding it hard to keep up with her. A twig got stuck under my toenail, but I kept going. I didn't dare say anything.

Mimi was muttering something in a language—God knows what. Looking up and shaking her head made me think she was complaining about me to someone. 'Stop talking about me,' I whined.

'Don't tell me you're fucking paranoid too!' But side-on in the moonlight, I saw a wry smile come to her lips and her eyes softened.

32. Nalaman – Shedding

We arrived at *Junki* and *Nypni's* rock pool. The reflection of the *mitimitis* (full moon) lit up half the waterhole like a stage spotlight. *Ramu* had followed us. *Mimi* led him to the water's edge. She bent down, cupped her hands, scooped up some water and put her hands under his large, soft lips. He slurped it up and she stroked him, reassuring him, that he was a good boy. Watching her with him melted the hardness in my heart towards her.

'Ready to go up?' *Mimi* asked.

I nodded.

She called out to the Spirits of the waterhole to accept us coming on their Country. Her voice echoed off the water and surrounding rocks and reminded me of *why* I was there and *who* I was with. Then she lightly sprinkled a handful of sand into the water and whispered a private greeting to her *yagu*. She took

263

some *mili* branches that were growing at the back of the rock base and used them to scrape the earth clean, and then she lit them with the cigarette lighter from her back pocket. 'Let's go.'

I nodded. She was a good climber but so was I. Keeping pace, I was proud of myself and felt like I was regaining a little respect.

It felt awesome standing on the ledge looking down. A ripple went through the still water below. 'What's that?' I whispered nervously.

'No problem, that's a keeper.'

I didn't ask any more. I didn't really want to know what creature was lurking under there watching us. We pushed back the rock that blocked the entrance and entered the cave.

Something had changed. *Junki* and *Nypi* were now bright red. 'Who did this? I asked, fearing some vandal had come in here.

'I dressed them in red ochre when I did the ceremony for *her* remains.'

'Where's *Jalbri*?' I asked.

Mimi shook her head in disbelief. She jabbed her *mili* (firestick) into the cave floor, and refusing to engage in *maminy* (stupid) conversation with me, she started to sing. She passed me two painted stones and clapped them together, indicating that I should continue clapping while she sang.

The firelight flickered against the painted walls. The *Jin.gis'* eyes looked kindly at us. *Mimi* got out *her* remains from a large crevasse in the wall. I'm sure I saw the painted *Jin.gi's* blink their eyes and nod their heads. I gasped. She placed the *ngurlurrbi* (paperbark) package on the floor and opened it. On top was *her* skull. It looked more alive than *her* fleshy, dead body.

Mimi continued to sing as she took one of *her* hands in hers and snapped off the pointer finger. The sharp sound was sickening. She looked up and handed it to me.

'WHAATT!' I said, like a complete idiot.

264

'It's an honour for you to continue her work,' *Mimi* said slowly and clearly.

'*Pararrka talu*,' I said sincerely, bowing down to her to receive my *Jalbri's* bone. I reached into my little pouch and took out *Jalbri's yagu's* finger bone. Looking at *Mimi* with the greatest respect, I asked, 'Would it be right to let *Jalbri's yagu's* bone rest here with *Junki* and *Nypni*?'

Mimi's eyes, her mouth and every bit of her, beamed with joy. 'Yes. That is the right thing to do.' She'd forgiven me for using *Jalbri's* name—she knew I was un-teachable.

Without her telling me what to do, I walked up and stood between *Junki* and *Nypni*. 'Would you look after my *Jalbri's yagu's* finger bone?'

A light breeze blew into the cave. The *mili* flickered and *Junki* and *Nypni* came to life.

They appeared not as skeletons but were fleshed-out and painted in red ochre. *Junki* was the dominant twin. She had a stylish air about her and her hair was queenly. *Nypni* looked a little spooky. Her eyes were starry and bulging and gave me the feeling she was expecting something bad was going to happen any minute. She had that real 'Cinderella complex'. I bet she painted a hundred *Jin.gi* stones to one of *Junki's*. *Nypni* carefully took the bone and placed it in a little slot in the rock face.

Junki's eyes twinkled with delight.

'*Kurntal murrung kurr, kalwarra jarriyarri miltiln* (Daughter a Spirit Child is being born to you).'

Nypni smiled timidly, making little humming sounds in soft agreement.

Suddenly the mood changed. *Junki's* eyes looked through me, past *Mimi* into the 'Beyond Beyond', where time stood still and vast distances were travelled in the single blink of an eye.

265

Junki's voice was low and her face mask like.

In Mangala she said:

'*Parrkana. Wangal ngana purrpun kakarrangu.*'

'Now times are cold, the wind blows in from the East.'

'*Yartarr, mingala gnana wutan.*'

'Everywhere, tears are running.'

'*Kakarranguna Kantinyarri mitimitila.*

'The full moon, she rises in the East.'

Nypni sang out,

'*Linkarra.Linkarra.*'

'True. True.'

Junki continued,

'*Kulpan Karrangu japartinyarri.*'

'*Kulpan Karrangu* (The Black Red Bellied Serpent) is coming.'

'*Paril ngana rrinya lanpuyangka.*

'He woke me up from sleep.'

The pitch of *Nypni*'s voice intensified as a chill wind whipped around us,

The Secret

'*Linkarra. Linkarra. Paril ngana rrinya lanpuyangka.*'
'It is true. It is true. He woke me up from my sleep,'

On that wicked wind, *Junki* whispered,

'*Milkanyarna yulpurru miparr.*'
'I have seen His face before.'

'*Balayi Biindamanah! Balayi!*'
'Watch out *Bindamanha* ! Watch out!'

When I heard my name, my heart missed a beat.
Nypni squawked, like a deranged *biyarrgu* (galah),

'*Balayi! Maranyan ngana jarri kuwipurri.*'
'Watch out. He is hungry for flesh.'

Junki took my hand, and looking deep into my rayi (soul), she said,

'*Pakatuju ngana jimanjimanarri mulnyi julatuja.*'
'The blind man feels his way across the ground with a stick.'

'*Bindamanha, Lipurra mil walpura.*'
'*Bindamanha,* you must open your eye.'

267

'*Pantaangka Lirra Larrka!*'

'Then you must open your mouth!'

Then in English she said,

'You must protect our people and our Country.'

'*Wakaj kanarri* (The finishing) has come.'

Nypni added excitedly. '*Linkarra. Linkarra* (True, true),'

Junki continued,

'*Ngijakura kututu Kurriji nyaltu karrpina ngarnan palyjarrangu.*

'With all my heart I am giving you this left turning boomerang.'

Junki placed the large *palyjarrangu* (boomerang) in my hands.

'*Palyjarrangu always return true*,' she said, looking deeply into my eye.

Feeling the weight of her words, I said, 'I promise to be true.'

Junki and *Nypni* both smiled.

'*Warrimparna* (Bye bye),' they said in unison.

Their images dissolved into the flickering firelight and they were gone.

Only their red-painted skeletons remained still and lifeless in their bush beds surrounded by thousands of painted *Jin.gi* stones.

'*Mimi?*'

'I'm still here,' she said, handing me her *mili* while she secured *Jalbri's* remains, covering the crevasses with a large painted stone.

I followed her out of the cave onto the ledge. *Mimi* sat with her legs hanging over the edge just like I did the first time I came here. She invited me to sit beside her. She took out a little cigar and lit it from the *mili,* drawing in a deep smoke-filled breath. 'See over there?' She pointed the glowing cigar tip in the direction we had come from. 'The women are holding the sacred space. They're a good strong mob. Can you see those white shapes moving between them and Help Canyon?'

'Yes,' I responded.

'That's the *Zalfinhi,*' she said, looking at me for a reaction. But I was calm as, just sitting there with my Mimi, hugging my *palyjarramgu* (boomerang).

'*Bindamanha,* are you ready to do this big work?'

'Yes, something has changed inside me, I'm not scared anymore.'

On cue, a painted rock fell from the ledge into the rock pool below. A ripple went out from where the stone entered the water. The reflection of the full moon was moving overhead. Suddenly the whole surface of the water moved as if something enormous had flapped its tail. The bright orb of the moon was shattered and a swampy smell filled the air.

'The keeper is stirring. *Wakaj Kanarri* (The Finishing) is here. We must return to the others.'

Without speaking, I followed *Mimi* down the rock face. *Ramu* was waiting for us at the bottom. From a rocky ledge, *Mimi* sprung onto *Ramu's* back. I handed her my gift and got on behind her. Then we galloped off, leaving *Junki, Nypni, Jalbri* and her *yagu* and the *Keeper* far behind.

When we got closer to the women holding sacred space, *Mimi* was careful not to break through the wall of energy they'd made. She slowed *Ramu* down to a walk. I didn't react to the *Zalfinhi* darting at us menacingly. They had no power over me now. The scaredy-cat kid had gone.

269

I walked into the circle in front of *Mimi* and *Ramu*. A new power had entered my limbs. *Waranmanha* was on the other side of the circle. We walked up to each other and hugged. I was back, but something deep inside me had changed. For the first time in my life I felt strong, centred and comfortable in my skin. *Waranmanha's* hug was different too. She had also changed. Her new-found strength was courage. She was calmly letting destiny have its way with her without resistance.

I've always been a watcher of people. Everyone's on the run, even me. Usually, its other people making you run, like Mum, my school and stuff. Only the old timers have got time. The rest of us run until the seconds turn into hours, days, months and years. Before you know it, all the shoulda, woulda, couldas turn into old baggage and it gets so heavy you can't carry it anymore, then we break. That's the real pain—not being able to put your baggage down and off-load some of ya shit along the way. We all need to sit down, take time and let the past catch up with the present.

I reckon there's only a few times when you're really in the *present,* when you can see the future a split second in front of you, like yesterday is properly finished, but tomorrow hasn't come yet. That's when you know things will never be the same ever again. There's no turning back. You just gotta meet it face on either in fear, or you give yourself up to that moment and trust whatever was on the other side of that next breath, was always meant to be.

Waranmanha and I were both at *that* point in time. Soon we would find the meaning of our life and our place in the universe. This was our portal to a different reality, our 'Star Trek' moment. She will travel with the stars through all the Dreaming Worlds. And me, I will stay in this world but not *be* of this world. But I will look up to the stars and never forget to Dream.

The *mama* (sacred song) the women were singing wound its way around us like swaddling cloth, like it was keeping us safe from the outside world. For those few precious moments, we were being *present* in the *present*.

In twinly unison, we reached into our pouches, took out our mother of pearl pendants, hung them around our necks and looked up.

High above us the *mitimiti* (full moon) was covered by layers of vapours that formed into wispy clouds obscuring its shape. The *mitimiti's* brilliance drenched the clouds that tried to block out its light in colours of turquoise and purple, and at the edge of each cloud spun long gaseous ribbons of gold.

All of a sudden a dark sinewy form like a *Dumaji's* dick, thrust into that light-filled realm. *Kulpan Karrangu's* massive head coiled around and came down real low as he bared his fangs at us. A burst of adrenaline shot up my spine into my throat. 'Get out!' I screeched.

He launched himself back up like an arrow, sinking his long, sharp fangs into *Pulanyi Bulaing's* throat. The high-pitched sound of dogs howling made my hairs stand on end. And in that eerie moment, reflected perfectly on my mother of pearl pendant, I caught a glimpse of Gofar and *Gulyi-Gulyi*, flexed backwards high on the rock, howling at the sky. They were howling for *Pulanyi Bulaing*. Her hissing was painful, like the sound of air escaping from a punctured balloon.

'*Birri! Birri!*' I yelled. The sulphurous smell of rotting eggs filled the air and burnt my throat and eyes. Looking away from the dazzling sky above, our approach to Help Canyon looked dark and gloomy, and the *Zalfinhi* seemed more menacing than ever before. Shrieking with delight, they mustered all the creatures of the night to come out of their hidey-holes into the moonlight.

Thousands of snakes and crawling creatures covered the ground in a slithering mass. Aunty Toots was screaming and Sister pulled her habit up tight between her legs.

'Double up, Double up!' *Mimi* shouted.

Sister leapt up behind me. Aunty Toots, Louanna and Polly got on poor old *Winthuly-Winthuly's* back. Mum and Barbara jumped onto *Ramu* with *Mimi* holding the reins. Patty Mae and Sandy Gibb were not daunted by the writhing mass on the floor.

Marissa was up a tree refusing to budge.

271

'I'll come back for you,' *Mimi* yelled.

Everyone knew *Waranmanha* had to ride alone.

'Get to the Canyon! Anyone who can climb, get to the top and hold your *milis* high. Call on the Ancestors and Spirits to remove all this evil, make Help Canyon a sacred place once more!' *Mimi* ordered us.

No one said a word.

Slowly we moved through the undergrowth. Our faithful, heavily laden *nguurru's* (brumbies) nervously set each hoof to earth, in spite of the hissing and spitting above and the shrieking *Zalfinhi* beside us. Although all this *mamany* (crazy) stuff was happening on all sides, I felt like I was encased in a thick bubble of silence that protected me from being my usual schizoid self.

As *Birri* approached the Burial Mound on the way to Help Canyon, she stopped and refused to move. I didn't try to urge her on. I just followed her lead. Sitting on her back with Sister Euphrates' little, cold hands holding onto my waist, I watched the others arrive at Help Canyon.

In the moonlight I could see them climbing, and as they climbed, Derwen's haunting screams rattled my eardrums. Wind from *Kulpan Karrangu's* whooshing tail blew my hair across my face. And on that wind rode the stench of *the one that feathers stick to*. Fear stifled my screams and my heart missed two beats. He was still alive.

Just to my left I caught sight of a rotting thing hanging on a low branch. It was a *wintiki* (curlew) with a *kuwa* (crow's) head. A wave of nausea hit the pit of my stomach.

'*Pilawal*!' I screeched. 'Leave me alone!' I threw up all over my foot.

I knew Sister was praying for something, but I couldn't hear what.

An old familiar squawk rang in my ears. '*Thubarnimanha* (Straighten up)!'

Birri heard it too and took off towards the Canyon.

272

We were flying—snakes, bugs and *Zalfinhi* were nothing to us now. My *Jalbri* was still with me; I wasn't alone. Inspirational quotes were pouring out of Sister like a broken tap.

Pulling up at the base of the Canyon, we were about to dismount when *Mimi* called out from above, 'Only Sister! You stay with *Birri* and *Gulyi* and look after *Ramu*, *Wilara* and *Winthuly-Winthuly*.'

Sister was down in an instant and began climbing up the rock face with the style and speed of her old circus days.

I stayed without a word of protest, even though inside my head I was screaming, 'Whaaatt? *Waranmanha's* the heroine and I'm the stable hand. Typical!' As I watched Sister and the others, I could see *Waranmanha* using the climbing tricks *Jalbri* had taught us.

Aunty Toots and Louanna climbed up awkwardly, passing their *mili* to each other as they lurched from rock to rock. On my right I could see Patty Mae, Sandy Gibb and Gofar arrive at the base of the rock, they were still yarning about the good old days. They were carrying a big stash of dead snakes over their shoulders, which they dumped at the base of the rock. This was a *blackfella* picnic for them. Patty Mae stroked her beard and gave me a nod before both women started their climb.

They'd all climbed up the eastern end of Help Canyon, at the back, along the ridge where it joined *Kuji Warnku* (Porcupine Rock). God forbid they'd trust me to do something exciting. I'd been left here like some reject to look after the livestock. And Marissa was still stuck up a gum tree. I bet *Mimi* had totally forgotten about her on purpose. She'd left us rejects behind.

Ramu and *Wilara* whinnied loudly. I looked around to see what was troubling them. A *malji* (wild tomcat) sprinted past us. *Gulyi-Gulyi* gave chase heading east.

'Come back!' I yelled, but he was off refusing to listen. 'Come on, *Birri*, after him.' She was reluctant to follow, but I was fed up and dug my heels in hard, making her gallop after him.

That big *fella malji* (wild tomcat) stopped and turned to face *Gulyi-Gulyi*. That *malji* coulda had *Gulyi's* eye out in a single swipe. I jumped off *Birri* and grabbed *Gulyi* by the scruff of his neck. He got a shock and swung around to bite me. 'No, bad dog.' I clipped him behind the ear like Mum often did to Frankie and me. I felt real bad though. The *malji* took advantage of the moment and leapt straight up the rock face and onto the *barlu* (rock ledge) where Derwen had once stood a hundred years before.

The sound of screeching laughter made my blood run cold. Petrified, I stood with my neck craned back looking up at *Kuji Wanku* (Porcupine Rock), trying to work out what was happening up there.

Two luminous stick figures peered menacingly over the edge of the Rock. Those *Zalfinhi* flashed a greenie-blue light down on me.

Already rigid with fear, I was stranded there without a fight in me. But suddenly, from deep inside my bones, my legs began to burn and my only instinct left was flight. I raised my foot to run, but instead jumped sideways. In the glow of the greenie-blue light cast by the *Zalfinhi*, I could see that I'd been standing on an enormous stack of writhing snakes. I froze.

Although I'd forgotten about *Gulyi* and *Birri*, they hadn't forgotten about me. *Gulyi* came charging in, lightly springing from one pile of snakes to the next, and then he launched himself at me. He rammed into my side, nipping me on the arm. Totally surprised, the shock and pain from that nip triggered my rage. My arm jerked in reaction and I literally flung him ten paces away into *Birri's* front legs. She was shifting her weight from one foot to the other, ready for action.

Then I suddenly realised what they were doing. 'Okay! You want tricks? Here goes!' I leapt up and out of the growing mound of serpents that were wrapping themselves around me. With amazing grace, I hopped, skipped and jumped my way outta there, kicking every raised snake's head that stood in my way.

33. Waranmanha

Gulyi was a compulsive hunter; he'd found something in the spinifex just ahead and was madly digging his way to China. When I got to him, he had a *pujarrpujarr* (desert mole) proudly hanging out of his mouth. 'Drrop! *Gulyi*, tarr, give it here! *Gulyi*!'

He didn't want to give it up. Huffing and puffing in protest, he finally let me have the *pujarrpujarr*. Dingo's jaws are so strong, you can't pull them open like a normal dog, they have to decide to let go.

As I held the poor little *pujarrpujarr* in my hands, he buried his little nose between my fingers and his strong front paws were digging flat out in mid-air. Being blind and everything, the little guy must've been scared as. He probably thought I was going to eat him. I ordered *Gulyi* to get his nose out of the tunnel and sit back. Then I knelt down and sat the little fella on the ground in front of the opening to his home.

I was about to stand up when I noticed something glisten, lit by the light of the full moon. Immediately, I recognised the simple curve of a gold ring sticking out of the dirt. I gently pulled it free. Looped through the ring was a necklace made of knotted string. The string was all bunched up and stuck together like it had been burnt. Fascinated, I ran my finger and thumb along the melted waxy string. Caught in the curved bit at the end was a shiny black locket. As I held it up to the moonlight, on the front I could see a small ten-pointed gold star with a moonstone set in the centre.

I held my precious find close to my heart. In the tumultuous sky above, I could see that *Kulpan Karrangu* had his red neck feathers unfurled and his massive fangs planted deeply into the throat of *Pulanyi Bulaing*. Their gyrating bodies obscured the light of the moon. Some of the women were terrified, screaming for protection, while others sang the *mama* (sacred songs).

Although I was standing right in the middle of the danger zone, I'd been sucked up into a different reality. Somehow the call of the ring and locket was more important than anything else. The tingling sensation in the centre of my palm was becoming so intense that my clenched fingers wanted to spring open to reveal their treasures. I needed a torch so I could have a good look. Us bloody *blackfellas*—we go bush, but no one's ever got a torch and my *mili* was way up the canyon with Polly.

Suddenly, a massive fireball hurtled out of the sky and ignited the tree beside me. Ignoring the immediate danger, my obsessive mind saw the flames as an answer to my desire for light.

I opened my hand and angled the ring towards the inferno. As my eyes scanned each word, I heard Derwen's soft lilting voice recite the verse.

'Ever Thine, Ever Mine, Lucy Starchild 1913.'

My hands were trembling like a newlywed, and before I knew it I'd slipped the ring on my finger. It was a perfect fit.

Excitedly I turned over the locket and read aloud the words etched deeply into the smooth black onyx:

We'll meet again

My Starchild

Lest we forget

RIP 1917

Forever Mine

Derwen

'What the hell are you doing?' *Mimi* roared, flying towards me. *Ramu's* face was like a ghost mask hovering above me in the thick acrid air. 'Get on that bloody horse. MOVE!'

I stuffed the locket and string into my pouch, leapt onto *Birri* and galloped after *Mimi*. I was boiling hot, frustrated and ashamed.

'*Gulyi*!' I shouted, looking around for him.

'SHUT UP!' *Mimi* was furious.

I knew I'd messed up, but a lot of stuff was running though my head.

Mimi pulled *Ramu* back so we were side by side. 'Because you never listen, Toots has been injured and Patty Mae got burnt trying to get her to safety. Why? Because you'd fucking gone off. What's bloody wrong with you?'

I couldn't say anything.

She rabbited on at me, but her fury had no power over my burning desire to look inside the locket.

We galloped further west, past the place where I was meant to stay and wait. The vast plains on either side were burning up. *Kulpan Karrangu's* rage spread across the land.

Our mob was gathered in the area I'd burnt back when I met *the one that feathers stick to*. I could see Patty Mae and Aunty Toots stretched out on the ground. My fault. *Garndi* (Shame), too much *garndi*. Sister was tending their wounds.

'Can I go see them?'

Mimi just nodded.

The air was thick with smoke. Aunty Toots didn't look good. 'Sorry Aunty,' I said softly and left her with Louanna, Sister and Barbara.

I felt real bad when I saw Patty Mae's burnt hands. Even her beard was burnt down to the skin with just the sides left like enormous sideburns.

She could see I was really upset. 'Won't shake your hand at the minute.' She smiled. 'Thought me beard needed a trim. Ya gotta admit, I'm still deadly as?' She winked.

'Yeah, your skin's like a baby's bum.'

'Nuf cheek from ya. You're in deep shit,' she said, pointing off to the side with her lower lip.

Mimi was coming.

I was expecting a telling off. Instead, she called out to everyone, '*Thubarnimanha*! (Straighten up!) We got to get back to ceremony. No one's focusing, we gotta call Mother Goddess—*Bulari*, and the heroes and heroines to help us restore the balance. *Pulanyi Bulaing* must not die.' She was real emotional and finding it hard to go on.

Another enormous fireball streaked towards the canyon. Us mob turned towards the light. The intense glare was too much, we all cast our eyes to the ground. There, on the hot red earth were hundreds of stones. Instinctively, every hand reached down and grabbed a couple to clap together. The call went up.

As I clapped and called out to *Bulari*, I realised that one side of each stone was painted. '*Jin.gi* stones!' I yelled.

In the flickering light, smiles spread from face to face and fired up our courage. We sang the *mama* (sacred song) with a renewed strength in our bones.

The *jurdu* (smoke) cleared, and the ten heroes and heroines above danced across the sky. On the ground, all was still except for the flickering fire around which we stood. Every face had turned its gaze to the Heavens. *Pulanyi Bulaing* was in her death throws.

'SING LOUDER!' I shouted. 'I'm going up, she has to hear us.'

'No!' *Mimi* commanded. '*Bindamanha, Waranmanha* get on your *nguurru* (brumbies). Mary, take *Winthuly-Winthuly* and ride right around Help Canyon. *Bindamanha* you ride *kakarra* (east) and *Waranmanha* you ride *kara* (west). Mary, go *kakarra*. I'll ride *kara*. The rest of you, stay, do *mama* (sacred song). Barbara knows the Lore, she'll lead you, follow her.' I was totally amazed that Barbara actually knew stuff and that us mob were following her lead.

I jumped on *Birri* and was ready to go. '*Gulyi*, stay!'

'Go, as fast as you can! Keep going around and around, don't stop! We'll keep the evil spirits contained.' *Mimi's* eyes flashed with excitement. '*Lipurra mil walpura*! (Keep your eyes open!) *Kantiyala*! *Kantiyala*!' (Ride em! Ride em!)

Two enormous rumps, one pure white and the other pitch black, thundered off side by side. They headed *kara* while Mum and I pushed forward into the easterly wind, she on her camel and me keeping pace on *Birri*.

Mum and I hadn't spent much time together lately. I thought all was forgiven, but I wasn't sure. I started to feel like she'd traded me in for my sister— the newer, perfect model. As we rode past the Burial Mound on the outer edge where the women were gathered, a shudder went through me.

'You okay, daughta?'

'Suppose so,' I answered.

'You gave me the biggest shock when you took off from Broome. I'd die if somethin' happened to you.'

'Really?' It made me happy thinking she'd die if something happened to me.

'Real sorry, Mum.'

'I'm sorry too. All them *walhi* (no good) family secrets. I should've been brave and 'fessed up to you kids about everything. Would've been a better life for all of us I reckon. Too much shame. Too many secrets.'

I glanced over at her. 'All forgiven, Mum. Really, all forgiven.'

Looking at me, she smiled and said, 'Thanks Lu … *Bindamanha* .'

'Guess what? I found a ring and a locket.'

Just at that moment, *Pulanyi Bulaing's* head landed with a thump on the ground in front of us. *Birri* pulled up sharp. The serpent's head was so massive, we were at eye level. *Birri's* ears went flat back against her neck and she started prancing on the spot getting ready to bolt. *Winthuly-Winthuly* bared her teeth at the gigantic rainbow serpent. Light green, pink, purple, turquoise, and cobalt-blue scales shimmered like shot Thai silk, changing colour as *Pulanyi Bulaing* struggled to draw an inward breath.

'*Gurugarra*, friend. *Birri*, she's our friend.'

Birri's ears pricked up.

'C'mon *Birri*.' Slowly and gently I coaxed *Birri* to walk up with me so that I could reach out and touch *Pulanyi Bulaing*. Dying, *Pulanyi Bulaing's* breathing was shallow and her large eyes; the size of dinner plates, were covered with a milky glaze.

Trying to comfort her, I gently lay my hand on one of her enormous blue scales. It shimmered and changed into vibrant lavender beneath my touch. The milky film that covered her eyes slid back to reveal the most beautiful green I had ever seen. Lost in its colour, a wonderful sense of peace flowed over and through me. Bathing in the sight of her glorious green eyes, I couldn't tell if I was alive or dead and I didn't care.

Finally, I spoke to her like we were lovers in a green meadow. '*Yanka kati ngarnana jiyanku* (I will follow you).' Touching her and gazing into her eye, my resistance to the pull of destiny fell away. '*Pulanyi Bulaing*, the *mamas* (sacred songs) are for you. Don't leave. We believe in you.'

Floating in that sea of green, moments in my life of pure, intense love flashed before my eyes, like the first time Mum clutched me to her breast when I was born, Frankie and Dad singing in front of the TV, Louanna with a handful of treasures I'd scrounged from the beach, Sister dancing with her purple drapes, and again when I saw her lily-white hand on mine.

Suddenly, I was sitting on the green grass of Wales. 'Forever entwined,' I heard Derwen whisper. And then, from the bright-green fields of England, I found myself over the darkest green ocean. 'Manu!' I sang out. 'Manu Tollie, I love you. '*Yanka kati ngarnana jiyanku* (I will follow you).' Looking up to my *Jalbri's* star, I thought I saw her twinkling eyes. And then I heard her voice as clear as the night sky. '*Thubarnimanha* (Straighten up), follow me.'

Suddenly, my sister's face appeared before me. *Pulanyi Bulaing's* eye had become the moon behind her. Even though a chill ran up my spine, I felt loved up, like I was in some drug-induced sixties movie. Destiny was calling her, but I could not follow.

I walked down a long psychedelic passage where everything had a light greenish hue. Nobody was there, just me in this 'Groovy Heaven'. I thought I must be dead. I was trippin', and sang out at the top of my lungs, 'I forgive you, Mum.' I giggled, high as a kite on the green stuff. 'I forgive you Dad, Frankie, Tina, Megan and Rachael from school, and even Sturchy, our Mother Superior.' Every week, she'd belt us kids to punish us for the evil thoughts we hadn't had yet. She was God's '*Just in case* Police force'.

This groovy 'Heavenly Love Space' was a new filter for all my memories. Old, deep wounds that were crippling my soul, defining my personality and holding me back were suddenly and miraculously healed. Not a trace of bitterness, hatred or self-pity remained. Freedom felt so sweet. As *Pulanyi Bulaing's* love healed me, my love healed her.

Dr Pilawal's name popped onto my lips a few times, but I couldn't forgive her. That was Derwen's right, not mine. Then I yelled out at the top of my lungs, 'I forgive you *Kulpan Karrangu*!'

Pulanyi Bulaing's whole body contracted and that little tripped-out-me was shot like a cannon ball back into my dazed body.

Pulanyi was re-energised by the power of *forgiveness*. A sacred, soulful serpentine song left her throat. Lifting her exquisitely beautiful head high into the sky, her flicking tongue tasted our love.

Revived, she swished the long, lacy feathers at the rear of her jaw, and with a contraction of her long sinewy form, she hurtled herself into the *Banharnigardi Banharnigardi*, 'Beyond Beyond', to meet her twin soul, *Kulpan Karrangu*. Enraged, he was not amused to see her enlivened by our love.

With her serpentine body returned to the Heavens, the path was open for us to continue riding. *Mimi* and *Waranmanha* galloped towards us.

Mimi said, '*Wakaj Kanarri* (The Finishing) is near. Be strong.'

Waranmanha stretched her arm out towards me and our fingers met and our eyes and hearts knew that our time together was also *finishing*. We all rode on—she and our grandmother going west, and me and our mother going east.

The sweet smell of burning *nirliyangarr* (dune wattle), gumarnu (sandalwood), *gungkara* (conkerberry) and *bilabirdi* (eucalyptus) was a comfort and made us feel like we were on our homeward journey.

I realised what *Mimi* was up to. She was trying to create balance by using counterbalance. We learned about counterbalance at school. Cos we each had an equal but opposite strength; our balance would undo the turmoil in the Heavens above. The placement of each and every one of us—the sacred sounds, the clapping stones, even the animals—all designed to create order in this chaos, to call down peace. Peace had left us so long ago, now we were calling her back home with open hearts.

As on Earth, so above.

Our troop thundered around again and again. The hissing and venting of *Kulpan Karrangu* was deafening. He walloped *Pulanyi Bulaing* with the long side of his body and wrapped his tail around her and dragged her down with his weight. Then *Kulpan Karrangu* sunk his fangs into her throat.

We pulled up our horses, every head was straining skyward.

His fangs were in deep and he wasn't letting go. A sad serpentine song of defeat escaped from *Pulanyi Bulaing's* open mouth. The sound resonated with all the world's sad sounds. It was airy, like an abandoned squeezebox falling open in drunken hands. A sorta back to front half cry, half song.

I grabbed my *Jin.gi* stone from my pouch; it felt wet to the touch. I glanced down to see the painted *Jin.gis* crying tears of blood red ochre.

All thoughts of counterbalance were gone. Our *mama* (sacred song) dried up. Staring dumbfounded at the sky, we saw the ten heroes and heroines arrive, singing and thrusting their firesticks at *Kulpan Karrangu's* massive jaws.

From the far west pointer stars *Wadjemup* (Rottnest) and *Mandungu Yabu* (The Pinnacles), we heard a loud *dumbulmanmamha* (thumping sound). And then we saw the three thousand initiated men who'd been killed at *Wadgemup* (Rottnest) dance across the sky. Following them were the ghostly keepers of *Mandungu yabu* (The Pinnacles).

From the *Gumbarri Jingi* (Twelve Apostles) in the south came the soft-lipped ones—the *Girai Warrung*—and their *mama* (sacred song) was like bush honey dripping from a newly opened leaf. The keepers of *Karlu Karlu* (Devils Marbles) flew in from the east.

They, like us, were enacting destiny.

And then upon a soulful wind I heard the *Bulyaman's* voice recite our history. Story after story, all the message from the stone of *Walhahna* (Wave Rock). But us mob waited with drawn breath to hear of this time of the *Wakaj Kanarri* (The Finishing).

283

We, *Waranmanha* and I heard our names. We were the ones foretold so long ago—this was our time.

Sister Euphrates' scream hooked my heart. I swung around to see her surrounded in flames. *Kulpan Karrangu* had released *Pulanyi Bulaing*, whose shrivelled body was floating to Earth like an empty balloon whilst he spat flames in all directions.

Birri was fast and sure-footed, so we flew past the area where the women were gathered to the space between the Burial Mound and Help Canyon. The surrounding spinifex was taller than Sister. Black plumes of thick smoke took on sinister shapes as they rose into the air.

'*Birri* …?' I was about to ask her to go into the flames to get Sister. Without hesitation, she ran in. I was relieved to see Sister and surprised that she wasn't burnt. Then she smiled ... I'd seen that smile before on the mouth of *the one that feathers stick to*.

Was she him? His *muridung* (evil ghost)? The *Birrinja's* trick?

'*Birri*! *Birri*!' I cried.

She'd sensed the evil presence too. She turned and galloped out of there. Her neck, underbelly and tail were on fire. She wasn't running out for herself. She was trying to protect me. She stormed out of the flames, up over the Burial Mound and fell.

As she crashed to the ground, I flew through the air and lay winded beside her. I wanted to get up but my life force was draining out of me. *Birri* lay twitching beside me; she'd taken a heavy fall. Her nervous system was shutting down. The smell of singed hair and burnt flesh hung heavily between us. My eyes were fixed on hers and hers on mine.

All I could do was reach out and stroke her frothing muzzle. Wide eyed, she was telling me a million things.

'*Birri*, you're my best friend.'

She blinked and blew out a long, wet purr from her lips. She loved me too.

'Stay calm *Birri*. I'll look after you.' I smiled, trying to comfort her.

Then in one violent convulsion, she was gone. Her lifeless eyes stared past me.

'*Birri*! *Birri*!' I cried. 'Come back!' I looked up past her stiffened legs to the lavender-coloured sky. A chill ran through me.

There, lit by a light-greenish full moon was my sister, *Waranmanha*, sitting tall on *Wilara's* back. She turned to look at me one final time. In my twin sister's eyes, there were a thousand goodbyes. But I couldn't bear even one.

From that high point on the ancestral red dirt, Burial Mound, *Waranmanha* and *Wilara* readied themselves to enter the raging inferno within the cavernous den of *Kulpan Karrangu*.

'NO!' I yelled, screamed and screeched. 'NO! NO! NO! PLEASE! NO!'

Silent, *tharlbarra* (strong), without hesitation, she rode her snow-white steed *Wilara* into that fire. The fire flared, fed by her saintly fuel.

My *Waranmanha* and her *Wilara* outshone that fire's light and extinguished *Kulpan Karrangu's* raging fury. Sweet-smelling plumes poured out of the cave that night.

Their sacrifice had mended the ancient crack that had let the darkness in.

Kulpan Karrangu had coiled himself around her dazzling form. '*Pararrka talu* (I'm sorry and ashamed),' *Kulpan Karrangu* cried out loud, holding onto her, trying to stop her leaving. He was *nalaman* (shedding) his old skin and *Waranmanha* was *nalaman* (shedding) her earthly life and returning to her Home to be a *biriny bundarra* (shiny white star) in the *Jirdulingu* (Milky Way).

In tears, I told him to 'Let her go.'

Now we understood each other.

'*Warrimparna*

Bye-bye.

Waranmanha,

285

I love you *Ngijakura kututu kurrji* (with all my heart).

    Mirninypunka (I will speak) and then *Yanka kati ngarnana jiyanku* (I will follow you).'

286

34. Mum and Manu

The voices of the women singing the *mama* (sacred songs) were a bittersweet comfort. Thick plumes of fragrant smoke filled our nostrils and encircled Help Canyon. *Waranmanha's jurdu* (smoke plume) wound its way to the upper reaches of *Kuju Warnku* (Porcupine Rock), and then departed for her new *Home* in the *Jirdilungu* (Milky Way).

I saw the strong, slender frame of our mother, Mary, standing on the highest point. Around me, grieving women's voices sang in ancient tongue—primitive harsh sounds from when the Dreamtime had begun.

Mingling with that earthly sound, Mary's voice was so strong and pure. Her *biru* (cosmic song) rose high above our sacred land into the endless sky. Sister took hold of my right hand and *Mimi* grabbed the other. She *yayiliri* (wailed), '*Bidi-Bidi* (Butterfly). My *Bidi-Bidi*.'

Then it struck me like a *jakiny* (barbed spear) through the heart. Us kids had heard Sister play 'Madame Butterfly' on her old gramophone a hundred times or more. Leaning into *Mimi,* I asked, 'How did Mum learn to sing like that?'

Tears streamed down *Mimi's* cheeks. Softly, she whispered the story of how Sister Josepha, the music teacher, noticed that Mum had a natural talent for singing, so she decided to teach her opera. From then on, everyone called her *Bidi-Bidi*. At the age of sixteen, *Bidi-Bidi* was invited to sing 'Madame Butterfly' with Harold Blair[46], the famous Aboriginal Tenor, at the Sydney Opera House, but Mum threw it all away when she met Dad and got pregnant.

Hearing Mum's story made my legs turn to jelly and my heart turn to mush. I had never heard her sing—not at church, not even to comfort Jonnie when he was a baby. Dad was the one who'd sing him to sleep. She'd been tongue-tied my whole life. But now that *julgia* (broken) woman looked strangely radiant, joyful and magnificent standing there, tall, dark and slender, dressed in rags. She raised her arms to the *Jurdilingu* (Milky Way) and spread them wide.

Spellbound, like a small child at a circus, I stood wide eyed and opened mouthed, watching my mum. As the volume and intensity of her voice increased, on her tippy toes she leaned out from the rock towards me, just like a trapeze artist on the long swing. In response, I leaned forward trying to inhale her energy like a *Bidi-Bidi* (butterfly) sipping nectar. I wanted to fly to her, but *Mimi* and Sister anchored me to the earth with a firm grip on each arm.

As Mum hit the last high, pain-filled note, *Gulyi-Gulyi*, Gofar and a *kuli kunyarr* (wild dog) howled loudly. Her voice soared above theirs and lifted her feet off the rock. For a split second I believed she could fly. And then, with arms spread like angels' wings, she fell. Her head hitting the rocks as she plummeted towards the ground.

---

46   Harold Blair - Opera singer and Aboriginal activist, was taken from his mother and placed on a mission run by the Salvation Army where he trained to be a farm hand but loved to sing. Served in the army in 1942 and was discovered singing on the cane fields. He married a white woman and worked tirelessly for the advancement of Aboriginal people and the arts.

We screamed.

Mimi mounted *Ramu*. 'I'm coming,' I pleaded, 'She's my mum.' Without hesitation, *Mimi* bent down and offered me her hand. I sprang up onto *Ramu's* rump and we took off. I held on so tight. My tears and snot flowed freely down *Mimi's* straight back, but this time she didn't complain.

Ramu jumped a boulder and the moment his front hooves hit the ground; *Mimi* swung him around real sharp. I leapt off his back, I had to see her. I stumbled and fell to my knees in prayer. 'Mummy, you'll be okay,' I said, not noticing that her head was at a strange angle. It was broken. Her eyes were wide open and a sweet smile graced her lips. I knew she'd seen *Bulari*, our Mother Goddess. Her arms were still spread out wide, and *warrimpa* (bauhinia) flowers spilled from her open hands.

Mimi was shaken—even she wasn't ready for this. She still had so much to say to her *Bidi-Bidi*. As I looked at Mum's broken body, I started trembling uncontrollably. We weren't finished! I had so much to tell her and a million things to ask. It was like we'd only just met. I didn't even get to tell her and *Waranmanha* about the ring and locket. They'd gone up to the *Jirdilungu* without me. 'It's not fair!' I whimpered, over and over, 'It's not fair ...'

'Shush,' *Mimi* whispered.

I'd forgotten about the battle. Staring open mouthed at the sky above, I could see *Bulari* surrounded by the ten heroes and heroines. She was greeting a tall, slender woman with open arms. The woman turned to bless us with a parting smile—it was my Mum, our *Bidi-Bidi*. With ceremony and song, they left our view for their starry Home in the *Jirdilungu* (Milky Way). 'Come back! Come back! Please ... don't leave ... me!' I cried, as they disappeared into the Banharnigardi, Beyond, Beyond.

Kulpan Karrangu uncoiled himself, rose up and launched into the inky blue sky. A cluster of *bundarra* (stars) gathered around his huge noble head. Standing in all his serpentine glory, the lustrous red stripe on his belly made him look a thousand metres tall. Twisting left and right, he saw the chaos he had caused.

Our suffering and sacrifice had warmed his blood and melted his cold heart. Lakes of tears formed in his enormous eyes and dropped to Earth. His tears revived *Pulanyi Bulaing* and restored the balance. As each droplet fell, she diverted the torrent into the dry river beds and filled the underground caverns. The sacred *jilas* were full once more.

As his tears cleared, *jinmiri* (light rain) fell. Under the soft light of the *mitimiti* (full moon), the *jinmiri* (light rain) extinguished the many fires that remained. Pleased, he *yunguyiti* (generously) returned his gift of sleep. Everyone lay down right where they stood as if they'd been given a sleeping potion. Our mob slept, even the dogs.

Everyone, except me.

I could feel sleep rising up from my feet like a thick syrup, but I could not stop my *wanayiti* (restless) mind. Feeling the water on my skin reminded me that Manu Tollie, my Bird Boy, was still on the open sea. My cold fingers fumbled in my waistband pouch for my *Milkanarri* (Seeing Stone).

Rain was falling here, there, and everywhere. Global warming was being undone. The planet was awash and seas were filling fast. Manu was in his tiny dugout canoe facing a huge wall of water.

'Manu,' I cried, losing sight of him in the valley of a wave.

'Lucy ... I love you ... can't go on ...'

'Please, Manu, you must...' My words were swallowed by the thunderous waves.

He said something about *our baby*. I felt her kick. The sea had sucked back, and in the moonlight I could see Manu flopped forward on his ores taking a break in the calm. His broad shoulder muscles twitched with fatigue.

'Look behind you!' I screamed.

A monstrous wall of emerald green rose out of the Timor Sea driven by a bitter wind heading towards Van Diemen Gulf.

Manu turned around in his dugout and knelt to face the king wave like a prince. Making the sign of the cross, he called on his Ancestors in the traditional way. Closing his fists, he beat his chest and prayed. Looking up at the king wave's foaming crown, he opened his arms wide like an albatross riding the wind. He called my name once, twice, three times before the emerald wall broke. The sea sucked him and his canoe up into her dark watery body and rolled them upside down. He and his dugout parted ways.

Clutching my *Milkanarri* (Seeing Stone) tightly, I peered helplessly through the barrelling wave and watched her have her way with him. She tossed him like a rag doll, over and over, until fed up with that game, she crushed him and he was gone. With my left hand on our *kurntal* (daughter) in my tummy, I blew her father, Manu Tollie, a single kiss.

Sobbing, I returned to loudly snoring women lost in deep sleep. Overwhelmed, I walked away and threw up near where I had found the ring and locket. I wandered in a daze, and found myself walking down the same track that the old Mardu mob had taken Derwen to find that wretch Dr Pilawal almost a hundred years before.

Strangely, I remembered Derwen as if he were Manu. I stopped walking. Sobbing uncontrollably, I reverently kissed my *Milkanarri* and placed it back into my pouch. The sun's golden head rose slowly above the purple haze from the far off battle smoke. Before I knew it, the locket was in my hand, the little moonstone set upon its golden star shone brightly in the morning light. Bub fluttered inside me as I flipped the clasp open.

The locket looked like the wings of a butterfly sitting open in the palm of my hand. Inside on the left I recognised the photo of Derwen taken before he got burnt. The picture on the right was of his late wife Lucy. The creepiest thing was, I knew she was a white woman from Wales, but in the photo, she looked just like me, even her skin was black. The heat from the fire must have been so intense that it reversed the tone in the photo making her white skin black and her dark dress white.

The question, 'why did she look like me?', kept running through my head.

Slowly and loudly, again I read the engraved words on the back:

We'll meet again my Starchild.

Lest we forget.

RIP 1917

Forever Mine,

Derwen.

I struggled to get my head around just what our connection was and why me? Why did she look like me? Was she a Starchild too? Who was Derwen to me? Remembering their wedding ring, I quickly slipped it off my finger and read those words again:

'Ever Thine, Ever Mine, My Lucy Starchild 1913.'

It felt like an omen from some weird horror movie. Suddenly, I heard *mugurimanha* (an evil thumping sound). A surge of adrenalin swept away all thoughts of Derwen and his Starchild. My blood trickled coolly down my spine and I slipped their wedding ring back onto my trembling finger, its warmth was a comfort to my racing heart.

Blue flashing lights and sirens shattered the early morning stillness of the bush and woke the sleeping women and dogs. *Gulyi* ran to my side growling.

Coppers. Heaps of them.

Police cars ploughed through the scrub, doors swung open and coppers jumped out of the moving vehicle screaming orders at us, 'Fucking move or we'll fucking shoot ya!'

I couldn't move. I tried.

Mimi must have heard the *mugurimanha* too, she'd removed *Ramu's* rope halter and was yelling at him and *Winthuly-Winthuly* to leave. A copper started running towards her. *Ramu* was confused. He was snorting loudly and pawing the red dirt. He'd only been spoken to like that once before when them fellas wanted to break him. *Mimi* wacked his shoulder as hard as she could. *Ramu* grunted. He rubbed his head on her, pleading for her forgiveness, even though he didn't know what he'd done wrong. I'd seen Lightning do the same when Dad flogged him after a drunken binge. *Ramu* cried, his whinnying echoed our grief for him. This gentle giant might'a looked menacing, but he was a big softy. So to see 'her' flogging him, was like watching bulldozers take to a forest.

Mimi couldn't keep it up. She swallowed deeply, put her long arms around his neck and kissed him on the cheek. I reckon *Ramu* was the only male she'd ever loved. She just stood there holding onto his massive head waiting for the copper to break 'em up.

Pointing at me, he called out to another cop, 'Got a freak show here. Cuff the bitch!'

I'd forgotten how strange I looked.

A fat female cop strode up to me. Her muffin top gut hung over her belt that sported a flash-looking gun, a taser and a baton; she was tooled up—just in case she needed to give me a good clout on the head after zapping me with the taser and shooting me dead. The radio on her shoulder crackled with copper's speak. She took me by the arm and twisted it behind my back, snapping cable ties to both my wrists. 'What you on love, meth?'

I shook my head, unable to speak. Anyway, there was no point, in her eyes I was a druggie.

'Yeah and I'm the Virgin Mary,' she said mockingly as she shoved me in the back, directing me towards the cop car. 'C'mon, move it!' Another shove. 'We'll sort it out at the station, shall we?' The thud between my shoulders was a bit too hard, but I wasn't stupid enough to complain.

Gulyi was stressed out and he bared his teeth at her.

'It'll be the bullet for you if you don't behave,' she said, extending the back of her hand for him to sniff. 'Actually, I'm a dog lover. I'd have a dingo any day over one of you *blackfellas*.'

One of the cops had fixed a bright-blue nylon rope to the trunk of a tree with big steel clips attached to it. The fat female cop walked me over and clipped the cable ties that bound my wrists to the rope. *Gulyi* stayed close beside me, growling softly.

Another cop had driven around to the Burial Mound and was yelling his head off, 'Murder scene. Call backup.' He'd found the bodies of my sister and mother. I let out a single squeal. I realised that this was no dream, they were really dead and we hadn't done proper "Sorry Business" for them. Proving to the coppers that we didn't kill 'em would be impossible.

One by one our mob was gathered up and clipped onto the rope that was tied to the tree. Aunty Toots was pulled along by her hair by a big, nasty-looking white bastard. She was trying to protect her dignity. After all, 'respect and dignity' was her thing, even if she was topless and hadn't had a shower for days. She wasn't gonna get respect from that *kartija* (*whitefella*). Not even if she got down on her knees in front of him and begged like a dog.

All of us mob were tied to the tree except *Mimi*. She'd quickly put some lippy on, spruced herself up a bit and was talking legal speak faster than a runaway road train. They didn't dare put a hand on her. *Mimi's* trusty pencil, like Mrs Lee before her, came in real handy. She was writing down everything. *Ramu* was walking close to *Mimi* with his head over her shoulder while she was baffling them with bullshit. She was deadly as—*Jalbri* would have been real proud.

We sat there tied up under that tree in the boiling hot sun for hours, waiting for backup to arrive. I started to think about my sister and all the *mamany* (crazy) things that had happened since we left Broome. Coppers wouldn't understand that all this stuff that happened was '*spiritual*'. These *kartija* were never going to believe us. How could we tell 'em that global warming, depression, anger and all that stuff came from a battle between two great mythical snakes? And that we were here saving the planet, and that's why my twin sister, my mother, my great grandmother, and Loke were dead.

Finally, backup arrived—two big lock-up vans and more police with guns. A butcher from Looma[47] came with a cold storage van to pick up the dead bodies. A huge man got out of one of the vans. He was black, blacker than any of us mob, and mean as. 'Put the juvie (juvenile) in van 404 and the others in 104.' From his accent, I knew he wasn't from here, not from anywhere near here.

Suddenly, I realised that the juvie they were gonna shove in 404 was me. '*Mimi, walhi kartija ngurliyimanha* (I'm terrified of these no-good *whitefellas*)!' I pleaded with *Mimi*, hoping she would protect me.

'Speak English, no Language,' she barked.

Suddenly, I realised that although we were standing in Our Country, when we were with these guys it wasn't Our Country no more. These fellas couldn't even bear to hear our Language in their ears.

Sister, who was also tied up, spoke up for me, 'You must understand! She is just an innocent child.'

The big black guy heard Sister's strong accent and walked over to her. We all held our breath. Towering over her, he let her have a mouthful in French. Everyone was stunned. Even the *kartija* (*whitefella*) coppers at least offered nuns some respect. Sister's face got redder and redder and her blue eyes were ablaze. The big guy turned his head to look at us mob, and then he turned back, leaned in closer to Sister and spat right in her face.

Without flinching, she jumped up like a champion volleyball player and smacked him right in the mouth with her head.

He braced himself like he was going to hit her back. *Gulyi* went ballistic. 'Shoot it!' he ordered. The fat female cop, the one who had pushed me in the back said, 'I got it.'

---

47   Looma - Western Australian town in the Kimberleys.

My heart stopped. I thought I was going to faint. She raised her gun and shot above *Gulyi's* head. He took off. She really was a dog lover, and at that moment I was so grateful she loved dogs more than us.

The big black guy wasn't happy at all. Our mob laughed when our little Sister gave him a head butt and even louder when *Gulyi* high-tailed it outta there. Seething with rage, he stormed over, unclipped me from the rope. He gripped my arm real hard and I could feel the power of his rage as he hoisted me off the ground and headed towards the van.

From out of nowhere, Marissa ran at him screaming her head off, 'Let her go, she didn't do nothin'!'

The nasty *kartija* cop drew his taser and shot her. She hit the dirt whimpering and writhing in pain. 'Again!' the black bastard ordered.

We all yelled for mercy but no one cared. Three tasers fired all at once. Marissa let out one final yelp and her eyes rolled to the back of her head. Her whole body stiffened and then her jaw locked tight and she was gone.

In the fear of the moment, I managed to slip my right hand out of the cable tie. Dad had shown me and Frankie how to place our wrists so that we could get our hands free just in case we ever needed to. The fat copper wasn't the smartest tool in the shed, so mine was loose anyway. Quickly and ever so quietly, I opened my pouch, grabbed my *Milkanarri* (Seeing Stone) and gently nestled it between my breasts.

The *Milkanarri* showed me a movie of the black copper's life.

Oh no, *Bulgardu* (God of the Universe)! Ouno Justenbaste was born in Sierra Leone at the time of the civil war and the rise to power of *'child soldiers'*.

In my mind's eye, I could see that day when the children's army marched into his little village to recruit more kids. All the parents in his village managed to hide their kids, but Ouno was the only kid who was smart enough to go to school and was walking home, just as the child soldiers were about to leave.

His parents were terrified when they saw their nine-year-old son round the corner. 'OUNO! RUN!' They screamed.

A strange skinny boy about Frankie's age wearing a wedding dress splattered with blood threatened to kill Ouno's parents if he ran away. Ouno clutched his mother's hand tightly. His father offered the soldiers pink diamonds for his son's life. The boy in the blood-stained wedding dress took the diamonds. Laughing insanely, he shoved the machine gun in Ouno's hand and ordered him to kill both his father and his mother. Ouno couldn't do it. The boy placed his hand over Ouno's and pressed the trigger. In just a few seconds his father, his mother, his Aunty and two uncles were blown to pieces.

I watched and felt the rest of his wretched life pass before me as if it were mine. As a child soldier, drugged to the max, he did terrible, unspeakable things—raped and killed young girls and boys, cut them up and ate their flesh. Ouno's soul became sick, drunk with evil, madness set in.

How the war ended, I don't know, but for Ouno it was still raging inside of him and we were all at the mercy of this merciless one. Switching from the nightmarish world of his childhood to mine.

Cool, calm and collected, Ouno grabbed his gun from his holster and shot *Ramu* in the diamond shape between his pale-blue eyes. In a heartbeat, *Ramu's* pure white face was covered in blood and a red river flowed down his strong black chest. His legs went out from under him and he fell forward, landing on the rope between Polly and Barbara. His body shuddered again and again.

Mimi was hysterical. She fell to her knees beside him, held him, begging him over and over not to leave her. She rubbed her face on his until the jerking stopped. *Ramu's* huge adoring eyes gazed at *Mimi* one last time before they glazed over.

I reached into my pouch and grabbed the little red ace of diamonds card and shoved it in his face. 'Ouno Justenbaste! I know *who* you are! I have seen *what* you've done!' I screeched.

He was terrified and so was I.

Then an old woman's voice reached up and out of my throat to teach him to *'straighten up'*. At first I thought it was my *Jalbri*, but it was his grandmother's voice.

297

'It is easier to build a child than repair a man. Ouno Justenbaste!

You must be like the moon. People complain when there is too much sun, but no one grumbles when the full moon shines.

Be gentle my son. Be gentle like moonlight.

Not fierce like sun.

Bring your gentle light into the darkness.'

He snatched the Ace of Diamonds from me. Shaking his head slowly, he said, 'Are you *mende*? Witch Doctor? Magician Man?'

My sister's words came flooding back to me, 'Yes I am *Jala-Jala Jura Mabarnyuwa* (Lucky-Child Sorcerer and Faith Healer Magician).' Startled by my response, part of me was happy, but the other part of me was scared shitless. My mind was screaming, *"Help me Jalbri, help!"*

'*Thubarnimanha* (Straighten up),' she whispered back.

He flung me onto his shoulder. 'Back in Freetown, I didn't have a choice,' he said quietly as he carried me to the lock-up van.

'I know,' I whispered back, 'but now you're in a new country, you can be a new man, be like the full moon.' I felt his body stiffen. Somehow, he and me were in our own little world, even though, in the background, I could still hear *Mimi's* distress and Sister trying to comfort her. Sandy Gibb and Gofar were wailing.

'In front of my eyes, day and night, I still see the little children, and the women, and the old people I killed. Those ghosts wave their hands at me and cry, saying, "How could you do this to me?'

I could feel his body tremble slightly as he held back his tears.

I felt sorry for him. 'I know what that feels like. You think once you start crying, you'll never be able to stop.'

The moment those words left my lips, the most beautiful smell wafted past my nose. It was sweet like roses but spicy like cinnamon, with a hint of cloves, cardamom, *bilabirdi* (eucalyptus) and *bardinyu* (pine). I'd smelt it before when I was hovering before Derwen's inward breath. And when *Jalbri* died and I saw the *Djulpan* (Southern Cross) reflected in *Jalbri's* dead eyes.

I suddenly remembered how strong that perfume was when Mum put her arms around *Mimi's* waist as they rode off together on *Ramu's* back, and again when we were 'The Magnificent Seven'. Ahh, and it was super strong when Old Jimmy Howard was talking to his parents before he topped himself. And when *Waranmanha* rode into the flames. And again, when my mum, our *Bidi-Bidi,* sang. My eyes were full of tears and my heart felt so swollen, it was hard to breathe.

Ouno reached the van and gently took me down off his shoulders as he opened the door. There was a real sense of peace between us. Glancing for a moment at the other coppers, his eyes narrowed, the spell was broken. Suddenly he was back to his cruel distant self. 'Goodness has never been my friend.' With one shove from his large black hand, he pushed me into the lock-up van and slammed the door.

Is that really how quickly goodness evaporates? Grieving for his loss, I heard the women outside begin the 'Sorry Business' song for Mum, *Waranmanha*, Manu, Marrisa and Ramu. *Mimi* was singing out the loudest. I knew it was for all the lost loves in her life.

I felt sorry for Ouno Justenbaste who was lost in the *walhi* (no good) business of his life. I sang and asked *Bulari* to forgive him. I pleaded with her to make him *thubarnimanha* (straighten up) and asked her to show him 'what's up' so he could find his way Home.

It was too hot in the back of the stinking van. There were no windows, only flickering glimpses of light flashing through an air vent. I lay on the floor staring at the vent spin around and around. Entranced by the flickering

299

light, I slowly entered a dream world as the vent morphed into a small barred window in a prison door.

I could still hear raised voices just outside the van. A woman with a broad white Australian accent said, 'The nun said the kid's pregnant.'

Some redneck answered, 'Yeah, knocked up good and proper. Probably spread her legs for petrol or glue. You know what they're like. She's one scary-looking bitch. If she were a dog, I'd put her and the kid out of their misery. Nah, but we gotta pussyfoot around cos she's a *blackfella*. As soon as that freak show of a mother drops that poor little bastard we'll give it away. Mark my words. Then it'll turn out to be a real lucky child.'

Shocked by what I'd heard, I realised I couldn't defend the way I looked. Placing both hands on my tummy, I told Bub that I loved her. I felt overwhelmed with emotion and my mind was swimming. 'Being taken' was a recurring nightmare for my family and our people, now that same nightmare was visiting me. Ever so softly, I sang to my little one and slowly entered a bewitching daydream of cautionary conundrums foretelling things to come.

The heat in the paddy wagon was intense. In the stifling air, the van became my prison and the voices outside faded away.

35. The Finishing

A loud thump on the side of the van grabbed by attention. 'What's her name?' Ouno demanded.

I heard someone get a good slap; Polly squealed.

'Yeah, that's right, pick on the kid, *Lulja* (Cockrag),' *Mimi* hissed.

'What's her name?' he bellowed, cutting her off. He started banging wildly on the side of my paddy wagon. 'Who is she? Who is she? Tell me now!'

'*Bind...a...manha* (Lightning Strike).' Mimi's voice trailed off, I knew she didn't want him to hear my spirit name.

Then she shouted real loud, like she was presenting a prize or something, 'She's a Lucky-Child... Lucy Lucky-Child.'

The biggest grin came to my face, so wide I thought my jaw was going to snap and drop off. That's how full up with pride I was. Tell ya what, I made up my mind right there and then, I'm gonna hold up high that Lucky-Child name and I'm never gonna put it down again.

'For God's sake, open the door!' I heard her scream.

Then the call went out in Mangala, Wajarri, English and even French. 'Show respect! Show respect! Respect!'

Them women were fired up something chronic, protesting at the disrespectful way the butcher from Looma was dragging Marissa's dead body into the meat van. Patty Mae was giving him a mouthful in real colourful language and old Sandy Gibb wasn't letting her have the final say either. I got real worried about my mum and my sister too. They didn't deserve no *whitefella* disrespect. This is a really big thing for us mob.

All of a sudden, a deafening burst of static from the satellite radio in the front of the cab made everyone shut-up and pay attention. There, in the middle of the Great Sandy Desert, the sound of a proper English woman's voice rang out loud and clear.

'With breaking news, it's Dalphine Dolittle for the BBC.'

'What the—' one of the coppers started to say, but someone must have shut him up.

'In a world first, the Federation of Bakers has issued an apology for the no show of bakers throughout the northern hemisphere this morning. It is reported that they all slept in, triggering wide spread bread shortages.'

All us *blackfellas* cheered.

'Shut up!' some half-witted copper shouted.

Polly piped up, 'My mum could learn their Queen how to make damper?'

I couldn't mistake Aunty Toot's belly laugh, she was cacking herself.

302

Gently rubbing my tummy, I shrieked, 'Bub, this is it. *Wakaj Kanarri* (The Finishing). He's given back the gift of sleep.' Bub wriggled. I was just about to explain when a familiar voice echoed off the paddy wagon walls.

'*Nganggurmanha* (Listen-up)!' Shit, that old *wintiki* (curlew) *Jalbri* was still bossing me about.

That posh Dolittle woman was still yapping, so I listened up real quick.

'In headline news there has been a surprising turn of events in the Israeli– Palestinian conflict. It would seem that mothers can do what world leaders cannot. At midday, mothers from both sides of the divide stepped unarmed into the no-go zone.

'Israeli and Palestinian women were pictured hugging their sons and taking their weapons from their hands.

'In emotional scenes, both Israeli soldiers and Palestinian militants then embraced each other and vowed to end the conflict and reinstate peace in the region. The newly formed group, Proactive Mothers, have also taken over the Knesset, the Israel's Parliament, and are holding the podium as we speak. Updates are on the BBC feed.'

See Bub, it's really happening.' I whispered, half expecting another telling off.

'The internet has gone into meltdown with footage showing ISIS troops in Syria throwing down their weapons and cleaning up the once besieged township. The terrorists are begging for forgiveness and assisting the injured in hospitals throughout the captured Territories.

'The world press is mystified by accounts that two large serpents, one with rainbow-coloured scales and the other black with a red belly, appeared to ISIS members worldwide in a dream and have apparently promised to forgive the terrorists if they change their ways, otherwise retribution will be swift. Experts believe that the two serpents resemble the creatures *Pulanyi Bulaing* and *Kulpan Karrangu*, who feature in Australian Indigenous Mythology.

'General Trustlove, a high-ranking official from the British Security Service MI5, had this to say: "Someone's got on that bloody Dark-web and hypnotised the lot of them. Mark my words, all this lovie dovie bullshit just won't last. It's unnatural."

'The Headlines coming up:

- Rare snow fall in the Sahara Desert.
- World-wide call for a ban on all blood sports.
- Proposed reduction in real working hours, as concerns mount over modern-day paid slavery.

'Which brings us to an interesting International Summit held in Bhutan to examine the meaning of Happiness and True Freedom. But before we look at these stories, world-first research out of Australia suggests that the trauma imposed on children taken from their parents, takes five generations of unbroken family stability to re-instate a sense of belonging. The study went on to say that the displaced person requires intensive emotional and community support to find security and acceptance within society.'

Finally, someone had said what we'd always known. The stunned silence of our mob was broken by, 'Struth Sharlene, can't ya do something?'

I felt the van sway and heard the flick of a switch. The radio in the front of the cab was silenced and the front door slammed shut. My little prison seemed to shrink and get hotter. I was melting from the inside. The air was too hot to breath and my tongue was so swollen, I couldn't swallow or call for help. Even my ears were filling with sweat and my skin seemed glued to the paddy wagon floor.

'Open the bloody door! She'll die in there!' *Mimi* screamed.

Someone held the door ajar. Gasping for life, I devoured the hot desert air. Into my flared nostrils came that hideous, familiar smell. I let out a withering screech cos even my my tongue could taste that nauseating stench of the *one that feathers stick to*.

Suddenly I couldn't see, but I felt myself freefalling into that terrifying space where nightmares are born. Then I heard her, *Bulari* (Mother Goddess), her songline was so pure, so true, it swaddled me like a newborn baby… like a butterfly in its cocoon. Her song raised me up ever so gently, back into the light. There, she lay me at peace on the paddy wagon floor.

'Open it now!' *Mimi* yelled, 'I wanna her. Now!' She was screaming somethin' powerful.

'Go on then, have a last fuckin look!' The nasty cop bellowed.

I didn't see what happened next, but I heard a sickening thud and recognised the familiar sound of the copper kicking her head in.

Mustering my last bit of strength, I lifted my head a little off the paddy wagon floor to catch a glimpse of Mimi's bloodied hand clutching in vain as it slowly slipped down the edge of the paddy wagon door.

A haunting wail went up, the Sacred *Mama* (Ceremonial Song) vibrated through the hot metal walls into my soul. I took a deep breath, listening for the words that would announce her death.

A heavy body plomped down into the driver's seat. It wasn't the fat female copper who loved dogss, cos she smells real sweet, like powder or somethin'. Just thinking of her made my thoughts fly to *Gulyi*.

Before my eyes, I could see *Gulyi-Gulyi* running with Gofar and *Winthuly-Winthuly*. She was trailing behind them. Her head raised up and thrown back with her top lip curled towards the sky. From her open mouth, massive yellow teeth stood proud like the old head stones at Pearler's Cemetery in Broome. And as she moaned about her life as camels do, the wind blew white gozzy stuff from her wobbling lips.

I knew exactly where they were heading. Disaster Well.

'No, don't go there!' I yelled. It was no place for them animals to be.

It's so bad, only *walhi* (no good) comes from there. Even if us mob were dying of thirst, we wouldn't drink water from that well. Them fellas who made the Canning Stock Route learnt pretty quick cos a real strange sickness followed them outta there. Disaster Well is *walhi bagi* (no good for nothing).

305

The cab door slammed. The seat belt clicked. The key turned. The engine fired. The copper put his foot to the floor. My paddy wagon took off, revving loudly with each gear change.

Fine red sand pelted me from the tiny spinning air vent above the back door. The whirling dust stung my eyes. Rubbing them with my sweaty hands only made it worse. So, I just lay there with eyes closed tight, but I couldn't wipe the last thing I'd seen from my mind. My *Mimi* having her head kicked in and our four-legged friends heading off to that *walhi bagi* (no good for nothing) place.

The panic set in. A million questions hit me all at once. Would I see them women again? Why did Ouno want to know my name? How come I was alone in this van? Where the hell were they taking me…? What were they gonna do with Bub? Kill her? Abort her, or kill both of us with poison, or kick us to death? How does taking her away work? I still have months to go before I give birth. Oh God, how can I give birth knowing they're gonna take her?

Shit, I gotta get outta here. That one obsessive thought bit me like a troop of flesh-eating bull ants. Lying flat on my back in this bloody paddy wagon wasn't gonna help. So, I hoisted myself up onto my elbows, commando style, crawled into the far corner of the van and sat snuggled in tight between the walls. The rhythm of the van slipping sideways and bumping over ridges as we raced through the desert reminded me of sitting in the back of Jackie's ute. Gaw, that seemed such a long time ago.

The heat on my back was strangely comforting, but after a while, I felt like my brain was boiling dry. I was just sitting there, like a stunned mullet, starring at the corrugations of the metal floor, when suddenly, them strong hard lines became soft, fluid like the *wurrja* (mirage) ya get on them blistering hot days in the middle of the Great Sandy Desert.

My mind was swimming. I blinked, and in a split second, the paddy wagon expanded, the floor turned into a giant chess board and the roof peeled off. Bedazzled by the night sky, I rose up and out of my crouching body.

Standing tall, just like Alice in Wonderland, I stepped into my Dreaming World, not knowing If I'd ever return.

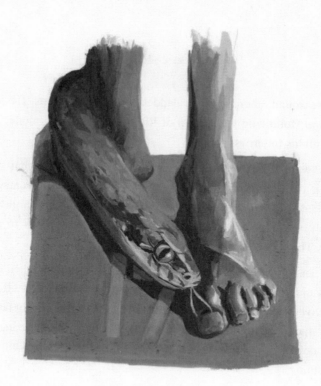

36. Life Board

'Tnick! Tnick! Hey daugha!'

Those four words threw open the door to the nuthouse in my head. Dad was standing there, large as life, on the 46th square of the checkered board. I was so happy to see him.

As he spoke, piles of snakes appeared, writhing at his feet. 'Remember what I said?' He asked. But before I could answer, he repeated his old catch cry.

'A *whitefellas*' life is full of ladders.

But a *blackfellas* life is full of snakes.'

I smiled at him, but inside my heart was breaking, cos instantly I could see as clear as anything his life spread out on the board in front of me.

He had lots of ladders at the beginning of his life. The ladders of Love and Learning, of Family and Culture, but on the 7th square of his life, a nasty looking snake took him back to the start.

Next time round, there was no ladder of Love for him. He was just *wandanmanha* (following the tracks) of life, mighty sad and alone. I reckon that's when all his bitterness set in.

But there were so many long, strong ladders he'd climbed that gave him strength in his darkest hours. Like the ones for Nature and Country, and of course Mother Mary's ladder of Compassion. He rose up real high when he became a proud stockman, and scaled his greatest ladder of all to meet my mum, Mary. The *Bidi-Bidi*. Our butterfly.

But that deadly snake of Wrong Ways took him way down when he had to separate me and *Waranmanha* at our birth and took up with his wife's sister. Then, the two headed snake of Unemployment and Disappointment landed him on another snake square where he was weakened by her slipperiness Grief. Further inflamed by the serpents of Hatred and Rage, they turned him to drink and self-loathing.

Sliding down the back of Despair, he landed heavily on his final square. Hissing with delight, the Taker slithered between him and himself, and everyone else. She piled him with booze, then hopelessness snatched him off the board into the jaws of a cruel death.

With an insane serpentine grimace, the Taker then rested her head on the 17th square. Helplessly, I watched my brother Frankie stumble onto that same square and disappear.

My eyes were filling up with tears so fast, I couldn't see Dad and Frankie's board any more. 'Why?' I cried, looking up to the stars and begging God for an answer, I needed a sign, anything that would show me that me and Bub weren't gonna end up the same way.

In a flash, Dad's Life Board slipped away, just like when Aunty Rosie does her party trick and pulls the tablecloth off, leaving the cups and plates just sitting there with nothing *julgia* (broken). That's exactly how Dad's Life Board slipped away and was replaced by a forest of ladders.

And then I noticed *her*. Swaying gently in the moonlight. She stood gracefully on the 2nd square of the 7th row. Her head was tilted slightly to the left, and her lips moved in silent prayer. Large wooden rosary beads hung down to her knees from the tight white belt around her tiny waist. In her right hand, a darning needle glistening like a sword, and from her other hand, a hemp rope uncoiled onto her Life Board.

An excitement grew inside me… I knew her… I had seen her… I loved her. Sister Euphrates stood tall and elegant, surrounded by her forest of ladders. She was my Joan of Arc. I knew that she would fight for Bub and me. Bub moved and together we stepped forward, willing to defend her, or burn beside her.

All her snakes, even the deadly ones, like the serpent of War from her time in Vietnam, led to squares from which enormous ladders soared, like those of Faith, Hope and Courage. What Dad had said was right, but I couldn't work out why.

Then, like an angel, she sang.

'Baby's birth.
Faith on Earth.

Serpents young and old bow down.
A dozen years, a Royal Crown.

With eloquence and grace and charm
She'll dispel darkness and do no harm

One by One on the eleventh hour
Resurrection of the people's tower.

Her voice chimed like chapel bells, and it reminded me of when I travelled through time and felt the universe open within me.

Then, I heard that familiar old crusty voice.

'This *jakiny's* (barbed spear) blood has passed,
Justice in your hands at last.'

Jalbri was at the end of the 9th row, on a square that had morphed into a waterhole. I could hear myself breathe in deeply. The low dark rush of air into my nostrils and the whirr as it left my lips made me realise that *Jalbri* and I had somehow become *one*.

Sister's voice floated high above us.

'Borderless through time and space
Justice comes for every caste and race.'

Jalbri's bottom lip jutted out towards me. She was asking me to come sit beside her. Respectfully, I walked slowly through her Life Board. It was unreal, every ladder was entwined with her snakes, and every snake confined by her ladders.

On her Life Board, there was no going back... and there was no easy way up. Everything looked too hard, but I could see how it made her work out what the real stuff of life was. She had to keep going up and forward. No breaks to lick life's wounds and feel sorry for herself. Nah – no holiday on her board, she just kept going and it made her an awesome person. Drop off her ladder and its *game over*.

I sat down beside *Jalbri*. Her left hand took hold of my right with surprising strength. She dragged it up to her papery lips and kissed the back of my hand so firmly, it spoke to me more clearly than a million words of just how much she'd missed me.

Then, without releasing her grip on my hand, she placed it firmly high on her lap. I could feel the warmth of her fleshy palm against mine. I put my head onto the top of her shoulder and snuggled in. Once again, I was her *gantharri* (great granddaughter).

Feeling safe and loved, I played the game that every young hand has played with the old. Gently picking up a long fold of skin off the back of her hand, I watched how long it took for the skin to sink back down again.

'*Milkanarri*,' her whisper echoed through my skull. Obediently, my left hand slipped into my pouch. Pushing past Derwen's locket, I could already feel the heat from the *Milkanarri* firing up with my intention to *see*.

Quickly and quietly I closed my eyes real tight and slipped my *Milkanarri* onto the cool skin between my breasts. *Jalbri's* chest expanded with mine as we breathed in deeply. Slowly I released that breath and opened my eyes to see my sister, *Waranmanha*.

She looked gorgeous, standing on the high reaches of a ladder soaring into the night sky. Wound around the top rung of her ladder, a single serpent raised itself beside her, looking at her adoringly as if bewitched by her.

Like a magnolia she glistened softly in the moonlight and around her hung a heady fragrant mist. I breathed her in and my heart seemed to beat with love for her at a rate I could hardly bear.

Our eyes locked and as we gazed into each other's hearts, I knew deep down that something had changed inside both of us. Then, bewildered, I watched as an unfamiliar voice left those lips that I knew so well.

'The carved-bone shark swims again

Salt water floods Kings blood shall reign

The clans of Mel clash in the streets of scorn

Cities burn that once were Bourne

Sins of the past will spore a new war

Two zero three four, then It'll be no more.'

As each phrase left her lips, I could see everything play out in front of me. But my mind was distracted by how different we had become.

I had an overwhelming urge to look down at our Life Board. I wanted to see exactly how Twin Star Children could start out on the same square but have life paths that were so different. Why did she get the *high road* and I got the *dirt track*? Why is she... what Sister Euphrates would call... magnolious, while I'm the good for nothing wretch? She's off with *Bulari* (Mother Goddess) while I'm sitting here with old *Jalbri* in the back of a paddy wagon, on my way to the lock-up.

I reckon they'll try and charge me with murder, maybe even mass murder, and soliciting for sure. They've already got it in their heads that I'm a druggie, and not fit to be a mother.

I was terrified of what them *kartijas* (*whitefellas*) were gonna do to me, and wild at the injustice of being handed the short straw. The *mungawarri* (little hairy men that live in mounds and cause mischief) kept saying in my ear, 'Go on, take a look at ya board. Carmon girl, see ya fate. Ya got nothin' to lose.'

Taking an uncomfortably deep breath, I clenched my jaw like the black pearlers would've done a hundred years before me, and decided to stuff the odds and dive into the cesspool of my destiny, and face my Life Board, snakes and all.

My *jinjamarda* (little baby) was kicking like crazy, warning me not to look. *Jalbri* vanished, and my twin sister evaporated into that magnolious mist. My *Milkanarri* (seeing stone) fell from my breast into my now cold empty hands. Our Life Board dissolved into a fine mist and caught my breath as it swept past me to form a little cloud that hovered just outta my reach.

'Heello?' I called, my voice echoing in the cavernous space.

'Heellooo?' I called again, enjoying the sound of my voice.

Suddenly, as if responding to my call, a circular pool of light appeared way below me, just like a waterhole on a moonlit night. Surprised, I saw a serpentine shadow slide across the surface, and a wooden ladder glide past and disappear gently into the pool of light.

As the serpentine and ladderish ripples met, I lost my balance and tumbled through the ripples, landing heavily, too heavily… and there, darkly coiled, I lay cool and motionless like a brooding snake in the bottom of an abandoned mine shaft.

A loud creaking sound made my ear drums quiver and an incredibly bright light drenched my whole body. My heart missed two beats, then a third, and a fourth. I waited for a fifth. A flash of sheer joy shot through my stiffened frame.

This is it! The bright light at the end of the tunnel. I'm dead! Properly dead!

I lay as still as a starfish, as quiet as a mouse and as dead as our doorbell. My *jinjamarda* (little baby) fluttered in my tummy like a *Bidi-Bidi* (Butterfly) preparing its wings for flight. Before I knew it, I was swept up by my little *Waranmanha*, and soared into the wild blue yonder, leaving behind that little cloud that seemed to haunt me my whole life.

Below, the desert lands of my Country were dressed up in a hundred billion flowers, welcoming me to Dragon Tree Soak, where my heart longed to be. Drifting up over Help Canyon, Mum's voice chimed in my ears like the chapel bells at St Mary's.

Black smoke still hung heavily over the canyon, the burial grounds, and the vast tracks of burnt out land. I winced, remembering my sister's death and our separation. In that instant of recall, bubs and me started to plummet.

'*Thubarnimanha* (Straighten-up)!' *Jalbri* cried out to us. We did an about face and swiftly entered *Banharnigardi Banharnigardi* (The Beyond Beyond).

Pushing through the fabric of time, we made contact with the *Beginning*.

There, me and my bub became one dot and a dash, slowly rotating and tumbling through space.

We were the Thingy-ma-jig

In the Watcha-ma-call-it

In the Place with No-name

With the One with No-name

Who made Every-thing

But needed No-thing.

For a trillion Dreamtime years, we learnt Every-thing about No-thing, and then, just when we believed that No-thing was that Some-thing called Peace, my heart beat… one… two… three… and… four.

The steady drumming of that heart of mine unhinged me, and my connection with the other side was lost.

I hurtled awkwardly into the darkly coiled human on the concrete floor. At the very moment of impact, I gasped a lung full of putrid air. My legs shot straight out in front of me, and my eyes sprung wide open. I was back inside my pathetic teenage self and its tedious life. The hollow thud in my chest was the unwelcome visitor who'd snatched from me my *get out of jail free* card.

37. The Flower and The Petal

'C'mon me little Petal. C'mon back to ole Delores Flower. She's been waitin' real patient like... I gotta get some tucker in ya... there's more bones sticken' outta ya than a dead dingo,' she said, giggling at her own joke, 'C'mon, Delores is gonna look afta ya real good.'

'*Guwardi Thubarnimanha* (Now straighten-up),' she said sweetly. The moment I heard those word leave her lips, I straightened myself up and tried to focus my eyes.

Sitting there, right in front of me, was a skinny old woman whose head moved to the beat of a slight tremor. I watched her snow-white hair dance lightly against her brown skin, but before I knew it, her sparkling blue eyes wooed me, like a waterhole on a hot summer's day.

Bum down and knees out, she sat traditional blackfella style on the ground. Her thin bony legs stuck up like tent poles that hoisted up the large folds of her brightly coloured skirt.

In between her legs, sat a small, half empty bowl of runny porridge. The head of an old metal spoon was buried, its handle pointed to the heavy barred cell door, and freedom. But there was no freedom here, it was locked up good and proper.

'Somethin' botherin' ya me girl?' I didn't answer. 'When that mob dragged you in here, you weren't up for knowin' nothin' about nothin'. But I'm tellin' ya now, you're in the lock-up at Fitzroy Crossing.

The old woman lifted the spoon out of the porridge. A dollop plopped back into the sky-blue bowl. I watched the slow goozy ripple try to make its way to the edge, just like the one at the entrance of *Junki* and *Nypni*'s cave.

I sat, stunned, just staring at Delores Flower with my mouth hanging open like some poor old fella in a nursing home. Before I knew it, a loaded spoon approached my lazy lips. As soon as the back of the metal spoon landed on my tongue, my mouth automatically closed. As I swallowed, a goozy dribble escaped from the corner of my pouting lips and headed down my cheek.

'Good girl,' she said. Using the edge of the cold metal spoon with the skill of a cut throat barber, she scraped the spill clean before it reached my chin.

Being fed like a baby made me think about all us kids, my bub, my sister, my brothers, Manu, Louanna, Polly and me. Suddenly, the shakes took hold of me real bad.

'Shussh… me Petal. It's okay, look 'ere,' she said, running her long brown, bony finger around the shiny edge of the bright blue bowl, 'You and me, we're just sittin' 'ere on Country. Look at this 'ere waterhole,'.

Drawing breath and pausing her feeding ritual, she leant forward and softly but firmly, said, 'You and me, we're gonna do lock-up Dreaming. Stick with me Petal, there's a real strong magic in the air.'

'See this 'ere blue fella?' her eyes twinkled like fairy lights as she tapped the bowl three times. 'See, Heaven never leaves ya on ya own. She's always comin' down stairs, showin' ya somethin'. Leavin' a sign for ya everywhere.

316

But ya eyes and heart gotta be wide open… lookin' out for her. That one. She's not showy or nothin'. Nah, quiet as anythin', she'll show ya the way.'

A calm like I'd never felt before enveloped me and a delicious warmth made me feel like I was sitting near a campfire on a cold desert night. When my eyes cleared, I noticed a large pile of long grasses in the right-hand corner of the cell.

Following my gaze, she said, 'Ya know 'bout grass?' Dropping the spoon on the floor and muttering excitedly in language, she hoisted herself up, shuffled over, grabbed two fists full of grass from the pile and bounded back. The little walk to the corner loosened up her old bones and gave her a new lease of life.

'String Petal! String! It can tell ya everythin' ya wanna know 'bout anythin'. Over and under, in and through, and together. There's nothin' more ya need to know.'

I watched, mesmerised by her lightning fast fingers as she twisted the long lengths of grass into a fine twine. Suddenly, my mind flashed to Sister Euphrates. The sweet smell of twining grass suddenly turned into the metallic taste of terror. It was bitter on my tongue, it squeezed my throat shut and loosened my bowels.

Terrified, I grabbed hold of her hand and whispered, 'Where is everyone?'

The last thing I remembered was my *Mimi's* (grandmother's) bloodied hand slipping slowly down the edge of the closing paddy wagon door, followed by the familiar thud of the copper's boot against her proud head… and Sister's blood curdling screams.

'Shit!' I screamed.

'Nooo… No, No… No, No…' Delores Flower whispered, pulling out a darning needle that was threaded through her t-shirt high above her breast. In one foul swoop, she jabbed at my forehead, right between my eyebrows. I bled.

With her needle hooked in the crook of her thumb, her long strong bony finger drew a line of fresh blood straight down my nose, across the centre of my lips, over my chin, and all the way down my throat, stopping firmly in the crease between my breasts.

317

I felt angry and taken advantage of. What right did these bloody *blackfellas* have just taking ya blood whenever they wanted to?

But before I could draw a breath, she raised that same bloody finger to her lips and said, 'Shush.' Then, pointing to her right ear with that same finger, she whispered, '*Nganggurnmanha* (Listen-up).'

Then, a light, airy, quivering, high pitched voice left the old Flower's dusty lungs.

'If you're happy and you know it, clap your hands!'

She clapped her hands like a little child in kindy.

'If you're happy and you know it, clap your hands!

If you're happy and you know it, then your face will surely show it.'

She leant over and pinched both my cheeks… I felt like knocking her out and making a run for the door.

'If you're happy and you know it, clap your hands (clap, clap).'

Shit, you're even more crazy than *Jalbri*,' I snapped at the old girl, feeling sure as anything that I was sitting in a looney bin, not in the lock-up.

Then I heard it… a woman's voice responding. Then another… and another. Thanks to the nuns, we've been singing that stupid song on Country, in schools, and in orphanages for over a hundred years. But I never thought I'd be happy to hear it here in this lock-up.

I started singing out real loud. I couldn't hold back my joy, cos coming back at me through the wall was Sister Euphrates's sweet French accent and Polly Tipple's awesome harmony; and them deep *yurla* (macho male) voices of Patty Mae and Sandy Gibb made me cry laughing. Of course, that bitch Aunty Barbara was her usual posh self.

But someone was missing… Mimi.

I strained my ears real hard, but I still couldn't hear her. Then I sorta half recognised a croaky smoker's cough… It had to be Mimi. Her words were slurred and I could tell it was an effort for her to sing out loud enough for me to hear her.

But those words, 'eef yaw harpie and yuoo no eet clarp yaw hhanns,' broke my heart into a million pieces. Bitter-sweet tears filled my heart with the joy of knowing that my *Mimi* was alive.

With a knowing smile, Delores Flower's voice got louder. The other women must have known what she was up to cos they started to sing in rounds against her. Then Delores dropped her voice down to a real low hum, looked me straight in the eye, and sang her message to me cloaked within the woven words and rich harmonies of those amazing women.

'In a little while
You'll be outta here (clap, clap)

Your bub will be safe
Me Petal don't you fear. (clap, clap)'

Then she joined the others in song.

'If you're happy and you know it, clap your hands.'

I clapped, she clapped and a cascade of clapping filtered through the wall from the other cell.

'Shut the fuck up!' A copper yelled.

'Shhh…! She said, holding me in her gaze with her long finger held against her pounting lips. Her bright blue eyes darted towards the door. '*Kuli Kunyarr* (The wild dog) has got his ear to the door.'

Like an old squeeze box reluctantly grinding to a halt, the women's voices trailed off.

Delores now pointed her finger at her left eye. 'Petal, you look in this here eye.' Without a moment's hesitation, my hands came together, and like the high diver of my childhood at Gantheaume Point, I launched myself from the *barlu* (rock ledge) of my life, into *the blue* and allowed it to consume me.

319

In that altered state, I became vaguely aware of her hand drifting down from above my head to ever so gently close my eyelids, one by one. That same gentle hand rolled me onto my side. I felt something soft shoved under my head. Then, like a little *winjinba* (field mouse) in its *manga* (nest) of warm, sweet smelling grasses, I snuggled down to sleep.

She laid her left hand onto my face. Her warm palm covered my right jaw and the vee between her thumb and fingers, nestled under my nose. The old woman's thumb pad rested lightly on my left eye and its base sat across my lips. Then she whispered, 'If you're happy and you know it, then your face will surely show it.'

Straight away, the corners of my lips curved upwards. Inhaling deeply, I could hear the air rush into my nose, and then, from the depth of my *rayi* (soul), my warm breath poured into her palm, escorted by a long, whale like moan.

And just like those huge creatures from the deep, I plunged into the Dreaming, travelling to that non-place where all the worlds of time and space collide.

I heard Manu murmur, 'No fear, your friends are near.'

Breaking through the *blue*, I entered the theatre of my life.

And there, my story played out its tragic comedy, like some old movie that was stuck in a never-ending loop. Repeated over and over, in each generation, and hidden within a million situations, I recognised my life's unanswered questions.

So ridiculous, you'd wanna die.

So funny, you'd wanna cry.

With brain-numbing monotony, I watched each twist and turn tangle the back stories that made me *who I am*.

Suddenly, those moving images of the snippets of our days in the Great Sandy Desert started to speed up, like a film on fast forward.

Then, feeling dizzy and disoriented, I heard voices from every side, chanting in *wulala mirniny* (many languages), 'Who are you?'

What a stupid question. Now I was totally confused and really annoyed. Sighing, I reluctantly answered the question. 'Lucy Lucky-Child... *Bindamanha* ... Whatever.'

'And What are you?'

'Shit! Really?' After all I've been through, that's all you've got?' I was fed up big time.

Ignoring my comeback, the chorus of voices persisted.

'What are you?'

'Okay! Aboriginal! Got it!' I snapped back.

'Which part of you is Aboriginal?' The question repeated incessantly.

'What an insult!' I snapped. This was driving me insane. I wanted to punch someone. 'I don't have to prove myself to anyone!' I yelled into the thick curtain of sound.

'Which part of you is Aboriginal?' As the voices grew louder, I felt like they were taunting me.

Humiliated and embarrassed, I could feel my face burning up. And just when I thought I was about to explode, I stepped into an arena of icy cool rage. From the smouldering pit of my stomach, came a yell so loud, even my ear drums quivered.

'My Tongue... My Heart... and... My Womb!'

Instantly, my seething rage was replaced by a deep sense of *wulyu* (peace). An amazing feeling of expansiveness radiated in a straight line from the core of my pulsating womb, right up though my pounding heart, to the tip of my tingling tongue.

At that very same moment, I heard *Jalbri* whisper, '*Thubarnimanha* (Straighten-up).'

Now I understood. Straightening myself up, I spoke aloud my vow.

'In truth, my tongue will speak the collective wisdom of my heart, and within my womb, the alchemy of love will nurture the precious seed of destiny.'

Then, suspended in a multilayered universe of sound, the *mama* (sacred song) bathed and healed my *rayi* (soul). And in that hallowed space prepared eons ago, I understood *who I was,* and then I received my *Lore*.

Lucky-Child

The Secret

Lucky-Child

Glossary

Word	English Translation	Language
'em	Them	Aussie Slang
As cranky as a cut snake	Very annoyed/angry	Aussie Slang
As the crow flies	Aerial distance	Aussie Slang
B'fore	Before	Aussie Slang
Bacci	Tobacco	Aussie Slang
Bajayimanha	Becoming wild with anger	Wajarri
Balayi	Watchout	Wajarri
Bawling	Crying	Aussie Slang
Balygurr	Small branches	Wajarri
Bamburdu	Message stick	Mangala
Bán chúng tói	Shoot us	Vietnamese
Banharnigardi	Beyond	Wajarri
Bardinyu	Pine	Wajarri
Barlu	Rock ledge	Wajarri
Barlura	Acacia wattle	Wajarri
Barndagura	Bush bustard	Wajarri
Barndi	Good / Smart / Clever	Wajarri
Barndi wayilpila	Good White Man	Wajarri
Barndijunmanha	Putting things right	Mangala
Barnga	Small goanna	Wajarri
Bidi-Bidi	Butterfly	Wajarri
Bidjy	Bidyadanga	Karajarri
Bilabirdi	Eucalyptus gum	Wajarri
Bilbiny	Grevillea	Wajarri
Bindamanha	Lighting / strike	Wajarri
Binu	Cloud of smoke	Wajarri
Binyj	Slippery Jack Mushroom	Wawuru Ngan-ga

Biriny	White, shiny	Wajarri
Birla	Sky	Wajarri
Birrinja	Feather foot	Wajarri
Biyarrgu	Galahs	Wajarri
Bloke's tackle	Male genitals	Aussie Slang
Breakfast to asshole	Thoroughly, constantly, the full distance.	Aussie Slang
Bugura	Very dangerous little spirit men that live in the hills	Wajarri
Buiyi mangga	Hornet's nest	Mangala
Buju	Finished, ended	Mangala
Bukirri	Dream	Wajarri
Bulari	Mother Goddess	Mangala
Bularra	Eucalyptus tree	Wajarri
Bulgardu	God of the Universe	Mangala
Bulya-man	Healer/Sorcerer	Wajarri
Bundarra	The Stars	Wajarri
Bundarra Murungkurr	Star Child Spirits	Wajarri
Bungarra	Lizard	Wajarri
Burlagardu	God, creator	Wajarri
Bushies	Bushmen	Aussie Slang
C'mon	Come on	Aussie Slang
Carmon	Come on	Aussie Slang
C'est magnifique	That's wonderful	French
Chinks	Chinese people	Aussie Slang
Chippy	Carpenter	Aussie slang
Choccies	Chocolates	Aussie Slang
Chook	Chicken	Aussie Slang
Cock Rag	Penis covering	Aussie Slang

Come down on me like a tonne of bricks	When someone is extremely angry and lets you know.	Aussie Slang
Coulda	Could have	Aussie Slang
Crook	Unwell	Aussie Slang
D'accord! Bien sûr!	Okay, of course	French
Dead set	Correct	Aussie Slang
Deep shit	Big trouble	Aussie Slang
Djulpan	Southern Cross	Mangala
Djulpan Dumgdung	Southern Cross	Mangala
Dob	Tell on someone	Aussie Slang
Dolled up	Dressed to impress	Aussie Slang
Dreadies	Dread locks	Aussie Slang
Duthu	Crazy dog	Mangala
Dunny	Toilet	Aussi Slang
Effing and blinding	Swearing	Aussie Slang
Fags	Cigarettes	Aussie Slang
Fair dinkum	The truth	Aussie Slang
Fella	Person	Aussie Slang
Fricken	Polite word for 'fucking'	Aussie Slang
From breakfast to asshole	From top to bottom	Aussie Slang
Full pelt	As fast as able	Aussie Slang
Gagi	Birds	Mangala
Gagi mupinjarri	Bird Medicine Man	Mangala
Gan.gara	High above	Wajarri
Ganba	Giant scorpion	Wajarri
Ganganggamanha garndi	Take the stone knife	Wajarri
Gantharri	Great grand daughter	Mangala
Gardugardimanha	Sitting cross-legged	Wajarri
Garndi	Stone knife	Wajarri

Gawking	Staring	Aussie Slang
Gig	Event	Aussie Slang
Gooden	Good person	Aussie Slang
Gooz	Sticky substance	Aussie Slang
Gonna	Going to	Aussie Slang
Grog	Alcohol	Aussie Slang
Gula Warlugura	Come nearby girls	Wajarri
Gulanda	Don't be forgetting	Wajarri
Gulyba	Sick	Wajarri
Gulyi-Gulyi	Funny looking	Wajarri
Gumamu	Sandalwood	Yawuru Ngan-ga
Gumbarri	Many	Wajarri
Gumbarri Jingi	The Twelve Apostles	Wajarri
Gungkara	Conker-berry tree	Yawuru Ngan-ga
Gurlanda	Don't be forgetting	Wajarri
Gurndany	Shame	Wajarri
Gurrgurgu	Mopoke owl	Wajarri
Guwa	Yes	Wajarri
Guwardi	Now	Wajarri
Hack it	Deal with it	Aussie Slang
Hidey hole	Hiding spot	Aussie Slang
High tailed	Moved very fast	Aussie Slang
Hubnuru	Light rain	Mangala
Ija	True	Wajarri
Ija maraji	True Auntie	Wajarri
Jabu	Rock wall	Wajarri
Jakiny	Barbed spear	Mangala
Jalajala	Really good	Wajarri
Jalbri	Great grandmother	Mangala
Jama	The ground	Wajarri

Jaman	Run	Mangala
Jambarn	Quickly	Mangala
Jani	Pubic tassels	Mangala
Jarda	Old woman	Mangala
Jarda thuthamarda	Old woman little tits	Mangala
Je t'aime	I love you	French
Jigi-jigi	Sex	Mangala
Jij	Plant	Mangala
Jija	Sister	Wajarri
Jila	Soak, eternal water	Mangala
Jimpiri	Feathers	Mangala
Jin.ga	Spirit	Wajarri
Jindilungu	Milky-Way	Wajarri
Jinjamarda	Little baby	Wajarri
Jinkirala	Dragon-flies	Wajarri
Jirdilungu	Milky Way	Wajarri
Ju	Up	Wajarri
Juja	Old man	Wajarri
Julgia	Broken	Central
Julirri	Blue-tongue lizard	Wajarri
Juljul	Fresh water soak, not permanent	Mangala
Jumu	Surface water	Mangala
Junimanha	Laughing at something	Wajarri
Jura	Child	Wajarri
Jurdu	Smoke	Wajarri
Jurru	Snake	Wajarri
Jutinkarra Kawauarri	Sing out for forgiveness	Mangala
JutikKarra Kawanarri	Sing out for forgiveness to undo the past	Mangala

Kaditja	One that feathers stick to Feather foot	Wajarri
Kai Kanarri	The Finishing time	Mangala
Kakarra	East	Mangala
Kalakala	Diarrhoea	Mangala
Kali	Furious	Mangala
Kana	Digging stick	Mangala
Kantiyala	Ride them	Mangala
Kara	West	Mangala
Kapanarri	Is coming	Mangala
Karparli	Grandmother	Mangala
Karrikin	Body	Mangala
Karrmina	Barren women	Mangala
Karrpina	Combat shield	Mangala
Kartija	White person	Mangala
Kava	West	Mangala
Kawanarri	Singing out	Mangala
Kipara	Bustard bird	Mangala
Kuji Warnku	Porcupine Rock	Mangala
Kukamyuyiti	Cannibal	Mangala
Kuli	Angry	Mangala
Kuli Kunyarr	Wild dog	Mangala
Kulpan Karrangu	The black, red bellied snake	Mangala
Kuliyiti	Be Brave	Mangala
Kumbulhmanmanh	Thumping sound	Wajarri
Kunamyarri	Is drinking	Mangala
Kurntal	Daughter	Mangala
Kurr	On the sound of the wind	Mangala
Kurriji pa Yajula	Dragon Tree Soak	Mangala
Kuta	Naked	Mangala

Kuwa	Crow	Mangala
Laplap	Sarong	Tiwi
Linkarra	Tree	Mangala
Lippy	Lipstick	Aussie Slang
Lipurra mil walpura	Keep your eyes open	Mangala
Lirra larrka	Open your mouth	Wajarri
Lirringin	Soapy wattle	Wajarri
Love fest	Excessive mutual appreciation	Aussie Slang
Lulja	Cockrag	Mangala
Maaja Muni	Boss woman	Mangala
Mabarn	Have faith	Wajarri
Mabarnyuwa	Female magician, faith healer, witch doctor, sorceress	Wajarri
Mad as a meat axe	A crazy person	Aussie Slang
Malardi	Tired	Wajarri
Malardiyimanha	Exhausted	Wajarri
Malgar	Women's fighting sticks	Wajarri
Malji	Tomcats	Mangala
Mama	Sacred song	Wajarri
Mamany	Crazy	Wajarri
Maminy warlugura	Stupid teenager	Wajarri
Maminy	Stupid	Wajarri
Mamukati	Dark night	Mangala
Mandarrayimanha	Clouding over just before rain	Wajarri
Mandugu yabu	Pinnacles	Mangala
Mangarikarra	Dreamtime	Mangala
Mangga	Nest	Wajarri

Mangul	Hunting spear	Mangala
Manguny	Dreamtime lore law	Mangala
Mangunykarraji	Forever/always	Mangala
Manngi	Headband worn by initiated men	Mangala
Mara-irri	Animal with special powers	Wajarri
Maraji	Aunty	Wajarri
Marduwayimanha Balbaru	Growing madness	Wajarri
Marlamarta	Mixed race	Mangala
Marloo	Big red kangaroo	Wajarri
Marlu nirla nga-yu	I don't know	Mangala
Marraja ngapa	Get me water	Mangala
Mére	Mother	French
Mes chéris	My darlings	French
Miginy	Kestrel	Wajarri
Milara	Moon	Wajarri
Mili	Firestick	Wajarri
Milkanarri	Seeing stone	Mangala
Milyura	Big snake	Wajarri
Mimi	Grandmother	Mangala
Minga	Meat ants	Wajarri
Minggarri	Coolamon, wood bowl for carrying water	Mangala
Minyjil	A pubic tassel made of possum hair	Mangala
Miparr	Face	Mangala
Mirni	Vagina	Mangala
Mirninypunka	I will speak	Mangala
Mirriyin	Crickets	Mangala

Mirru	Spear thrower	Mangala
Mitily	Baby	Mangala
Mitily Mamga	Baby girl	Mangala
Mitimiti	Full moon	Mangala
Miyarnu	Knowing, knowingly	Wajarri
Mo	Mustache	Aussie Slang
Món chérie	My dear	French
Mugurimanha	An evil thumping sound	Wajarri
Mulgahu	Friend	Mangala
Mulgara	Bush rat	Mangala
Munda	Loner/orphan	Mangala
Muniwarri	The Seven Sisters	Wajarri
Muridung	Evil ghost	Mangala
Muta Wanti	Just sit down	Mangala
Myambi	Knee-shaking dance	Mangala
Naka	Loincloth	Mangala
Nalaman	Shedding	Mangala
Nam jarri jirra	Shut up your face	Mangala
Nganggurmanha widigunmanha	Listen up and don't forget	Wajarri
Nganiggurnmanha	Listen up	Wajarri
Ngapa Yakurr Juljul	Dirty water soak	Wajarri
Ngardubirla	The night-time sky	Wajarri
Ngarn.ga	Cavern	Wajarri
Ngarnam Jiyamku	I will follow you	Mangala
Ngarnamin'gil	The firestick tree	Wajarri
Ngarnmanha	Eat	Wajarri
Ngarrungu	Aboriginal activist	Mangala
Ngijakura Kututu Kurrji	I love you with all my heart	Mangala

Ngubanu	Dingoes	Wajarri
Ngula jimaha	Crying together	Wajarri
Nguri	A drawstring bag made from kangaroo hide	Wajarri
Ngurlurrbi	Paper bark	Wajarri
Nguurru	Brumbies (horses)	Wajarri
Nguwinatu	A special person who comes back	Mangala
Nhangan	Go, Look, Watch	Wajarri
Nicked	Stolen	Aussie Slang
Nila	You will know	Wajarri
Niriliyangarr	Dune wattle	Wajarri
Non	No	French
Nuf	Enough	Aussie Slang
Nyaan-nyaan	Secret whispers, secretive, secretly	Mangala
Nyarluwarru	The Stone Towers representing the Seven Sisters at Reddell beach	Broome Speak
Nyubarr	Sleep	Wajarri
Nyubarrimanha	Falling asleep	Wajarri
Pajalpi	Springs	Mangala
Pararrka	Sorry	Mangala
Pararrka talu	Sorry and ashamed	Mangala
Parranga	Hot weather	Mangala
Parrkana	Cold time	Mangala
Pauu	Enough	Mangala
Photo	Photograph	Aussie Slang
Pily	Red	Mangala
Pitimaararri	Painting in lines	Mangala

Plawal	Bloodwood	Mangala
Pujarrpajurr	Desert Mole	Mangala
Pulanyi Bulaing	The Rainbow Serpent	Mangala
Pulyarr	Ghosts	Mangala
Pulyarra	Half blind	Mangala
Pungarri	Paint in dots	Mangala
Punku	Immortal people	Mangala
Putijputy	Smoke announcing someone's arrival	Mangala
Rabbited on	To speak continuously	Aussie Slang
Ragging	Making fun of	Aussie Slang
Ramkunarri	Is breathing	Mangala
Ramu	Special patterns on a shield	Mangala
Rantangka	Alone	Mangala
Rayi	Soul	Mangala
Reckon	Think	Aussie Slang
Rellies	Relatives	Aussie Slang
Roll your owns	Tobacco	Aussie Slang
Roos	Kangaroos	Aussie Slang
Shabby	Untidy	Aussie Slang
Short arse	Short person	Aussie Slang
Shoulda	Should have	Aussie Slang
Starkers	Naked	Aussie Slang
Stoked	Very happy	Aussie Slang
Sunnies	Sunglasses	Aussie Slang
Ta	Thank you	Aussie Slang
Ta ta	Little lizard	Wajarri
Tad	Small amount	Aussie Slang
Tantalpal	Clap your hands	Mangala
Tarr	Thanks	Aussie Slang

TGres horrible	Terrible, horrible	French
Thabinmanha	Question	Wajarri
Tharlbarra	Strong/Be strong	Wajarri
The Minhan	The brave	Wajarri
Thubarnimanha	Straighten up	Wajarri
Thubarnimanha Nganggu-nganggunmanhu	Straighten up your thinking	Wajarri
Thuribirla	The daytime sky	Wajarri
Thuthamarda mimi	Little tits	Wajarri
Truckies	Truck Drivers	Aussie Slang
Two bob	Two dollars	English Slang
Vego	Vegetarian	Aussie Slang
Wabarnanga	Jump	Wajarri
Wadjemup	Rottnest Island	Noongar
Wajijinjamarda	No baby in arms	Mangala
Wakaj Kanarri	The Finishing	Mangala
Wakuyanupirri	Hide	Mangala
Walarda	Sandalwood	Wajarri
Walgahna	Walga Rock	Wajarri
Walhinanmanha	Stop making mistakes	Wajarri
Walypa	Bitter wind	Mangala
Wanayiti	Rest	Mangala
Wandanmanha	Following the tracks	Wajarri
Wandarri	Red sandy country	Wajarri
Wang-gi li-yan mingan-ngany-janu	Have you got bad feelings for me	Mangala
Wangnar	Happy	Mangala
Wanna	Want to	Aussie Slang
Waranmanha	Lightning	Wajarri

Waranmanha	Lightning strike	Wajarri
Warrimpa	Bauhinia tree	Mangala
Warrimparna	Goodbye	Mangala
Warrimparna	Bye bye	Wajarri
Warri-murdi	Homesick for my Country	Wajarri
Warritharra	Sad	Mangala
Watali	Poor man	Wajarri
Wayiliri	Cry	Mangala
Widigunwauha	Remember, don't forget	Wajarri
Wilara	Moon	Wajarri
Wilburu	September	Mangala
Willy-Willy	Whirlwind	Aussie Slang
Wilu	Sea	Wajarri
Winthu	Wind	Wajarri
Wintiki	Curlew	Mangala
Wirlu	Penis	Mangala
Wurrja	Mirage	Mangala
Wulkula	Soft	Mangala
Wulyu	Good	Mangala
Wongi's	Indigenous person from Kalgoorlie	Wongi
Woulda	Would have	Aussie Slang
Ya	You	Aussie Slang
Yaburu	People from the North of Australia	Mangala
Yagu	Mother	Mangala
Yalibirri	Emu	Mangala
Yanaji	Come	Wajarri
Yanajimanha	Come on, come here	Wajarri
Yanayimanha	Coming	Wajarri

Yangarda	Longtime ago	Wajarri
Yanka kati ngarnana jiyanku	I will follow you	Mangala
Yarapa kurrapa	Open you hand	Mangala
Yarlgu	Menstrual blood	Mangala
Yarn	Talking/chatting	Aussie Slang
Yarning	Talking	Aussie Slang
Yayiliri	Wailing	Mangala
Yilliwirri	The old rain makers	Mangala
Yirarr	Womb	Mangala
Youse	Both or all of you	Aussie Slang
Yuna	Circumcise coroboree	Mangala
Yuna Pulkun	Initiation scars	Mangala
Yunba	Identical	Mangala
Yungatha	Family	Mangala

References

1. Bundiyarra Aboriginal Community, Aboriginal Corporation, Wajarri Dictionary
2. http://www.bundiyarra.com.au/wajarriApp/
3. Burgman, Albert, McKelson, Kevin, Wangka Maya Pilbara Aboriginal Language Centre, Mangala English Dictionary, Mangala Finderlist & Topical Wordlist 2005
4. Dianne Appleby, Susan Edgar, Yawuru Language Team, Yuwuru Ngan-ga, a phrase book of the Yuwuru Ngan-ga language, Magabala Books 1998.
5. King James Bible, King James Version (KJV), Mathew 5:29, Mathew 18:8, https://www.kingjamesbibleonline.org

About the Author

Dr. Chelinay Gates, AKA Malardy, is an Australian Indigenous Doctor of Traditional Chinese Medicine (TCM), and is a practitioner of Hypnosis and Esoteric Acupuncture.

Chelinay is an internationally recognised, prize winning artist, who has been out of circulation since her husband was horrifically burnt in September 2001.

Lucky-Child: The Secret, the first of a trilogy, marks her foray into the literary world as an author.

She has illustrated 2 popular children's books;

'My Dog Mat', author Dr. Kiri Gates,

'Bushfire Dreaming', author and co-illustrator, Dr. Drewfus Gates.

2019 has been a huge year for Malardy

Jan 2019 – 'No Dogs, No Aboriginals Allowed (her father's life story) - Cultural Times

July 2019 – 'The Petri Dish of Life', Traditional Chinese Medicine - Cultural Times

July 2019 – 'Diamonds in the Dust', monologue written & performed under the guidance of dramaturgs, Hellie Turner and Polly Low, as a Yirra Yaarnz project.

July 2019 – Westerly Magazine 64.1, illustrated article, University of Western Australia.

Aug 2019 – Winter Nights Festival, performed a suite of poems, hosted by Yirra Yaakin Productions at the Blue Room, Western Australia.

August 2019 – Podcast - Unsung Heros, hosted by Winnie Lai Hadad.

September 2019 – AFTRS Talent Camp W.A (Writing for Film and television).

Dec 2019 – 'Toxic Emotions', Traditional Chinese Medicine article, Cultural Times, RedHead Communications.